AR

RS

TM

STAR WARS™

DOOKU

JEDI LOST

STAR WARS™

DOOKU

JEDI LOST

CAVAN SCOTT

DEL REY
NEW YORK

Copyright © 2019 by Lucasfilm Ltd. & ® or ™
where indicated. All rights reserved.

Published in the United States by Del Rey,
an imprint of Random House, a division of
Penguin Random House LLC, New York.

DEL REY and the HOUSE colophon are registered
trademarks of Penguin Random House LLC.

ISBN 978-0-593-15766-4
International edition ISBN 978-0-593-15859-3
Ebook ISBN 978-0-593-15767-1

Printed in the United States of America on acid-free paper

randomhousebooks.com

2 4 6 8 9 7 5 3 1

First Edition

Book design by Elizabeth A. D. Eno

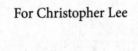

For Christopher Lee

THE DEL REY

STAR WARS™

TIMELINE

THE DEL REY
STAR WARS™
TIMELINE

A long time ago in a galaxy far, far away. . . .

DRAMATIS PERSONAE

VENTRESS: Dooku's assassin, recently recruited to his cause. Our narrator.

DOOKU: Sith Lord. Seen at various points in his life.

SIFO-DYAS: Male. Dooku's oldest friend.

TERA SINUBE: Male. Cosian. Jedi lightsaber instructor.

YULA BRAYLON: Female. Jedi Master.

KY NAREC: Male. Ventress's former Jedi Master.

LENE KOSTANA: Female. Altiri. Dooku's mentor.

ARATH TARREX: Male. Dooku's childhood rival.

COUNT GORA: Male. Dooku's father.

ANYA: Female. Dooku's mother.

RAMIL: Male. Dooku's brother.

JENZA: Female. Dooku's sister.

RAZ FELLIDRONE: Male. Portmaster.

PRIME MINISTER: Male. Bivall. Prime minister of Proto-branch.

PIRA: Female. Bivall. Doctor.

GRETZ DROOM: Jedi Knight. Seen as a sixteen-year-old and then as a young Jedi and eventually Master.

PRIESTESS: Presager dark sider.

QUI-GON JINN: Jedi Padawan.

JOR AERITH: Female. Mirialan. Jedi Master with a sharp tongue.

RAEL AVERROSS: Male. Dooku's first Padawan, seen as a Jedi Knight. Thick Ringo Vindan accent.

AIR-RACE COMMENTATOR: Fast-talking alien.

INSPECTOR SARTORI: Male. Coruscant Security officer.

CENEVAX: Female. Jenet. Crime lord. Skittish and ratlike, but deadly.

DROIDS

LEP-10019: Dooku's LEP droid.

D-4: Female. Gora's cantankerous protocol droid.

TACTICAL DROID

WAITRESS DROID

SECURITY DROIDS

BATTLE DROIDS

ENFORCER DROID

POLICE DROIDS

MED DROIDS

ATTENDANT DROID

QC-ME: CSF mortuary droid.

MINOR ROLES

CELEBRATION HOLOGRAM ANNOUNCER

BRY: Male. Hoopaloo. Birdlike alien thief.

JORKAT: Male. Karkarodon. Thug.

VELEK: Female. Askajian. Thug. Speaks alien language.

ZANG: Female. Jedi Initiate.

TEMPLE ATTENDANT: Female.

RESTELLY QUIST: Female. Elderly. Chief librarian at the Jedi Temple.

YEPA: Female. Portworker.

GRAN: Male. Thugs.

PENDAGO: Male. Thug. Speaks guttural alien language.

SENATOR TAVETTI: Male. Bivall senator.

RRALLA: Male. Wookiee child. Medcenter patient.

AID COMMANDER

TRADER

PROTESTOR #1

PROTESTOR #2

VARIOUS GHOSTLY VOICES FOR SINGLE LINES

PARS-VALO: Initiate.

AMBASSADOR KETAS: Male. Solodoe ambassador.

CHIEF TANU: Solodoe security chief.

DIVAD MASSPUR: Male. Holopresenter. Drunk.

CANDOVANT AMBASSADOR: Male. Speaks alien language.

DESK SERGEANT: Male. Human. Mid-forties.

TRANDOSHAN HEAVIES: Speaking both Trandoshan and Basic.

GUARD

GLUTE: Male. Cybernetic Crolute. Voice like Unkar Plutt but with a mechanical buzz beneath everything, as if his voice box is augmented.

SENATOR BULGESKI: Male. Sallichen senator.

CHANCELLOR KALPANA: Male. Elderly.

TRADE FEDERATION REPRESENTATIVE: Male. Human.

SENATOR PALPATINE / DARTH SIDIOUS: Does he really need an introduction?

SERGEANT ESON: Male. Serennian.

COUNTESS HAGI: Female. Serennian refugee.

ABYSSIN GUARD #1

ABYSSIN GUARD #2

ABYSSIN COMMANDER

ABYSSIN GENERAL

ABYSSIN MERC

HAL'STED: Male. Ventress's slave master.

REPUBLIC AGENT #1

REPUBLIC AGENT #2

PART ONE

CUE THEME

SCENE 1. INT. CASTLE SERENNO. KEEP. NIGHT.

Atmosphere: Wind whistles past a balcony, high in Dooku's castle.

VENTRESS: (NARRATION)
I hate it here.

I hate the castle. I hate the cliff. I hate the spikebats whirling above the forest far below. I hate the moons grinning down at me.

I hate the fact that night after night I stand on this ledge, feeling the breeze against my skin, wondering what it would be like to jump, to drop down into the trees.

Would the Force guide me?

Would it help me find that perfect branch that would take my weight so I could spring to safety, leaves crunching beneath my feet as I ran, rodents scurrying for their nests.

KY NAREC: (GHOST)
How did you get here, little one?

VENTRESS: (NARRATION)
Most of all, I hate that voice. The stupid, impossible voice. A voice of the past. A voice that doesn't belong.

KY NAREC: (GHOST)
I said . . .

VENTRESS:
I know what you said, Ky.

KY NAREC: (GHOST)
And yet you choose to ignore me, my Padawan.

VENTRESS:
I'm not your anything!

VENTRESS: (NARRATION)
I whirl around, expecting to see his face. Those crinkled eyes. That crooked smile.

But the room is empty, dust motes whirling in the moonlight.

He's not here. And yet . . .

KY NAREC: (GHOST)
How did you become this?

VENTRESS:
A monster?

KY NAREC:
(DISTORTED) Do not twist my words, little one.

VENTRESS:
Don't call me that.

KY NAREC:
(DISTORTED) What do you want me to call you?

VENTRESS:
You could try my name.

KY NAREC: (GHOST)
How did you become this, *Asajj*?

VENTRESS:
Actually, that's worse.

VENTRESS: (NARRATION)
I know I'm being contrary, but what does he expect? How *did* I come here? How did I become this woman? This *creature*?

He did this. He led me here.

He left me behind.

KY NAREC: (GHOST)
I never left you, Ventress. I never would.

VENTRESS:
Shut up! Get out of my head!

LEP-10019:
Mistress?

VENTRESS: (NARRATION)
The damn droid makes me jump. The castle is full of them, with their whirring servos and lifeless eyes.

VENTRESS:
I wasn't talking to you.

The droid looks around, its neck servos whirring.

LEP-10019:
There is no one else here.

VENTRESS:
No. No, there's not. (SIGHS) What do you want, droid?

LEP-10019:
My designation is LEP-10019.

VENTRESS:
I don't care.

LEP-10019:
Oh. Um. He needs you.

KY NAREC: (GHOST)
Ventress . . . please . . .

VENTRESS:
Lead the way.

SCENE 2. INT. CASTLE CORRIDOR.

The LEP-100197 droid clanks as it leads Ventress through the castle.

VENTRESS: (NARRATION)
I think of the ways I could destroy the waddling robot as it leads me through the castle. The corridors are long and as sterile as its workforce. As a building it's impressive, with its high vaulted ceilings and arched doors. We had nothing like it on Rattatak, nothing that wasn't pockmarked by laser burns anyway. But where are the portraits of long-dead ancestors? Where are the statues? Where is the stuffed rancor head mounted over a roaring hearth?

The castle is pristine but empty, devoid of warmth.

Like its master.

LEP-10019:
This way please.

VENTRESS: (NARRATION)
Dooku is in the great hall, standing on a raised dais. He stares through the circular window that dominates the far wall, his family's sigil etched into the stained glass.

LEP-10019:
Wait here.

VENTRESS: (NARRATION)
I fight the urge to separate the El-ee-pee's stupid rabbit-eared head from its narrow shoulders. It totters off, leaving me in Dooku's presence. The imposing man doesn't turn. He doesn't even acknowledge that I am here.

I wait, every muscle aching with the effort of appearing nonchalant.

As if I can fool him.

DOOKU:
Your feelings betray you.

VENTRESS:
I'm sorry. I—

DOOKU:
(STERN) Did I grant you permission to speak?

VENTRESS: (NARRATION)
I grit my teeth, trying to calm the fury that twists in my belly like a nest of bloodvipers.

DOOKU:
No. Let your anger grow. Let it seethe.

VENTRESS: (NARRATION)
Finally he turns, regarding me not with interest but with idle curiosity, the way a scientist examines a rodent to see if it has mastered a new trick, to see if it deserves a reward.

But there are no rewards here.

DOOKU:
Your burns are healing. Do they hurt?

VENTRESS:
No, Master.

DOOKU:
Liar. Try again.

VENTRESS:
Yes. They hurt very much.

DOOKU:
Good. Focus on the pain. Use it. It is the source of your power.

VENTRESS:
Yes, Master.

VENTRESS: (NARRATION)
Master. The word sticks in my throat. I vowed I would never call anyone Master again. Not after Hal'Sted. And especially not after Narec.

And yet, here I am.

KY NAREC: (GHOST)
Here you are.

VENTRESS: (NARRATION)
I clench my fists, nails biting into my palms. The voice has plagued me ever since I was brought here. A voice only I can hear. Unless this is another test? Has Dooku summoned a phantom to torment me?

I square my shoulders, raising my chin. I must appear strong.

Dooku's dark eyes narrow.

DOOKU:
You are troubled.

VENTRESS:
No, Master. It . . . It is nothing.

DOOKU:
I told you. Do not lie to me.

VENTRESS:
I wouldn't. I . . . I couldn't.

VENTRESS: (NARRATION)
A smile tugs at the corners of his mouth. The rat has performed well. Squeak, squeak, squeak.

DOOKU:
You wish to kill me.

VENTRESS:
No. I—

Force lightning crackles out from Dooku's fingers, striking Ventress.

VENTRESS:
(CRIES OUT)

VENTRESS: (NARRATION)
Dark lightning bursts from Dooku's fingers, coursing over me. In one agonizing, mind-shredding moment, he proves to me that nothing else matters. Not the droids. Not the castle. Not even Ky.

There is only his authority and his voice.

The lightning continues to flow throughout the scene as Dooku taunts her.

DOOKU:
Of course you want to kill me. You are a killer. That is what you do. That is why I chose you. Do you think I came to Rattatak by chance? That I somehow stumbled upon your pit?

VENTRESS:
(PAINED) No . . .

DOOKU:
The Force showed me. It showed me a Dathomiri sold to save her coven. A slave liberated from captivity. A Padawan forced to watch her Master bleed out in the dirt.

VENTRESS:
Please . . .

DOOKU:
Is that how they begged, your victims, as you took revenge, as you slaughtered every Rattataki who conspired to murder your Master? I wish I'd seen it, Ventress. I wish I'd seen their faces when they realized the storm they'd unleashed.

VENTRESS: (NARRATION)
Somehow, despite the lightning, despite the pain, I relive each and every moment. Feeling the fury swell inside me, my lightsabers a blur, their screams like music.

I never knew how sweet revenge would taste, how the fear in their eyes sated the anger in my belly.

Ky would have told me that it wasn't the Jedi way, but I didn't care. I had taken the Jedi way and rammed it down their throats along with my fist.

Zol Kramer. Rynn'k-lee. They all fell, one after another.

Until I faced Kirske. Until I faced the scumsnake who had ordered Ky's death.

I'd thought he'd be like the others. I thought he would pay. I thought he would suffer as I was suffering.

I was wrong. I was blindsided by my own vanity, so sure that I would emerge victorious. So convinced. I never expected Kirske to use himself as bait until it was too late, until I'd raced toward him, lightsabers blazing.

Until the trap had been sprung.

That's why Dooku found me, not surrounded by the corpses of my enemies, but forced to spill blood for the entertainment of others, a gladiator in a filthy pit, stun collar tight around my neck.

Could he sense my regret? My rage?

For my part, I had no idea who he was, just the latest in a long line of spectators enjoying the hospitality of Osika Kirske's viewing gallery. I had no idea he'd told Kirske he was looking for an assassin, or that he'd already made his choice.

I don't know who was more surprised when Dooku took Kirske's head, me or the Vollick himself. One minute Dooku was sipping wine from a crystal glass, and the next his crimson lightsaber was slicing through Kirske's neck.

The Vollick's head bounced down into the arena, a shocked expression on his face as it bounced once and then twice before coming to rest at my feet.

I couldn't celebrate. I couldn't revel in Kirske's death. *I* should've been the one to deal the killing blow, to snuff out his life, and yet this . . . this stranger with fine clothes and an imperious gaze had stolen my revenge.

I leapt from the arena floor, the Force propelling me up to the gallery, my lightsabers already burning. Dooku was waiting for me. Two blades against one. There was no way the old man should've been able to defend himself, and yet he did. He blocked every attack, parried every blow, giving no ground, taking no damage.

He didn't even spill his wine.

And then it came. His lightning. It felt like every atom in my body was being torn apart, every memory I had shredding beneath the onslaught. Mother Talzin. Hal'Sted. Ky. They were all gone, consumed in the pain of Dooku's dark magic.

I don't remember my lightsabers slipping from my hands. I don't even remember blacking out.

The next thing I knew, I was being grabbed by mechanical hands, dragged through unfamiliar corridors. My stun collar was gone, the air cool against my charred skin. I remember hearing birds as I was hauled past open windows. That's when I knew I was no longer on Rattatak. The only birds on Rattatak are the strike-vultures that strip bones clean on the dust plains.

He was waiting for me in the great hall, in the exact same place as he stands now, looking down at me with eyes as black as a starless sky.

"I will teach you the ways of the dark side, but first, you must prove yourself."

(A BEAT AS WE RETURN TO THE HERE AND NOW)

It takes me a moment to register that the lightning has stopped. Hands take my scorched arms. For a moment, I imagine it's Ky, helping me back to my feet, but then my vision clears and I'm looking into the face of my savior and tormentor.

I force myself to stand, telling myself I need to appear strong no matter what lessons Dooku inflicts.

DOOKU:
I don't want to have to do that again.

VENTRESS: (NARRATION)
That makes two of us.

He walks behind his desk, opening a drawer. As I struggle to draw air into my scorched lungs, he retrieves a disk no larger than a coin and tosses it toward me. It clatters and spins before coming to rest on the polished wood. I wait, not daring to move until he nods. Cautiously, I retrieve the disk, turning it over in my hand.

VENTRESS:
A data card?

DOOKU:
Place it in the holoprojector.

VENTRESS: (NARRATION)
I do as I am instructed, a hologram fizzing into existence. It's a boy, no older than ten years old, wearing the robes of a Jedi Initiate,

hair buzz-cut short. There's something about his face. Something familiar.

VENTRESS:
(REALIZATION DAWNING) It's you.

DOOKU:
I'd forgotten I was ever that young. It belongs to my sister.

VENTRESS:
Your sister?

DOOKU:
I had no idea she kept the recordings. I told her to destroy them. She disobeyed me.

VENTRESS:
But I don't understand. You were a Jedi.

DOOKU:
I was.

VENTRESS:
But I thought Jedi cut all ties to their family.

DOOKU:
They do. But my sister . . . let's just say . . . we found each other . . .

VENTRESS:
How?

VENTRESS: (NARRATION)
I tense, waiting for another burst of lightning, but instead Dooku's eyes drop away, focusing on the hologram of the boy in front of us. I sense conflict in him, memories long buried bubbling to the surface. When he speaks again, there is a . . . wistfulness in his voice, a vulnerability that I just haven't heard in him before.

DOOKU:
I never knew my family, for the reasons you mentioned. Like most of the Order, I was brought to the Temple by a Seeker, a Jedi who

was tasked to scour the galaxy for Force-sensitive infants. I had no recollection of my home, having been transported to Coruscant as a babe in arms, only to be told that I was to return as an Initiate.

VENTRESS:
Return to Serenno. Why?

DOOKU:
For a great celebration . . .

SCENE 3. EXT. CARANNIA. CAPITAL CITY OF SERENNO.

Atmosphere: As Dooku talks, we hear the sounds of a grand cele-bration behind the narration, music playing, crowds bustling, dem-onstrations being made. Think of it as a trade fair for the outer rim.

DOOKU: (NARRATION)
Serenno was hosting a showcase for the galaxy, an opportunity for the planets of the Outer Rim to demonstrate what they could bring to the ever-growing Republic. Merchants and traders flocked here to wander the pavilions and gawp at demonstrations. There were ship makers and weaponsmiths, droid manufacturers and agrifarmers.

VENTRESS: (NARRATION)
And Jedi?

DOOKU: (NARRATION)
The Council had debated the wisdom of sending Initiates to such an event, but it had been argued that the Celebration was too good an opportunity to miss, a once-in-a-lifetime opportunity for the young Jedi-in-training to observe the galaxy they had pledged their lives to protect . . .

What better way could there be for young Jedi-in-waiting to un-derstand the galaxy they would serve, but to see it with their own overeager eyes?

SIFO-DYAS: (TWELVE YEARS OLD)
Dooku. Dooku, can you believe this? Look at it all. There are so many people.

DOOKU: (TWELVE YEARS OLD)
Too many.

SIFO-DYAS:
(LAUGHS) You need to relax. Enjoy yourself. It's a festival!

DOOKU:
I am enjoying myself.

SIFO-DYAS:
Then you should tell your face.

DOOKU: (NARRATION)
It's safe to say that I was a . . . difficult person to know. I struggled
to make friends in the early days of my training. On arrival at the
Temple, Initiates are sorted into clans, an arbitrary grouping in
many ways, but one that is supposed to foster an atmosphere of
trust and kinship. Not so for me. I had no need of camaraderie,
even then. I was there to train, to be the very best I could be. While
my clan-mates huddled together after lessons, swapping tales of
the Nameless or whatever phantasmagoria had seized their over-
active imaginations, I could be found ensuring my tunic was
sharply pressed and boots polished. I had Masters to impress, after
all.

Only one boy saw through my bluster, an Initiate as likely to cause
trouble as I was expected to excel. Perhaps I needed someone to
burst my bubble. Perhaps I just needed a companion. But whatever
the reason, we became inseparable . . .

DOOKU:
Sifo-Dyas, remember where we are. People are staring.

SIFO-DYAS:
So? It's the Celebration. We're supposed to be enjoying ourselves.

DOOKU:
No. We're supposed to be representing the Jedi. What would
Master Yoda say if he saw you prancing about like a Floubettean
dancer?

SIFO-DYAS:

But he's not going to see, is he? He's too busy being wise and inscrutable and—

Sifo-Dyas barrels straight into Yoda, who is knocked from his feet.

YODA:

(CRIES OUT)

DOOKU: (NARRATION)

My heart sank as Sifo-Dyas wheeled around, knocking into the very Jedi Master he was mocking.

SIFO-DYAS:

M-Master Yoda! I'm so sorry.

DOOKU:

(HISSING) You idiot!

YODA:

Look where you are going, you should, young Sifo-Dyas.

DOOKU: (NARRATION)

As if they'd been waiting for disaster to strike, the other Masters appeared from the crowd, rushing to their Grand Master's aid. There was Tera Sinube, the beak-nosed Cosian who, like Yoda himself, seemed to have been born ancient and wizened . . .

TERA SINUBE:

Master Yoda? Are you all right?

DOOKU: (NARRATION)

And then there was Yula Braylon, a Seeker who had brought many of the Order's new recruits to the Temple doors.

BRAYLON:

Who did this? Show yourself.

SIFO-DYAS:

It was me, Master Braylon. I . . . I just got so excited with all the lights and the sounds and . . .

BRAYLON:
And this is why dragging Initiates halfway across the galaxy was a mistake.

YODA:
No harm was done. An accident it was.

DOOKU:
Sifo-Dyas really is sorry.

YODA:
Learned a lesson, young Sifo-Dyas has. Do it again, he will not.

SIFO-DYAS:
No. I promise. I'll . . . I'll look where I'm going.

YODA:
As all of us must. Yes. Everyone.

DOOKU: (NARRATION)
Not all the Masters were as quick to forgive. Braylon fixed us with a suspicious glare, as if convinced we would blunder into trouble the moment her back was turned.

Her instincts were to be applauded.

BRAYLON:
Now, don't go wandering off. The lightsaber demonstration takes place in less than an hour. Do you understand? Remember why we are here.

DOOKU:
To demonstrate the discipline and composure of the Jedi.

SINUBE:
See? They *were* listening, Braylon. Well done, Dooku.

DOOKU:
Thank you, Master Sinube.

DOOKU: (NARRATION)

We waited solemnly as the Masters headed back to the stage where the demonstration would be given. It was only when they were out of sight that I punched Sifo-Dyas sharply in the arm.

SIFO-DYAS:

Ow! What was that for?

DOOKU:

What do you think? Knocking Master Yoda over! You're lucky they didn't ship us back to Coruscant.

SIFO-DYAS:

I thought that's what you wanted. Come on, Doo.

DOOKU:

(SIGHING) Don't call me that.

SIFO-DYAS:

Why not? It's your name.

DOOKU:

No, it's not.

SIFO-DYAS:

(TEASING, SINGSONG) Doo. Doo. Dooku.

DOOKU:

Shut up.

SIFO-DYAS:

Doo. Doo. Doo.

DOOKU:

(UNABLE TO STOP HIMSELF FROM LAUGHING) You're an idiot.

SIFO-DYAS:

And you're home! This is Serenno, Dooku. How many Initiates get to visit where they were born?

ARATH: (TWELVE YEARS OLD)
(APPROACHING) What was that, Sifo-Dyas? This is where *His Eminence* comes from?

DOOKU:
(GROANS) Nice work, Si.

DOOKU: (NARRATION)
If I could have willed it, I would have urged the ground to swallow me up there and then.

From the day we met, Arath Tarrex had been determined to make my life a misery. He seemed to take offense at everything I did. The way I walked. The way I talked. And most important, the way I outshone his pitiful attempts to succeed in each and every one of our classes together.

Jedi are trained to suppress our emotions, but even then, Arath. He was jealous of me, and for good reason . . .

SIFO-DYAS:
Leave us alone, Arath. We weren't talking to you.

ARATH:
Is this really your home, Dooku?

DOOKU:
No. My home is the Temple. Just like you.

SIFO-DYAS:
(SOTTO) More's the pity.

ARATH:
What was that?

SIFO-DYAS:
Nothing, Arath. Nothing at all. What's the matter, anyway? Don't you like it here?

ARATH:

Are you kidding? It's a dump. Who would have thought that for all his airs and graces, little Lord Dooku comes from a shab-hole like this?

DOOKU:

I'm warning you, Arath . . .

ARATH:

What? What are you going to do, Dooku? Run off to Braylon like last time?

DOOKU:

I'll show you what I'm gonna do.

Dooku goes to shove Arath, but Sifo-Dyas stops him.

SIFO-DYAS:

Whoa-whoa-whoa! Discipline and composure, remember. Discipline and composure.

ARATH:

(WALKING OFF) Good luck with that. See you at the demonstration, Your Highness.

DOOKU:

One day I'm going to wipe the smirk off his stupid face.

SIFO-DYAS:

And what good would that do?

DOOKU:

It would put him in his place.

SIFO-DYAS:

Which is exactly the kind of talk that adds coaxium to his engines. Look, I know you're better than him. He knows you're better than him. Even the duraslugs back home know you're better than him, but there's no need to rub his face in it.

DOOKU:
What about rubbing his face in that dewback paddock over there?

SIFO-DYAS:
Okay, that I would like to see, but if you do, Braylon will make sure we spend the rest of the Celebration holed up on the *Ataraxia.* Come on, Doo. When do we ever get out of the Temple, let alone off Coruscant? Let's forget Arath and explore while we have the chance, yeah?

SCENE 4. EXT. CELEBRATION. JENZA'S POV.

DOOKU: (NARRATION)
I reluctantly agreed, allowing Sifo-Dyas to drag me farther into the crowd, unaware that, not far away, nobility was gracing the festivities.

HOLOGRAM ANNOUNCER:
People of the galaxy, welcome to Carannia. Here you will discover all the Outer Rim has to offer. Innovation. Exploration. A brave frontier awaits, worlds of opportunity and adventure, all accessible by safe and reliable hyperroutes . . .

We come upon Count Gora, the ruler of Serenno, who is sweeping through the celebration surrounded by his entourage.

GORA:
(SNORTS) "Safe and reliable hyperroutes"? What a load of Sith spit.

ANYA:
Gora, please! The children.

GORA:
What about them? I can't believe the Assembly talked me into this. It's an insult. That's what it is. A damn insult.

D-4:
Actually, Count Gora, the Celebration is a once-in-a-lifetime opportunity for Serenno.

GORA:

Anya, kindly remind your protocol droid not to lecture me, unless he wants to be smelted down with the next batch of Malvern's zersium.

ANYA:

Dee-Four, maybe it would be better if you buttoned your vocabulator.

D-4:

But Countess Anya, I sought only to remind His Grace that—

GORA:

I can still hear it talking!

ANYA:

Please, Dee-Four. The last thing we need is for him to go into another rage. Perhaps you could look after the children?

D-4:

The children? Countess, I'm programmed for diplomacy and etiquette . . .

ANYA:

And therefore the perfect babysitter for Ramil and Jenza.

RAMIL: (FOURTEEN YEARS OLD)
Mother! I'm not a baby!

D-4:

(SNORTS) That's a matter of opinion.

RAMIL:

Oh, shove it up your recharge coupling.

D-4:

Countess. Did you hear what he said?

ANYA:

(SIGHING) Yes, yes. Ramil, there's no need to be rude. (TO HERSELF) You're not your father.

GORA:

What was that?

ANYA:

Nothing, darling. I was just talking to the children.

JENZA: (ELEVEN YEARS OLD)

Can't we just look around, Mother?

ANYA:

Not by yourself, Jenza. You know that.

JENZA:

But—

ANYA:

But nothing. Dee-Four will stay with you.

RAMIL:

This is so humiliating.

ANYA:

You could always come to the Assembly and hear your father's speech?

JENZA:

Actually, Dee-Four will make fine company. (POINTED) Won't she, Ramil?

RAMIL:

I suppose. Come on then, Bolt-Head. Let's look around.

D-4:

But I must protest. My duty—

ANYA:

(CALLING BACK AS SHE WALKS OFF) Is to look after the children. Have fun.

D-4:

(CALLING AFTER HER) Countess. Countess, really. (TO HER-SELF) This is too much. I've half a mind to . . . (REALIZES THE

CHILDREN HAVE GONE) Where are they? Where have they gotten to? (CALLING) Lady Jenza.

SCENE 5. EXT. CELEBRATION. THE CHILDREN'S POV. (CONT.)

We shift farther into the crowd, D-4 now behind us.

D-4: (OFF-MIC)
Master Ramil! Come back here.

JENZA:
What do you want to see first, Ramil? I hear there are Jedi here.

RAMIL:
Why would anyone want to see those freaks?

JENZA:
Don't call them that.

RAMIL:
Father does.

JENZA:
Father does a lot of things. Come on.

They run off, D-4 finally catching up, just a moment too late.

D-4: (COMING UP ON MIC)
No. No. Wait for me, you pampered—Oh, what have I done to deserve this.

SCENE 6. EXT. CELEBRATION—JEDI DEMONSTRATION.

The children push through the crowds, heading toward the Jedi demonstration. Above the babble of the watching crowd, we can hear Yoda, Sinube, and Braylon performing a ceremonial demonstration in perfect unison, their lightsabers buzzing and swooping. Think of it as Tai Chi for Jedi.

DOOKU: (NARRATION)
At the Jedi stage, we stood watching Yoda, Sinube, and Braylon demonstrating basic lightsaber stances, plasma humming as

they moved in perfect synchronization, eyes closed and minds calm.

All around, the crowd gawped, the Masters just another spectacle to experience amid the noise of the revelry, but for one young observer the demonstration would be a life-changing moment . . .

Jenza pulls Ramil through the crowd. D-4 has caught up with them.

JENZA:
There they are! Wow. Just look at them.

D-4:
Yes. Yes. Very good. Shall we find your parents now?

RAMIL:
Is that it? Aren't they supposed to be fighting or something?

D-4:
No, the energy blades are purely ceremonial.

JENZA:
It helps them meditate.

RAMIL:
How do you know?

JENZA:
I saw a documentary on the HoloNet. The swords are called lightsabers.

RAMIL:
They look stupid.

D-4:
They look dangerous. They'll have someone's arm off in a minute.

RAMIL:
Here's hoping. At least that'll be more interesting. (LAUGHING) Look at that one. He looks like a slime-gnome.

JENZA:

Shush. He'll hear you.

RAMIL:

I'm not surprised with ears like that. Oh, come on, Jen. This is so boring. Let's find the Nalroni pavilion. Father says the Celanites are demonstrating their new security droids.

JENZA:

You go. I want to look around.

RAMIL:

Yeah, like Bolt-Head will let us split up . . .

D-4:

Bolt-Head certainly will not.

RAMIL:

See?

Jenza leans into her brother conspiratorially.

JENZA:

(WHISPER) What's the matter, Ramil? Scared of a protocol droid?

RAMIL:

(WHISPER) Of course not.

JENZA:

(WHISPER) Prove it.

RAMIL:

(WHISPER) Okay. Watch this.

He rummages around in his pockets.

JENZA:

(WHISPER) What are they?

RAMIL:

(WHISPER) Thunderburst caps.

JENZA:

(WHISPER) Mother said you weren't supposed to have them any-more. Not since the Frost-tide ball!

RAMIL:

(WHISPER) What's the matter, Jenza—*scared*?

JENZA:

(SMILING) Oh shut up.

RAMIL:

(WHISPER) Get ready to run. One.

JENZA:

(WHISPER) Two.

RAMIL:

Three!

He throws down the thunderbursts, which burst on the ground like little fireworks. The crowd reacts, spectators crying out in shock, the children laughing with glee as they run.

JENZA:

(CALLING TO HER BROTHER) Catch you later, Ram!

D-4:

Wait. Where are you going? Come back. Come back here this minute!

SCENE 7. EXT. CELEBRATION—JEDI DEMONSTRATION. DOOKU'S POV.

We hear the disturbance from the other side of the Jedi demonstration where Dooku and Sifo-Dyas are watching.

DOOKU: (NARRATION)

On the other side of the stage, the disturbance caused much excitement among the Initiates . . .

SIFO-DYAS:

What's going on?

ARATH:

Just local kids setting off fireworks.

SIFO-DYAS:

Doo, are you okay?

DOOKU:

That girl . . .

SIFO-DYAS:

What girl?

DOOKU:

She was just there. By the droid.

ARATH:

You found yourself a girlfriend, Your Majesty?

SIFO-DYAS:

Shut up, Arath.

ARATH:

He looks pretty keen to me.

SIFO-DYAS:

What? (REALIZES DOOKU IS GONE) Doo? Dooku. Where have you gone?

SCENE 8. EXT. FAIRGROUND.

Atmosphere: An alleyway full of game stalls. Dooku is pushing his way through the crowd.

(THE FOLLOWING WILD TRACKS ARE FOR USE IN THE BACKGROUND AS HE PUSHES THROUGH.)

GAME STALLHOLDER #1:

Take a leap of faith. Zero-gee diving. Just three credits. Why not have a go?

GAME STALLHOLDER #2:

Droid firing gallery. Hit the target to win a prize. Droid shoot-out. Hit those tin-heads between their photoreceptors.

GAME STALLHOLDER #3:

Whack-a-bloggin! Try your luck. Where will they pop up next? Only two credits. That's it, son. That's it!

GAME STALLHOLDER #4:

Prize every time. What have you got to lose? Everyone's a winner!

DOOKU:

Excuse me. Excuse me.

Sifo-Dyas chases after him.

SIFO-DYAS:

(APPROACHING) Dooku! Wait up. Where are you going?

DOOKU:

Si. Go back.

SIFO-DYAS:

And let you have all the fun? What's gotten into you?

DOOKU:

That girl . . . I sensed something . . .

SIFO-DYAS:

I don't believe it. Arath was right.

DOOKU:

No, not like that. It was like I knew her somehow.

SIFO-DYAS:

How? You were only a baby when Yoda came for you.

DOOKU:

I know. I can't explain it. (SPOTS JENZA) There she is!

SIFO-DYAS:

Doo, this is crazy. You can't just run off. If the Masters catch you . . .

Dooku runs after her.

DOOKU:
You go back. I'll be all right.

SIFO-DYAS:
No. No you won't!

SCENE 9. EXT. FAIRGROUND. JENZA'S POV.

Atmosphere as before.

STALLHOLDER #1:
Test your strength against the tractor beam. Only three credits. (SPOTS JENZA) What about you, little lady? Feeling strong today, are we?

JENZA:
(UNSURE) No. Thank you.

She hurries on.

STALLHOLDER #1:
(CALLING AFTER HER) Go on! Have a go. You never know your luck.

JENZA:
Really. It's fine. Thank you.

She bumps into an alien who answers angrily in Huttese.

ALIEN:
Chuba! Doompasha lo! [Hey! Watch it!]

JENZA:
I'm sorry! I didn't mean to walk into you.

ALIEN:
Oosa do nawee, eh? [Use your eyes, eh?]

She rushes off.

JENZA:
I really am sorry.

She wanders for a minute, totally lost.

JENZA:
Maybe this wasn't such a good idea.

She activates a comlink.

JENZA:
Ramil? Ramil, are you there?

RAMIL: (OVER COMM)
What do you want?

JENZA:
Where are you?

RAMIL: (COMM)
Heading toward the droid pavilion. Why?

JENZA:
I thought I might come with you after all. Can you wait for me?

RAMIL: (COMM)
Ha! I knew you'd get scared on your own. (TEASING) Perhaps you should ask the Jedi for protection?

JENZA:
Don't be such a smog-wart.

RAMIL: (COMM)
Where are you?

JENZA:
I don't know. There are games and—

Someone barges into her.

JENZA: (CONT.)
(REACTS) So many people.

RAMIL: (COMM)
Okay. Wait there. But you'll owe me. Do you hear?

JENZA:
Yes. I—

Someone else brushes past her, roughly.

JENZA:
(SHOUT) Hey!

RAMIL: (COMM)
What is it? Jenza?

JENZA:
Someone stole my purse.

RAMIL: (COMM)
What? Who?

JENZA:
A scraggy little Hoopaloo. I can see it. (SHE STARTS TO RUN, BARGING PAST PEOPLE) Excuse me! Let me through!

RAMIL: (COMM)
Jenza, no. Don't go after it. It could be dangerous. Jen—

Jenza trips.

JENZA:
(GASPS)

And there's a crunch as the comlink breaks, cutting Ramil off.

JENZA:
Oh no.

She scrabbles up to run after the thief, clicking the comlink button repeatedly.

JENZA:
Ramil? Ramil, can you hear me?

With more clicks, she realizes the unit is broken.

JENZA:
No. Mother's going to kill me. (SHOUTS AFTER THE THIEF)
Come back!

SCENE 10. EXT. FAIRGROUND—BEHIND THE STALLS.

Jenza runs between the attractions, finding herself behind a large tent.

JENZA:
Where did it go? (SPOTS IT) There you are!

DOOKU: (NARRATION)
The Hoopaloo was crouched behind a large repulsor tent, rifling through the contents of the girl's bag.

JENZA:
Give that back! It's mine!

She grabs the purse.

BRY:
(SQUAWKS) Don't snatch.

JENZA:
Don't snatch? You stole my purse. (SHE LOOKS THROUGH IT) Where's the crystal? What did you do with it?

BRY:
Don't know anything about a crystal.

JENZA:
Look, you can keep the credits. I don't care about them, but I need that crystal. It belonged to my grandmother.

A male Karkarodon—Jorkat—and a female Askajian—Velek—approach suddenly.

JORKAT:
Well, well. What have we here?

DOOKU: (NARRATION)

A shadow fell over Jenza. She turned to see a shark-faced Karkarodon and a substantial Askajian stalking toward them. The Karkarodon grinned, revealing four rows of tiny pointed teeth.

JENZA:

(GASPS)

BRY:

Jorkat. Stealing from me, she was. Got me purse.

JENZA:

That's a lie! It's *my* purse.

JORKAT:

Stealing from my friends, eh? A rich little thing like you. What do you think about that, Velek?

VELEK:

Keea milek. [Selfish little brat.]

JORKAT:

Yeah, she *is* selfish, isn't she? All those pretty trinkets, and poor Bry, not a credit to his name. Perhaps we'll have that coat of yours. How would you like that? That'll warm your feathers, won't it, Bry?

BRY:

Yeah. Nice and toasty.

JENZA:

No. You can't have it. It's mine.

VELEK:

(MOCKING) *"Minaar. Minaar."* ["It's mine. It's mine."]

JORKAT:

(GRABBING HER) Let's see what else you've got . . .

JENZA:

(SCREAMS) Let go of me!

Ramil runs up.

RAMIL:

Let her go!

JORKAT:

And what's this? A little rich boy to complete the set. Grab him.

Velek grabs Ramil.

RAMIL:

(STRUGGLING) Get off me! Let me go!

BRY:

Perhaps we should take 'em with us, Jorkat. See what Renza will give us for 'em.

JORKAT:

The Hutt? She likes more meat on the bones, that one. But I suppose we could—Ow! The little scutta bit me.

JENZA:

Leave my brother alone!

Jenza rushes at Velek, who swats her back.

JENZA:

(CRIES OUT)

JORKAT:

Get her, Bry.

BRY:

Come here, you little—

DOOKU: (NARRATION)

Without warning, the Hoopaloo was thrown through the air, crashing into the tent's heavy canvas.

BRY:

(CRIES OUT)

JORKAT:

What are you doing? Get back on your feet.

BRY:

Something knocked me over.

JORKAT:

Nothing touched you!

BRY:

I know what I felt.

JENZA:

Let us go!

DOOKU:

Do as she says!

JORKAT:

What the—?

DOOKU: (NARRATION)

Now it was the Karkarodon's turn to gape . . .

BRY:

It's a Jedi!

JORKAT:

(LAUGHS) It's a child! It hasn't even got a lightsaber.

DOOKU:

I don't need one.

DOOKU: (NARRATION)

I flicked my wrist, a telescopic rod extending from the hilt I'd hidden in my palm, a rod that crackled with unfettered energy.

JORKAT:

Ha! What's that supposed to be?

DOOKU:

It's called an electroblade. We use it to practice against dummies. Like you.

He strikes Jorkat with the blade, electricity arcing. Jorkat cries out as he falls.

DOOKU: (NARRATION)
I wheeled around, my blade smacking into the brute's legs . . . He crashed to the floor, staring up at me in disbelief.

DOOKU:
Do you want more?

JORKAT:
You wouldn't dare.

DOOKU: (NARRATION)
How wrong he was.

The young Dooku strikes Jorkat time and time again, electricity sparking with each blow.

JORKAT:
Argh! Stop it!

BRY:
I'll get him, Jorkat!

DOOKU:
No, you won't.

DOOKU: (NARRATION)
The Hoopaloo scrambled forward, only to be plucked from the ground and sent spinning the way he came . . .

BRY:
(CRIES OUT AGAIN)

DOOKU: (NARRATION)
Even the Askajian, for all her bulk, was no challenge. A flick of the wrist took her feet out from beneath her. Gravity did the rest.

Velek crashes forward, hitting the ground.

VELEK:
Carek nada khan? [How is he doing that?]

Jorkat grabs at Dooku.

JORKAT:
How am I supposed to know how he's doing it? Come 'ere, you little scumslug.

DOOKU:
I don't think so.

DOOKU: (NARRATION)
I buried my blade in his side, and sparks danced across his newly cracked teeth.

JORKAT:
(CRIES OUT)

DOOKU:
Haven't you had enough yet? (TO VELEK) And as for you, Askajian, what is it they say? The bigger they are ... the louder they scream!

DOOKU: (NARRATION)
And scream she did as she was thrown across the litter-strewn floor to slam into her Hoopaloo cohort.

VELEK & BRY:
(CRY OUT)

DOOKU: (NARRATION)
The Askajian took one last look at my blade and decided that no coat was worth further humiliation. She pushed herself up, all but crushing the Hoopaloo in the process, and fled like the coward she was.

JORKAT:
Velek! Come back!

DOOKU:
I'd run, too, if I were you.

JORKAT:
I'll rip yer head off.

BRY:
Jorkat. Please, let's get out of here.

JORKAT:
Gah! (SCRABBLING UP AND RUNNING) Jedi scum. Why don't you go back where you came from!

DOOKU:
(SHOUTING AFTER THEM) I already have. Unfortunately!

DOOKU: (NARRATION)
I stood there, scowling at the ruffians, so consumed with indignation that I failed to notice the girl reach out to me . . .

JENZA:
Are you okay?

DOOKU:
(STARTLED, SPINNING AROUND, ELECTROBLADE BUZZING)

JENZA:
I'm sorry. I didn't mean to startle you.

DOOKU:
You . . . you didn't. Are you hurt?

JENZA:
No. Thanks to you.

RAMIL: (OFF-MIC)
I'm fine. Thanks for asking.

Dooku goes to assist him.

DOOKU:
I'm sorry. Here, let me help.

RAMIL:
(PUSHING HIMSELF UP) I can manage. Jenza, are you—

JENZA:

I'm fine. Did you see it, Ramil?

RAMIL:

I saw.

JENZA:

The way you took on that . . . I don't know what it was. The shark-thing.

DOOKU:

A Karkarodon. You were lucky.

RAMIL:

I don't feel very lucky.

JENZA:

Stop moaning. We're safe, aren't we? Thanks to . . .

DOOKU:

Dooku. My name's Dooku.

RAMIL:

Well, yes. Thank you, Dooku. But we'd better be off.

JENZA:

I don't want to go.

RAMIL:

Dee-Four will be looking for us.

JENZA:

What about the security droids?

RAMIL:

What? Oh, we can see them another time.

JENZA:

Go and see them now. I want to stay.

RAMIL:

With *him*?

JENZA:
Bye, Ramil.

RAMIL:
Jenza. You were the one who called *me*!

JENZA:
And what good were you, exactly? I don't know what would have happened if Dooku hadn't come along.

RAMIL:
I could have handled those creeps.

DOOKU:
Looked like it.

JENZA:
(SNICKERS)

RAMIL:
What did you say?

DOOKU:
I mean, that Askajian . . . She was pretty scary. You could have been smothered.

DOOKU: (NARRATION)
Glaring, Ramil went to grab her hand.

RAMIL:
Come on, Jenza. We're leaving.

JENZA:
(PULLS AWAY) No, we're not.

RAMIL:
Fine. (HE STALKS OFF) Just don't blame me when you get eaten by a pack of ravenous Karkran or something!

DOOKU:
Your brother's an idiot.

JENZA:

You don't have to tell me.

DOOKU:

Karkran don't even eat humans.

JENZA:

Oh. They don't?

DOOKU:

They don't like the way we taste.

JENZA:

(GIGGLES) You know a lot about . . . well, all this.

DOOKU:

I . . . I like to study.

JENZA:

It's weird. You're going to think this is crazy, but I feel like I know you.

DOOKU:

Me too. I mean, I felt something similar when you were watching the demonstration.

JENZA:

You followed me?

DOOKU:

No. I . . . I sensed you were in trouble.

JENZA:

And I was. Thank you . . . for helping us. I'm grateful, even if my pig of a brother isn't.

DOOKU:

And your name is Junsa?

JENZA:

Jenza.

DOOKU:
Mine's Dooku.

JENZA:
(LAUGHS) I know. You said.

DOOKU:
(EMBARRASSED) Sorry.

JENZA:
Don't be. But Dooku . . . that's a Serennian name.

DOOKU:
I'm from here. At least, originally.

JENZA:
Where's your family?

DOOKU:
I don't know. I was just a baby when I was taken to Coruscant.

JENZA:
A baby?

DOOKU:
(SHRUGS) It's the Jedi way. I can't remember any of this.

JENZA:
Then you need a tour. Would you like me to show you around?

DOOKU:
What about your droid?

JENZA:
She can wait. (GRABS HIS HAND) Come on.

DOOKU: (NARRATION)
She held out her hand, and after hesitating for just one moment, I
took it.

We explored the Celebration together, tasting succulent lalaren
blooms from Carosi Eight and marveling at blatterborn and huna-

net-tre in the Dianectric Menagerie. We even tried our luck at the game stalls, Jenza winning a stuffed purrgil on the zero-gee shoot-out . . . with a little help from the Force . . .

It was like walking through a dream, the place of my birth both alien and yet eerily familiar.

For all my training, I struggled to keep my emotions under check as Jenza led us away from the pavilion, heading toward an imposing domed building in the heart of Carannia. I had known little of life outside the Temple, but here, as we climbed the magnificent marble steps, I felt a stirring deep within me, as if this was where I truly belonged . . .

SCENE 11. INT. ASSEMBLY HALL. SERENNO.

Atmosphere: The assembly hall is vast, a great cathedral with a massive domed ceiling. Dooku and Jenza's footsteps echo as they enter the main hall.

DOOKU:
(AWED) What is this place?

JENZA:
The Great Assembly. Our version of the Senate, I guess you'd call it.

DOOKU:
It's incredible.

He rushes to the far wall.

DOOKU:
What are these?

JENZA:
The seals of the seven houses. That's Borgin, that's Malvern, and that's Hakka.

DOOKU:
What about this?

JENZA:
Serenno.

DOOKU:
The planet?

JENZA:
The house. (RELUCTANTLY) My father's house.

DOOKU:
Your father?

JENZA:
He's the Count of Serenno. He . . . he rules the council.

DOOKU:
So the entire planet is named after your family?

JENZA:
I think so. I'm sorry. I really should pay more attention in lessons, but it's all so tedious, especially when Father starts harping on about our "birthright."

DOOKU:
But how did it happen?

JENZA:
(SIGHS) I could launch the hologuide . . .

DOOKU:
I'm sorry. I'm just interested.

JENZA:
Someone has to be. According to legend, the planet was part of the Sith Empire . . .

DOOKU:
The Sith!

JENZA:
And my great-great-great-great-something-grandfather led the charge against them.

DOOKU:

Your grandfather did? Surely it was the Jedi?

JENZA:

Like a Serennian would let someone else take the credit. If you believe the stories—and my father does, *passionately*—Granddaddy Serenno saw them off single-handedly, and the other houses submitted to his authority.

DOOKU:

Renaming the planet in his honor.

JENZA:

He formed the council, joined the Republic, and here we are. Although Father's never been too keen on the last part.

DOOKU:

Joining the Republic?

JENZA:

(PUTTING ON HIS VOICE) "Serenno can look after itself, Jenza!"

DOOKU:

(LAUGHS) Well, we know *you* can. Not many people try to take a bite out of a Karkarodon. It's usually the other way around.

JENZA:

(EMBARRASSED) We should probably get back. We're not even supposed to be in here. (BEAT) Dooku?

DOOKU: (NARRATION)

A carving had caught my attention—an immense beast, larger than any malosaur, crawling up toward the domed ceiling. The creature's crested head was thrown back, jaw stretched wide, roaring at the stars that were painted across the apex. Spines ridged its powerful back, wings spread wide as if ready to take flight.

And then there were its eyes . . . eyes, though fashioned in stone, that burned with an intensity that was all too familiar . . .

DOOKU:
What is that?

JENZA:
The Tirra'Taka? Just another legend. "The dragon that holds the world together . . ."

DOOKU:
It's beautiful.

DOOKU: (NARRATION)
I couldn't look away, walking toward the sculpture as if in a trance. It looked so alive, so vibrant, as if any minute it could spring from the wall to crash through the columns that held the domed roof in place.

I could feel the creature's heart beating in my own chest, its roar echoing at the back of my mind . . .

We also hear the roar of the Tirra'Taka. It's distorted, low, rising in volume beneath the following exchange.

JENZA:
Dooku, what are you doing? Don't—don't touch it, okay? It's supposed to be bad luck.

DOOKU:
So beautiful.

The ground shakes, dust falling from above.

DOOKU: (NARRATION)
I barely even noticed the ground shifting beneath our feet, flakes of paint falling from the ceiling high above . . .

JENZA:
What was that?

DOOKU:
(WHISPER) *Tirra'Taka . . .*

JENZA:
Dooku—don't!

DOOKU: (NARRATION)
My fingers brushed the stone . . . and the world was torn apart . . .

A groundquake hits, shaking the foundations of the assembly hall.

JENZA:
What did you do?

DOOKU: (NARRATION)
I snapped from my reverie, cracks snaking across the polished marble before us.

DOOKU:
Me? Nothing? What's happening?

Another rumble, stronger this time.

JENZA:
It's a groundquake.

DOOKU: (NARRATION)
But it wasn't the scrape of tectonic plates that caused me to clasp my head in pain, but an impossible bellow slicing through my mind as easily as plasma carves through flesh . . .

The beast roars in his head.

DOOKU:
(SCREAMS IN PAIN)

JENZA:
Dooku!

DOOKU:
So loud.

Another roar. More rumbles.

DOOKU:

I can't—(SCREAM)

The full force of the groundquake hits, the walls cracking.

JENZA:

We need to get outside!

Masonry tumbles from the domed ceiling, crashing to the ground nearby. All the time, the monster bellows in Dooku's head.

DOOKU:

(PAINED) Make it stop!

JENZA:

Dooku! Please. We need to move before the roof comes down! Dooku!

The assembly hall collapses on them.

DOOKU: (NARRATION)

Serenno's Assembly Hall had stood for generations, surviving invasion, storms, and revolution. But now it came tumbling down.

History is written in the blink of an eye. My story would have ended there if Jenza hadn't pushed me aside. Everything that has happened since . . . my life with the Jedi . . . my life now . . . it all hinged on that moment. All hinged on the bravery of an eleven-year-old girl . . .

SCENE 12. INT. ASSEMBLY HALL. BENEATH THE RUBBLE.

We're underneath the rubble. The stone is still settling above Dooku and Jenza.

DOOKU:

(COUGHS)

JENZA:

Dooku?

DOOKU:

Jenza? Where are you?

JENZA:

I'm trapped. I . . . I can't move.

DOOKU:

Me too. What happened?

JENZA:

You don't remember?

DOOKU:

You were telling me about your family, and I heard a noise and—
(CRIES OUT)

JENZA:

What is it?

DOOKU:

My leg. It's trapped. (CRIES OUT) I think it's broken.

JENZA:

What are we going to do?

DOOKU:

Do you have a comlink?

JENZA:

It got smashed. Back at the festival.

DOOKU:

I should have one. (SEARCHES FOR IT, PANICKING SLIGHTLY)
Where is it? Where is it?

The rubble shifts above them.

JENZA:

(CRIES OUT)

DOOKU:

Jenza!

JENZA:

The rubble. It's moving.

DOOKU:

It must be settling.

JENZA:

How are we going to get out?

DOOKU:

I don't know.

JENZA:

Your . . . powers.

DOOKU:

What about them?

JENZA:

Can't you lift the stones the way you shoved those aliens away?

DOOKU:

Master Yoda tells us that the only difference is our mind, but . . . (HE PUSHES WITH HIS MIND, IMMEDIATELY GASPING WITH FRUSTRATION) A few thugs are one thing. An entire building is very much another.

The rubble shifts again.

JENZA:

You've got to try!

DOOKU: (NARRATION)

I took a deep breath, closing my eyes, trying to ignore the pain in my leg. I could do more than try. I was a Jedi. Back on Coruscant, during levitation classes, Yoda had told me I was strong in the Force. I could see the truth of his words in those ageless eyes, and yet they had me shifting blocks and baubles around the practice gallery, good enough for Sifo-Dyas and the others, but I knew I could do more.

As my clan-mates played with the toys, I tried to shift the statues that lined the gallery, the equipment chests, even the chair on which Yoda was perched. (SNORTS) He told me I wasn't ready. That my time would come.

And this was it. This was my chance to show everyone just what I could do. I would save the girl. I would save myself. I would demonstrate, once and for all, my true potential.

Quieting my mind, I placed my palms against the rubble that pressed down upon me . . . and pressed back.

DOOKU:
(TRYING TO HOLD HIMSELF TOGETHER) "The Force surrounds me. The Force dwells in me."

JENZA:
What are you doing?

DOOKU:
"The Force flows through me, the Force protects me."

JENZA:
Dooku?

DOOKU:
You told me to try! I'm trying!

JENZA:
Sorry. Sorry. I'm just so scared.

DOOKU:
I know. I am, too. But I'll get us out of here. I promise.

JENZA:
I know you will.

DOOKU: (NARRATION)
She believed in me. She knew. Now I *had* to do it.

DOOKU:
(THROUGH GRITTED TEETH) "The Force surrounds me, the Force dwells in me."

DOOKU: (NARRATION)
Above us, the rubble started to shift, to grind against itself . . .

The stones begin slowly to separate.

JENZA:
Dooku. Dooku, it's working.

DOOKU: (NARRATION)
Of course it was.

Rubble scrapes against itself as the stones lift.

DOOKU:
(WITH EFFORT) "The Force surrounds me, the Force dwells in me. The Force flows through me. The Force. Protects. Me."

DOOKU: (NARRATION)
Dust was pouring through the shifting stones, streaming into my eyes, coating my gritted teeth, but what did I care? I could feel the heat of the sun against my grazed cheek, slivers of light breaking through gaps in the debris—gaps I was creating.

SIFO-DYAS:
(OFF-MIC) There he is!

ARATH:
(OFF-MIC) Where?

Sifo-Dyas and Arath scrabble through the levitating stones toward Dooku.

DOOKU: (NARRATION)
It was Sifo-Dyas and Arath. They were looking for me. They would see what I had accomplished. I should have concentrated on the rubble, but couldn't resist the urge to cry out. Sifo-Dyas would share in my victory and Arath . . . Arath would burn with envy . . .

DOOKU:
I'm lifting them!

SIFO-DYAS:
Dooku!

DOOKU: (NARRATION)
(VICTORIOUS) I pushed up, the stones lifting, rising into the air. My arms shook with the effort, even as my friend scrabbled toward me.

DOOKU:
Sifo-Dyas! Can you see what I'm doing?

ARATH:
He's delirious.

SIFO-DYAS:
Arath. Look at his leg!

DOOKU:
I'm lifting them, Si. I'm lifting them.

SIFO-DYAS:
Not you, buddy. Not you.

DOOKU: (NARRATION)
What did Sifo mean? How dare he belittle what I had achieved. I expected such petty jealousy from Arath, but never Sifo-Dyas. Sifo-Dyas was my friend. He . . . he *understood.*

And then, out of the corner of my eye, I saw a familiar figure in Jedi robes standing in the ruin of the Assembly Hall, hands outstretched, eyes screwed tight.

It was Yoda. Yoda was lifting the debris. He had saved us.

Not me.

YODA:
(WITH EFFORT) Pull him out.

DOOKU:
No.

YODA:
(WITH EFFORT) Hurry.

More Jedi make their way across the rubble.

DOOKU: (NARRATION)
They were all there. Braylon. Tera Sinube. Even the rest of the clan.

BRAYLON:
Careful. That injury looks serious.

DOOKU: (NARRATION)
I had failed. My pride . . . my pride had gotten the better of me. Yet, disappointed though I was, my thoughts went to my newfound friend. I twisted around, pain lancing up my back. Where was she? Where was Jenza?

JENZA:
Hello? Can you help me?

DOOKU: (NARRATION)
She was alive. I hadn't failed her.

SINUBE:
Let the rescue droids through. That's it. Stand back.

Several hovering droids sweep in to offer assistance.

DOOKU: (NARRATION)
I listened to them work, picking over the rubble, looking for other survivors. I tried to tell them that we had been alone, but my voice was hoarse, dust coating my throat.

DOOKU:
(COUGHS)

SIFO-DYAS:
Dooku. Try to relax.

DOOKU: (NARRATION)

Relax? How could I relax? I felt a presence sweep across the disaster site, a fury that was all too recognizable.

Gora hurries across the rubble.

GORA:

(OFF-MIC, CALLING) Jenza? Jenza, where are you, Daughter?

JENZA:

Father?

BRAYLON:

We have her, Your Grace.

GORA:

(APPROACHING) Out of my way.

He shoves Braylon aside.

GORA:

Let me see.

JENZA:

Father!

DOOKU: (NARRATION)

If Braylon was insulted, she didn't show it. She was hurrying over to Yoda, whose face had darkened with the effort of keeping the debris aloft.

YODA:

Yula . . . Some assistance . . . I require . . .

BRAYLON:

Of course. (CALLING) Tera!

SINUBE:

(APPROACHING) I am here.

DOOKU: (NARRATION)

The Masters mirrored Yoda's stance, palms lifted to the open sky.

SINUBE:
In the Force we trust.

BRAYLON:
In the Force we believe.

YODA:
In the Force we are!

DOOKU: (NARRATION)
With the sound of a rushing gale, the rubble was blown clear.

SINUBE:
Master Yoda. Are you—?

YODA:
Look not to me.

DOOKU:
(CRIES OUT)

SIFO-DYAS:
Try not to move. (CALLING OUT) Someone help him. He's really hurt.

DOOKU: (NARRATION)
I barely heard Sifo's voice. Barely felt Yoda's fingers pressing against my temples . . .

YODA:
No pain, there is. No torment.

DOOKU: (NARRATION)
Tears cut through the grime and gore on my cheeks, such was the relief.

DOOKU:
(BREATHING MORE EASILY) Thank you.

Gora scrabbles over to Jenza.

GORA:

Daughter. Are you hurt?

JENZA:

I . . . I don't think so.

DOOKU: (NARRATION)

The count swept the child into his arms.

BRAYLON:

Careful. She may be injured.

GORA:

Stay back. This has *nothing* to do with you.

YODA:

(GENTLE, WARNING) Master Braylon.

GORA:

What were you doing here, Jenza? When they said you were in the hall . . . ?

JENZA:

I was showing Dooku the family crest—

DOOKU: (NARRATION)

I heard Gora's intake of breath, felt the sliver of ice that ran through his soul.

GORA:

(BLOOD RUNNING COLD) Showing *who*?

DOOKU:

(WEAK) Jenza . . .

GORA:

(POISONOUSLY) You!

DOOKU: (NARRATION)

The count whirled around at my voice, his dark thoughts clear for all to see, Jedi or otherwise. Yoda stepped into his path, smiling benignly.

YODA:

A long time it has been, Your Grace. Good to see you it is.

GORA:

Good to see me? My daughter was nearly killed!

YODA:

The Force protected her.

GORA:

The Force? You said you would never bring him back here. You said you would keep him away.

DOOKU:

(CONFUSED) What does he mean? Keep who away?

SIFO-DYAS:

Shhh. Don't talk. They're fetching a stretcher.

GORA:

I knew this was a mistake. This pantomime. Having you people here.

YODA:

Count Gora . . .

GORA:

No. You don't get to talk to me. You don't get to even look at me. Get off my planet. Get off it now.

YODA:

This was not your son's fault.

GORA:

(SHOUTING) He's not my son!

JENZA:

Father?

DOOKU: (NARRATION)

And then I knew. I knew why Jenza had seemed so familiar. Why I had felt so comfortable in her presence. We had never met, and yet she had called to me—blood to blood.

Gora was my father.

D-4 totters over to them.

D-4: (COMING UP ON MIC)
Your Grace? Oh, Your Grace! Is Lady Jenza all right?

Gora stalks away from the Jedi, taking Jenza with him.

GORA:
Call the guard. Have them escort the Jedi from the system.

JENZA:
(CALLING BACK) Dooku!

DOOKU:
Jenza!

YODA:
Shhh, young Dooku. Quiet now.

DOOKU:
Master Yoda. Is that—?

YODA:
Your sister, she is. But now, care for your injuries we must.

DOOKU:
My sister . . .

A hover-stretcher buzzes over.

SINUBE:
Sifo-Dyas. Arath. Help me lift him onto the stretcher. That's it. Use the Force.

DOOKU:
(CRIES OUT AS HE IS LIFTED)

SINUBE:
Careful.

BRAYLON:

Yoda . . .

YODA:

Not now, Master Braylon. Return to Coruscant we must.

BRAYLON:

But Count Gora . . .

YODA:

Count Gora. Count Gora. Full of bluster, Count Gora is. Bluster and fear. Worry about Dooku we must. Great confusion I sense in him.

DOOKU: (NARRATION)

(WITH A BITTER LAUGH) Confusion? Could he blame me? I had met my family, seen their faces, felt the kinship of a sister I never even knew existed.

And now they were gone.

SCENE 13. INT. CASTLE SERENNO. GREAT HALL.

VENTRESS: (NARRATION)

Dooku falls silent, lost in his memories. He's never looked so old. So . . . human.

KY NAREC: (GHOST)

Now is your chance, Ventress. You can strike him down.

VENTRESS: (NARRATION)

I ignore the voice. It's not real. Instead, I focus on the hologram, imagining a mag-brace locked around the boy's leg.

VENTRESS:

Your injuries . . .

VENTRESS: (NARRATION)

Dooku straightens, adjusting an already immaculate cuff. His jaw clenches beneath that neat white beard, his gaze once more like steel.

DOOKU:

They healed. The wonders of modern medicine. Yoda visited me in the infirmary. Apologized. Said he had been wrong to take me to Serenno.

VENTRESS:

But the damage was done . . .

DOOKU:

Before the festival, I never thought of my family. I knew they existed, somewhere out there, in the stars. But what did they matter to me? The only family I needed was within the Temple walls.

But now, now everything had changed . . .

SCENE 14. INT. JEDI TEMPLE. INITIATES' TRAINING GALLERY.

Dooku trains, sweeping his buzzing electroblade around in an arc. It is painful for him, his injuries still raw, but he doesn't care.

DOOKU:

(WINCES IN PAIN)

Sifo-Dyas enters.

SIFO-DYAS:

Dooku. There you are. You missed supper.

DOOKU:

I need to train.

SIFO-DYAS:

You need to relax.

DOOKU:

I've already missed too much.

SIFO-DYAS:

Stop pushing yourself. Give it time.

DOOKU:

(ANGRY) Why?

Dooku sweeps his electroblade around once more, nearly striking Sifo-Dyas, who is forced to jump out of the way.

SIFO-DYAS:
Careful. You nearly hit me that time.

DOOKU:
(BREATHING HEAVILY) How did you come to the Temple, Si?

SIFO-DYAS:
The same as you. A Seeker found me. Master Maota.

DOOKU:
You're lucky. I asked Master Yoda about how I was found. Do you know what he told me?

SIFO-DYAS:
No.

DOOKU:
The Council received a message from my father, telling them what I was, instructing them to take me away.

SIFO-DYAS:
What?

DOOKU:
Perhaps it shouldn't be a surprise. The way he looked at me in the rubble . . .

SIFO-DYAS:
I know. Look. I'm sure it was just shock. He nearly lost his daughter.

DOOKU:
He nearly lost his son. A son he didn't want. A son he hated.

SIFO-DYAS:
You don't know that.

DOOKU:

Don't I? Do you know what he did? Yoda said Gora left me outside his castle's walls. With no clothes. No shelter. With nothing to identify me at all.

SIFO-DYAS:

Dooku.

DOOKU:

I did some research. There are spine-wolves in that forest, Sifo. If I hadn't had been found . . .

SIFO-DYAS:

You need to stop this, Dooku. None of that matters. Not anymore. You're here, with me. You're one of us.

DOOKU:

But I could have been so much more!

An awkward silence, then . . .

SIFO-DYAS:

(FIRM) You don't mean that.

Another beat, then Dooku sighs, collapsing his electroblade into its hilt.

DOOKU:

No. No, I don't. But I can't help but think . . .

SIFO-DYAS:

You can't help but think what might have been. (LAUGHS) You're royalty, Doo. It's in your blood. It's probably why you've got an ego the size of Hudalla.

DOOKU:

(SNICKERS) I really thought I'd lifted that rubble.

SIFO-DYAS:

I know you did, you shaak-head.

DOOKU:

I could've, you know. If my leg hadn't been so busted . . .

SIFO-DYAS:

(TEASING) Yeah, yeah. Come on. Let's find you something to eat.

Footsteps approach. It is a female Temple attendant.

ATTENDANT:

Excuse me. Initiate Dooku?

DOOKU:

Yes?

ATTENDANT:

A parcel has arrived for you.

DOOKU:

For me?

ATTENDANT:

Here.

He takes it.

DOOKU:

Where did it come from?

ATTENDANT:

I don't know. I was just asked to bring it to you.

DOOKU:

Thank you.

ATTENDANT:

You're welcome.

The attendant leaves.

SIFO-DYAS:

Well, what are you waiting for? Open it up.

DOOKU:
Okay, okay.

He rips open the paper, throwing it down.

DOOKU: (NARRATION)
It was a wooden box, the seal of Serenno carved into the lid.

Dooku opens it.

DOOKU:
A holocomm?

SIFO-DYAS:
There's a message. Look, the light's flashing.

Dooku presses a button, a hologram activating.

SIFO-DYAS:
It's her. Your sister.

DOOKU:
Jenza.

Another beep as he presses play.

JENZA: (HOLORECORDING)
Dooku. I hope this gets to you. I'm sorry that I couldn't say good-bye. Father was so angry . . . he told me to forget about you, forbade me from even mentioning your name. But I couldn't forget you . . . not now . . . my brother . . .

SCENE 15. INT. CASTLE SERENNO. GREAT HALL.

DOOKU:
My sister. (BEAT)

VENTRESS: (NARRATION)
Dooku raises a hand, using the Force to click off the hologram.

It fizzes out.

DOOKU:

We communicated for years, sending messages back and forth across the stars.

VENTRESS:

Using holomessages. Was that allowed?

DOOKU:

No. But it didn't stop us. I had no idea that she'd kept the recordings. Not until I . . . finally . . . came home.

VENTRESS:

Where is she now?

DOOKU:

Gone. Taken from me. I have many enemies, Ventress. The things they would do to her to learn my secrets . . . the torture they would inflict . . .

VENTRESS:

But not the Jedi. They do not torture.

DOOKU:

Are you sure?

VENTRESS:

It is not their way.

VENTRESS: (NARRATION)

That amuses him. A smile tugs at his mouth, but there is no warmth to it. *This* is the Dooku I have come to know. The mask is back on.

DOOKU:

Is that what he told you? Your Master, Ky Narec? About the Jedi who abandoned him on Rattatak?

VENTRESS: (NARRATION)

I feel a presence stir at the back of my consciousness . . .

KY NAREC: (GHOST)

Don't listen to him, little one.

VENTRESS: (NARRATION)
Dooku continues, unaware of the voice in my head.

DOOKU:
The Jedi who could have rescued him anytime they wanted, but left him to rot instead.

KY NAREC: (GHOST)
That's not how it was.

DOOKU:
They knew he'd taken a Padawan.

VENTRESS:
What?

DOOKU:
They could have come for you when he breathed his last. They could have saved you. But they didn't. They left you to die on that Force-forsaken planet, rejecting you, just as they rejected him.

KY NAREC: (GHOST)
It's all lies!

VENTRESS:
I . . . (TAKING A BREATH)

VENTRESS: (NARRATION)
I force myself to calm, blanking out Ky's outrage at Dooku's claims.

VENTRESS:
What do you want from me?

DOOKU:
I want you to find my sister.

VENTRESS:
She could be anywhere.

DOOKU:
No. She is still on Serenno. I can sense her.

VENTRESS:
Then why can't *you* find her?

VENTRESS: (NARRATION)
Lightning crackles around Dooku's fingers. I take an involuntary step back. Again, Dooku smiles, satisfied.

DOOKU:
That disk was recovered in Carannia, in the Trannon district.

VENTRESS:
Near the spaceport.

DOOKU:
(AMUSED) You've done your homework.

KY NAREC: (GHOST)
It's always wise to have an escape route.

Dooku throws more data disks down on the table in front of Ventress.

DOOKU:
Here are more recordings. You may study them.

VENTRESS:
To know you better.

DOOKU:
To know *her*. Do not fail me, Ventress. You know what will happen if you do.

PART TWO

SCENE 16. EXT. DOOKU'S AIRSHIP. THE *WINDRUNNER.* DECK.

Ventress is standing on the deck of Dooku's airship. The ship's engines are almost silent, a slight whirring in the background, all but drowned out by the rushing wind.

VENTRESS: (NARRATION)
Dooku insists I take the *Windrunner*. It will give me an opportunity to study the holograms, he says, as well as view his kingdom the way he sees it. From above.

I shiver, my breath fogging in the high altitude. Who has an airship? Like the castle, it's impressive enough, its hull carved from burnished wood with portholes so clear you find yourself reaching out to check if there's glass in the frames. But for all his finery, Dooku obviously cares little for luxury. The castle, the airship . . . it's all a show, like his tailored capes and polished boots.

No. Dooku likes the *Windrunner* because it's silent. No boosters. No repulsors. You'd never even know it was coming until it sounded its guns.

That is Dooku. The *real* Dooku.

He doesn't belong here. Not really. He's a man playing king, but for what end? His Sith beliefs? He already has power. Already has riches. What else does he need?

KY NAREC: (GHOST)
What do any of us need?

VENTRESS:
(SIGHS) Go away.

KY NAREC: (GHOST)
It's quite a view, isn't it? Look at all those birds. They're beautiful.

VENTRESS:
You're not really here. You're not real.

KY NAREC: (GHOST)
Aren't I? You know, that was the one thing I missed on Rattatak.

VENTRESS:
What?

KY NAREC: (GHOST)
The birds. I used to feed them in the training ground back on Coruscant. Song sparrows. Crown finches. You should have seen them flitting around the Great Tree, so many colors, darting this way and that.

VENTRESS:
Don't worry. You fed them on Rattatak as well. Or at least your flesh did.

KY NAREC: (GHOST)
That's not true. You had me cremated.

VENTRESS:
Oh. There, were you? Watched me do it?

KY NAREC: (GHOST)
You think I'd miss my own funeral? I was standing beside you. I saw you cry.

VENTRESS:
You were dead!

KY NAREC: (GHOST)
I saw everything.

VENTRESS:
That's why you're here, isn't it? To judge me. To make me suffer.

KY NAREC: (GHOST)
No. I would never do such a thing.

VENTRESS:
Why not? It's only what I deserve, isn't that what you think?

KY NAREC: (GHOST)
Because you took revenge? Because you forsook everything I taught you?

VENTRESS: (NARRATION)
I don't have to listen to this. I look around the deck, calling over to a chromium-plated astromech.

VENTRESS:
You. Droid. Where can I find a holocomm?

The astromech whistles back.

VENTRESS:
The count's private cabin. Do I have access?

The astromech bloops.

VENTRESS:
How generous of him. Take me there.

The astromech trundles off, Ventress following.

SCENE 17. INT. THE *WINDRUNNER*. DOOKU'S CABIN.

A door slides open, and the astromech leads Ventress into Dooku's sanctum.

VENTRESS: (NARRATION)
The cabin is a surprise. I'd expected it to be sparse like the castle, but the dark-paneled walls are lined with glittering holos: jagged mountain ranges, rushing rivers, even a desert that almost looks as arid as Rattatak. I feel a pang in my chest. Who thought I could feel homesick for that dust bowl?

The droid leads me to a slab of a desk, a twisting dragon etched into its polished sides. A holocomm lies beside a golden stylus, neatly arranged alongside gleaming datapads and bound files.

The desk of a statesman.

He must have meetings here. That would explain the cabinet replete with bottles and decanters, the bookshelves expertly arranged, Serenno's greatest works, I assume, displayed for all to see. This is exactly the kind of room people would expect from the Count of Serenno.

Another lie.

Another deceit.

A chair creaks as she sits.

VENTRESS: (NARRATION)
I drop into his oversized chair. Into his *throne.* Run a finger along the arm, the leather squealing beneath my nail.

I could get used to this. Perhaps I should ask for an airship of my own.

The droid beeps.

VENTRESS:
You can go.

The droid trills, its beeps telling Ventress that there's no need to be rude. It wheels from the room, the door sliding shut.

VENTRESS:
(SIGHING) Alone at last.

KY NAREC: (GHOST)
A Jedi is never truly alone.

VENTRESS:
(ANNOYED) So it seems.

KY NAREC: (GHOST)
You can't hide from me, Asajj. You might as well try to hide from yourself.

VENTRESS:
I'm not hiding. I have a job to do.

She scatters data disks onto the table.

KY NAREC: (GHOST)
More of Dooku's messages to his sister . . .

VENTRESS:
If they're boring you, please feel free to leave.

VENTRESS: (NARRATION)
I load the next disk into the player and scroll through the contents. The same boy appears, older now, maybe thirteen or fourteen. A lightsaber has replaced the electroblade on his belt. His shoulders are broader, his smile more confident.

I lean in, examining his face as he speaks, his voice so eager and bright . . .

The hologram beeps and plays.

DOOKU: (FOURTEEN YEARS OLD, HOLO-NARRATION)
Hello, sister. You asked me about my day. Well, there isn't much to tell. We wake at dawn to meditate on the three pillars—that's the Force, Knowledge, and Self-Discipline. Then we file through to the refectory for breakfast. I always sit next to Sifo-Dyas. I think you'd like him. He's my best friend, although Master Braylon insists we shouldn't form attachments. Most of the time I don't have any problem with that, but Si's different. He's from Minashee, at least originally. The son of a fisherm—

Ventress fast-forwards through the message, the young Dooku's voice becoming gibberish.

VENTRESS:
Seriously. Why would anyone care . . .

KY NAREC: (GHOST)
If they're boring you . . .

VENTRESS:
Shut up.

KY NAREC: (GHOST)
You would have done well there. At the Temple.

VENTRESS:
Not that you gave me a chance.

KY NAREC: (GHOST)
It wasn't like that.

VENTRESS:
That's not what Dooku says . . .

KY NAREC: (GHOST)
Dooku says a lot of things . . .

We hear Ventress forwarding through more holo-letters under the next speech.

VENTRESS: (NARRATION)
That's true enough. I keep fast-forwarding through the messages, swapping disk after disk. Talk about oversharing. Who would have thought that Dooku was so . . . chatty. Not that his sister seems to care. The disks also contain her replies, message after message, asking inane questions, urging him to holo more. More? Who could bear it? Was her own life that dull?

Another disk is clicked into the holocomm. More fast-forwarding.

VENTRESS: (NARRATION)
And there she is again. Her perfect hair cascading over a perfect fur-trimmed collar in perfect ringlets. Why would he care about her? Why would he care about any of it?

She resumes the recording, the message kicking in halfway through, leading us into the next scene . . .

YOUNG DOOKU: (HOLO-NARRATION)
. . . you should see the libraries, Jenza. So much knowledge, there for the taking. We were there today, being led to the Room of a Thousand Fountains by Yoda. I wished I could have stayed, to explore the shelves for myself, but we were on a tight schedule, not that it stopped Zang asking a question . . .

SCENE 18. INT. JEDI ARCHIVES. CORUSCANT.

Yoda and Braylon lead Dooku's clan through the Archives, Yoda's cane tapping on the floor. The Archives echo, and there's a slight buzz of computers in the background as Jedi work all around them.

ZANG: (FOURTEEN YEARS OLD, FEMALE)
Master Yoda?

YODA:
Yes, Initiate.

ZANG:
These busts? Who are they?

YOUNG DOOKU: (HOLO-NARRATION)
It was something I had often wondered myself. I couldn't help but feel a flush of frustration. I should have been the one to ask the question.

BRAYLON:
We haven't time for this now.

YODA:

No, Master Braylon, an important lesson this is.

Yoda halts, tapping his cane three times to get everyone's attention.

YODA:

Initiates. Stop here we will. Yes. Yes. Gather 'round.

They do as he says, gathering around the Grand Master.

YODA:

Youngling Zang asks about the busts. These are some of the Lost.

SIFO-DYAS: (FOURTEEN YEARS OLD)

Lost. Lost how?

ARATH:

He means killed, Sifo-Dyas.

BRAYLON:

No, he does not. Why don't you try listening for once, Arath, rather than running that mouth of yours?

YODA:

Masters they once were, before disillusioned they became.

DOOKU:

Disillusioned? How?

YODA:

A good question, Initiate Dooku. A good question indeed. Master Braylon, perhaps explain you will?

BRAYLON:

Gladly.

Braylon walks over to one of the busts.

BRAYLON:

They became disillusioned about our principles. Of our very way of life. Take Radaki here, for example. He questioned the belief that to serve, Jedi must sacrifice everything about their lives. Their family. Their riches.

SIFO-DYAS:
Radaki? Excuse me, Master, but didn't he turn to the dark side?

BRAYLON:
Someone's been reading their history.

YODA:
Yes, seduced by the dark side of the Force, Radaki was. A powerful Sith he became.

DOOKU:
Is that what happened to all of them? They became Sith?

Yoda walks toward the next bust.

BRAYLON:
No. Some became leaders. Others taught, while most simply vanished into history, never to be heard of again.

YOUNG DOOKU: (HOLO-NARRATION)
As Braylon talked, Yoda hobbled toward the bust of a female with a proud, defiant expression.

YODA:
(QUIETLY, LOST IN THOUGHT) Master Trennis. Hm. Sad, that was. Yes. Sad indeed. (TURNING BACK TO THE STUDENTS) Remember them, we must. Honor them, yes. Learn from our failure.

DOOKU:
Our failure?

YODA:
To keep them where they belonged.

He continues to walk, the students following. We stay with Dooku and Sifo-Dyas.

YODA:
But the past they are. Our future you will be. Come. Much Master Odell has to teach you. Hurry we must.

YOUNG DOOKU: (HOLO-NARRATION)
I held back, fascinated by the bronzium heads . . .

SIFO-DYAS:
(SHUDDERS) Don't they give you the creeps?

DOOKU:
They're just statues.

SIFO-DYAS:
Reckon there's one of Teradine?

DOOKU:
(SNICKERS) Yeah, like they'd commemorate an expelled Padawan.
If he ever existed at all.

SIFO-DYAS:
Oh, he existed all right.

DOOKU:
Just imagine it: (IMPERSONATING YODA) "Thrown out they
were. Honor them we must."

SIFO-DYAS:
(LAUGHING) Your impression gets better all the time.

DOOKU:
We hear his voice often enough.

SIFO-DYAS:
Would you like to hear Teradine's?

DOOKU:
What do you mean?

SIFO-DYAS:
I found this.

YOUNG DOOKU: (HOLO-NARRATION)
Glancing about to make sure no one was looking, Sifo drew a rusty
datapad from his robes.

DOOKU:
What is it?

SIFO-DYAS:
Teradine's holojournal. I found it in the dormitory, stashed away for future troublemakers.

DOOKU:
Troublemakers like you?

SIFO-DYAS:
Troublemakers like *us*.

YOUNG DOOKU: (HOLO-NARRATION)
If you believe the stories—which Sifo-Dyas does, passionately—Teradine was a Padawan from the time of the High Republic. He'd always been what you'd call problematic, testing the boundaries of his Masters, and repeatedly bringing the name of the Order into disrepute. No one really knows why or even if he was expelled. Some say he stole records from the Archives, while others believe he had an affair with the chancellor's aide. Either way, he vanished from Jedi history, only remembered . . . well, only remembered by us and every other Initiate that likes to gossip by the light of a glow lantern late at night.

I always believed that he was legend, a story, but if this was truly his journal . . .

SIFO-DYAS:
You should see the stuff in here, Doo. New ways to sneak down to the stacks. How to find your way into the Bogan Collection.

DOOKU:
The what?

SIFO-DYAS:
(DRAWING HIM IN EVEN CLOSER) The Archive of Forbidden Artifacts.

DOOKU:

Like what?

SIFO-DYAS:

I don't know. But how do you think I found out all that stuff about Radaki?

DOOKU:

It's in here?

SIFO-DYAS:

Radaki became a Sith Lord called Darth Krall. It was Krall who won the Battle of Wasted Years. Who tamed the Nightmare Conjunction. Teradine was *obsessed* with him.

DOOKU:

Teradine was a Sith?

SIFO-DYAS:

No, of course not. He just liked mucking around with stuff he wasn't supposed to. Apparently Krall's lightsaber is in this Bogan Collection, somewhere in the Temple. Teradine saw it. And we could, too.

SCENE 19. INT. THE *WINDRUNNER*. DOOKU'S CABIN.

Atmosphere as before.

VENTRESS: (NARRATION)

A serving droid slinks into the cabin, its tray heaped with fruit and cheese. The master is obviously pleased with his rat, or at least knows that she needs to keep her strength up.

I wave for the droid to leave the food on the desk, picking at grapes as I continue the recording. I'm warming to this Sifo-Dyas. Not only does he seem to be the only one willing to stand up to Dooku, but he has a rebellious streak so large you could fly a Dreadnought along it.

Not that Dooku was impressed when he was woken in the middle of the night . . .

SCENE 20. INT. DORMITORIES. NIGHT.

SIFO-DYAS:
(WHISPER) Doo. (BEAT) Doo, are you awake?

DOOKU:
(SLEEPILY) I am now. What's the matter?

SIFO-DYAS:
We have to go. Now.

DOOKU:
Go where?

SIFO-DYAS:
The Bogan Collection.

DOOKU:
It's the middle of the night.

SIFO-DYAS:
So old Quist will be tucked up in bed. The library will be empty.

DOOKU:
You hope.

SIFO-DYAS:
Do you want to come or not?

DOOKU:
And if we get caught?

SIFO-DYAS:
You worried about getting a black mark on that impeccable record of yours? I think you kinda blew that when you dropped an Assembly Hall on your sister.

DOOKU:
Sifo!

SIFO-DYAS:
Oh come on. We need to do this. We need to do this now!

SCENE 21. INT. JEDI ARCHIVES. NIGHT.

YOUNG DOOKU: (HOLO-NARRATION)
The Archives were in shadows as we crept through the doors, glow rods gripped in our hands . . .

DOOKU:
Are you sure Quist isn't still up? Arath says she never sleeps.

SIFO-DYAS:
Arath's an idiot. There's no one here but creepmice. This way.

They creep around a corner.

SIFO-DYAS:
There. What do you see?

DOOKU:
A stained-glass window.

SIFO-DYAS:
And what's different about it?

DOOKU:
I don't know. Nothing.

SIFO-DYAS:
Are you sure?

DOOKU:
(REALIZING) It's on an interior wall.

SIFO-DYAS:
Exactly. Then how is moonlight streaming through?

DOOKU:
It's fake.

SIFO-DYAS:
Illuminators behind the glass. It's not a window. It's a *door.*

DOOKU:
To the collection.

SIFO-DYAS:
According to Teradine's journal.

A squeak of fingers against glass as Dooku checks the window.

DOOKU:
But how do you open it?

Sifo-Dyas rummages about in his robes.

SIFO-DYAS:
With this.

He produces a small tub.

DOOKU:
A tub of sand.

Sifo-Dyas unscrews the lid.

SIFO-DYAS:
I scooped it up when Odell wasn't looking.

DOOKU:
And what are we supposed to do with it?

There's a sudden noise from nearby. A scrape of a chair.

DOOKU:
What's that?

SIFO-DYAS:
Quick. Get back here.

They hide and we hear their nervous breathing close to the mic as they wait. A droid stomps past, and we listen to its whirring servos and heavy feet as it leaves the Archive.

DOOKU:
(WHEN IT'S GONE) That was close.

SIFO-DYAS:
It's just a maintenance droid.

They go back to the window.

DOOKU:
Which means it'll probably come back. We should go back to the dormitory.

SIFO-DYAS:
You can't. I need you for this bit.

DOOKU:
Me? Why?

SIFO-DYAS:
Remember levitation, when Yoda taught us to focus on small particles?

DOOKU:
The Shifting Sand meditation. What about it?

SIFO-DYAS:
You were the top of the class.

DOOKU:
But how will that help?

SIFO-DYAS:
The door has a magnetic lock. Slide the sand between the frame and the wall, and it'll break the connection.

DOOKU:
It can't be that easy.

SIFO-DYAS:
You don't think you can do it?

DOOKU:
(SIGHING) Hold out the tub.

SIFO-DYAS:

I knew you wouldn't let me down.

DOOKU:

Shut up and let me concentrate.

Dooku regulates his breathing.

YOUNG DOOKU: (HOLO-NARRATION)

I held out my hand, the sand stirring in the pot.

DOOKU:

I feel the Force in everything. Flowing through me. Flowing through the sand.

The sound of the sand scraping in the container.

YOUNG DOOKU: (HOLO-NARRATION)

Sifo-Dyas grinned as the individual grains rose in the air, twisting and turning like a swarm of beta-flies.

SIFO-DYAS:

That's it. Now push them toward the door.

A bucket clatters at the back of the library.

SIFO-DYAS:

Stang! It's that damn droid again.

DOOKU:

The Force is forever in motion. Rising. Flowing.

The droid starts clanking toward them.

SIFO-DYAS:

Can't you make it flow any quicker?

DOOKU:

I'm trying!

The droid is nearer.

SIFO-DYAS:

That's it. Into the gap.

DOOKU:

I don't think I can.

SIFO-DYAS:

I thought you could do anything! Why else do you think I hang around with you?

YOUNG DOOKU: (HOLO-NARRATION)

The droid squeaked closer, its joints in desperate need of lubrication.

The slightest scrape of sand against metal.

SIFO-DYAS:

(HISSING) Dooku!

DOOKU:

I can't find the lock.

SIFO-DYAS:

You have to!

DOOKU:

I can't . . . Hang on. There!

The clunk of a magnet releasing.

SIFO-DYAS:

You did it.

DOOKU:

Did you have any doubt?

YOUNG DOOKU: (HOLO-NARRATION)

I yanked open the secret entrance and ushered Sifo inside, convinced we were going to get caught any second.

SIFO-DYAS:

Okay, okay, I'm in. Close the door.

DOOKU:

I'm trying.

They pull the door shut and we're in the corridor with them, listening as the droid passes by.

DOOKU:

(BREATHES A SIGH OF RELIEF) That was close.

SIFO-DYAS:

You were brilliant.

DOOKU:

What if it sees the sand?

SIFO-DYAS:

It'll fetch a broom.

DOOKU:

So much for the illuminators. It's so dark in here.

SIFO-DYAS:

Where's your glow rod?

Dooku clicks on his glow rod.

DOOKU:

I think I preferred it when I couldn't see.

SIFO-DYAS:

It's just a few spinner-webs.

DOOKU:

A few?

SIFO-DYAS:

Come on.

SCENE 22. INT. THE BOGAN COLLECTION.

YOUNG DOOKU: (HOLO-NARRATION)

The corridor came out into a vault filled with cabinets, relics of the past suspended on repulsor pads, some behind glass, others protected by crackling force fields.

SIFO-DYAS:

This is *unbelievable*. Look at all this stuff.

DOOKU:

Master Yoda told us the holocron was the only Sith artifact to survive the war.

SIFO-DYAS:

Master Yoda lied. And it's not just Sith. Look at this. The Sorcerers of Tund. The Yacombe. Where did this all come from?

DOOKU:

Sifo. Here it is.

He rushes to a cabinet.

DOOKU:

(READING) "The Saber of Darth Krall."

SIFO-DYAS:

Hmmm.

DOOKU:

What do you mean—"hmmm"?

SIFO-DYAS:

I thought it would be spikier.

Dooku takes a few steps.

DOOKU:

Hey. Look at this.

SIFO-DYAS:

Seriously. *That's* what you want to look at? There's all these . . . scrolls and weapons and whatever that creepy mask thing is, and you want to look at a lump of old metal?

DOOKU:

There's something about it . . . something I've felt before.

SIFO-DYAS:
Doo. Look at this. I think it's a parang.

We start to hear a noise inside Dooku's mind, a growl like he heard in the assembly hall on Serenno. Low. Ominous.

DOOKU:
(WINCES)

SIFO-DYAS:
Dooku?

DOOKU:
Can't you hear it?

SIFO-DYAS:
Hear what?

DOOKU:
The beast below.

SIFO-DYAS:
Okay. Very funny. Drop the act. This place is spooky enough as it is.

The growl intensifies.

DOOKU:
It's coming.

SIFO-DYAS:
What?

DOOKU:
Coming for us. Coming for me.

SIFO-DYAS:
Okay, now you're freaking me out. Let's look at something else, shall we?

The growl becomes a roar.

YOUNG DOOKU: (HOLO-NARRATION)

And then it was in front of me, Jenza, fangs bared, wings out-stretched. The same creature you showed me in the Assembly Hall. The Tirra'Taka. I can't explain how but I could see it, feel its breath against my skin, its spines bristling, ready to attack, ready to tear us apart.

DOOKU:

(SCARED) No.

SIFO-DYAS:

Doo, calm down.

DOOKU:

Stay back!

SIFO-DYAS:

Dooku, there's nothing there.

DOOKU:

Can't you see it? Why can't you see it?

Sifo-Dyas goes to grab Dooku, as—in the young Jedi's head—the monster prepares to attack.

DOOKU:

(CRIES OUT IN FEAR)

YOUNG DOOKU: (HOLO-NARRATION)

I pushed out with the Force, every cabinet in the Archive shattering at once. Sifo-Dyas was thrown back, smashing into a wall as artifacts tumbled to the floor.

SIFO-DYAS:

(GRUNTS)

Alarms blare.

SIFO-DYAS:

(GROANS) Why did you do that?

DOOKU:

It's gone. The creature.

SIFO-DYAS:

What creature?

DOOKU:

You couldn't see it?

SIFO-DYAS:

I don't know what you're talking about. (WINCES)

Dooku scrambles up, running to his friend, glass crunching beneath his feet.

DOOKU:

Are you all right?

SIFO-DYAS:

(WHIMPERING) My arm. I can't move it.

DOOKU:

That doesn't look good.

Nearby a door slides open. There are running footsteps, a lightsaber humming.

QUIST: (COMING UP ON MIC)
Who's there?

DOOKU:

Oh no.

QUIST:

Show yourself!

DOOKU:

Librarian Quist. We're over here. My friend, he's hurt.

QUIST:

Younglings? What happened here?

SCENE 23. INT. JEDI TEMPLE. INFIRMARY.

YOUNG DOOKU: (HOLO-NARRATION)
It was a good question, and one I struggled to answer, even as Yoda and Braylon confronted us in the Temple infirmary . . .

YODA:
Explain you must.

DOOKU:
We're really sorry.

BRAYLON:
Sorry you were caught, you mean.

SIFO-DYAS:
(WINCES IN PAIN)

YODA:
Let the healer work. The bacta cast will mend your bones, if not our trust in you.

SIFO-DYAS:
It wasn't Dooku's fault.

BRAYLON:
No. He didn't destroy the collection?

DOOKU:
I don't know what happened. I was looking at the artifacts and then—

BRAYLON:
(INTERRUPTING) And then you threw your friend through a cabinet.

YODA:
Teradine's legacy lives on. Destroy this journal we must.

SIFO-DYAS:
Are you going to expel us?

BRAYLON:
Don't tempt me.

YODA:
Punished you must be. Disgrace you have brought upon the Hawk-Bat Clan. Upon yourself.

DOOKU:
We'll never do anything like it again.

SIFO-DYAS:
We promise.

Doors sweep open and Lene enters.

LENE:
Master Yoda.

DOOKU: (NARRATION)
We looked up. The doors of the infirmary had swept open to admit a purple-skinned Altiri. Her head was shaved, a single lock of hair curled behind her right ear.

LENE:
I hear there was a disturbance in the Archives.

YODA:
Master Kostana.

BRAYLON:
I wasn't aware you'd returned.

LENE:
Not before time, it seems. Was anything damaged?

BRAYLON:
Nothing that we can't incinerate.

LENE:
Incinerate? You can't be serious.

BRAYLON:

Lene, for the last time, there really is no cause for alarm. It was just a couple of Initiates, getting themselves in trouble. Again.

LENE:

How did they get in?

YODA:

Through Kaneer's window.

LENE:

In the Archives? Hasn't that been blocked up?

BRAYLON:

Obviously not.

YODA:

Said the same we did, after you and Braylon broke in.

DOOKU:

You did, Master Braylon?

BRAYLON:

It was a long time ago.

LENE:

And these are the culprits, I assume. That was quite a storm you whipped up in there.

YODA:

Strong in the Force, Dooku is.

LENE:

So I can sense. Tell me, Dooku . . . what did you see?

YODA:

Now is not the time.

LENE:

Really? The boy obviously disturbed something down there. We should understand what it was.

DOOKU:

I can't remember. I've tried but . . .

SIFO-DYAS:

(SULKILY) I saw something. The wall, when I hit it.

DOOKU:

(TO SIFO) I'm really sorry.

BRAYLON:

You'll have to forgive Master Kostana, Initiates. She has a particular interest in esoteric beliefs and arcane trivia.

LENE:

There is nothing trivial about the dark side, Yula.

DOOKU:

That's what it was? The dark side?

YODA:

Not ready for such a test are you. Dangerous those artifacts are.

BRAYLON:

Which is why they are in a vault!

YODA:

Your punishment you will serve.

YOUNG DOOKU: (HOLO-NARRATION)

And serve it we did, hunched over Archive monitors under the watchful eyes of Restelly Quist . . .

SCENE 24. INT. JEDI ARCHIVES.

Atmosphere: Back in the cloistered Temple Archives. Dooku and Sifo-Dyas are writing with styluses on datapads.

DOOKU:

Why did I let you talk me into all this?

SIFO-DYAS:

I didn't. You came of your own free will. And then threw me through a cabinet.

DOOKU:
How's your arm?

SIFO-DYAS:
Getting better. *Slowly.*

QUIST:
That's enough chatter.

DOOKU:
Yes, Librarian Quist.

SIFO-DYAS:
Sorry, Librarian Quist.

DOOKU:
Three days of translating agricultural treatises. No artifacts are worth this. If I ever meet Klias Teradine . . .

SIFO-DYAS:
Who knew there would be so much to say about crop rotations . . .

Lene Kostana enters the Archive behind them.

QUIST: (OFF-MIC)
Master Kostana. It is good to see you.

LENE: (OFF-MIC)
And you, Chief Librarian.

SIFO-DYAS:
(WHISPER) Doo. It's her. The Altiri.

LENE: (OFF-MIC)
I wonder if you can help me find this?

QUIST: (OFF-MIC)
The Sands of Elath? My. No one has asked for that for decades.

LENE: (OFF-MIC)
You know where it is?

QUIST: (OFF-MIC)
Yes, yes. It might take some time, that's all.

LENE: (OFF-MIC)
I can wait. Thanks, Restelly. What would I do without you?

QUIST: (OFF-MIC)
Find someone else to flatter? I'll be right back.

Hobbles off. Lene approaches the boys.

LENE:
Good to see you two hard at work. What did the old goblin have you do?

DOOKU:
You can't talk about Master Yoda like that!

LENE:
It's a term of endearment, but your loyalty does you credit. Let's see what you've got there . . .

She picks up the scrolls.

LENE:
(LAUGHS) The Lothal Papyri? He's still having Initiates translate these?

SIFO-DYAS:
You mean they've been deciphered before?

LENE:
Only every time someone steps out of line. Took me and Yula at least three months. Good luck.

She passes the papers back to Sifo-Dyas.

SIFO-DYAS:
T-thanks.

Lene walks off, calling back to them.

LENE:

Tell Restelly I'll pick the book up later. I need to see a man about an akk.

SIFO-DYAS:

(CALLING AFTER HER) O-okay.

DOOKU:

What was that all about?

SIFO-DYAS:

Beats me. She's an odd one, that's for—

He finds something in the papers.

SIFO-DYAS:

Hang on, what's this?

DOOKU:

What's what?

SIFO-DYAS:

A fragment of a book. Kostana must have—

He flicks through pages.

SIFO-DYAS:

Wow!

DOOKU:

What is it? Let me see.

SIFO-DYAS:

Look.

Dooku takes it and looks through the pages.

DOOKU:

(READING) Silooth . . . tuk'ata . . . veergundark . . . krastenane . . .

SIFO-DYAS:

You know what those are, don't you?

DOOKU:
Hideous, by the looks of things.

SIFO-DYAS:
They're Sith warbeasts.

He snatches the book back.

DOOKU:
Sith? Are you sure?

SIFO-DYAS:
Yes. *The Bestiary of Darth Caldoth*—see?

DOOKU:
But what's Kostana doing with Sith texts?

Quist returns.

DOOKU:
Quist's back. Hide it!

Sifo-Dyas shoves it beneath the papers. Quist walks over to them.

QUIST:
Where's Master Kostana?

SIFO-DYAS:
She, er, she said she'd come back later.

DOOKU:
For her book.

SIFO-DYAS:
(QUICKLY) The one you were fetching.

QUIST:
Hmmm. Well, get on with your work, you two.

The librarian walks away.

QUIST: (OFF-MIC)
Plenty more documents where those came from.

SIFO-DYAS:

(SOTTO) And don't we know it.

DOOKU:

What are you going to do?

SIFO-DYAS:

About what?

DOOKU:

About the *Bestiary*!

SIFO-DYAS:

What do you think? Read it.

DOOKU:

But shouldn't we tell someone?

SIFO-DYAS:

No!

YOUNG DOOKU: (HOLO-NARRATION)

But I couldn't let it go, Jenza. Something wasn't right about Master Kostana, and it was my duty as a Jedi to investigate . . .

SCENE 25. EXT. JEDI TEMPLE. MAIN SPIRE. CONTEMPLATION BALCONY. NIGHT.

Atmosphere: A balcony halfway up the main spire. Coruscant air traffic zipping past in the background.

Lene Kostana is waiting as her pet Altirian convor flaps down to land on the balcony railing.

LENE:

There you are, girl. Been off hunting?

The convor chirps in response, Lene ruffling her feathers.

LENE:

Yes. Yes. I've missed you too. Here.

She feeds the convor, the bird chirping.

LENE:

Do you like that? Yes? Good girl. Good girl.

She waits a couple of beats and then . . .

LENE:

(CALLING OUT) It's hard to sneak up on a Jedi, you know, especially in the Temple. If you needed to meditate, you only had to ask me to vacate the contemplation balcony . . .

Behind her, Dooku steps out from his hiding place and activates his lightsaber. Lene turns.

DOOKU:

I'm not here to meditate.

LENE:

Really? You're challenging me to a duel, Dooku?

DOOKU:

Why did you give Sifo that book?

LENE:

Well, technically it was *part* of a book. Eight pages at most.

DOOKU:

(MORE FORCEFULLY) Why?

LENE:

Who said it was for him?

She ignites her own lightsaber. Her convor chirps, worried, flapping from its perch.

LENE:

Calm yourself, Ferana. There's nothing to worry about, is there, Initiate?

DOOKU:

Was it a test? Is that what it was?

LENE:

Why would I be testing you?

DOOKU:

To see if we're like you.

LENE:

Like me? What about me?

DOOKU:

I can . . . feel it inside you. Frustration. Anger.

LENE:

Is that so?

We hear the roar of the Tirra'Taka in Dooku's mind. Distant, but insistent all the same.

DOOKU:

(WINCES)

LENE:

Initiate?

DOOKU:

I sense the dark side.

LENE:

You do?

Another roar.

DOOKU:

It must be stopped.

LENE:

And you're the one to do it?

DOOKU:

Yes.

YOUNG DOOKU: (HOLO-NARRATION)

I launched myself at Kostana, my lightsaber slashing through the air only to be blocked . . .

LENE:

Not bad. Tera Sinube said you showed promise.

They duel more, lightsabers crackling.

Each [strike] in the text indicates where their lightsabers meet.

LENE:

And as for that lightsaber. A curved hilt. I haven't seen one of those in a while. [STRIKE] Do you know who else had a curved hilt? [STRIKE] Darth Sakia. By all accounts, she was quite the swordswoman.

DOOKU:

I knew it. [STRIKE] You *are* a Sith.

LENE:

There haven't been Sith [STRIKE] for a thousand years.

DOOKU:

They haven't been discovered, you mean? [STRIKE]

LENE:

Ha. I like you, Dooku. A good fighter. [STRIKE] Brave. Willing to go toe-to-toe with a [STRIKE] Dark Lord. Or should that be Dark Lady? [STRIKE] I never know.

DOOKU:

[STRIKE] I won't let you win.

LENE:

And what exactly will you do? Summon the beast you heard in the collection? [STRIKE] The beast you hear now?

DOOKU:

(SUDDENLY UNSURE) I . . . I didn't hear anything.

LENE:

Are you sure? [STRIKE] You've locked it away. [STRIKE] But it's still in there. In your memory. I can feel it.

DOOKU:

Stop it. [STRIKE] You're evil. [STRIKE] And I will stop you.

The fight intensifies, Dooku forcing Lene back against the railing as he strikes again, and again, and again.

YOUNG DOOKU: (HOLO-NARRATION)

I don't know what came over me. I'd always been so careful to keep my emotions in check, just as I'd been taught, but . . . I couldn't control myself. I hacked at her time and time again, forcing her back to the edge of the balcony. All I could feel was her anger. Her rage . . . at least, I thought it was her. I couldn't think, I could only act . . . and all the time, her convor flapped around our heads. Cawing. Screeching. Ready to claw out my eyes, anything to protect its mistress . . .

LENE:

(DROPPING THE ACT AS SHE REALIZES HE'S LOSING CONTROL) Okay. That's enough, Dooku.

DOOKU:

No, it isn't.

He's becoming frenzied.

LENE:

Dooku. Stop. [STRIKE] Stop! [STRIKE]

YODA:

(FIRM) Stop.

Yoda's sudden appearance stops the fight dead.

YOUNG DOOKU: (HOLO-NARRATION)

The voice stopped us dead, our lightsabers centimeters apart. *His* voice. He didn't shout. Didn't yell. One word was all it took.

LENE:

(BREATHLESS) Master Yoda.

DOOKU:
(OUT OF BREATH) Master Yoda . . . Kostana . . . She's a Sith . . .

YODA:
A Sith, you say. Hmm. Sure of that, are you?

DOOKU:
She admitted it herself . . . She was talking . . . about Darth . . .
Darth Sakia . . .

YODA:
Sakia? There was no such Sith.

DOOKU:
How do you know? We can't have known them all.

YODA:
But know Kostana we can. Reach out with your feelings.

DOOKU:
I did.

YODA:
No. Reached inside you did.

DOOKU:
What?

Lene extinguishes her lightsaber.

LENE:
Go ahead. I won't resist. Tell me . . . have I been touched by the
dark side, Initiate?

We focus on Dooku's still-ragged breath for a beat and then . . .

DOOKU:
I feel . . . I feel nothing.

YODA:
Dooku. Your lightsaber.

DOOKU:

I'm sorry. I . . .

He extinguishes his own blade.

DOOKU:

I was so sure.

YODA:

Jumped to assumptions, you did. As Master Kostana expected you to.

DOOKU:

This was all a test? The way you goaded me? The book?

YODA:

Book?

DOOKU:

*The Bestiary of Cal-*something.

YODA:

(SIGHS) Caldoth. (TO LENE) Return that to the Archives you should. Along with young Teradine's holojournal. You it was who hid it in the dormitory, I assume?

LENE:

Master Yoda. Dooku saw something down there. We need to know what it was.

YODA:

What's done is done. Repressed the memory, his mind has. The way he should. The way he has been trained. Much darkness dwells in that collection. That he felt something, surprising it is not. But gone it now has. And gone it will remain.

DOOKU:

(SOFTLY, GUILTILY) I heard it roar.

LENE:

Dooku?

DOOKU:

A great beast. It was . . . terrifying.

YODA:

Hmm. Meditate you must. Cleanse your mind. Help, we will.

LENE:

Ignoring the past as always.

YODA:

Not the time, now is, Master Kostana.

DOOKU:

I don't understand.

LENE:

It's quite simple, Dooku. I believe the Jedi must be prepared for a Sith uprising, whereas Master Yoda thinks such preparations are—

YODA:

Unnecessary.

LENE:

See what I mean?

YODA:

Gone, the Sith are.

LENE:

Yes, but what if we're wrong. What if reducing them to a footnote of history is playing into their hands. Younglings like Dooku should be trained to identify and combat their relics—relics that are still scattered across the galaxy.

YODA:

Found more you have?

LENE:

(HESITATING) No. Not yet. But they're out there, I know they are. It's all right for you and the Council, sitting safe in your spire. Something's coming, Master Yoda. I can . . .

YODA:

You can feel it.

LENE:

(SIGHING) If we could just examine the prophecies . . .

YODA:

Unknowable, the future is. Only to the dark side, prophecy leads.
To doubt and fear. An old argument this is.

LENE:

(SIGHS) An argument you always win.

YODA:

What was it you used to call me, hmm, when an Initiate you were?
What do you call me still, when you think I cannot hear?

LENE:

(SLIGHTLY EMBARRASSED) I don't know what you mean.

DOOKU:

She called you an "old goblin."

YODA:

Ha! Old goblin. Yes. Old, I am. Seen much. Understand more than
you think I do, in my safe spire. Come here, young Dooku.

DOOKU:

(UNSURE) Master?

YODA:

Look into your mind, I must. To see if justified, Master Kostana's
fears are.

DOOKU:

Will it hurt?

LENE:

No. Just relax.

YODA:

Yes. Relax. Relax.

There is a moment's silence and then . . .

LENE:

And?

YODA:

No lasting damage, there will be. Strong in the Force, the boy is. A great future he will have.

LENE:

(SMILING) I thought the future was best unknown.

YODA:

Evident, some things are, whether prophesied or not.

DOOKU:

I'm sorry, Master Kostana. I could have hurt you.

LENE:

(LAUGHS) Probably not. But you're good with a lightsaber. You'll make someone a fine Padawan someday, Dooku. A fine Padawan indeed.

SCENE 26. INT. THE *WINDRUNNER*. DOOKU'S CABIN.

Ventress rifles through the disks.

VENTRESS: (NARRATION)

And then it began, Dooku filling message after message with news of Lene Kostana. Of her increasingly frequent visits to the Temple. Of her work, her theories, even her damn convor.

The young Initiate had found himself a hero.

She slips another disk into the reader.

KY NAREC: (GHOST)

You could stop, you know. Haven't you learned enough to complete your mission?

VENTRESS:
I'm nothing if not thorough.

KY NAREC: (GHOST)
Are you sure that's all this is? Perhaps I was wrong to keep you on Rattatak? Perhaps you should have trained at the Temple, with a clan of your own? Is that why you're so . . . fascinated?

VENTRESS: (NARRATION)
I ignore him, continuing through the disks. He's speaking non-sense, though I can't help but feel a sense of thrill as I come to what is obviously one of the most important days in the young Initiate's life, the culmination of years of hard work . . .

A hologram activates.

VENTRESS: (NARRATION)
Dooku is older again, only by a year or so, but his eyes have lost none of their hunger. Their ambition.

DOOKU: (SIXTEEN YEARS OLD, HOLO-NARRATION)
I'm sorry I haven't been in contact, sister. I have been preparing for the tournament. It's tomorrow, in the training gallery. I haven't slept for days thinking about it all. The rumors are that some of the Masters are ready to take their Padawans, that they're coming to the duels. If that's true . . . and Lene is there . . . Do you think she'll choose me?

VENTRESS: (NARRATION)
I want to mock him. To jeer at his youthful enthusiasm, but Ky is right, no matter how hard that is to admit. Try as I might, I can't stop myself from imagining what it would have been like to stand in that chamber myself, skin prickling with anticipation, waiting to see what the future held . . .

SCENE 27. INT. JEDI TEMPLE. OUTSIDE THE TRAINING GALLERY.

Atmosphere: The babble of excited younglings.

SIFO-DYAS: (SIXTEEN YEARS OLD)
Where is he?

ARATH: (SIXTEEN YEARS OLD)
What's the matter, Sifo? Worried His Lordship won't turn up?

ZANG: (SIXTEEN YEARS OLD)
I'd like to see you call him that to his face.

ARATH:
Who? Dooku? I'm not scared of him.

SIFO-DYAS:
Yeah, yeah, Arath. We get it. You're not scared of anyone.

ARATH:
You bet I'm not.

ZANG:
He'll be here, Sifo. Don't worry.

ARATH:
Sure about that? Three credits says he won't show.

Footsteps as Dooku runs up.

DOOKU:
(RUNNING UP) Have they started yet?

ZANG:
Should've taken that bet.

SIFO-DYAS:
You're late.

DOOKU:
I know.

SIFO-DYAS:
You're never late.

ARATH:
We thought you'd chickened out.

DOOKU:
I was practicing. I'm still not happy with my riposte.

SIFO-DYAS:

Says the guy who aced lightsaber class for, oooh, I don't know . . .

ZANG:

. . . the last ten years!

DOOKU:

You know what Braylon says. You can never be too prepared.

ARATH:

What does she know? Stupid old mynock.

ZANG:

Arath!

ARATH:

Well, she is.

SIFO-DYAS:

Ignore him, Zang.

SINUBE: (OFF-MIC)

Hawk-Bat Clan.

DOOKU:

This is it.

SINUBE: (CONT.)

Enter the arena.

SCENE 28. INT. JEDI TEMPLE. TRAINING GALLERY.

We follow the Initiates in. They gather in front of the Masters.

SINUBE:

Younglings. From the anticipation in your faces, I see you know why you are here today.

BRAYLON:

A ceremonial lightsaber duel to demonstrate your aptitude in the Force.

SINUBE:

A tradition of the ages. But one that changes with every year. As you have learned with Master Radorm, tournaments of the past have been held underwater.

BRAYLON:

Or in zero gravity.

SINUBE:

Do you remember the year we held it in a simulated hurricane? That *was* exciting.

BRAYLON:

Yes. Thank you, Master Sinube. This year, as ever, we sought guidance from the Force. You will be glad to know that the contest is to be held on dry land.

SIFO-DYAS:

Thank the stars.

BRAYLON:

However, you will all be blindfolded.

SIFO-DYAS:

Oh no.

DOOKU:

Shhh!

BRAYLON:

Your eyes can deceive you. As Jedi, you must rely on your feelings. You must rely on the Force.

SINUBE:

An extra benefit of the blast visors is that you won't be able to see your potential Masters studying your every move.

DOOKU:

So it's true . . .

ZANG:
(WHISPER) No pressure there.

YODA:
Interfere the Council will not. Sacred the bond between Master and Padawan. Guide us all, the Force will. Focus, you must.

Yoda strikes the floor with his cane.

YODA:
Let the tournament begin.

VENTRESS: (NARRATION)
I listen as Dooku describes dropping back with his fellow Initiates, huddled in groups around the walls. He paints the picture so vividly, I can see myself standing alongside him, shifting nervously while still trying desperately to remain nonchalant . . .

The Initiates gather around the walls.

SIFO-DYAS:
(GROANS) I feel sick.

DOOKU:
You'll be fine.

SIFO-DYAS:
Who are you looking for, anyway?

ARATH:
Can't you guess? Master Kostana . . . blessed be her name.

DOOKU:
(PUSHES HIM) Shut up, Arath.

ARATH:
Hey!

SIFO-DYAS:
Cool it, you two.

DOOKU:
I just thought she would be here.

SIFO-DYAS:
Perhaps she doesn't want a Padawan.

SINUBE: (OFF-MIC)
The combatants will be chosen by the Force.

Braylon picks up a small round stone from a large container in front of her.

BRAYLON: (OFF-MIC)
Each Initiate's name is inscribed on one of these Vagni stones.

She throws it back into the container.

BRAYLON: (OFF-MIC)
We shall pick one at random, using only the Force. Come forward when your name is called.

The stones whirl around in the container, rattling together as if they're being stirred.

SINUBE: (OFF-MIC)
The first combatant is . . .

ARATH:
Let me see.

DOOKU:
Quit shoving!

The stones stop stirring as one is chosen.

SINUBE:
Initiate Dooku!

ZANG:
You're first.

SIFO-DYAS:
Congratulations. I guess.

BRAYLON:
And his opponent will be . . .

The stones start churning again.

DOOKU:
Please let it be Arath. Please let it be Arath.

The stones stop.

BRAYLON:
Initiate Sifo-Dyas.

SIFO-DYAS:
You're kidding. I don't stand a chance against you.

DOOKU:
Of course you do.

YODA: (OFF-MIC)
Forward, the combatants will come.

SIFO-DYAS:
Just promise you won't go easy on me. I don't need any favors.

DOOKU:
Don't worry. I won't give any. May the best man win.

SIFO-DYAS:
That's what I'm worried about.

VENTRESS: (NARRATION)
Dooku describes taking to the arena, the two of them turning to face each other, hands resting on their hilts. I can imagine what was going through Dooku's mind as he attempted to focus, his eyes darting around the gallery, searching for the woman he had pinned his hopes upon. How his heart would have sunk as he realized she wasn't there, how he would force himself to concentrate, staring deep into the eyes of Sifo-Dyas.

And they say the Sith are cruel . . . Pitting a child against his friend and expecting them to see it as an honor, just as Narec welcomed his exile on Rattatak.

The Jedi are fools, each and every one . . .

YODA:
Masters Sinube and Braylon—apply the blast visors.

Sinube walks over to Dooku.

SINUBE:
(QUIETLY) There's no need to worry, Dooku. You've always been my finest student.

DOOKU:
But Sifo . . .

SINUBE:
Ah-ah-ah. None of that. Jedi must concern themselves only with the will of the Force. Remember what Master Niobaya wrote.

DOOKU:
"Do not let attachment cloud your vision, not of possessions . . ."

SINUBE:
"Nor people."

DOOKU:
"There is only the Force."

SINUBE:
Only the Force. Right then, on it goes.

He slips the blast goggles over Dooku's eyes.

SINUBE:
There. Can you see anything?

DOOKU:
N-no. Nothing at all.

SINUBE:

Excellent. Trust your feelings, Dooku. I have faith in you.

Sinube hobbles away.

BRAYLON:

Contenders, prepare for conflict.

Both boys ignite their sabers, Ventress narrating over it.

VENTRESS: (NARRATION)

I close my eyes as Dooku describes the battle, seeing myself in his place, feeling the power pulse through my lightsaber hilt before the blade bursts into life, my opponent doing the same, feet apart, lightsaber held low, its blade thrumming with energy.

Would I have done as he did, strategies racing through my mind, every sensation amplified, every emotion heightened? The beating of my heart. The cold tickle of sweat running down my back.

Who will make the first move? Who will take control? Recalling the lessons of a hundred training sessions, the repetition and discipline. Reminding yourself that the tournament is ceremonial and your strikes must be measured. There can be no injuries, no fatal blows. You must disarm, not disable.

I could have done this. I should have.

YODA:

Let the tournament begin.

On "Begin," Yoda brings his stick down heavily on the floor.

VENTRESS: (NARRATION)

Dooku's words are intoxicating now. As I sit here, surrounded by his trophies, I am no longer listening to his account, I am experiencing it, living each and every moment of the duel, Dooku striking first, the Initiates' lightsabers meeting accompanied by the sharp tang of crackling plasma. Sifo-Dyas throwing himself back, kicking at Dooku's wrist, almost knocking his lightsaber from his fingers. He staggers back, meeting Sifo-Dyas's blade as his opponent twists. Dooku blocks every blow, one arm tucked neatly be-hind his back, eyes closed behind the visor. Sifo-Dyas thrusts and lunges, every attack a story in its own right, revealing his tactics, exposing his weaknesses.

Sifo-Dyas somersaults over Dooku's head—the moment Dooku has been waiting for. He slices up, not to spear his opponent, but to force Sifo-Dyas to twist in midair to avoid the humming blade. The boy lands awkwardly, his ankle folding beneath him. He crashes to the floor, his extinguished lightsaber skittering across the ancient flagstones.

This is it. The moment of victory.

ARATH:
(SHOUTING FROM THE SIDELINES) What are you waiting for? Finish him!

VENTRESS: (NARRATION)
If I were there, I would have been screaming the same. And yet Arath's cry gives Dooku a moment to pause. He senses Sifo-Dyas in front of him, sprawled on the floor, waiting for him to call for his surrender.

Instead, Dooku reaches out with the Force, sending Sifo-Dyas's lightsaber sliding back to his hand.

DOOKU:
Take it. Get up.

SIFO-DYAS:
Doo?

DOOKU:
We finish this together.

Sifo-Dyas's lightsaber reignites and he jumps up.

VENTRESS: (NARRATION)
And that's what they did, completing the duel in front of their clan, neither holding back or pushing the advantage. It sounds

like a glittering display, and when they are finished, hair slick with sweat, lightsabers locked together, the gallery erupts into applause.

The clan applauds, cheering as the lightsabers shut off.

SIFO-DYAS:
We did it! We did it!

DOOKU:
Sifo, behind Yoda—she's . . . she's here. She must have seen everything.

SIFO-DYAS:
(LAUGHING) Saw *you,* you mean. (BEAT) Thank you.

DOOKU:
For what?

SIFO-DYAS:
You know. You could have finished me, there and then, just like Arath said.

DOOKU:
Since when have I ever listened to him?

BRAYLON: (OFF-MIC)
Settle down. Settle down. We must prepare for the next duel. Please. We must have silence.

VENTRESS: (NARRATION)
Dooku describes the duels of each of his clan-mates in excruciating detail, fascinated even at this young age with form and technique. I don't need to listen to all of it, scrolling through the files until I reach the moment Dooku has waited for. The same gallery on a different day. The same Masters standing in front of the same pupils, the anticipation in the room at an all-time high . . .

BRAYLON:
The time has come, Initiates. I will ask each of the Masters to choose their Padawans. This is a solemn moment, but also a joyous

one. You are about to embark on the next stage of your journey. May the Force guide us all.

SIFO-DYAS:
(WHISPER) This is it, Doo.

DOOKU:
Shhh!

SIFO-DYAS:
I can't. It's too exciting.

BRAYLON:
Who will make the first declaration?

SINUBE:
I will. By the will of the Force, I choose Zang Arraira as my Padawan.

ZANG:
(GASPS) It will be an honor to train with you, my Master.

BRAYLON:
Is there anyone else?

LENE:
Yes. I wish to claim a Padawan.

DOOKU:
(TO HIMSELF) The Force will be with me. The Force will be with me.

There is excited babble among the younglings.

LENE: (CONT.)
I choose . . .

ARATH:
(SNICKERS) Look at Dooku. All a-flutter.

DOOKU:
Seriously. One more crack and I'll . . .

LENE:
. . . Sifo-Dyas.

DOOKU:
What?

LENE:
Come, Padawan. Join me.

SIFO-DYAS:
(LOW, TO DOOKU) Dooku. I'm sorry.

DOOKU:
It's fine. (IT'S NOT, BUT HE DOESN'T WANT HIS FRIEND TO KNOW) Congratulations. Go, go.

Sifo-Dyas approaches Lene.

SIFO-DYAS:
Thank you, Master.

ARATH:
(LEANING IN TO DOOKU) Awww, is someone going to cry?

LENE:
What of you, Master Braylon?

BRAYLON:
I will not elect a Padawan this year, but if there is anyone else . . . ?

YODA:
Yes. Chosen, I have.

An excited buzz goes around the gallery.

SINUBE:
The Grand Master is to take a Padawan. This is a rare honor.

YODA:
Dooku, I choose. My Padawan he will be.

DOOKU:
(SHOCKED) Thank you, Master.

YODA:

Arduous the training will be. Much I expect of you.

DOOKU:

And I won't let you down. I promise.

YODA:

A promise not to me you must make, my young Padawan, but to yourself. The Force will guide you. Yes. The Force will guide us all.

VENTRESS: (NARRATION)

But the Force had little to do with the glee in Dooku's voice as he talked to his sister later that night . . .

SCENE 29. INT. THE *WINDRUNNER*. DOOKU'S CABIN.

DOOKU: (HOLO-NARRATION)

You should have seen Arath's face, Jenza. His name wasn't even called. Yoda said he wasn't ready, that he would continue to train as an Initiate for another year. Another year! ·

I know it's wrong of me, but I can't help but think he got what he deserved.

VENTRESS:

So much for Jedi compassion.

She turns off the hologram, swapping another disk into the player.

KY NARAC: (GHOST)
More?

VENTRESS:

Can't a girl be curious?

DOOKU: (HOLO-NARRATION)
Yoda has told me that our training will be delayed . . .

VENTRESS:

No.

The recording scrubs forward. She clicks the button.

DOOKU: (HOLO-NARRATION)
. . . tied up with negotiations with the—

VENTRESS:
No.

She fast-forwards again.

DOOKU: (HOLO-NARRATION)
This is it, Jenza.

VENTRESS:
This sounds more promising.

DOOKU: (HOLO-NARRATION)
Yoda has told me to meet him in the training garden. My apprenticeship begins today . . .

SCENE 30. EXT. JEDI TEMPLE. TRAINING GROUND.

Atmosphere: A gentle wind rustling through the leaves of the kukra tree. Birds singing.

Dooku approaches a meditating Yoda.

DOOKU:
Master Yoda.

There is no response.

DOOKU:
Master Yoda. I am ready to commence my training.

Still no response.

DOOKU:
Hello?

SCENE 31. INT. THE *WINDRUNNER*. DOOKU'S CABIN.

VENTRESS: (NARRATION)
It was obviously not what the new Padawan was expecting.

The sound of a recording fast-forwarding.

VENTRESS: (NARRATION)
And yet, if his next few holomessages were anything to go by, the following days brought little change.

She presses play.

DOOKU: (HOLO-NARRATION)
I don't understand it. It's the same every time.

SCENE 32. EXT. JEDI TEMPLE. TRAINING GROUND.

As before, Dooku approaches.

DOOKU:
Master Yoda?

DOOKU: (HOLO-NARRATION)
I go to the training garden at the allotted time to find Yoda sitting, cross-legged, on the floor. Just meditating.

DOOKU:
I'm sorry, Master, but I thought we might begin today.

Nothing but the birdsong.

DOOKU:
I'm eager to begin my apprenticeship.

Nothing.

DOOKU:
I have so much to learn. Master Yoda.

Nothing.

DOOKU:
Master Yoda.

DOOKU: (HOLO-NARRATION)
It was the same yesterday, and the day before. I might as well be talking to the statues of the Four Founders.

Again, we hear Dooku approach on another day, his step just that little bit more brusque, and when he speaks, his tone is just a little more frustrated.

DOOKU: (HOLO-NARRATION)
And then today . . . today he was floating! A meter from the floor! Still with his eyes closed. Still not moving. Not talking.

DOOKU:
Master. Have I displeased you, somehow? Have I done something wrong? Why will you not talk to me? (BEAT) Master, please.

DOOKU: (HOLO-NARRATION)
It's all right for Sifo-Dyas. I've seen him every day this week, in the training gallery, practicing with Lene. Zang too. Just this morning, she was performing soothing rituals in the atrium. Soothing rituals! Master Sinube was right there alongside her, talking to her, encouraging her, like he's supposed to be. But not Yoda.

We hear the swipe of solitary lightsaber practice, Dooku showing off in front of his meditating teacher.

DOOKU:
(WITH EFFORT FROM THE MOVES) Look, Master.

DOOKU: (HOLO-NARRATION)
Never Yoda.

More swipes.

DOOKU:
I have been practicing.

And more.

DOOKU:
I have perfected the forestalling stance. Do you see? Do you see?

DOOKU: (HOLO-NARRATION)
He sits and he meditates and he floats and he doesn't even acknowledge my presence!

Another day. More footsteps. Angry now. Dooku's voice raised as he marches forward.

DOOKU:

Why are you doing this? Why did you even choose me?

More fast-forwarding.

DOOKU: (HOLO-NARRATION)

I don't know what to do. Do I talk to Braylon? Do I go to the Council? It's not right, Jenza. It's not fair. Master Sinube said it himself. I was his best pupil. His best! Is this how the best are treated?

DOOKU:

(SHOUTING) Why won't you answer!

Another hologram of Dooku opens.

DOOKU: (HOLO-NARRATION)

I've had enough of it now, Jenza. It's been almost a month. I talked to Lene, asked her advice, but she said it wasn't her place to interfere. Not her place. Since when has that stopped her? But I'm not standing for it anymore. Oh no. Yoda said, on the day of the tournament, he said that the bond between a Padawan and his Master was sacred. And this is how he treats me. How he . . . how he *insults* me. He demands respect. Oh, how he demands respect, but he doesn't give. Doesn't earn it. I'm going to show him, Jenza. If he won't teach me, I'm going to show him what I can do.

Back in the training garden. Same atmosphere. The breeze. The birds. Dooku marches up.

DOOKU:

I'm ready for my lesson, Master. Look.

More fast-forwarding.

DOOKU: (HOLO-NARRATION)

I did it. Just as I said I would. I marched up in front of him and reached out with the Force.

DOOKU:
(GRUNT OF EFFORT)

DOOKU: (HOLO-NARRATION)
I lifted everything I could around us. Stones. Leaves. Blossoms. I even lifted some of the soil from the roots of the Great Tree, molding it as we were taught in Master Veleckra's Force-sculpture lesson; a perfect icosahedron, fashioned out of dirt. Do you know how difficult that is? And still . . . and still he ignored me! He might as well have laughed in my face.

I couldn't take it anymore. I had to show him. I had to make him open his eyes.

I let everything else fall and focused on the tree. They say it is old, even older than Yoda, that it originally stood on Ossus, at the heart of the First Temple. I don't know how many Jedi have trained beneath its branches, or how many birds have roosted among its leaves, but I knew it would get his attention.

I imagined my hand, huge and strong, closing around that gnarled trunk, the rough bark beneath my fingers. I could feel the Force running through the kukra's sap, radiating out, sweeping over the ziggurat, over the entire district. Yoda loves that old tree. Growing up, I had seen him standing at its base day after day, looking up into the twisted boughs. I'd felt the connection between the two of them, each impossibly ancient. Now he would see the tree afresh. He would open his eyes as I pulled it from the ground, roots and all, as easy as if I'd plucked a fresh shoot from its bed. He would remember why he chose me. He would remember my strength in the Force.

DOOKU:
(NOISES OF EFFORT)

DOOKU: (HOLO-NARRATION)
I pulled, recalling Yoda's own words as my guide. The only difference was my mind. The only difference was my mind.

The branches began to shake, leaves tumbling to the ground. I would show him. I would show him I was ready, once and for all.

The noises of effort become an almost bestial roar that is at first intent and then frustration.

Dooku has to stop. We hold on the silence for a moment as he breathes heavily, the leaves continuing to fall.

DOOKU: (HOLO-NARRATION)
I couldn't do it. It was too much.

Dooku slumps to the ground.

DOOKU: (HOLO-NARRATION)
I sat down, hard, in front of him. Exhausted in both body and spirit.

DOOKU:
(BREATHING HARD, TRYING NOT TO CRY)

DOOKU: (HOLO-NARRATION)
I had failed. I wasn't strong enough.

And yet, when I looked up, Yoda's eyes were open, and they were settled on me.

YODA:
Ready, are you, my Padawan? Ready to learn what you do not know?

DOOKU: (HOLO-NARRATION)
And finally I understood.

DOOKU:
Yes, Master. Yes, I am.

YODA:
Then begin, we shall.

SCENE 33. INT. THE *WINDRUNNER*. DOOKU'S CABIN.

Ventress switches off the holocomm.

KY NAREC: (GHOST)
A good lesson.

VENTRESS:
Like you would know.

KY NAREC: (GHOST)
I could say the same of you, sitting there. Have you so easily forgotten the lessons I taught you?

VENTRESS:
You didn't teach me anything, because you aren't real.

KY NAREC: (GHOST)
Never waste an opportunity. Keep your senses open.

VENTRESS:
(IRRITABLE) What are you talking about?

KY NAREC: (GHOST)
You want to learn about Dooku, but you can't see what is under your nose. Where are you sitting, Asajj? Whose desk is that? What secrets does it hide?

VENTRESS: (NARRATION)
I look down at the wooden table, at the files, arranged neatly.

VENTRESS:
They are for show.

KY NAREC: (GHOST)
Yes, they are.

VENTRESS:
Then what am I supposed to be looking for?

VENTRESS: (NARRATION)
Drawers. There are drawers in the desk. I hadn't even thought to look in them. Ky is right. He may be an annoying fiction, but he

has a point. If I want to truly know my new Master, maybe I should display a little more . . . initiative.

I reach out with the Force, letting my hand be guided to the drawers on the right, third one down. It's locked. Unsurprising. But locks can be broken.

We hear Ventress break the lock using the Force. The drawer opens.

VENTRESS: (NARRATION)
A datapad. Old by the look of the design. Well worn. I lift it out, activating the screen, hearing the device hum to life.

Beeps as she scrolls through the leather-bound datapad.

VENTRESS: (NARRATION)
No. It can't be. Why would he leave it here, on his airship? I scroll through the contents to make sure and yes, yes it is. It's Dooku's journal, written while he was training, chronicling his lessons with Yoda, long after the Jedi Master had tried to teach him humility. Voyages to Mantooine, Lahsbane, and Kashyyyk. Diplomatic encounters, rescues, mercy missions, and even a time when the pair liberated an entire solar system from the thrall of a necrotic queen.

KY NAREC: (GHOST)
Worth finding.

VENTRESS:
To see how a real teacher operates? Yes.

KY NAREC: (GHOST)
Ouch. If I weren't already dead.

There's a buzz at the door.

VENTRESS: (NARRATION)
I deactivate the device, slipping the pad into my pocket.

VENTRESS:
Come.

The door slides open.

TACTICAL DROID:
We have arrived at the spaceport.

Ventress scrapes up all the data disks.

VENTRESS:
Finally.

KY NAREC: (GHOST)
Do you think it saw you?

VENTRESS:
(SOTTO) Shush.

KY NAREC: (GHOST)
Do you think it knows you've taken it?

VENTRESS:
(SOTTO) I won't tell you again.

TACTICAL DROID:
Tell me what?

VENTRESS:
I was clearing my throat. Please. After you.

SCENE 34. EXT. THE *WINDRUNNER*. DECK.

The droid leads Ventress out onto the deck. She peers over the edge.

VENTRESS:
Is that it?

TACTICAL DROID:
You were expecting something else?

VENTRESS:
I was expecting something grander. Where is the main terminal?

TACTICAL DROID:
That building there, ma'am. Next to the control tower.

VENTRESS:
Then that is where I shall go.

TACTICAL DROID:
We will make preparations to land.

VENTRESS:
There's no need.

TACTICAL DROID:
Ma'am. Wait—

VENTRESS: (NARRATION)
The droid holds out a metallic hand to stop me as I vault over the side of the airship. I plunge down to the ground, landing unseen behind a duracrete hangar.

She lands nimbly.

VENTRESS: (NARRATION)
The place stinks of hyperfuel and desperation. Every spaceport is the same. Yes, they can gild the buildings, play jaunty tunes, even fly holographic flags from the towers, but scratch the surface and you'll find the dregs of the galaxy. It's easy to see why. Everywhere is noise and bustle. Cargoes unloaded, passengers keen to be on their way. Loved ones are reunited and families torn apart, hope and despair in equal measures. Perfect for those who want to slip beneath the sensor. Thieves and smugglers, cutthroats and bounty hunters, all happy to relieve you of your wallet or your life, most often at the same time.

I head to where the disks were found, a greasy back alley, a deactivated droid slumped against a graffiti-strewn wall like a spice-addled junkie. The heat of a furnace spills from a nearby repair pod, the constant din of hammered metal all but drowning out the roar of ships rocketing toward the stars.

Dooku's sister was a senior member of the ruling house. There was no way she would've chosen to come to a place like this of her own accord.

SCENE 35. INT. PORTMASTER'S OFFICE.

Atmosphere: An office far from the shipyard. The portmaster—Raz Fellidrone—is operating a computer when his in-ear comm beeps. It chirps as he answers it.

FELLIDRONE:
Portmaster's office. Raz Fellidrone speaki— Erbelene, you old space-dog! When did you get in? What's that? A problem with customs? (MOCK GASP) I can't believe it. (LAUGHS) No, it's fine. I can make that go away. For the usual price, of course. (PAUSE) From Zeltros? You're spoiling me, Erb. Just give me a minute.

Beeps as he operates the computer.

FELLIDRONE:
Just make a few adjustments to your docking authorization and . . .

One last beep.

FELLIDRONE:
You've been added to the fast track. No, no, there's no need to thank me. Just have the consignment sent to the usual . . . yeah, you know the drill.

How long are you in town? There's a new club in the marina that—

There's a sudden thump from outside, followed by a tinkle of droid parts.

FELLIDRONE:
What the—

The door slides open and Ventress slinks in, followed by a female portworker—Yepa.

YEPA:
You can't go in there!

VENTRESS:
It appears I can.

FELLIDRONE:
Erb. I need to go. I have a . . . visitor.

He deactivates the comm.

FELLIDRONE:
What in Rylon's name is going on here, Yepa?

YEPA:
I'm sorry, Portmaster. She just barged in. Cee Zee Ninety-Four—

VENTRESS:
Cee Zee Ninety-Four is no longer operational.

YEPA:
I'll call security.

VENTRESS:
You don't want to call security.

YEPA:
I don't want to call security.

VENTRESS:
You want to make your boss a nice cup of caf. In Saffia.

YEPA:
I want to make him caf.

VENTRESS:
Shut the door behind you.

Yepa leaves, shutting the door.

FELLIDRONE:
Saffia is over a hundred kilometers away.

VENTRESS:
Your caf might not be warm when she gets back.

FELLIDRONE:
What do you want?

VENTRESS:
I'm after information.

She activates a hologram.

VENTRESS:
Jenza. Sister of your beloved count. She came here yesterday.

FELLIDRONE:
I wouldn't know anything about that.

VENTRESS:
You're the portmaster with the big office and the . . . ugh . . . terrible aftershave. What *is* that?

FELLIDRONE:
You need to leave.

VENTRESS:
No. You need to check if she had a ticket.

FELLIDRONE:
You could at least say please.

Ventress ignites one of her lightsabers.

FELLIDRONE:
(QUICKLY) I'll check.

He works the computer.

FELLIDRONE:
Yes, I've found it. A ticket was purchased three days ago.

VENTRESS:
Heading where?

FELLIDRONE:
To the Core systems. To Coruscant.

VENTRESS:
And did she use it?

He presses more buttons.

FELLIDRONE:
No. She never made the flight.

VENTRESS:
You have facial recognition on your security system?

FELLIDRONE:
Of course we do.

VENTRESS:
Step aside.

FELLIDRONE:
What? Look, you can't just—

VENTRESS:
Move.

He gets up. Ventress extinguishes her lightsaber and sits at the desk, operating the computer.

FELLIDRONE:
What are you doing?

VENTRESS:
Looking for our aristocratic friend.

The computer beeps.

VENTRESS:
There she is.

A hologram of a street scene appears.

VENTRESS:
Where is this?

FELLIDRONE:

The approach to the main terminal. Are you sure that's her?

VENTRESS:

Looks like a match to me.

VENTRESS: (NARRATION)

As we watch, Jenza hurries toward the domed building, sidestepping a man in shabby clothes who shuffles up, holding out a grimy hand.

FELLIDRONE:

Damn beggars. We try to move them on, but there are so many. It's the droids, you see, taking all the jobs—

VENTRESS:

Don't care.

VENTRESS: (NARRATION)

Security droids swarm in, grabbing the vagrant, restraining him. They don't notice a figure lurching out of the crowd toward Jenza. The pair are lost in the crowd for a second, a school party of hulking Togorian younglings blocking the view. I try to adjust the holo's angle, but the flea-bitten brats are everywhere at once. When their teacher finally gets them under control, the mysterious figure is gone, as is Jenza.

I scrub back through the recording, zooming in at the moment where the alien lists toward Dooku's sister. The holo pixelates, but the intent in his fragmented eyes is obvious.

VENTRESS:

What is that?

FELLIDRONE:

A Crolute, I think. Horrible things.

VENTRESS:

With extensive cybernetics.

FELLIDRONE:

Where is it taking her?

VENTRESS:

A more pertinent question would be why your droids didn't notice.

FELLIDRONE:

They were focused on the beggar I suppose. Yepa is responsible for the droids. I'll have her look into it . . . when she returns from Saffia.

VENTRESS:

While I look for the Crolute.

FELLIDRONE:

That shouldn't take you long. There can't be many on Serenno.

Ventress stands.

VENTRESS:

We never had this conversation.

FELLIDRONE:

(TRYING TO BE BRAVE) Your mind tricks won't work on me.

VENTRESS:

Who's using a mind trick? Tell anyone about this and I'll rip out your tongue.

KY NAREC: (GHOST)

It's amazing how persuasive you can be . . .

PART THREE

SCENE 36. INT. BELSALLIAN CANTINA.

We come up on the sounds of a spaceport cantina. Music in the background. Drinks being poured. Glasses clinking. General babble of clientele.

Ventress is sitting alone at a table.

VENTRESS:
Can't a girl enjoy a drink in peace?

VENTRESS: (NARRATION)
Searching for the Crolute has proved trickier than Fellidrone suggested. It's hard to believe but no ones's seen a seven-foot thug with gelatinous skin and more implants than a Guavian rigger. Funny that.

My only lead has brought me here, to the Belsallian Cantina, an establishment so disreputable that it advises its patrons to arm themselves before entering its premises.

The last thing I need is the return of my spectral stalker, or the walrus-faced Khormai who staggers toward me, drooling through his drooping whiskers.

KHORMAI:
(SLURRING) *Kora oron ba sandre?* [Looking for fun, beautiful?]

Ventress takes a sip of her drink.

VENTRESS:
I suggest you turn around and walk away.

KHORMAI:
Oona ke marak-ne. [You could come with me.]

VENTRESS:
(SIGHS) Do you see that serving droid over there?

KHORMAI:
(GRUNTS, TURNING TO SEE)

VENTRESS:
That's right. The one with a squeaky wheel. Do you like her tray? Here . . .

Suddenly the tray whips through the air, clanging into the Khormai's face. The brute goes down, hard.

VENTRESS: (CONT.)
. . . take a closer look.

The waitress with the squeaky wheel trundles over.

WAITRESS DROID:
Want me to get rid of that for you, honey?

VENTRESS:
No. Leave him where he is. It'll act as a warning.

The waitress droid squeaks off.

WAITRESS DROID:
I wouldn't bet on it.

Ventress takes another sip.

KY NAREC: (GHOST)
You bring me to all the best places.

VENTRESS:
I didn't bring you anywhere. You followed me. (TAKES AN-OTHER SIP) Shame I can't hit you with a tray.

KY NAREC: (GHOST)
It reminds me of that place in Velenki.

VENTRESS:
I'm surprised you can remember.

KY NAREC: (GHOST)
That was a dive, too.

VENTRESS: (NARRATION)
He's not wrong, even if he can't possibly know. Ky . . . the *real* Ky had received word that a small settlement called Velenki had been having problems with Weequay raiders. I knew something was wrong the moment we walked into the tavern, the way the barkeep never met our gaze, even as he asked for help.

KY NAREC: (GHOST)
You can't blame them.

VENTRESS:
They betrayed us. They betrayed *you*.

KY NAREC: (GHOST)
They had been threatened. Kirske promised to torch their village unless they handed us over.

VENTRESS: (NARRATION)
Kirske. Everything always came back to Osika Kirske.

VENTRESS:
He burned it anyway.

KY NAREC: (GHOST)
I tried to warn them. All those barrels!

VENTRESS: (NARRATION)
I can still hear him, calling out, desperately trying to warn the villagers.

KY NAREC: (A FLASHBACK, DISTORTED)
Look out, the paralene. It's going to blow.

We hear an echo of an explosion, the paralene erupting.

VENTRESS: (NARRATION)
The Weequay came from all directions at once. I tried to fight them off, but there were too many, even for Ky. I never saw the blaster lance until it was too late.

We hear the echo of a shot and then the young Ventress's cry, her voice distorted by time.

YOUNG VENTRESS: (DISTORTED)
Master!

VENTRESS: (NARRATION)
That was the moment when my path was set. Not when the Nightsisters handed me over to Hal'Sted, not when Ky rescued me all those years later. I took the first step toward Dooku when I grabbed Ky's bloodied lightsaber and ignited the blade.

Again, the echo of both lightsabers igniting.

YOUNG VENTRESS: (DISTORTED)
Noooo!

KY NAREC: (GHOST)
You didn't have to kill them all.

VENTRESS:
You wouldn't have avenged the villagers?

KY NAREC: (GHOST)
Never out of hatred.

VENTRESS:
(MOCKING) Because, repeat after me, younglings, hate leads to suffering and suffering leads . . .

KY NAREC: (GHOST)
Yes?

VENTRESS:
To the dark side. Do you know what? Yes. Yes, it does. (TAKES A DRINK) And I for one like it here.

KY NAREC: (GHOST)
You don't mean that.

VENTRESS:
Believe that if it makes you feel better.

The squeaky-wheeled waitress returns.

WAITRESS DROID:
Er, hun. That blob-head you're looking for. He runs with the Razorclaw Gang. That's them over there.

VENTRESS: (NARRATION)
Thugs are huddled by the bar, two Gran and a multi-limbed Pendago. I take one last drink and slink over to them, letting the Gran's eyes linger on my hips. The Pendago glances at my would-be suitor, still comatose beside my table. I position myself between its suspicious gaze and the unconscious Khormai.

VENTRESS:
Hey, boys. Care to help a girl find what she's looking for?

GRAN:
And what's that?

VENTRESS:
A Crolute. You can't miss him. Sagging skin, rusting implants. A real catch.

PENDAGO:
(GUTTURAL) *Uhh-uh-na-na!*

VENTRESS:
What was that?

GRAN:

He said we don't know any Crolutes.

PENDAGO:

(SUGGESTIVE) *Uh na-u-na.* [But you can have fun with us.]

VENTRESS:

No need to translate that. I got the general idea.

She activates her lightsabers and takes off one of the Pendago's limbs.

PENDAGO:

(BELLOWS IN PAIN)

VENTRESS:

Touch me again and you'll lose another tentacle.

GRAN:

You're crazy.

VENTRESS:

And you're one answer away from being dead, so let's try again. The droid says you know the Crolute. Is she lying, or are you?

SCENE 37. EXT. ROOFTOP. NIGHT.

Atmosphere: The sounds of the spaceport in the background. Ships arriving and leaving, speeders zooming past below on the street, a slight wind blowing across the roof.

VENTRESS: (NARRATION)

Turns out that the droid was telling the truth. The Crolute's name was Glute. He'd fallen out of favor with their boss and no one had seen him for weeks. It took three more tentacles until I believed them.

The Gran told me where he lived, a room in a crumbling res block near the cargo stores. There was no one home, the front doors bolted, not that the rusted locks proved too much of a problem.

She kicks it open.

VENTRESS: (NARRATION)

But once inside, the trail grew cold. The building was a maze of dank corridors, mold and spirit knew what else climbing up the walls. Glute could have been hiding behind any of the warped doors, but I knew in my gut that he wasn't here. Maybe it was the Force. Maybe it was a hunch, but I decided to wait, sheltering on the roof of a nearby warehouse as it started to rain.

There's the rumble of thunder, the pattering of rain, which continues in all scenes in this location.

VENTRESS:

Unfortunately, I wasn't alone . . .

KY NAREC: (GHOST)

This all comes so naturally to you.

VENTRESS:

Still wish you'd taken me to the Temple?

KY NAREC: (GHOST)

They could have done so much for you. Unlike me.

VENTRESS:

Please. Spare me your self-pity.

KY NAREC: (GHOST)

I failed you.

VENTRESS:

Yes. Yes, you did.

VENTRESS: (NARRATION)

At least that silenced him, but I couldn't let it go, like picking at a scab.

VENTRESS:

Dooku says they abandoned you.

KY NAREC: (GHOST)

He's Sith. He lies.

VENTRESS:

Really? All the time we were together, all the time we trained, you never contacted them, and they never contacted you. Why was that?

There's no answer.

VENTRESS:

Hello? Are you there? Or are you pulling a Yoda. I'm ready to learn, Master! Why won't you open your eyes!

KY NAREC: (GHOST)

You're mocking me.

VENTRESS:

Only because you make it so easy.

VENTRESS: (NARRATION)

He chuckles. Actually chuckles. I find myself smiling. I can't let myself get sucked in. I need to stay focused, to remember why I'm here.

She pulls the data disks from her pouch.

KY NAREC: (GHOST)

What are you doing?

VENTRESS:

Following orders. Maybe you should've done the same.

KY NAREC: (GHOST)

Then I wouldn't have met you.

VENTRESS:

No, but you'd still be alive.

She pulls the projector from her pouch.

KY NAREC: (GHOST)

That's the reader from Dooku's cabin.

VENTRESS:
What he doesn't know won't kill me. Do you mind?

KY NAREC: (GHOST)
Could I stop you if I did?

VENTRESS:
Better men have tried.

She slips a disk into the reader. A hologram activates.

VENTRESS: (NARRATION)
I wince when I say it. Better men? Like Dooku? He stopped me quickly enough. He stares back at me from the hologram, now a Padawan, seventeen, maybe eighteen years of age, no sign of the cruelty that will follow.

Why am I doing this? If Ky really is there, if he's found a way to come back, surely I should be spending every moment I can with him, rather than wading through the past of the man who's enslaved me all over again. Because that's what I am, isn't it? A slave. Back where I began.

I could run right now. I could jump on a cruiser and never look back.

But where would I go? Rattatak? Dathomir?

I'd thought I'd come so far.

She presses play.

DOOKU: (SEVENTEEN YEARS OLD, HOLO-NARRATION)
Jenza. I hope you are well. I . . . I have just returned from a mercy mission, but things did not go to plan. There is much we could have done differently . . . much we *should* have done, but they wouldn't listen. They never listen . . .

SCENE 38. EXT. JEDI TEMPLE. MEDITATION BALCONY.

Atmosphere as before, traffic zipping past, et cetera.

DOOKU: (SEVENTEEN YEARS OLD)
Ferana, come on, girl. Where are you?

DOOKU: (HOLO-NARRATION)
I've been caring for Lene's convor while she's offplanet, which turns out to be more often than not . . .

The convor flies down to roost on a rail, chirping.

DOOKU:
There you are. Hello, girl. Yes, hello. Hello. Are you hungry? Do you want something to eat?

There's a rustle of a bag of seed.

DOOKU:
There you are. Do you like that, eh?

The bird trills.

SIFO-DYAS: (SEVENTEEN YEARS OLD)
Careful. Last time I fed her she nearly took off my fingers.

DOOKU:
Sifo-Dyas!

SIFO-DYAS:
Good to see you, old friend.

They embrace, slapping each other's backs.

DOOKU:
Old?

SIFO-DYAS:
It must be the beard. Very distinguished. One might almost say . . . regal.

DOOKU:
Don't start. When did you get back?

SIFO-DYAS:
This morning. Zang said you were up here.

DOOKU:
Like she'd know.

SIFO-DYAS:
I have something for you.

He rifles through his robes, producing a crystal.

SIFO-DYAS:
There you go.

DOOKU:
Thank you. It's . . . it's beautiful. (HE TURNS IT OVER) Is it kyber?

SIFO-DYAS:
No. I got it on Palek. The Palekians use them to meditate. Here, let me show you. (HE TAKES IT BACK) You hold it in your hand like this and focus on the vibrations in the cortex. Go on. You try.

Dooku takes it.

SIFO-DYAS:
Can you feel them?

DOOKU:
Yes. Yes, I can.

SIFO-DYAS:
It's incredible, isn't it? A hyperstorm hit when we were there, and even in the middle of it—

(CRIES OUT IN SUDDEN PAIN)

DOOKU:
Sifo. Sifo, what's wrong?

Sifo drops the crystal. It shatters.

SIFO-DYAS:
(PAINED) The storm.

DOOKU:

On Palek?

SIFO-DYAS:

No. Flames. Flames rushing in. The planet is burning.

DOOKU:

Planet? What planet? Sifo. Look at me. Focus on me.

SIFO-DYAS:

I can't stop them. Why can't I stop them, Dooku?

A door slides open. Lene enters.

LENE:

Dooku?

DOOKU:

Lene. Something's wrong with Sifo-Dyas.

LENE:

Not again.

DOOKU:

It's happened before?

LENE:

Too many times. Sifo. Sifo, listen to me. You need to come back. You need to center yourself.

SIFO-DYAS:

Master?

LENE:

That's right. Breathe. Focus. The Force is with you.

SIFO-DYAS:

The Force is with me.

LENE:

What did you see?

SIFO-DYAS:

(SHAKEN) The sky was falling. There were screams. So many screams.

LENE:

Where were you?

SIFO-DYAS:

I don't know. A planet. Not far from here. Millions will die.

LENE:

It's a warning.

DOOKU:

What do you mean?

LENE:

Sifo-Dyas suffers from . . . premonitions.

DOOKU:

Since when?

LENE:

Since he learned to open his mind.

DOOKU:

Does Yoda know?

LENE:

I was hoping we could keep it . . .

DOOKU:

Secret?

LENE:

Under wraps.

SIFO-DYAS:

This was different, Master. I've never seen such devastation.

DOOKU:

We should tell the Council.

SIFO-DYAS:
Dooku, no.

DOOKU:
We must.

LENE:
Dooku's right. It's too important.

SIFO-DYAS:
They won't listen.

DOOKU:
Then we'll make them.

SCENE 39. INT. JEDI COUNCIL CHAMBER.

Atmosphere as in the prequels.

YODA:
Worrying, this is, Master Kostana.

LENE:
Yes, yes. I know what you're going to say. The future should remain unseen, but unfortunately Sifo-Dyas has little choice in the matter.

SINUBE:
How long have these visions been plaguing you, Padawan?

SIFO-DYAS:
A few months.

BRAYLON:
And yet your Master didn't think to bring it to our attention.

LENE:
I've been training Sifo how to withstand his . . . episodes.

BRAYLON:
(EXASPERATED) Why?

LENE:

Because they come from the Force. What right do we have to ignore its warnings?

BRAYLON:

If this has something to do with your obsession with the Sith . . .

LENE:

It has to do with saving lives! Millions upon millions of lives. He saw entire cities wiped out, Yula. Can you imagine that? Can you imagine the pain and the suffering? Because Sifo-Dyas can. He saw it. He felt it.

YODA:

Hmm. Come forward, Padawan.

SIFO-DYAS:

Yes, Grand Master.

YODA:

Visualize the disaster, you must. Painful it may be.

SIFO-DYAS:

I . . . I understand.

YODA:

Pinpoint the disturbance we shall. You, too, my Padawan. Join the circle, you should.

DOOKU:

Master.

BRAYLON:

Tell us what you saw, Sifo-Dyas.

SIFO-DYAS:

It was . . . a paradise. Long grass blowing in the wind. Fields the size of countries.

SINUBE:

Show us. Picture it in your mind.

SIFO-DYAS:

(BECOMING AGITATED) The wind . . . it turned into a storm. A terrible storm. People were falling. Screaming. Flames reaching up to catch them. Burning fingers reaching into the sky.

LENE:

You're safe, Sifo-Dyas. Remember that.

SINUBE:

He can't take much more.

DOOKU:

But I can. Sifo-Dyas, draw on my strength.

YODA:

No. Too dangerous it is.

DOOKU:

Master, we need to see.

SIFO-DYAS:

It's all right. I can manage.

BRAYLON:

Where is it, Sifo-Dyas? Show us the planet.

LENE:

It doesn't work like that.

SIFO-DYAS:

No. I can do it.

SINUBE:

Anything you can give us. Constellations? Suns?

SIFO-DYAS:

Sun. One sun. Bloated. Old.

YODA:

I sense . . . a Core world.

LENE:

Or the Colonies. Somewhere central.

BRAYLON:

Open a holomap.

A hologram shimmers on.

BRAYLON:

Bardotta?

LENE:

No. That's not right. The grass Sifo described . . . they're . . . they're crops.

YODA:

Hmm. An agriworld, then.

BRAYLON:

Remove all other planets from the display.

There's a beep. The hologram shifts.

YODA:

Focus. Focus on what Sifo-Dyas saw.

DOOKU:

There. Protobranch.

BRAYLON:

Are you sure?

SIFO-DYAS:

Yes. Yes, that's it. I know it is.

YODA:

Hmm. And what do we know of Protobranch? Dooku?

A datapad beeps.

DOOKU:

The homeworld of the Bivall. Traditionally agricultural. Main exports include grain and bacta.

BRAYLON:
Have there been reports of any unusual meteorological phenomena?

More beeps.

DOOKU:
Not that I can see.

SIFO-DYAS:
We should warn them.

YODA:
No.

DOOKU:
But Master, if they could prepare themselves . . .

YODA:
No, I said.

DOOKU:
But why?

YODA:
Because misleading visions can be. Never certain the future is. Meditate on this we must.

LENE:
Meditate? And what will we do if disaster strikes while we search for answers? Will we meditate on the lives that could have been saved?

BRAYLON:
The Council's decision is final, Master Kostana.

LENE:
Then the Council is wrong.

DOOKU: (HOLO-NARRATION)
Lene stormed from the Chamber. I watched as she swept from the Temple, her robes billowing as she crossed the Republic Plaza, marching toward the Senate . . .

SCENE 40. EXT. OUTSIDE THE SENATE BUILDING.

Atmosphere: The busy hubbub of the Senate. Crowds of people. Air traffic above.

Lene is walking purposefully up the steps, Dooku chasing after her.

DOOKU:
Lene. Wait.

LENE:
You're supposed to be at the Temple, Dooku.

DOOKU:
I could say the same about you.

LENE:
Just go back. You don't have to be a part of this.

DOOKU:
A part of what?

TAVETTI:
(CALLING OVER) Master Kostana!

Lene walks toward him.

LENE:
Senator Tavetti, it's good to see you.

DOOKU:
(WHISPER) That's the Bivall senator.

LENE:
(WHISPER) Yes, it is.

DOOKU:
(WHISPER) But Yoda said . . .

LENE:
(HISSED) I know what he said. (TO TAVETTI) Senator. You've had opportunity to review my message?

TAVETTI:

You think I would agree to meet if I had not? If what your apprentice saw is true . . .

LENE:

There is no way to be certain. It was only a vision.

TAVETTI:

But the landscape he described.

LENE:

You recognize it?

TAVETTI:

Of course. The Tabor Plains.

DOOKU:

Where the majority of your bacta is produced.

TAVETTI:

And this is?

LENE:

Padawan Dooku.

TAVETTI:

The Padawan who had the vision?

DOOKU:

No, but I was there. Sifo said there would be a fire. A fire that would rage over the entire globe.

TAVETTI:

A disaster of this scale would be catastrophic to the planet's economy.

DOOKU:

Not to mention all the people who would die.

TAVETTI:

Without our bacta, the galactic death toll would be much worse. What does the Council intend to do about it?

LENE:
We cannot be seen to interfere.

TAVETTI:
Interfere?

LENE:
Not without definite proof that something is about to happen. Have you contacted Protobranch?

TAVETTI:
Straightaway. But the weather is strictly regulated. No storms are scheduled until well after harvest.

LENE:
There must be something we can do.

TAVETTI:
I will talk to the chancellor. Maybe she can order the Council to investigate.

LENE:
Whatever you think is best, Senator.

TAVETTI:
I shall see her at once.

Tavetti hurries off.

TAVETTI:
(CALLING BACK) But your mission must be kept secret, Master Jedi. We mustn't cause panic among the people.

LENE:
Of course, Senator.

DOOKU:
Master Yoda isn't going to like this, you know.

LENE:
Not in the slightest.

SCENE 41. EXT. SPACE.

A Jedi shuttle zips by.

SCENE 42. INT. JEDI SHUTTLE.

Atmosphere: The interior of a Jedi shuttle coming down through clouds.

Yoda is meditating, Dooku nervously hovering at the door.

DOOKU:

(CLEARS HIS THROAT) Master Yoda. We have arrived in the Protobranch system.

YODA:

Aware of that, I am. Thank you, Padawan.

DOOKU:

Sorry. I . . . Master Kostana asked me to let you know.

YODA:

Prepare we must. Waiting on the surface, the prime minister will be.

DOOKU:

Master, I . . .

YODA:

Yes?

DOOKU:

I'm sorry Master Kostana went behind your back.

YODA:

Hm. As am I. Yes. As am I.

DOOKU:

She was just so angry about what happened in the Chamber . . .

YODA:

Angry, was she? Hmm? Ask you to speak to me, did she? To explain?

DOOKU:
No. But I thought . . .

YODA:
Yes? Speak your mind, you should.

DOOKU:
(HESITATING, AND THEN . . .) If I was on the Council, I would listen to what the Force had to say. I would heed its warning . . .

YODA:
Hm. Is that right? Is that right? If on the Council the Padawan was . . .

DOOKU:
I . . . I meant no disrespect.

YODA:
No? Hmm. Always knows best, Dooku does. Never listens. Maybe on the Council one day you will be. Maybe, in my chair you will sit. Although, a little on the small side you may find it . . .

DOOKU:
(EMBARRASSED) Master . . .

YODA:
Always rushing ahead, you are. Always eager to prove your worth. *Too* eager. *Too* keen. A Jedi, you are. Worth enough for anyone that should be.

A comm chimes.

SIFO-DYAS: (OVER COMM)
We're coming in to land, Master Yoda.

YODA:
Thank you, Padawan. On our way, we are.

The comm line shuts off. Yoda starts toward the door.

YODA:
What's done is done. Act now we must.

DOOKU:

I understand.

YODA:

Make sure you do, young Dooku. Make sure you do.

SCENE 43. EXT. TABOR PLAINS. DAY.

The shuttle lands. It is a pastoral scene, albeit one marred by the hum of gigantic city-sized repulsor disks in the air.

DOOKU: (HOLO-NARRATION)

Our shuttle touched down on Protobranch on a bright, balmy day, a gentle breeze rippling through crops that stretched on forever. I'd never seen anything like it, Jenza. The sky was dotted with cities built on top of sprawling antigrav platforms. They cast huge shadows over the swaying cereal, the thrum of repulsors a constant drone in the air . . . much like the voice of the planet's prime minister.

The prime minister's voice comes up on the mic as he walks his guests through the crops.

PRIME MINISTER:

I fear your journey has been wasted, Master Yoda. We have conducted extensive tests, but our weather is strictly regulated.

LENE:

My Padawan witnessed a storm.

PRIME MINISTER:

And yet none are scheduled.

DOOKU:

Could it be a malfunction in the control matrix?

PRIME MINISTER:

Certainly not. We pride ourselves on total environmental control.

YODA:

Second only to Coruscant itself. Hm.

SIFO-DYAS:
But this is where it was.

PRIME MINISTER:
In your vision.

SIFO-DYAS:
Yes.

PRIME MINISTER:
Then I can only suggest that you were mistaken, thank the stars.

LENE:
Protobranch is certainly impressive, Prime Minister. I've never seen agriculture on such a scale. Entire continents turned over to cultivation.

PRIME MINISTER:
Thank you, Master Kostana. The decision to transfer the population to sky-disks was controversial but has paid off in the end.

DOOKU:
An ingenious solution.

PRIME MINISTER:
We needed more land, it was as simple as that. Production has tripled in the last decade, and with it, the need for more crops. Think of the lives our bacta has saved across the galaxy.

YODA:
And the buildings above us?

PRIME MINISTER:
One of our smaller production plants, and Tabor Hospital, of course.

LENE:
Where you test new strains of bacta.

PRIME MINISTER:
Yes. Exactly.

SIFO-DYAS:
(GASPS) Master.

LENE:
Sifo?

PRIME MINISTER:
Is anything wrong?

DOOKU:
I feel it, too.

PRIME MINISTER:
Feel what?

YODA:
A disturbance in the Force.

An alarm sounds on the prime minister's datapad.

LENE:
What's that?

PRIME MINISTER:
A solar storm has been detected, headed straight for Protobranch.

SIFO-DYAS:
A storm?

YODA:
How big?

More warning beeps.

PRIME MINISTER:
It's . . . it's off the scale.

SIFO-DYAS:
But, Master Kostana. If that's what I saw, the magnetic pulse . . .

LENE:
Will knock out every circuit on the planet.

The prime minister's datapad crackles and dies.

PRIME MINISTER:
My datapad!

YODA:
Begun, it has . . .

Above them the repulsors flicker and cut out.

DOOKU:
The cities!

LENE:
The repulsor platforms have failed!

The platforms creak and then fall.

PRIME MINISTER:
They're coming down!

DOOKU: (HOLO-NARRATION)
All around the planet, cities that had been suspended in the air for decades dropped as one. Where once there had been the perpetual buzz of repulsorlift engines, now there were crashes and explosions and terrible screams . . . screams that Sifo-Dyas had already endured.

The disks plowed into the endless fields, plumes of dirt rising up to greet the bodies falling to their deaths.

DOOKU:
Look out!

DOOKU: (HOLO-NARRATION)
I threw myself at Sifo-Dyas, knocking him clear as a crumbling tower block flattened the grass behind us. The falling hospital had crashed into the Tabor Plains, columns of fire igniting a blaze that swept hungrily through the dry crops. The cries of a million souls cut through me, a tremor in the Force that threatened to send us all into a spiral of grief and dispair.

LENE:

Is everyone all right?

SIFO-DYAS:

(ANGUISHED) We were too late.

The prime minister tries to open a comm channel.

PRIME MINISTER:

Hello? Can anyone hear me?

YODA:

Down, the comm network will be.

The fires intensify.

DOOKU:

The fire is spreading.

SIFO-DYAS:

Just like I saw.

PRIME MINISTER:

We're going to be burned alive.

YODA:

Hold back the flames we will.

PRIME MINISTER:

How?

YODA:

The Force is strong.

DOOKU: (HOLO-NARRATION)

Yoda and Lene stood back-to-back, their eyes closed and arms outstretched. I felt the Force swell around us, providing an invisible barrier to the flames. The heat was intense, but at least the fire was stopped in its tracks . . . for now.

PRIME MINISTER:

But that's . . . that's impossible.

YODA:
Dooku. Sifo-Dyas. Check for survivors you must.

DOOKU:
In the hospital?

LENE:
Send them to us.

DOOKU:
But what then? We have no way to get them offplanet.

PRIME MINISTER:
The early warning system would have sent a distress call before it shut down.

YODA:
On its way, help will be.

SIFO-DYAS:
But the flames. Surely you won't be able to hold them back for long.

LENE:
Let us worry about that. Go now. And may the Force be with us all.

SCENE 44. EXT. OUTSIDE HOSPITAL.

DOOKU: (HOLO-NARRATION)
Most species have their own Armageddon myths. We learned many of them as Initiates. Understand someone's fears, we were told, and you will know how to help them. Zang used to hate it, all that fire and damnation, but me . . . I reveled in it. I never took them seriously, you see. They were stories. Fables. I knew the universe would endure, and if it didn't, it wouldn't be because of gods or powers beyond our understanding.

And yet . . . the scene that greeted us as we raced toward the entrance of the hospital was worse than any apocalypse. It was real. It was raw. Droids lay in crumpled heaps, the sick and infirm trying to help those who had been injured in the crash.

DOOKU:

(SHOUTING) Everyone. Keep moving. Head toward the plantation.

DOOKU: (HOLO-NARRATION)
The pain and terror were overwhelming . . .

SIFO-DYAS:

(CRYING OUT, CLUTCHING HIS HEAD)

DOOKU:

Sifo?

SIFO-DYAS:

(PAINED) Everyone is going to die.

DOOKU:

No, they're not. We can do this. The Force is with us.

SIFO-DYAS:

What if that's not enough?

DOOKU:

It will be. It has to be.

SIFO-DYAS:

I'm sorry. It just . . . it just hurts.

DOOKU:

You can do this, I know you can. People are relying on us.

SCENE 45. INT. HOSPITAL RECEPTION.

Atmosphere: The hospital is largely deserted, everyone having either fled or been killed. Fires burn. Cables spark.

DOOKU: (HOLO-NARRATION)
It's fair to say that I've always been . . . overconfident, but even I was daunted as we ran inside what remained of the building. Cables hung exposed, sparks cascading like falling stars while fires

burned in the debris, consuming those who hadn't survived the crash.

Dooku and Sifo run in.

SIFO-DYAS:
(COUGHING ON SMOKE) Hello? Is there anyone in here?

DOOKU:
It's so dark.

SIFO-DYAS:
Reckon our lightsabers still work?

DOOKU:
Only one way to find out.

Both lightsabers burst on.

SIFO-DYAS:
Thank the Force for kyber insulators.

DOOKU:
Shame they didn't install them here.

There's a banging nearby. Fists against metal.

PIRA: (CALLING OFF-MIC)
Hello? Is someone there?

DOOKU:
Yes. Yes, we're here. We're coming.

They run deeper into the complex.

SCENE 46. INT. CORRIDOR.

Dooku and Sifo-Dyas run up to a door, their lightsabers humming. There's knocking on the other side.

PIRA: (MUFFLED)
Hello? Is anyone there?

DOOKU:
(CALLING THROUGH THE DOORS) Yes. Can you open the doors?

PIRA: (MUFFLED)
No. They're jammed.

DOOKU:
Stand back.

He thrusts his lightsaber into the door, cutting a hole.

DOOKU: (HOLO-NARRATION)
My lightsaber flared as I pierced the duraplast.

PIRA: (MUFFLED)
Hurry!

DOOKU:
I am.

He finishes burning his way through the door.

DOOKU:
Are you clear?

PIRA: (MUFFLED)
Yes.

DOOKU:
I'm going to knock it through.

He kicks the door, a perfect circle clattering to the floor on the other side.

DOOKU: (HOLO-NARRATION)
We leapt through the hole, finding a Bivall doctor, her once crisp uniform blackened with soot and blood.

PIRA:
Thank the stars.

DOOKU:

Are you hurt?

PIRA:

No, but there are younglings in the emergency ward. I can't move them.

SIFO-DYAS:

You're gonna have to.

There's an explosion nearby. More flames roar.

DOOKU:

This place isn't safe.

PIRA:

Will you help?

DOOKU:

Show us.

SCENE 47. INT. CORRIDOR.

Footsteps run toward us.

PIRA:

They're down here. Past the bacta reserves.

More sparks. More small explosions.

PIRA:

(CRIES OUT IN ALARM)

The tanks start to crack.

SIFO-DYAS:

The tanks. They're cracking.

DOOKU:

That's a lot of bacta.

PIRA:
We need to hurry.

They continue to run.

SCENE 48. INT. OUTSIDE WARD.

They reach the door, lightsabers still burning.

DOOKU: (HOLO-NARRATION)
We came to the doctor's ward, the door wedged tight against the smoke and dust.

Pira bangs on the door.

PIRA:
It's Dr. Pira. I've brought help.

Behind them, the tanks rupture, bacta rushing down the corridor.

DOOKU:
The bacta tanks. They've ruptured.

The doctor bangs on the door again, even more frantically.

PIRA:
Open up!

The door opens, the bacta rushing toward them.

RRALLA:
(SHYRIIWOOK)

PIRA:
Rralla? Where's Nurse Volkan?

RRALLA:
(SHYRIIWOOK)

PIRA:
She went to get help? I told her to stay with you.

SIFO-DYAS:
Why don't we worry about that when we're inside, eh?

RRALLA:
(SHYRIIWOOK)

DOOKU:
Move!

SIFO-DYAS:
Get that door shut.

DOOKU: (HOLO-NARRATION)
Sifo's warning came a moment too late. Bacta surged through the open door, drenching us all.

The bacta hits, rushing into the room. The patients cry out in alarm, especially Rralla.

DOOKU:
(CHOKING ON THE BACTA) Pira. Get the children as high as you can. Sifo, help me with the door.

SIFO-DYAS:
It won't budge.

DOOKU:
Trust the Force.

Both Jedi make sounds of effort as they use the Force, the door scraping as it slowly begins to shut.

SIFO-DYAS:
It's moving!

DOOKU:
Keep focused.

The door continues its painfully slow progress.

PIRA:
The bacta's rising.

DOOKU & SIFO TOGETHER:
We noticed!

DOOKU: (HOLO-NARRATION)
The door finally slid shut, but there was no time for celebration.
Bacta was already seeping through the seal.

SIFO-DYAS:
We did it.

PIRA:
The bacta's still getting in.

DOOKU:
There can't be much left in the tanks.

SIFO-DYAS:
You sure about that?

PIRA:
How are we going to get out?

DOOKU:
We'll have to go up.

PIRA:
Up?

DOOKU:
What's above us? On the next level.

PIRA:
I don't know. The delivery suite, I think.

DOOKU:
It'll have to do. Sifo, help me with that med table.

They drag a table through the bacta.

PIRA:
That's delicate equipment.

SIFO-DYAS:
Not anymore it's not.

DOOKU:
That's it. Get it into the middle of the room.

RRALLA:
(SHYRIIWOOK)

PIRA:
I know, Rralla. I'm scared, too. But we have to be brave for the other children.

DOOKU: (HOLO-NARRATION)
I jumped onto the table, ready to thrust my lightsaber into the ceiling.

DOOKU:
Right. Watch out for the sparks.

He starts cutting a hole in the ceiling.

DOOKU: (HOLO-NARRATION)
Sifo-Dyas positioned himself between the doctor and the molten metal that splashed steaming into the bacta from my blade.

SIFO-DYAS:
Now, about these kids.

PIRA:
We can't move them.

SIFO-DYAS:
So you said, but we can't leave them here, either.

Dooku continues cutting his circle.

DOOKU:
Nearly done. Stand back.

He finishes cutting, the circle of metal splashing down.

DOOKU:

I'll see what it's like up there.

He jumps up through the hole, his robes rustling as he leaps.

PIRA:

How can he jump like that?

SIFO-DYAS:

Regular exercise. (CALLING UP) Dooku?

DOOKU:

(CALLING DOWN) It's clear. Doctor, we need to keep moving. We've no idea if the building is sound. It could come crashing down at any moment.

PIRA:

Okay. But how are we going to get them up there?

DOOKU:

Get them beneath the hole.

PIRA:

But . . .

DOOKU:

Just trust me.

PIRA:

Fine. Rralla, help me with Apina.

RRALLA:

(RUMBLES HIS AGREEMENT)

DOOKU: (HOLO-NARRATION)

With bacta slopping around their knees, the bedraggled Wookiee guided his friend into position.

PIRA:

That's it. You're doing great.

DOOKU:
(STILL CALLING DOWN) All right. Apina, was it? Don't be scared. I'm going to pull you up, okay?

PIRA:
Pull her up. How?

DOOKU:
I'm going to use the Force.

PIRA:
You're going to *what*?

DOOKU:
Just relax. That's it, Apina. One. Two. *Three!*

DOOKU: (HOLO-NARRATION)
The child let out a frightened squeak as she shot up like a homing missile.

On three, he pulls her out of the bacta.

RRALLA:
(SHYRIIWOOK)

DOOKU:
I've got you. I've got you.

PIRA:
I don't believe it.

DOOKU:
Now the next one.

DOOKU: (HOLO-NARRATION)
Pira glanced worriedly at a Fluggrian slouched in a diagnostic hovercot.

PIRA:
He can't walk.

DOOKU:
Then we'll take the bed with us.

DOOKU: (HOLO-NARRATION)
The doctor helped drag the cot beneath me.

PIRA:
Will you be able to take the weight?

SIFO-DYAS:
I can help. What's his name?

RRALLA:
(SHYRIIWOOK)

SIFO-DYAS:
Sorry, my Shyriiwook's a little rusty.

PIRA:
Cuhoon.

SIFO-DYAS:
Okay, Cuhoon, you're gonna need to hold on as tightly as you can.
Are you ready? Yeah?

DOOKU:
Here we go. One. Two. (WITH EFFORT) *Three!*

DOOKU: (HOLO-NARRATION)
I visualized the boy floating toward me, and the cot wobbled before rising unsteadily . . .

PIRA:
Careful.

RRALLA:
(SHYRIIWOOK)

SIFO-DYAS:
I've got it.

PIRA:
Let me help.

DOOKU: (HOLO-NARRATION)
Pira clambered onto the table to support the heavy bed. She may have not been able to use the Force, but as the stars were her witness, she wasn't about let her patient fall.

She climbs onto the table.

DOOKU:
(EFFORT) That's it. Just a little higher.

PIRA:
Have you got him?

The cot is pulled through.

DOOKU:
Yes. Yes, I have. Good to meet you, Cuhoon.

SIFO-DYAS:
Who's left?

PIRA:
Only Rralla.

DOOKU:
Are you ready?

DOOKU: (HOLO-NARRATION)
The Wookiee loped forward, eagerly holding his thin arms up toward me.

RRALLA:
(SHYRIIWOOK) [Yes.]

DOOKU:
Good. On three. One. Two. *Three!*

RRALLA:
(SHYRIIWOOK—COUNTING WITH HIM) [One. Two. *Three!*]

DOOKU: (HOLO-NARRATION)
I almost laughed at the Wookiee's delight as he was yanked into the air, bacta dripping from his fur. I grabbed his arms, swinging him to safety.

DOOKU:
Can you look after the others, Rralla? That's it. (CALLING BACK DOWN) Time for you, Doctor.

The door creaks.

SIFO-DYAS:
Take her now, Dooku!

DOOKU: (HOLO-NARRATION)
The door buckled, liters of thick bacta flooding into the ward.

The door gives way, bacta rushing in.

PIRA:
(SCREAMS)

SCENE 49. INT. DELIVERY SUITE. (CONT.)

DOOKU: (HOLO-NARRATION)
I pulled Pira toward me before the deluge could take her.

RRALLA:
(SHYRIIWOOK) [Dr. Pira!]

DOOKU:
It's all right. I have her. That's it. Up you come.

PIRA:
What about your friend?

DOOKU:
I don't know. (CALLING DOWN) Sifo-Dyas!

DOOKU: (HOLO-NARRATION)
There was no reply. My friend was nowhere to be seen.

DOOKU:
Stay here.

PIRA:
Why? What are you . . .

DOOKU: (HOLO-NARRATION)
Holding my breath, I plunged into the churning bacta.

RRALLA:
(SHYRIIWOOK)

PIRA:
I don't know. I can't see him. The bacta's too thick.

The bacta slops around below them, time ticking by far too slowly.

PIRA:
Come on. Come on.

Dooku breaks the surface, carrying Sifo-Dyas.

DOOKU:
(SPLUTTERING) I've got him!

RRALLA:
(SHYRIIWOOK)

PIRA:
Thank the stars.

DOOKU:
Help me get him up.

PIRA:
What happened to him?

DOOKU:
He hit his head. (WITH EFFORT AS HE LIFTS HIM UP) Only
Sifo-Dyas could hurt himself in a sea of bacta. Have you got him?

PIRA:
Yes.

SIFO-DYAS:
(GROANS)

DOOKU:
Careful.

PIRA:
That wound doesn't look good.

DOOKU: (HOLO-NARRATION)
I leapt up to rejoin them, running a hand through my damp hair.

DOOKU:
Just another crisis to add to the list.

The building creaks, dust falling down.

PIRA:
What was that?

DOOKU:
The building isn't safe. We need to get out as soon as possible.

PIRA:
There's a repulsorlift in the next section.

DOOKU:
I doubt it'll be working. We'll have to do it the old-fashioned way.

PIRA:
What do you mean?

DOOKU:
I was hoping you wouldn't ask that. Out a window?

PIRA:
You're joking.

More creaking.

RRALLA:
(WHIMPERS)

DOOKU:

The floor's giving way.

PIRA:

Actually, a window will be fine. I'll carry Apina. Rralla, can you push Cuhoon?

RRALLA:

(SHYRIIWOOK) [Yes.]

PIRA:

You take your friend.

DOOKU:

Yes, ma'am.

Another creak, but this time accompanied by a monstrous roar.

DOOKU: (HOLO-NARRATION)
I froze, staring into the gloom ahead.

PIRA:

What was that?

DOOKU:

It appears we're not alone.

Another roar, which makes Rralla whimper in fear.

PIRA:

It's right outside. What are we going to do?

DOOKU: (HOLO-NARRATION)
There was really only one choice; the floor was finally collapsing under its own weight.

DOOKU:

Run!

Rralla whines as they run, the floor collapsing.

SCENE 50. EXT. THE PLANTATION.

Flames crackle all around.

DOOKU: (HOLO-NARRATION)
Outside, a crowd of survivors had gathered around Yoda and Lene . . .

PRIME MINISTER:
The heat. It's unbearable.

LENE:
Master Yoda. Dooku and Sifo-Dyas? Can you still sense them?

YODA:
No. Only the blaze.

PRIME MINISTER:
You must hold it back.

LENE:
(WITH EFFORT) A task, Prime Minister, that will be a lot easier if you'd stop talking!

PRIME MINISTER:
I'm sorry. I only thought—

There's a rumble from behind as the hospital collapses in on itself.

DOOKU: (HOLO-NARRATION)
With a final groan, the hospital's structure collapsed, the sudden rush of air fanning the flames.

PRIME MINISTER:
Oh no.

LENE:
Do you think they got out?

A monster roars.

PRIME MINISTER:
What's that?

A giant beast is charging toward them.

LENE:
Something very big!

PRIME MINISTER:
It's a monster!

YODA:
No. On its back.

LENE:
Dooku!

DOOKU: (HOLO-NARRATION)
My mount skid to a halt within the protective circle, snorting superheated air from four expansive nostrils.

DOOKU:
(CALLING DOWN) Masters! Meet Rolettan. He was giving birth when the pulse hit.

LENE:
Where's the baby?

DOOKU:
(CALLING) Bringing our friends.

DOOKU: (HOLO-NARRATION)
A smaller and yet equally commanding creature carried the doctor and her young charges into the enclosure. You should have seen them, Jenza. Thick scarlet scales, clubbed tails, and six legs apiece.

PIRA:
(CALLING) Look at the flames.

RRALLA:
(WHIMPERS)

DOOKU:

(CALLING) Get the younglings down to the ground.

PIRA:

(CALLING) How's your friend?

DOOKU:

(CALLING) Still unconscious.

DOOKU: (HOLO-NARRATION)

Rolettan bayed as I dropped from his back, Sifo-Dyas cradled in my arms.

LENE:

What happened?

DOOKU:

He got knocked out, that's all. He'll be all right.

LENE:

Half an hour in a hospital and he thinks he's a doctor.

DOOKU:

A hospital that nearly killed us.

YODA:

Grateful I am that it did not. Help us, my Padawan.

DOOKU:

(WITH EFFORT) How long will we be able to hold them back?

LENE:

As long as we need to.

DOOKU:

And how long is that?

There's the thunder of a spaceship overhead.

PRIME MINISTER:

(JOYFUL) I don't believe it. The distress call. It must have gotten through.

Pira runs up.

PIRA:
Is that a Republic ship?

AMPLIFIED VOICE:
Please remain calm. We are deploying flame suppressant. We will begin evacuation procedures once the fire is under control.

DOOKU:
That could be some time.

Water starts gushing from the ship.

RRALLA:
(SHYRIIWOOK)

PIRA:
Don't worry, Rralla. It's putting out the fire. See?

YODA:
(RELAXING) The Force has protected us.

DOOKU:
I'm just sorry we weren't able to get more people out.

LENE:
You did your best.

YODA:
All any of us can ask, that is.

DOOKU: (HOLO-NARRATION)
A hatch opened in the belly of the ship, and an aid worker in protective clothing jetpacked down to us.

AID COMMANDER:
Master Yoda.

YODA:
For your timely arrival we thank you, Commander.

The aid commander lands.

AID COMMANDER:
More ships are on the way.

LENE:
Best news I've heard all day.

AID COMMANDER:
Prime Minister, are you hurt?

PRIME MINISTER:
No. The Jedi kept me safe. Unfortunately, I fear the same cannot be said for much of the population.

AID COMMANDER:
Senator Tavetti wishes to know how much bacta you will be able to salvage.

PRIME MINISTER:
T-there is no way of knowing. Not yet. The loss of life must be—

AID COMMANDER:
He will need a full report as soon as possible.

His comm beeps.

AID COMMANDER:
Excuse me.

PRIME MINISTER:
Yes. Yes, of course.

AID COMMANDER:
(IN BACKGROUND, QUIET, BENEATH EVERYONE ELSE)
Yes. I have located the prime minister. There are a handful of survivors here. When will the rest of the fleet arrive? (BEAT) Very well. Are the Jedi sending any support? (BEAT) Then we will have to make do until we hear. I will ask the Grand Master. Focus on the main fires and protect any surviving bacta.

PIRA:
Is that all they care about?

PRIME MINISTER:
(TRYING TO MAKE SENSE OF IT) I . . . er . . . I can understand his concern.

PIRA:
But what about the people? What about survivors?

YODA:
Do all we can, we will. This I promise.

SIFO-DYAS:
(GROANS)

Dooku moves to him.

DOOKU:
Sifo.

SIFO-DYAS:
What hit me?

Rolettan roars nearby.

SIFO-DYAS:
And what is *that*?

DOOKU:
A friend.

SIFO-DYAS:
The children . . . did we . . . ?

LENE:
You saved them.

Rolettan roars again, indignant.

LENE:
(HURRIEDLY) With a little help.

DOOKU:
It's not enough.

LENE:

Dooku?

Dooku stands.

DOOKU:

If we had acted sooner . . . when Sifo-Dyas first had his vision . . .

LENE:

What's done is done. We must now concentrate on making sure Protobranch receives as much aid as possible.

DOOKU:

(BITTERLY) Because of the bacta?

LENE:

No. Because of the people.

DOOKU: (HOLO-NARRATION)

I moved in closer to Lene, lowering my voice . . .

DOOKU:

(SOTTO) And what about next time? What happens when Sifo-Dyas receives another premonition?

LENE:

Then maybe the Council will listen. Maybe they'll act.

DOOKU:

Do you honestly believe that?

LENE:

(AVOIDING THE QUESTION) Your compassion does you credit, Dooku. Focus on that.

SCENE 51. EXT. ROOFTOP. NIGHT. RAIN.

VENTRESS: (NARRATION)

I pause the hologram, scanning the street for any sign of the Cro-lute.

VENTRESS:

Dooku had compassion. Who would have thought?

KY NAREC: (GHOST)

If he did, it was lost the day he turned to the dark side.

VENTRESS:

Are you sure? The way he talked about his sister. Maybe the heart of that young Padawan is still there . . .

KY NAREC: (GHOST)

Underneath the surface.

VENTRESS:

It's possible. Isn't it?

KY NAREC: (GHOST)

Anything is possible, little one.

VENTRESS:

I've told you not to call me that. I'm not your little one. I'm not your anything. You're not even real.

KY NAREC: (GHOST)

Are you sure about that?

VENTRESS:

Please. Next you'll be telling me you can see the future like poor deranged Sifo-Dyas.

KY NAREC: (GHOST)

What if I can?

VENTRESS:

Go on then. Tell me. What will I become?

KY NAREC: (GHOST)

You will become lost.

VENTRESS:

(LAUGHS) That happened a long time ago.

KY NAREC: (GHOST)
When you were taken by Hal'Sted?

VENTRESS:
Leave him out of this.

KY NAREC: (GHOST)
Why? He stole you from Dathomir. You were just a child.

VENTRESS:
He protected me. Gave me a home.

KY NAREC: (GHOST)
A home on Rattatak? He made you his slave, Ventress . . . he used you. You never told me, did you? Not really. Never explained what he forced you to do.

VENTRESS:
He never forced me to do anything.

KY NAREC: (GHOST)
No? Never used you as a living torture device? I told you. I see things now. Like the day he dragged you in front of a Weequay who refused to pay his dues . . .

VENTRESS:
Don't.

KY NAREC: (GHOST)
Why? Is it painful to remember? The crack of the Weequay's skull as you applied the pressure? Or the blaster shot as Hal'Sted put him out of his misery?

VENTRESS:
I did what I needed to survive. Hal'Sted . . . Hal'Sted looked after me. He treated me like a daughter.

KY NAREC: (GHOST)
He made you a weapon.

VENTRESS:
No. That was you.

KY NAREC: (GHOST)
I rescued you. When I saw what you could do . . .

VENTRESS:
How I could aid your crusade, you mean.

KY NAREC: (GHOST)
The Force led me to you.

VENTRESS:
Shame it didn't help you stick around. But nothing lasts forever. Not Hal'Sted. Not you.

KY NAREC: (GHOST)
And neither will Dooku.

VENTRESS:
You don't know that.

KY NAREC: (GHOST)
Don't I?

VENTRESS: (NARRATION)
I can't listen to this. Ky . . . Ky is dead. This thing in my head is a delusion. Nothing more. I reactivate the final data disk, another hologram shimmering into life. I concentrate on Dooku, older again, although his Padawan's braid still rests on his shoulder. But something is wrong. His expression is guarded, his stance awkward and stiff. Even in the holoform I can see the shadows beneath his eyes. Something has happened.

DOOKU: (TWENTY YEARS OLD, HOLOGRAM)
Sister. I do not know if you will play this message, but I want to explain. I *need* to explain. I meant you no harm, you have to believe that. I only wanted to help. To support you. If I had only known what would happen the day I received your message . . .

PART FOUR

SCENE 52. EXT. JEDI TEMPLE. MEDITATION BALCONY.

LENE:

That's it, Dooku. Concentrate on the convor.

High above, the convor hoots as she flies through the air.

DOOKU: (TWENTY YEARS OLD)

She keeps flying out of reach, Master Kostana.

LENE:

Because I have trained her well. Just as I am training you.

DOOKU:

Shouldn't Master Yoda . . .

LENE:

Master Yoda is busy with the Council and has asked me to take you through the basics of animal kinship, if you'd ever stop talking.

DOOKU:

I'm sorry.

LENE:

Good. Now concentrate. Others call this beast control. They are mistaken. Jedi never control. We influence. We persuade. Reach out to Ferana. Feel the Force flowing through her, feel it flowing through you. Yes. That's it. One mind. Two bodies. What do you feel?

DOOKU:

Her wings ache when she flies.

LENE:

Poor old thing.

DOOKU:

She trusts you. Knows you will never do her any harm. But isn't so sure about Sifo-Dyas.

LENE:

I believe the feeling's mutual. Okay. Touch her mind. Know what it's like to fly above the Temple. Share the experience with her.

DOOKU:

It's . . . thrilling. The air beneath her . . . beneath *my* wings. Soaring down. Twisting around. Turning. So many colors.

LENE:

Ask her to fly from one spire to the other. From the Tower of First Knowledge . . .

We hear her flying high above.

DOOKU:

To the Reassignment Spire.

LENE:

That's good. Now, send her to the Tower of Reconciliation, but . . . quick, change her mind. Persuade her to fly to the Tranquility Spire. That's it. You're doing it, Dooku. You're doing it.

There's a beep from Dooku's holoreceiver, hidden in a pouch on his belt.

LENE:
Concentrate.

The beeping continues.

LENE:
What is that?

High above them, Ferana squawks and flies away.

DOOKU:
I lost her.

LENE:
Because you were distracted.

Dooku fumbles with his belt.

DOOKU:
I'm sorry. I'll switch it off.

LENE:
Is that a holocomm?

DOOKU:
Yes. But—

LENE:
It's not standard issue.

DOOKU:
I know, but I can explain.

LENE:
Give it to me.

DOOKU:
(SIGHS) It's not what it looks like.

LENE:
Let's see, shall we?

She activates the holocomm. A hologram of an eighteen-year-old Jenza appears. She is upset. Crying.

JENZA:

(SOBBING) Brother.

LENE:

Brother?

JENZA:

Mother . . . Mother has passed. She is to be buried in the family mausoleum on Mantero. Will you come to the funeral? Father is . . . well, he's worse than ever and Ramil doesn't care one way or another. I know I shouldn't ask, but I need you here. I need someone who understands. Please come. Please come home.

The recording ends.

LENE:

Home.

DOOKU:

Serenno. That is Jenza. My sister.

LENE:

So I gathered. How long have you two communicated?

DOOKU:

Ever since Carannia.

LENE:

(DISBELIEVING) The Celebration . . . but that was years ago. And you've never told anyone.

DOOKU:

No. I mean, I told . . . (REALIZING WHO HE'S TALKING TO) No one. I told no one.

LENE:

You told Sifo-Dyas. Of course, you did. (SIGHING) Yoda is going to be . . .

DOOKU:

Livid?

LENE:

Disappointed. Which, trust me, is worse. What were you thinking?

DOOKU:

She sent me the receiver. What was I supposed to do?

LENE:

Not keep secrets.

DOOKU:

Oh. Because you *always* tell the truth.

LENE:

Dooku! You're the Grand Master's Padawan.

DOOKU:

What difference does that make?

LENE:

(SIGHS) It doesn't.

DOOKU:

Jenza and I have a connection, Lene. We've had it from the moment we met. And that's what I don't understand—the Jedi are supposed to protect the galaxy and yet we remove ourselves from it. Cut ourselves off.

LENE:

So our judgment isn't clouded.

DOOKU:

But what if that's wrong? My sister's in pain and I can help her. I . . . I owe it to her. She's listened to me all these years. Whenever I've been angry. Whenever I've struggled. She's always been there, my guiding light.

LENE:

The Force should be your guide.

DOOKU:

And the Force is in all things. Who's to say that it hasn't been working through her all these years? Who's to say it can't work through me, now. She needs me.

LENE:

It's not me you need to persuade.

DOOKU:

Will you talk to him? On my behalf?

LENE:

To Yoda? No. (BEAT) But I'll stand beside you, when you address the Council.

SCENE 53. INT. JEDI COUNCIL CHAMBER.

DOOKU: (HOLO-NARRATION)

The last time I stood before the Council, all eyes had been on Sifo-Dyas, but now they were firmly set on me. There was nowhere to hide. The Masters listened to my confession, their condemnation palpable. I told them everything, about you, our messages beamed back and forth across the stars, and what you had asked of me. And then I waited, the silence damning. When he finally spoke, the sorrow in Yoda's voice was like a lightsaber in my chest . . .

YODA:

What have I always tried to teach you, my Padawan?

DOOKU:

That a Jedi must be strong—

YODA:

No. The Force is strong. A Jedi listens. A Jedi understands. A Jedi respects.

DOOKU:

I do respect you.

YODA:

Not I. Respect the *Force*. Respect its teachings. How many times must the same things I repeat. *Away* from the past a Jedi must turn. Only in the present you should dwell.

BRAYLON:

Familial attachments are strictly prohibited. You know that, Dooku.

DOOKU:

I do, Master Braylon. I just thought—

YODA:

Thought? Tell you what you thought, I will. Thought you were different, hmmm? That the rules you could break.

LENE:

I don't think it's so much break, as bend them a little.

YODA:

Your influence, this is, Master Kostana. Not mine.

DOOKU:

Masters, please. I was wrong to hide the holocomm from you, I know that. I was wrong to keep my relationship with Jenza a secret. But none of this is my sister's fault. Punish me, yes, but please, don't punish her.

SINUBE:

What would you have us do, Padawan?

DOOKU:

Let me go to her, Master Sinube.

YODA:

Hmh!

DOOKU:

Let me stand by her side as she buries our . . . as she buries her mother. And then I swear, I will break all contact.

YODA:

True to your vows you will be?

DOOKU:

I promise.

YODA:

Hmm. A fine speaker, you are. A great politician you would make.

DOOKU:

Then you will let me go?

YODA:

Leave the Temple I cannot.

DOOKU:

But—

BRAYLON:

Master Yoda is negotiating a treaty between the Forta and the Lerall.

YODA:

At a delicate stage, the talks are.

LENE:

What if I take him?

YODA:

You?

LENE:

I have business in the Gordian Reach. Serenno isn't that far out of my way.

YODA:

Business? What business?

LENE:

There have been worrying reports along the Hydian Way, a rise in lawlessness and disorder.

BRAYLON:

That's true. Reports that the Senate has chosen to ignore.

YODA:

Investigating these reports, you are?

LENE:

That was my plan. And Dooku is a native of the region. He may be able to sense something that others have not.

SINUBE:

And if the Senate asks?

LENE:

He is visiting his home for a state funeral.

BRAYLON:

It *is* the perfect cover.

YODA:

Happy about this I am not, Master Braylon . . . but my permission I give.

DOOKU:

Thank you, Master.

YODA:

Do not thank me yet, my apprentice. Fickle the past can be. The pain of tomorrow, the comfort of yesterday is. Only in the present should we trust. Only in today . . .

SCENE 54. INT. THE *TRUTHSEEKER*.

Atmosphere: The interior of a spaceship.

DOOKU: (HOLO-NARRATION)

I had often wondered what it would be like to take to the stars in Master Kostana's shuttle, the *Truthseeker*, to soar away from Coruscant time and time again. And now I knew, and the reality of the situation weighed heavy on my heart as we sped toward Serenno . . .

SIFO-DYAS: (TWENTY YEARS OLD)
Doo?

DOOKU:
Please don't call me that.

SIFO-DYAS:
You never used to mind.

DOOKU:
Yes. Yes, I did.

SIFO-DYAS:
I'm sorry.

DOOKU:
No. I am. I just keep thinking about what Yoda said.

SIFO-DYAS:
About your sister?

DOOKU:
For as long as I can remember, I've felt . . . I've felt like I don't belong.

SIFO-DYAS:
Dooku, that's ridiculous.

DOOKU:
Is it?

SIFO-DYAS:
You're the most accomplished Padawan in a generation. Everyone says so. *You* say so, most of the time.

DOOKU:
I know I am . . . difficult to be around at times.

SIFO-DYAS:
(WARMLY) Only at times? That's one way to put it.

DOOKU:
You're teasing me.

SIFO-DYAS:
Yes, because sometimes we all need a little teasing. As long as I've known you, you've strived to be the best. No, actually it's more than that. You've known you *are* the best. Remember when Yoda chose you as his Padawan?

DOOKU:
It's hard to forget.

SIFO-DYAS:
The others were surprised. But not me. It made complete sense. *Of course* Yoda would want to shape you.

DOOKU:
But what if I don't want to be shaped?

SIFO-DYAS:
You don't?

DOOKU:
Everyone is so sure of my future. Yoda. The Council. I'll become a Jedi Knight and one day take a Padawan of my own.

SIFO-DYAS:
(SMILING) May the Force be with them.

DOOKU:
It's not funny! Become a Master. Join the Council. And then what?

SIFO-DYAS:
Rule the galaxy?

DOOKU:
I could do a better job than the Senate.

SIFO-DYAS:
You'd do a better job than anyone. But this isn't about your future.

DOOKU:

Then what is it?

SIFO-DYAS:

Your secret. Everyone knows now. Jenza. The holocomm. You can't control it anymore. Can't decide when or where you talk to her. You've even agreed to give her up. And why? Because whatever you say, however resentful you feel at this moment, you are a Jedi, Dooku. Through and through. More Jedi than I'll ever be. This is where you belong. This is where you make a difference. I don't think your future is mapped out at all. You're going to change everything.

DOOKU:

For the better?

SIFO-DYAS:

This is you we're talking about.

DOOKU:

(QUIETLY) Thanks, Si.

SIFO-DYAS:

(TEASING) Please don't call me that.

DOOKU:

(SMILING) You never used to mind.

There's the creak of a deck plate.

LENE:

Knock knock.

The Padawans stand.

DOOKU:

Master Kostana.

LENE:

We're approaching Serenno. Should we land at Carannia?

DOOKU:
No. Take us straight to Mantero.

LENE:
The Funeral Moon, coming up.

They follow her through to the cockpit.

SIFO-DYAS:
Funeral Moon?

LENE:
Serennians bury their dead on the smallest of their moons.

DOOKU:
So our ancestors can gaze upon us forever.

SIFO-DYAS:
That's amazing. I mean, it's ghoulish, but that's what makes it so great. I like your planet.

DOOKU:
And guess who has the largest plot of all?

SIFO-DYAS:
House Serenno?

DOOKU:
Who else?

SCENE 55. EXT. THE MANTERO ATMOSPHERE.

A cut scene of the Truthseeker *zooming past.*

SCENE 56. EXT. MANTERO CEMETERY SPACEPORT.

Atmosphere: A busy spaceport, full of the usual bustle.

A landing ramp lowers and Count Gora clomps down, followed by D-4.

GORA:

Tell those two to hurry up will you, Dee-Four?

D-4:

At once, Count Gora.

Ramil and Jenza come down the ramp.

RAMIL:

No need. We're here.

GORA:

About time. The sooner we get this done, the better.

JENZA:

The sooner we get this done? You're talking about Mother's funeral!

GORA:

Damn circus.

JENZA:

How can you say that?

D-4:

Please don't make a scene, Lady Jenza. The cam droids are watching.

GORA:

What did I tell you?

RAMIL:

Let's just play the grieving family and get back home. I've a race tonight.

JENZA:

I'm not playing, Ramil.

GORA:

Good for you.

He strides off.

GORA: (CONT.)

Dee-Four, inform the newsnet to focus on my daughter. She's the best bet, if it's tears they're after.

JENZA:

Monster.

RAMIL:

Now, now. You know what he's like.

JENZA:

And you're just as bad. Racing, today of all days.

RAMIL:

It's what Mother would have wanted.

TRADER:

Memory Stone, sir? To remember your loved one?

RAMIL:

(HAUGHTILY) No, thank you. We don't need any of your funeral tat. (THEY CARRY ON) Damn grief-mongers.

JENZA:

He's just trying to make a living, Ramil.

RAMIL:

Vultures, the lot of them. (LOOKS AT HIS SISTER) Jenza? Jenza, now what are you looking for?

JENZA:

Nothing. I'm just seeing which of the houses have sent representatives.

RAMIL:

Every single one, if they know what's good for them. Great and small. You know Father. He'll be taking notes.

SCENE 57. EXT. SERENNO MAUSOLEUM.

A sharp wind is blowing through the sprawling cemetery. Alien crows caw in the trees, but only one person is crying—Jenza.

CELEBRANT:
And now we commit Countess Anya to her ancestors. She will rest here, in their company, in the Serenno vault. But before we light the final flame, her daughter, Lady Jenza, would like to say a few words.

GORA:
What? Dee-Four—what's going on? This wasn't part of the ceremony.

D-4:
No, it certainly was not. I worked long and hard on the order of the service.

GORA:
What in the seven gods is she thinking?

JENZA: (AMPLIFIED)
On behalf of my father, I would like to thank so many of you for coming here today.

GORA:
On behalf of her father? Of all the nerve.

JENZA: (AMPLIFIED)
My mother would be proud to see so many of the houses represented today. You honor her, and us, with your presence.

GORA:
Like they had any choice.

JENZA: (AMPLIFIED)
Mother always liked Mantero. Not only because she could walk with our ancestors, but because she could look up and see Serenno in the sky. That planet was her life. She worked tirelessly, caring for those less fortunate than us.

RAMIL:
Most of the planet then.

JENZA: (AMPLIFIED)
Caring for the outsider. The . . . (SHE PAUSES, HAVING SPOT-
TED SOMEONE)

GORA:
Now what's wrong with the girl? What's she looking at?

RAMIL:
Over there. By the Demeci Memorial. It can't be . . .

GORA:
It is! I don't believe it. How dare he come here.

D-4:
Count, please. People are looking.

JENZA: (AMPLIFIED)
(SMILING, EMOTIONAL) I'm sorry. As I was saying, my mother
was a compassionate woman. She cared passionately for the outsider and for the lost.

PROTESTOR #1:
(SHOUTING) Don't make me laugh!

GORA:
Now what?

JENZA: (AMPLIFIED)
I'm . . . sorry?

PROTESTOR #1:
It's all right for you, Lady Jenza, standing there in your furs. But
what about the rest of us? If your mother cared so much, why
didn't she stop the Assembly taking our jobs?

PROTESTOR #2:
Yeah, where was she then?

GORA:
Damn protestors. This is an outrage. (CALLING TO THE COUNT
OF MANTERO) Hakka. Hakka, do something.

JENZA: (AMPLIFIED)

I . . . This is my mother's funeral.

PROTESTOR #1:

Might as well bury the entire planet.

PROTESTOR #2:

You've said enough. It's time for us to be heard. (CHANTING) Hear our voice. Hear our voice.

The chant is picked up by protestors in the crowd.

CROWD:

Hear our voice. Hear our voice. (REPEAT)

GORA:

They're everywhere. They planned this.

JENZA: (AMPLIFIED)

Please. This is not the time. We can talk about this.

GORA:

Like hell we can. Get her off the comm.

D-4:

Lady Jenza. Please. Take your seat.

Gora grabs the comm. There's a burst of feedback.

GORA: (AMPLIFIED)

Now listen. This is a disgrace. You dishonor my wife. You dishonor my family.

PROTESTOR #1:

You dishonored us when you brought in all those droids.

D-4:

Oh dear.

PROTESTOR #1:

We won't stand for it anymore. Do you hear? It is time for a reckoning. Hear our voice! Hear our voice!

The protestors start throwing moonrocks at the count. One strikes him in the head.

GORA:

(CRIES OUT IN PAIN) Maniacs!

D-4:

Count, are you all right?

GORA:

What do you think? They're throwing rocks! Where's Hakka's security?

D-4:

I doubt it was deemed necessary, Your Grace.

GORA:

Not necessary? Luckily, I plan ahead. (OPENS COMLINK) This is Gora. Send them in. Send them in now.

SCENE 58. EXT. SERENNO MAUSOLEUM. JEDI POV.

DOOKU: (HOLO-NARRATION)

My hand went to my lightsaber as the mob surged forward . . .

The chanting continues.

DOOKU:

We need to do something.

LENE:

No, Dooku. It's not our place.

DOOKU:

That's exactly what it is. That's my family out there. They're in danger.

LENE:

And what do you intend to do about it?

DOOKU:
We're peacekeepers, aren't we? We keep the peace.

We hear the rumble of hovertanks.

DOOKU: (HOLO-NARRATION)
The argument became moot as the hovertanks approached, their doors swinging open . . .

Doors open and squadrons of security droids march out in perfect step.

SIFO-DYAS:
I don't believe it. Are those . . . ?

DOOKU:
Security droids!

SIFO-DYAS:
At a funeral?

DOOKU:
This can't happen.

SCENE 59. EXT. SERENNO MAUSOLEUM. JENZA'S POV.

More tramping of robotic feet.

JENZA:
Father? What is this?

GORA:
Protection. (TO THE DROIDS) Surround the protestors.

SECURITY DROIDS:
Order confirmed.

Droids clank.

RAMIL:
Father, we need to get out of here.

GORA:
The HoloNet wanted a show. Well, we'll damn well give them one.
A show of strength.

COMMAND SECURITY DROID:
Protestors, desist.

PROTESTOR #1:
Like hell we will!

A rock is thrown and bounces off the command security droid.

COMMAND SECURITY DROID:
This unit has been struck. Protect the family. Open fire.

SECURITY DROIDS: (IN UNISON)
Confirmed.

The droids' blasters click, ready to fire.

Dooku runs up, putting himself in front of the droids' guns.

DOOKU:
No! Wait!

JENZA:
Dooku?

DOOKU: (HOLO-NARRATION)
It was hardly the reunion I had hoped for, you all standing open-
mouthed as I positioned myself between the droids and the protestors.

GORA:
What is the meaning of this?

DOOKU:
I could ask the same question, *Father.*

DOOKU: (HOLO-NARRATION)

One word, that's all it took. One powerful word. I felt the ripple going around the crowd, the surprise and speculation, the other houses wondering if they'd heard correctly . . .

Sifo-Dyas and Lene run up.

LENE:

Dooku. Stop this.

DOOKU:

No, Master. I need to understand what's happening here.

PROTESTOR #1:

What's happening? Those damn droids, that's what's happening. When they're not pointing blasters at us, they're working the mines, transporting the ore, serving his kind.

GORA:

They're serving Serenno!

LENE:

Your Grace. May I suggest that your guards stand down.

GORA:

No. You may not.

PROTESTOR #2:

They're not even the guard. He disbanded the guard and brought in machines. More lives ruined so he can line his pockets!

PROTESTOR #1:

People are starving. His people. Not that he cares.

DOOKU:

Father, is this true?

GORA:

I'm not your father.

Dooku ignites his lightsaber, speaking over the noise.

DOOKU:
Is it true?

GORA:
Is that what you're going to do, freak? You're going to cut me down where I stand? Droids. Shoot him.

DOOKU: (HOLO-NARRATION)
It all happened so fast. The droids' blasters coming up. The screams from the crowd. I didn't even see you run forward until it was too late, until you had thrown yourself in front of me. When I reacted, calling on the Force, it was to protect you, Jenza. Not me.

I wanted to push the droids back, but I was so . . . so angry. I didn't even realize what I had done, not at first, not even as you and Father and Ramil were thrown back . . . not even as the crowd scattered, mob and mourners running for their lives. Running from me.

Then Father came at me, lips drawn back into a snarl. I acted on instinct, ready to strike, my lightsaber drawn . . .

JENZA:
Dooku, no!

DOOKU: (HOLO-NARRATION)
You stopped me, Jenza. Your cry stopped me. But it didn't stop him.

GORA:
I'll kill you.

Gora slams into Dooku, knocking him to the ground, striking him over and over.

DOOKU: (HOLO-NARRATION)
I could have fought back even as he pummeled me into the ground. Could have snapped his neck. But I knew that was wrong, even as Ramil pulled him away.

LENE:
Dooku, are you—

DOOKU:
Leave me alone.

LENE:
We need to go.

DOOKU: (HOLO-NARRATION)
I knew pushing Lene back was wrong, but all I cared about was you . . .

DOOKU:
Jenza. I . . .

JENZA:
No. Dooku. Please. Stay away.

DOOKU:
But I—

JENZA:
I mean it!

DOOKU: (HOLO-NARRATION)
And that's when I saw it, Jenza, the coffin lying on its side, the lid open, our mother's body . . .

It was an accident, Jenza. You have to believe me. I tried to put it right.

DOOKU:
Jenza, I'm sorry. Here, we can . . .

JENZA:
(SHOUTING) Leave her alone!

DOOKU:
Jenza.

JENZA:

Your friend is right. You need to go.

DOOKU:

But . . .

JENZA:

Just go, Dooku!

SCENE 60. INT. THE *TRUTHSEEKER*.

DOOKU: (HOLO-NARRATION)

I expected Father to be angry. To sense his rancor and fear, but I never expected it from you. It haunted me even as the *Truthseeker* sped from the sector . . . It haunts me to this day . . .

We hear Dooku practicing his lightsaber moves, shifting from one stance to another, grunting, and breathing hard as he drops into every position.

Lene enters.

LENE:

Need a sparring partner?

DOOKU:

I am practicing.

LENE:

So I can see. Put down the lightsaber.

DOOKU:

No.

LENE:

(FIRM) I said put it down.

The lightsaber clatters to the floor.

DOOKU:

Why did you do that?

LENE:
Because I need to ask you something.

DOOKU:
What?

LENE:
Do you trust me?

DOOKU:
I'm sorry?

LENE:
Do you trust me?

DOOKU:
Yes.

LENE:
Good. Sit with me.

Chairs are pulled up.

LENE:
I've checked the HoloNet and all official channels. There has been no mention of the fracas at your mother's funeral.

DOOKU:
Fracas?

LENE:
It is my opinion that Count Gora is suppressing the scandal. He won't want the Senate to know . . .

DOOKU:
That I'm his son?

LENE:
How bad things have become on Serenno.

DOOKU:
But when we tell the Council—

LENE:

When we tell the Council, you will face a hearing, as will I for allowing you to assault your family.

DOOKU:

It was an accident.

LENE:

I know, but I also know how the Council thinks. I will be shackled to the Temple, Sifo-Dyas reassigned.

DOOKU:

But none of this is your fault.

LENE:

Nor is it yours, Dooku.

DOOKU:

Lene. The way Jenza looked at me . . .

LENE:

She was confused. Scared.

DOOKU:

Master Yoda was right. The past must be left alone.

LENE:

You truly believe that?

DOOKU:

Yes.

LENE:

Then you should cease communication, as you promised the Council, at least until passions have cooled. I propose we keep this to ourselves. Count Gora obviously doesn't want the galaxy to know what happened.

DOOKU:

But I failed. Master Yoda . . .

LENE:
Master Yoda would overreact. And if he doesn't, the rest of the Council certainly will. Do the right thing, Dooku. Make amends.

DOOKU: (HOLO-NARRATION)
I am truly sorry for what has happened between us, Jenza. You will never know how much I have cherished our friendship, how much I have . . . relied on our communication. You have been my rock, my confidante, but now it must end.

Cut straight into:

SCENE 61. EXT. ROOFTOP. RAIN.

DOOKU: (HOLOGRAM, CONT.)
I wish you well, Lady Jenza. You are a strong woman . . . stronger than you give yourself credit. May the Force be with you, now and forever.

The hologram cuts off.

VENTRESS: (NARRATION)
I stare into the space where Dooku's holoform had been, the rain hissing on the still-warm projector.

KY NAREC: (GHOST)
What's wrong? Asajj?

VENTRESS:
Their story isn't over.

KY NAREC: (GHOST)
Well, obviously. He sent you to find her.

VENTRESS:
No. It's more than that.

She reaches into her pocket, pulling out a leather-bound datapad.

KY NAREC: (GHOST)
Dooku's journal.

VENTRESS: (NARRATION)
I shift under the cover of a cooling tower to protect the screen.

She swipes through pages.

KY NAREC: (GHOST)
What are you looking for?

VENTRESS:
(DISTRACTED) The Force will guide me.

More swipes.

VENTRESS:
Here.

KY NAREC: (GHOST)
What is it?

VENTRESS:
The rest of the story. (READING) "Lene is correct. I know she is, but it still hurts. And if we are to keep it from Yoda . . ." This is it, the missing link.

KY NAREC: (GHOST)
Missing link?

VENTRESS:
If I am truly to serve Dooku, I must understand him. I thought I understood you, but I was obviously mistaken . . .

KY NAREC: (GHOST)
Asajj . . .

VENTRESS:
Don't you see? *This* is Dooku. The holo-letters, they were meant for someone else. But this . . . this was for him. His thoughts. His truth. The Force led me to it.

KY NAREC: (GHOST)
I led you to it. Oh, I forgot. I'm not real, am I?

VENTRESS:
(SUDDENLY NOT SO SURE) No. You're not.

KY NAREC: (GHOST)
Then humor me. Tell me what it says. If I'm only a delusion, you'll be talking to yourself. Does that really matter? We all do it, after all.

VENTRESS:
Some more than most, it seems.

She swipes another page.

VENTRESS:
"I had thought that Lene would take me straight back to Coruscant, but she reminded me that we still had work to do, her mission in the Gordian Reach, or so I thought. It turned out . . ."

As she reads, we hear the twenty-year-old Dooku echoing the words, taking up the narration.

DOOKU: (NARRATION)
. . . that we still had work to do, her mission in the Gordian Reach, or so I thought. It turned out Lene had been somewhat economical with the truth. I don't know why I was so surprised . . .

SCENE 62. EXT. THE PLANET ASUSTO. HIGH ATMOSPHERE.

The Truthseeker *soars through the sky.*

SCENE 63. INT. THE *TRUTHSEEKER.* COCKPIT.

DOOKU:
What is this place?

LENE:
Sifo-Dyas?

Sifo pilots the ship as he talks, pressing buttons and pulling levers.

SIFO-DYAS:
Asusto, a heavily forested planetoid in the Tamsis Nebula.

DOOKU:
Sentient life?

SIFO-DYAS:
Not that we know of.

LENE:
Although it's a regular haunt of smugglers and weaponrunners.

DOOKU:
The disorder along the Hydian Way?

LENE:
Possibly, although the Council's concerns run deeper. As we just saw, tempers are running high in the Outer Rim.

SIFO-DYAS:
The Trade Federation has worked hard to attract prospectors . . .

DOOKU:
I've seen the posters. A brave new frontier.

SIFO-DYAS:
But what the posters don't tell you about is the growth in organized crime.

LENE:
Growth that neither the Republic nor the Jedi can handle.

DOOKU:
So you're here to stop it?

SIFO-DYAS:
Yes.

DOOKU:
But that's not all, is it? You're keeping something from me. I can sense it.

LENE:
It isn't the *only* reason we're here. As you know, the Council and I don't always see eye-to-eye.

SIFO-DYAS:
On anything.

LENE:
But the one thing they know all too well is that the galaxy is littered with relics of the Sith Empire.

DOOKU:
I thought you'd never found any.

LENE:
You've seen the Bogan Collection.

SIFO-DYAS:
It's doubled in size since we broke in, Dooku.

LENE:
Something is coming. Something dangerous. The last few years have seen an explosion of artifacts being sold on the black market.

SIFO-DYAS:
Most are fakes.

LENE:
And the rest are worthless. But all it would take is one genuine artifact falling into the wrong hands . . .

DOOKU:
So you're trying to find them first. So they can be studied.

LENE:
Unfortunately the Council isn't that progressive. They're locked away.

SIFO-DYAS:
Where even young troublemakers can't find them.

LENE:
I still think it's a mistake, but one battle at a time, eh?

DOOKU:
And you think there are relics here? On Asusto?

LENE:

We infiltrated a smuggler ring on Karazak. They had no idea what they were dealing with.

SIFO-DYAS:

We've been following their supply routes. Many converge here, on this planet.

LENE:

Can you feel it, Dooku? The dark side?

DOOKU:

Yes. Stronger than ever before.

LENE:

The entire planet is drenched in it.

SIFO-DYAS:

Must be why so much trash is drawn here.

LENE:

Like stink-flies to bantha fodder.

DOOKU:

Do you know what we're looking for?

LENE:

"We"?

DOOKU:

I'm not just along for the ride.

LENE:

Glad to hear it. And no, not yet. But we'll know when it finds us.

SCENE 64. EXT. ASUSTO.

Atmosphere: A full-on horror soundscape. Wind moaning through twisted trees. Weird insects chirping. The sudden cry of alien birds. And above it all, the slow, omnipresent creeping of living moss over everything. Trees. Rocks. The floors. The atmosphere should be claustrophobic, especially as they move farther into the forest.

We focus on this soundscape for a few seconds until the Truth-seeker swoops in and lands, the landing gear deploying and ramp lowering.

The three Jedi descend.

DOOKU:
Are you *sure* there's no sentient life?

SIFO-DYAS:
You feel it, too.

Lene steps off the ramp into the spongy moss.

LENE:
I think it's all this.

The others follow, the substance squelching beneath their boots.

SIFO-DYAS:
Some kind of moss.

DOOKU:
It's . . . moving.

LENE:
I certainly wouldn't stand still for too long.

SIFO-DYAS:
You're not kidding. It's already halfway up the landing rig.

LENE:
Close the ramp.

SIFO-DYAS:
Yes, Master.

He presses a control on his sleeve. The ramp rises and locks shut.

DOOKU:
So where do we start?

LENE:
We close our eyes.

DOOKU:
We do what?

LENE:
Think back to your training, Dooku. Why do we use blast visors?

DOOKU:
To focus on what we feel.

LENE:
Rather than what we see.

DOOKU:
(UNSURE) Okay. Eyes closed, it is.

LENE:
Now reach out with your emotions. But this time, open your mind to everything, not just the light. Remember how you felt on Mantero.

DOOKU:
What?

LENE:
The anger you felt. The betrayal. Remember how your sister looked at you. Remember her fear.

DOOKU:
No. We shouldn't.

SIFO-DYAS:
We're not in the Temple now, Dooku.

LENE:
Like stink-flies, remember? Like calls to like.

DOOKU:
But anger and fear—

SIFO-DYAS:
Will find what we're looking for.

LENE:
You don't have to embrace the dark side, Dooku, but you need to know it's there.

SIFO-DYAS:
I see it, Master. A path through the wood.

LENE:
Then lead the way.

Sifo-Dyas heads farther into the spooky wood, the moss crunching and squelching beneath his feet.

LENE:
Are you coming, Dooku?

DOOKU:
I . . . I do not know.

LENE:
Are you scared?

DOOKU:
(HESITATING) Yes.

LENE:
Good. Then you'll probably come out of this alive.

SCENE 65. EXT. THE ASUSTO FOREST.

The soundscape has become even more claustrophobic and intense. The Jedi continue creeping cautiously through the woods.

DOOKU:
Lene?

LENE:
I'm still here. Keep focused.

Something sweeps past Dooku, a whooshing intangible sound.

DOOKU:
What was that?

LENE:
Your mind is playing tricks on you. It is the dark side, trying to take hold.

GHOSTLY VOICE:
Dooku.

DOOKU:
Did you hear that?

GHOSTLY VOICE: (YODA)
Dooku.

DOOKU:
Master Yoda?

LENE:
No. He's tucked up safely on Coruscant. The voices aren't real.

DOOKU:
You can hear them?

LENE:
Not necessarily the same ones. We all have our demons to face.

GHOSTLY VOICE: (VENTRESS)
Master.

GHOSTLY VOICE: (ELEVEN-YEAR-OLD JENZA)
Brother.

GHOSTLY VOICE: (SIDIOUS)
Apprentice.

DOOKU:

I-I can't do this.

SIFO-DYAS:

You can, Dooku. I know you can.

GHOSTLY VOICE: (OBI-WAN)

Traitor.

GHOSTLY VOICE: (ARATH)

Idiot.

GHOSTLY VOICE: (MOTHER TALZIN)

Count.

SIFO-DYAS:

(URGENT) Wait.

DOOKU:

What is it?

SIFO-DYAS:

We're not alone.

DOOKU:

But Lene said they weren't real.

SIFO-DYAS:

Not the voices. Can't you feel it? A presence.

DOOKU:

Yes. They don't belong here.

LENE:

None of us do.

SCENE 66. EXT. THE ASUSTO FOREST. NEARBY CLEARING.

Two Abyssin gunrunners—Lyo and Creethe—are unloading crates from a shuttle, while a third cyclops messes around with a comm unit, the device cycling through different frequencies with bursts of static and white noise.

DOOKU: (NARRATION)
We crept on, finding a freighter cooling its engines in a clearing. White-whiskered aliens were unloading crates from the back of the craft, each with a single eye set deep in a cadaverous face.

The three Jedi whisper.

LENE:
Abyssin.

DOOKU:
Your smugglers?

DOOKU: (NARRATION)
There was no way for Lene to know, although it was obvious that the thugs were waiting for a buyer. As we watched, one of the Abyssin activated a wrist-com, informing their contact that the samples had been unloaded. It turned out they weren't smuggling dark side artifacts, but weapons almost as deadly . . .

SIFO-DYAS:
Nerve disruptors?

LENE:
Illegal in every civilized system.

DOOKU: (NARRATION)
Lene swore. If artifact hunters were plundering Asusto, the last thing she needed was for the Abyssin to get in the way. She needed to act, and I was only too happy to oblige.

DOOKU:
I'll deal with them.

SIFO-DYAS:
No. Dooku. Wait.

DOOKU: (NARRATION)
I burst through the foliage, my lightsaber flashing. The Abyssin drew their pulse-blasters, but I was too fast for them, slicing through first barrels and then limbs. But then . . . I couldn't stop. I

don't know what it was, my shame over what had happened on Mantero or the dark side amplifying my fury as kyber focuses plasma. By the time my companions reached the clearing, the Abyssin were dead. I've read that the lumbering aliens can regenerate limbs, but there was no coming back from these injuries.

Cautiously, Lene ignited her own lightsaber, as if wary of me . . .

LENE:
Dooku. It's over. They're done.

DOOKU:
No. Their evil remains.

DOOKU: (NARRATION)
I turned, slicing down the piled crates, cleaving the nerve disruptors in two.

We hear Dooku breathe hard for a few moments before extinguishing his lightsaber.

SIFO-DYAS:
You feeling better now?

DOOKU:
No. Not while scum like this still exists. This is what we should be doing, Sifo. Not meditating, safe within Temple walls. We should be out here, restoring balance by whatever means possible.

LENE:
(WARNING) Dooku.

DOOKU: (NARRATION)
It was as though she feared I would turn my ire upon her. Perhaps I would have, blinded by emotions I could barely control, emotions she had stirred by bringing me to Asusto. But I couldn't have moved if I'd wanted to. None of us could. The moss Sifo-Dyas had first noticed had been slowly creeping into the glade, smothering the Abyssin's corpses, rolling over our boots . . .

SIFO-DYAS:
Master! I can't pull free.

LENE:
Don't struggle.

SIFO-DYAS:
It's dragging me down.

Dooku swipes his lightsaber around to no avail.

DOOKU:
Burn it off.

LENE:
Dooku, no!

DOOKU: (NARRATION)
I sank my blade into the writhing morass.

DOOKU:
Burn it clear!

DOOKU: (NARRATION)
I could barely hear Lene screaming at me to stop, couldn't even hear the squelch of the moss as it traveled up my legs and over my back, drawing me into a cocoon.

My head was ablaze with voices, ghosts of the past and echoes of the future.

The ghostly voices assault him again, repeating, overlapping, becoming a cacophony.

GHOSTLY VOICE: (JENZA)
Brother.

GHOSTLY VOICE: (YODA)
Padawan.

GHOSTLY VOICE: (ARATH)
Idiot.

GHOSTLY VOICE: (ANYA)
Son.

GHOSTLY VOICE: (GORA)
Freak.

GHOSTLY VOICE: (SAVAGE)
Master.

DOOKU:
(STRAINED) Stop them!

LENE:
(PAINED) Padawans . . . this is an illusion . . . the dark side . . .

DOOKU:
You can hear them, too?

SIFO-DYAS:
The Force is with me. The Force is with me. (SIFO-DYAS RE-PEATS THIS OVER AND OVER AS A MANTRA, ADDING TO THE CACOPHONY.)

DOOKU:
Lene. I can't block them out. Help me.

OVERLAPPING GHOSTLY VOICE: (JENZA)
Help him.

OVERLAPPING GHOSTLY VOICE: (YODA)
Help him.

OVERLAPPING GHOSTLY VOICE: (ARATH)
Help him.

OVERLAPPING GHOSTLY VOICE: (ANYA)
Help him.

OVERLAPPING GHOSTLY VOICE: (GORA)
Help him.

OVERLAPPING GHOSTLY VOICE: (SIDIOUS)
Help yourself.

DOOKU:
Lene! I can't block them out.

DOOKU: (NARRATION)
But Lene was gone, consumed by the moss. Sifo-Dyas, too, was swallowed up, the moss pouring into his eyes, into his mouth. My lightsaber was sucked from my hands, the lichen numbing my skin. I thrashed and twisted, trying to free myself, but there was no escape . . .

OVERLAPPING GHOSTLY VOICE: (JENZA)
No escape.

OVERLAPPING GHOSTLY VOICE: (ARATH)
No escape.

OVERLAPPING GHOSTLY VOICE: (YODA)
Escape.

OVERLAPPING GHOSTLY VOICE: (GORA)
No escape.

DOOKU:
(CHOKING) Help me. Somebody, please. Help—(GAGS AS HE'S SMOTHERED)

The moss squelches.

DOOKU: (NARRATION)
I couldn't see. I couldn't hear. I couldn't even breathe. I was completely cocooned, consciousness slipping away . . .

We hear Dooku's beating heart in a deadened soundscape.

SCENE 67. INT. CAVERN. ASUSTO.

DOOKU:
(GASPS VIOLENTLY AS HE WAKES)

Atmosphere: We're in a cold cave. Water drips. We're high, near the stalactites. A ritual is being performed below, the constant drone of a song being sung in an alien tongue. We can hear the crackle of blazing torches.

DOOKU: (NARRATION)
I woke in a vast cavern, slick walls illuminated by flickering flame. I was suspended from on high by the same clinging moss that had overcome us.

Sifo-Dyas and Kostana hung lifelessly beside me. I had no idea if they were alive or dead, my senses overwhelmed by the pungent incense drifting up from the chamber below . . .

DOOKU:
(HISSING) Sifo . . . Lene . . .

PRIESTESS: (FROM BELOW)
Ah—*tt-tt-tt*—the conduit wakes.

The priestess, a human-sized insectoid alien, flies up to Dooku, her wings buzzing. The priestess's mandibles clack together when she talks. She adds little insectoid ticks into her speech pattern, indicated by tt *in the dialogue.*

Dooku struggles against the moss.

DOOKU:
Conduit? What are you talking about? Who are you?

PRIESTESS:
Do not struggle—*tt-tt-tt*—the moss holds you tight. You will only injure yourself.

DOOKU:
My lightsaber.

PRIESTESS:
You have been disarmed—*tt-tt-tt*—nothing must disrupt the ritual.

DOOKU:
You haven't answered my question. Who are you?

LENE:
(GROGGILY) The Presagers of Hakotei.

DOOKU:
Lene.

The priestess flits over to Lene.

PRIESTESS:
You have heard of us, Master Jedi.

LENE:
I thought you were extinct.

PRIESTESS:
We survive—*tt-tt-tt*—hidden from the universe. The last coven.

LENE:
You must be very proud.

PRIESTESS:
It was foretold. As was your coming.

DOOKU:
The relics came from you?

PRIESTESS:
You followed the trail.

DOOKU:
And fell into your trap.

LENE:
It was all a lure.

PRIESTESS:
The sacrifice was required.

SIFO-DYAS:
(GROGGILY) Why don't I like the sound of that?

DOOKU:

Sifo.

SIFO-DYAS:

Is this as bad as it looks?

LENE:

The Presagers were obsessed with prophecy. They sacrificed millions to be rewarded by visions of the future.

SIFO-DYAS:

Death magic.

DOOKU:

And now they need fresh blood.

PRIESTESS:

This planet—*tt-tt-tt*—it is a nexus point. We have foreseen it. The source—*tt-tt*—of all change.

DOOKU:

What change?

PRIESTESS:

We do not know. Your blood will open our eyes—*tt-tt-tt*—Every future laid bare.

SIFO-DYAS:

And is there a future where we survive?

The priestess flies down to her sisters.

PRIESTESS:

The ritual must begin.

SIFO-DYAS:

She didn't answer my question. Did anyone else notice that?

DOOKU:

They've taken our lightsabers.

LENE:
We still have the Force.

SIFO-DYAS:
Are you sure about that? My head feels like it's full of wampa wool.

LENE:
(WITH EFFORT AS SHE TRIES TO USE THE FORCE) It has to be this moss. Dampening our abilities.

The moss starts to slide over them.

DOOKU:
And it's on the move.

SIFO-DYAS:
(SPITTING) I don't think I can take being smothered again.

LENE:
I don't think you have much choice.

PRIESTESS:
Give yourself willingly. Let the moss absorb you.

LENE:
Resist it.

SIFO-DYAS:
I can't.

LENE:
The Force is with us. Repeat the mantra. The Force is with us.

DOOKU & SIFO-DYAS:
The Force is with us. The Force is with us.

Lene joins in.

DOOKU, SIFO-DYAS, & LENE:
The Force is with us. The Force is with us.

The Jedi struggle as the moss covers them, repeating the mantra, gagging as their mouths are flooded.

PRIESTESS:

You will be consumed so all futures will be ours—*tt-tt-tt*—
Everything that may come to pass.

DOOKU: (NARRATION)

I find it hard, even now, to describe what I saw. Was this what Sifo-
Dyas endured every time he was visited by days to come? I saw the
future. *Futures.* Every prospect. Every possibility. And all of them
a living nightmare.

SCENE 68. INT. THE VISIONSCAPE.

*Atmosphere: Nightmarish images flooding through Dooku's mind.
Behind it all we can hear the Presagers' chant, the visions folding
over one another, becoming more crazed, snatches of dialogue from
the films alongside things we haven't heard before.*

DOOKU: (REVERB)

What is this? (CALLING OUT) Master Kostana? Lene? Can you
hear me?

*Dooku sees a battle, turbolasers firing. Explosions. The tramp of
troopers' boots. Starfighters roaring above.*

DOOKU: (NARRATION)

I saw battles. So many battles. The future bleeding out on a thousand worlds.

SIFO-DYAS: (DISTORTED)
(SCREAMS)

DOOKU: (REVERB)
(CALLING OUT) Sifo-Dyas!

The vision shifts to the Temple chamber.

DOOKU: (NARRATION)

And faces. Faces I knew, faces that were new to me. All of them
changed from the way they should be . . .

YODA: (DISTORTED)
Wrong this is.

GRETZ DROOM: (DISTORTED)
We have no choice. The Senate has been corrupted. The Jedi must take control.

YODA:
Control?

We shift to the Senate Building. Jedi boots marching forward.

CHANCELLOR PALPATINE: (DISTORTED)
Master Jedi. What is the meaning of this?

GRETZ: (DISTORTED)
Our destiny.

Gretz Droom kills Palpatine with a lightsaber thrust, the vision of the Senate Building whizzes past Dooku as he hears Droom say . . .

GRETZ: (DISTORTED)
The rule of the Jedi has begun.

DOOKU: (NARRATION)
The Jedi as conquerors. It couldn't happen. Couldn't be. There had to be a different way. And there was . . .

The sounds of a clone wars battle.

CLONE COMMANDO:
One-Eighty-Fourth Attack Battalion, move out.

Blasterfire.

BATTLE DROID:
Roger Roger.

More clone war battles.

JOR AERITH:
Commander Crane?

CLONE COMMANDER:
Order 66 must be executed.

Blaster shots are fired, deflected by Aerith's lightsaber.

JOR:
No! Don't!

The shots find their target.

JOR:
(SCREAMS)

DOOKU: (NARRATION)
The futures were colliding, overlapping, my mind on fire.

There's the scream of a tie fighter swooping by, leading into a space battle, the familiar scream of tie fighters against X-wings.

DARTH SKRYE: (FEMALE)
The Cauldron opens.

The sound of a planet tearing in two.

DARTH SKRYE:
The Sith reborn.

A massive explosion.

DOOKU: (NARRATION)
Only one voice was true . . .

LENE: (DISTORTED)
(CALLING) Dooku . . .

DOOKU: (REVERB)
Lene?

LENE: (DISTORTED)
I've lost Sifo . . .

Lightsabers clash.

DOOKU: (REVERB)
Lene. Where are you?

LENE: (DISTORTED)
It's up to you . . . Dooku.

As she says his name, we hear the roar of the Tirra'Taka and become aware of a name chanted over and over by a crowd.

CROWD:
Doo-ku! Doo-ku! Doo-ku! Doo-ku!

DOOKU: (REVERB)
What?

The chanting continues behind the sound of battles and explosions. And then there is another sound—the crackle of Force lightning.

DARTH SIDIOUS:
I have chosen you, my apprentice.

More Force lightning. It plays out through all this, building in intensity, as does the chant of "Doo-ku, Doo-ku," the roar of the Tirra'Taka, and the sounds of battle.

DARTH SIDIOUS:
You serve a higher purpose.

QUI-GON:
My only conclusion . . .

DARTH SIDIOUS:
My purpose.

Everything—including the following increasingly overlapping dialogue—builds to a crazy, overwhelming crescendo like the end of the Beatles' "A Day in the Life," Dooku becoming increasingly agitated, in great pain.

QUI-GON:
It was a Sith Lord.

KI-ADI-MUNDI:
The Sith have been extinct for a millennium.

DARTH SKRYE:
The Sith reborn.

KI-ADI-MUNDI:
Extinct.

DARTH SKRYE:
Reborn.

LENE: (DISTORTED)
Dooku!

GRETZ:
The rule of the Jedi.

YODA:
Wrong this is.

LENE: (DISTORTED)
Dooku! Please!

QUI-GON:
(OVERLAPPING) The Sith have returned.

GRETZ:
(OVERLAPPING) Must take control.

YODA:
(OVERLAPPING) Wrong this is . . .

YODA #2:
(OVERLAPPING) Right.

YODA:
(OVERLAPPING) The Jedi rule . . .

YODA #2:
(OVERLAPPING) Jedi serve.

DARTH SIDIOUS:
(OVERLAPPING) All is as it should be.

DOOKU: (VISION)
(OVERLAPPING) The future is ours . . . my Master.

VENTRESS: (VISION)
Master. No.

Force lightning crackles.

VENTRESS: (VISION)
(SCREAMS)

The lightning builds into a storm, everything else swirling around it, and beneath it all, the emperor's manic laughter.

GRETZ:
(OVERLAPPING) Control . . . control . . . control . . . control . . . control . . .

DARTH SKRYE:
(OVERLAPPING) Reborn . . . Reborn . . .

QUI-GON:
(OVERLAPPING) Have returned . . . have returned . . . have re-turned . . . have—

And beneath the crescendo, Dooku screams in pain and fury.

DOOKU:
(PRIMAL SCREAM)

CUTTING STRAIGHT TO:
SCENE 69. INT. CAVERN OF THE PRESAGERS.

Dooku's scream dies in his throat like a man waking from a nightmare. He breathes hard as he finds himself back in the cavern. All is quiet. The chanting has stopped. Only a few of the torches are still burning, the others having gone out.

Force lightning crackles over the rocks.

LENE:
(COMING AROUND) Dooku? How did we get down?

DOOKU:
(SHAKEN) I don't know.

She pushes herself up.

LENE:
(DISGUSTED) What's that smell?

DOOKU:
(NOT SHOCKED) The Presagers.

LENE:
They're . . . They've been burned to a crisp. But how . . . ?

Dooku turns.

DOOKU:
(SCARED) Master . . . I . . .

LENE:
Dooku. Your hands.

DOOKU: (NARRATION)
I looked down at the indigo light crackling around my fingers . . .

DOOKU:
In my vision. I saw . . . lightning, coursing through bodies . . .

LENE:
Dooku, you're going to be all right . . .

DOOKU:
It's a mark of the dark side.

LENE:
Not always.

The lightning surges as his anger flares.

DOOKU:
Don't lie to me!

LENE:
Tell me what you saw.

DOOKU:
So many things.

LENE:
Different futures collapsing in on one another? The Jedi storming the Senate?

DOOKU:
Yes. And weapons . . . terrible weapons . . .

LENE:
The things you saw. They're not certainties. They're only possibilities.

DOOKU:
I saw the Sith.

LENE:
Things we can prevent.

DOOKU:
But the lightning . . .

LENE:
Your mind locked on to something.

DOOKU:
My future?

LENE:
No. Definitely not.

DOOKU:
But the dark side . . .

LENE:
Runs through this place like a seam. Dooku, it used you. Not the other way around. It latched on to your concern, for us, twisting it, weaponizing it. This wasn't you, Dooku. The Presagers brought it upon themselves.

More lightning crackles.

DOOKU:
I saw it, dancing from my fingertips . . . There was a woman. With bone-white skin.

LENE:
It was just a vision. And visions fade. We'll get away from this place and purge the memories, I promise.

SIFO-DYAS:
(GROANS, HIGHLY DISTRESSED)

DOOKU:
Sifo-Dyas!

DOOKU: (NARRATION)
I ran to Sifo-Dyas. He was gripped by a seizure, his face contorted in silent agony.

DOOKU:
What's happening?

LENE:
Sifo. Remember your training. Sifo.

DOOKU:
He can't hear you.

LENE:
Then we need to make him.

SIFO-DYAS:
(DELIRIOUS) Can't be happening. Can't be happening.

LENE:

It's no good. We need to get him to the *Truthseeker*.

DOOKU:

But I—

LENE:

(FIRMLY) But nothing. Look at your hands, Dooku.

DOOKU:

The lightning. It's gone.

LENE:

It was never there. But Sifo-Dyas is real and needs your help. Your *friend*, Dooku. Will you help him?

DOOKU:

Yes. Of course I will.

LENE:

We're going to have to carry him. That's it. Carefully.

SCENE 70. EXT. SPACE. ABOVE ASUSTO.

The Truthseeker *flies by.*

SCENE 71. INT. THE *TRUTHSEEKER*.

Sifo-Dyas is writhing on a bunk.

DOOKU: (NARRATION)

Sifo-Dyas's torment continued long after we'd left the planet's atmosphere.

SIFO-DYAS:

(AS IF HAVING A NIGHTMARE) No . . . You can't . . . It cannot be.

DOOKU:

Sifo. Listen to me. You're safe. You're safe.

Lene runs in.

LENE:
How is he?

DOOKU:
The same. I can't get through to him.

LENE:
He's lost in the visions.

She kneels beside him, gripping Sifo-Dyas's arms.

LENE:
(FIRMLY) Padawan. That is enough. You need to come back to me. The Force is strong in you. Do you hear? The Force is strong.

SIFO-DYAS:
Master?

LENE:
I'm here.

SIFO-DYAS:
Master . . . There were soldiers . . . hundreds of thousands of soldiers. So much blood . . . washing over me, washing over us all.

LENE:
It wasn't real. It was the dark side. Nothing more.

SIFO-DYAS:
You didn't hear the explosions. Didn't hear the screams.

LENE:
Sifo, do you remember the cleansing ritual I taught you?

SIFO-DYAS:
No.

LENE:
On Rishi. After we uncovered the Hand of Skrye.

SIFO-DYAS:
The Ritual of the Three. Yes. I remember.

LENE:
We need to teach it to Dooku. Do you understand? The dark side washed over him, too. You want to help your friend, don't you? You want to save him?

SIFO-DYAS:
Yes. Yes, of course I do.

LENE:
Then we must prepare. Can you stand?

SIFO-DYAS:
I think so.

He pushes himself off the bed.

LENE:
Stand in a circle, so we can see one another's eyes. Look inside yourself. Can you feel the Force within?

DOOKU:
Yes.

LENE:
Describe it.

SIFO-DYAS:
It is . . . it is cold.

DOOKU:
Dark.

LENE:
That will change. You have to believe it. Now . . .

We hear Lene walk to a locker, opening the door.

LENE: (CONT.)
. . . we need these,

She recovers three rolls of fabric.

DOOKU:

Bandages?

LENE:

The Balm of the Luminous. Do you see? Their words are woven into the gauze. As we wrap them about our arms, we bind ourselves in the light.

DOOKU:

It . . . it sounds like witchcraft.

LENE:

It's a tool, nothing more. A means to find balance. Here.

DOOKU: (NARRATION)

Almost reverentially, she passed both of us a roll of cloth.

LENE:

Starting at the wrist, you wind the fabric up your arm, like this. Do you see?

DOOKU:

Yes.

SIFO-DYAS:

K-keep your palm open and raised toward the stars.

LENE:

That's right, Sifo. Can you remember the invocation?

SIFO-DYAS:

Yes. Yes, I think so:

"We call upon the Three . . ."

LENE:

"Light. Dark . . ."

SIFO-DYAS:

"And Balance true."

LENE:
"One is no greater than the others."

SIFO-DYAS:
"Together they unite, restore, center, and renew."

LENE:
"We walk into the Light. Acknowledge the Dark."

SIFO-DYAS:
"And find Balance in ourselves . . ."

LENE:
"For the Force is strong."

SIFO-DYAS:
"For the Force is strong."

LENE:
Excellent. Dooku. Are you ready?

DOOKU:
Yes.

DOOKU: (NARRATION, SPEAKING OVER THE INCANTA-
TION)
Together, we repeated the ritual, binding our arms.

As the autopilot sped us back to the Core, I felt the shadows lift, the memory of what had happened, while still fresh, weighing lighter on my mind. On my heart.

ALL THREE TOGETHER: (UNDER NARRATION)
"We call upon the Three.

Light. Dark. And Balance true.

One is no greater than the others.

Together they unite, restore, center, and renew.

We walk into the Light. Acknowledge the Dark. And find Balance in ourselves . . .

For the Force is strong.

For the Force is strong."

We hold on the silence for a moment.

LENE:
(CALM) There. Is that better? Look inside yourself again. Describe what you see. What you feel.

SIFO-DYAS:
Warmth.

DOOKU:
Warmth and light.

LENE:
Keep the bandage under your sleeve. No one will see it or question it. And if you are troubled in future . . .

SIFO-DYAS:
Repeat the ritual.

LENE:
As often as you need. The ancient Jedi did this every day. We have forgotten so much.

DOOKU:
And what now?

LENE:
We return to Coruscant. The journey will give us opportunity to meditate.

SIFO-DYAS:
I feel so tired.

LENE:

You must rest, my Padawan. You've been through a lot. We all have.

SIFO-DYAS:

Yes, Master.

DOOKU:

Would you like me to stay with you, Sifo?

SIFO-DYAS:

No. I need to be alone.

DOOKU:

Only if you're sure.

LENE:

I'll let you know when we're almost home.

She leaves the room, Dooku hurrying after her into the corridor.

DOOKU:

Lene, wait.

LENE:

I suggest you do the same, Dooku. Get some rest.

DOOKU:

But . . . what are we going to tell Master Yoda?

LENE:

Nothing.

DOOKU:

But this isn't like Mantero. The things we saw. (ASHAMED) The things we did.

LENE:

Dooku, listen to me. Yoda already has doubts about my work. He tolerates what I do, but if he found out I exposed two Padawans to the dark side . . .

DOOKU:

He'd shut you down.

LENE:

In an instant. This has to be our secret. Do you understand?

DOOKU:

It doesn't feel right. He's my Master.

LENE:

And it pains me to ask you, Dooku. But the work is too important, to the Order, to the galaxy as a whole. You see that, don't you? Especially now. You've seen the dark side. You know what it's capable of.

DOOKU:

What I'm capable of, you mean.

LENE:

No. No, I don't. The visions. (DROPS HER VOICE) The lightning. That wasn't you. It was that place. But you're stronger.

DOOKU:

"The Force is strong."

LENE:

"The Force is strong." Don't worry. Please. The future you saw, whatever it was, won't come to pass. I can guarantee it. You're a good man, Dooku. A good man.

SCENE 72. EXT. ROOFTOP. RAIN.

VENTRESS:

A good man . . . (SNORTS)

She swipes through to another page.

KY NAREC: (GHOST)
Are you all right?

She swipes back.

VENTRESS:
"A woman. With bone-white skin." Sound familiar?

KY NAREC: (GHOST)
It could be a coincidence.

VENTRESS:
Says the dead man. (THOUGHTFUL) Maybe everything has already been written, none of us with a choice.

KY NAREC: (GHOST)
He did. Dooku. The man I knew would never have hurt you.

VENTRESS:
You knew him? You knew Dooku?

KY NAREC: (GHOST)
He taught me. He taught us all.

VENTRESS:
Maybe you told me that. I can't remember.

KY NAREC: (GHOST)
The Dooku I knew was older. He'd been a Jedi a long time. Still had the beard from the holos, but it had already turned to gray. And a Knighted Padawan of his own, for that matter.

VENTRESS:
Ah. Dooku has mentioned him. Qui-Gon, wasn't it?

KY NAREC: (GHOST)
Qui-Gon Jinn. But he wasn't Dooku's first. Oh no. First came Rael. Rael Averross. As untidy as Dooku was smart, and as friendly as he was stern. A hyperstorm waiting to happen, that's what Master Sinube called him. And he was right. But I liked Rael. We all did.

VENTRESS:
Even Dooku?

KY NAREC: (GHOST)
See for yourself.

VENTRESS:
What? How?

KY NAREC: (GHOST)
Dooku's journal. He'll be in there. We all will . . .

PART FIVE

SCENE 73. EXT. JEDI TEMPLE. TRAINING GROUND.

Atmosphere: A gentle wind rustling through the leaves of the kukra tree.

Dooku, now a Jedi Master—and nearer than ever to the Dooku we know—is putting a group of Initiates through their paces, each facing a holographic opponent.

DOOKU: (FIFTY-SOMETHING)
That's it. Very good. Now . . . Let's cycle through the marks of contact. *Sai cha.*

Ten lightsabers sweep and stop.

DOOKU:
Excellent. *Cho sun.*

Again, there are ten swipes.

DOOKU:
Cho mai.

And again.

DOOKU:

Hmm. A little more precision if you please, Ovana. (BEAT) *Sun djem.*

And again.

DOOKU:
Mou kei.

And again, one lightsaber slightly out of step.

DOOKU:

I said *mou kei*, Pars, not *cho mok*. If these were your trials, you would have failed.

Rael walks into the garden.

RAEL:

Don't let him give you a hard time, kid. You're doing just fine.

DOOKU:

Rael. Now is not the time for coddling, my former Padawan. If the Initiates are to be ready . . .

RAEL:

They will be. Won't you, younglings?

PARS-VALO:

With Master Dooku's guidance, Jedi Averross.

RAEL:

Ha-ha! See. You have them well trained already, Master. Total obedience.

DOOKU:

If only the same could have been said of you. Look at the state of those robes. And that sash . . .

RAEL:

(SHAKES HEAD) Same old Dooku.

DOOKU:
I beg your pardon.

RAEL:
Tell me, kids, would ya rather play with training holograms all afternoon or witness a practical demonstration?

Rael activates his lightsaber.

DOOKU:
You're challenging me to a duel?

RAEL:
For old times' sake.

Dooku ignites his lightsaber.

DOOKU:
Holograms off.

The training holos shimmer off.

RAEL:
That's better. What style shall we use?

DOOKU:
Whichever you like. It'll make little difference.

RAEL:
You've always been too confident. It will be your undoing. *Sun djem!*

He sweeps his lightsaber as he announces the cuts, Dooku easily blocking every move.

DOOKU:
Whereas you talk too much. *Shiim!*

Another block. And then Rael performs three swift moves, each blocked by Dooku.

RAEL:

That's true, I guess. While no one could accuse you of being chatty. *Cho sun! Mou kei! Sai tok!*

Their lightsabers sizzle as they lock.

DOOKU:

Really? The Bisecting Blow? I taught you better than that, Rael.

RAEL:

Eh. Sometimes I like to play dirty. As do you!

They go into a full lightsaber battle, forgetting about the marks now, just reveling in the duel, ribbing each other as they fight.

DOOKU:

You should be careful, my former pupil. You don't want to tire yourself out. You have a long journey ahead of you.

RAEL:

Don't worry on my account, Master. I could do this all day.

DOOKU:

That won't be necessary.

Dooku performs a skilled maneuver, getting the upper hand.

RAEL:

Ha-ha! Okay, okay. I yield. *Solah! Solah!*

They extinguish their lightsabers.

DOOKU:

You need to work on your lateral extension. You leave yourself open to attack.

RAEL:

And there you have it, Initiates. Always the teacher. Always knows best. And don't any of ya forget it.

DOOKU:

(TO THE YOUNGLINGS) That will be all for today, younglings, but before you go, remember, while we may practice the marks of contact, a Jedi preserves life above all else. In combat we seek only to disarm, never to destroy. Do you understand?

INITIATES: (TOGETHER)
Yes, Master Dooku.

DOOKU:
Very good. Now off with you. Master Braylon is waiting in the Hall of Discovery.

The Initiates file out, talking among themselves.

RAEL:
You're hard on 'em, you know that?

DOOKU:
Too hard?

RAEL:
They still have plenty of time. Besides, as you always told me, lightsaber conflict is purely ceremonial.

DOOKU:
More's the pity.

RAEL:
You don't mean that.

DOOKU:
And you know as well as anyone that the galaxy is a dangerous place.

RAEL:
Is that your way of tellin' me to be careful?

DOOKU:
You will be. I trained you. Just remember, diplomacy can quickly fail.

RAEL:
When neither party hungers for peace. I know. But I'm sure Yanis will be different.

DOOKU:

I hope so. For everyone's sake. I'll walk with you to the hangar.

RAEL:

(MOCK SURPRISE) You're comin' to see me off? I didn't know you cared, Master.

DOOKU:

Just don't tell anyone. I have a reputation to protect.

SCENE 74. EXT. JEDI TEMPLE. SHUTTLE HANGAR.

Atmosphere: A busy shuttle bay, ships being prepared for departure, droids bleeping and rolling about.

Doors swish open, and Rael and Dooku enter.

RAEL:

Ah, *now* I see why ya wanted to be here. I'll try not to be too disappointed.

LENE:

Dooku.

DOOKU:

Master Kostana. I'm glad I caught you.

LENE:

And I you. (CALLING OVER) Sifo. Dooku's come to wave us off.

SIFO-DYAS: (OFF-MIC)

Oh. I'm ... er ... a bit busy. I'll ... um ... I'll be over in a minute.

RAEL:

Well, that's not awkward at all.

DOOKU:

(WARNING) Rael.

RAEL:

I know when I'm not wanted. If you need me, I'll be on my interceptor.

Rael walks off, calling to an astromech.

RAEL:

(CALLING) Aitch-Sixteen! You fitted those laser capacitors yet?

An astromech burbles back.

RAEL:

Don't give me that. You've had plenty of time.

LENE:

He hasn't changed.

DOOKU:

And I hope he never does.

LENE:

Dooku, listen. About Sifo. It's not you . . .

DOOKU:

I know. It's just been so long.

LENE:

It's one of the reasons we stayed away.

DOOKU:

You still travel together.

LENE:

He needs me.

DOOKU:

You're not responsible for him anymore.

LENE:

We both know he's vulnerable. And we work well together. We always have.

DOOKU:

And his visions?

She doesn't reply.

DOOKU:

Lene.

LENE:

They're getting worse.

DOOKU:

You should talk to the Council.

LENE:

What good would that do? They'd lock him away.

DOOKU:

He's not a criminal.

LENE:

No. But in their eyes, he's dangerous. I've heard . . .

DOOKU:

What?

LENE:

(LEANING IN CONSPIRATORIALLY) They've opened a new correctional unit on Lola Sayu. For those with foresight.

DOOKU:

Within the Citadel? I find that hard to believe.

LENE:

You haven't been there. The thought of Sifo-Dyas ending up in a place like that. No, he's better with me. And it's not that unusual. The Jedi of old traveled together, sometimes in pairs. Sometimes more.

DOOKU:

(HESITANT) The last thing I'd want is to cause him distress.

LENE:
Thank you. But there is something you can do.

DOOKU:
Name it.

LENE:
(LOOKING AROUND) Where is she? Ah, there we are. (WHIS-TLES)

A convor flies down to land on Lene's arm.

DOOKU:
(LAUGHING) You've trained a new convor.

LENE:
She'll never replace poor Ferana, but she's beautiful, aren't you, girl?

She ruffles the convor's feathers, the bird chirping happily.

DOOKU:
She's certainly very striking.

LENE:
And that, Calleen, is as near a compliment as you're ever going to get from Master Dooku.

DOOKU:
Calleen. The Altiri goddess of wisdom.

LENE:
I'm impressed.

DOOKU:
Even a teacher must study.

LENE:
Will you look after her for me? She gets skittish around Sifo.

DOOKU:
It will be my pleasure. I shall construct a roost in my chambers.

LENE:

There's no need to go to any trouble.

DOOKU:

There's every need. It is good to meet you, Calleen.

The convor chirps and jumps to Dooku's arm.

DOOKU:

(LAUGHS)

LENE:

(LAUGHING, TOO) Will you look at that? The beginning of a beautiful friendship. You look after him as well, eh, Calleen?

The convor chirps.

LENE:

Good. I'll see you soon, Dooku.

DOOKU:

I hope so.

Lene returns to her ship as Rael walks back up to his old Master.

RAEL:

If I hadn't taken a vow of celibacy . . .

DOOKU:

It's never stopped you before . . .

RAEL:

She's a fine woman.

DOOKU:

I think you mean, a great Jedi.

RAEL:

'Course I do. (BEAT) You all right?

DOOKU:

Why wouldn't I be? Meet Calleen.

The convor squawks.

RAEL:

Don't think she likes me.

DOOKU:

Then it appears she has excellent taste.

RAEL:

But seriously, your friend . . . I know what Sifo-Dyas means to you.

DOOKU:

We've known each other for a long time, but the Force has led us down different paths. Sifo-Dyas is an explorer, while I am doomed to endure ridicule from my former students.

RAEL:

Quite right, too. Just promise me one thing. Don't wait too long.

DOOKU:

For what?

RAEL:

To take another Padawan.

DOOKU:

As if you could be so easily replaced.

RAEL:

You know what I mean.

DOOKU:

Worry about Yanis, Jedi Averross. Your old Master will take care of himself.

Dooku walks away.

RAEL:

(CALLING AFTER HIM) I thought we weren't saying old?

SCENE 75. EXT. ROOFTOP. RAIN.

VENTRESS:

According to this, he would take another Padawan, sooner than anyone expected.

KY NAREC: (GHOST)
Himself included?

She swipes through to another entry.

VENTRESS:
I thought you would remember. Looks like you were there . . .

SCENE 76. INT. JEDI TEMPLE. TRAINING GALLERY.

A lightsaber duel is in process, a group of Initiates watching from the side of the gallery.

KY NAREC:
Gretz? Is he here? Can you see him?

GRETZ:
Stop panicking, Ky. He's there. Behind Master Aerith.

KY NAREC:
I thought he wasn't coming.

GRETZ:
Dooku never misses the tournaments.

KY NAREC:
Yeah, but he never picks a Padawan, either. Not since Rael.

GRETZ:
Maybe this year will change all that.

KY NAREC:
And I suppose you think he'll pick you.

GRETZ:
Can you think of any reason why he won't?

KY NAREC:
Yeah. You're looking at him.

GRETZ:
You?

KY NAREC:
Why not?

GRETZ:
Ky, you yield in every duel.

KY NAREC:
I do not!

GRETZ:
What do you think, Qui-Gon?

QUI-GON:
I think you should be quiet. I'm trying to watch Ima-Gun and Yeeda.

KY NAREC:
Gretz says I always yield.

QUI-GON:
And? Sometimes to win you must lose.

KY NAREC:
Exactly. (BEAT) I think.

GRETZ:
Please don't pretend you know what that means.

The lightsaber duel ends in one of the sabers going off.

IMA-GUN: (OFF-MIC)
Solah!

SINUBE: (OFF-MIC)
Well done, Initiates.

BRAYLON: (OFF-MIC)
The next combatants will be chosen.

We hear the stones whirl as before until one is chosen.

SINUBE: (OFF-MIC)
Initiate Narec.

GRETZ:
Time to prove yourself.

BRAYLON: (OFF-MIC)
And his opponent will be . . .

The stones whirl until . . .

SINUBE: (OFF-MIC)
Initiate Droom.

KY NAREC:
(GROANING) Oh, great.

GRETZ:
What's the matter, Ky? Nervous?

QUI-GON:
There is no need to be. The Force will be with you.

GRETZ:
(TEASING) Yeah. It'll need to be.

SCENE 77. INT. JEDI TEMPLE. TRAINING GALLERY. JEDI MASTERS' POV.

Another duel is under way.

YODA:
Impressive. Most impressive. Trained them well you have, Master Dooku.

DOOKU:
Master Sinube deserves the credit. He has spent more time with Heliost Clan. My time has been taken up with Thranta, as usual.

YODA:
And yet one youngling interests you, I think.

DOOKU:
He has great potential.

YODA:
An inquiring mind. That is what he has.

BRAYLON:
More like a total disregard for authority, if you ask me.

DOOKU:
That is unfair, Master Braylon.

BRAYLON:
You haven't taught him.

YODA:
Yet.

DOOKU:
I am not ready to take another Padawan.

SINUBE:
I don't see why not. Unless you're thinking of sitting on the Council?

YODA:
Welcome, my former Padawan would be. That he knows. But other plans I sense he has. Chosen for him, the Force already has.

SCENE 78. INT. JEDI TEMPLE. TRAINING GALLERY.

The tournament is over, the Initiates milling around.

KY NAREC:
I don't believe it.

GRETZ:
Maybe he couldn't choose between us?

KY NAREC:
So he chose *him*?

Gretz spots Dooku approaching.

GRETZ:
Shhh.

DOOKU:
Padawan Droom. I trust you are pleased with your mentor.

GRETZ:
Yes, Master Dooku.

DOOKU:
Jor Aerith is a fine Jedi, Gretz. You will learn much from her. As will you from Master Mana, Padawan Narec.

KY NAREC:
Thank you, sir.

Qui-Gon approaches.

DOOKU:
And here is *my* Padawan. I hope you are ready for a challenge, Qui-Gon?

QUI-GON:
Always, Master Dooku.

DOOKU:
Then we shall begin immediately.

QUI-GON:
Master?

DOOKU:
Meet me in the training ground, in ten minutes.

Dooku strides off.

DOOKU: (GOING OFF-MIC)
A Jedi is always punctual. Remember that, Padawan.

QUI-GON:
I will.

GRETZ:
You better run along, Qui-Gon. You've got yourself a real task-master there.

JOR: (APPROACHING)
Is that so, Padawan Droom?

GRETZ:
(JUMPS) Master Aerith. I didn't see you there.

JOR:
Obviously. Let's take a leaf out of Master Dooku's book, shall we? The Hall of Endurance, in *five* minutes.

GRETZ:
Five? I mean, yes, Master. I'm looking forward it.

QUI-GON:
Shouldn't you have already left?

GRETZ:
Very funny.

Gretz rushes off.

SCENE 79. EXT. ROOFTOP. RAIN.

VENTRESS:
You don't remember it at all?

She swipes another page beneath his dialogue.

KY NAREC: (GHOST)
Sometimes it is difficult . . . my memories are clouded . . .

VENTRESS:
Then maybe this will clear things up for you . . . "I must admit at first I was concerned. Had I misread the Force? Qui-Gon and I struggled in the early days of our partnership. Everything about us

seemed at odds, more so than it had ever been with Rael. Perhaps we were too alike. I needn't have worried. Trust in the Force, Master Yoda used to tell me, and as in most things he was correct. Now it feels as though we were born to serve together, Qui-Gon the student and I, the teacher . . ."

As before, fade into:

SCENE 80. EXT. JEDI TEMPLE. TRAINING GROUND.

DOOKU: (NARRATION)
. . . and I, the teacher. Aerith says we have become inseparable, and I for one welcome it . . .

QUI-GON:
I am ready, Master.

DOOKU:
Are you sure?

QUI-GON:
Yes.

DOOKU:
Very well. This technique is not one I learned from Master Yoda. And yet I will share it with you, as I shared it with Rael. Who knows. Perhaps you will share it with your Padawan one day.

QUI-GON:
But if you didn't learn it from Master Yoda . . . Ah. You learned it from Lene Kostana.

DOOKU:
You've heard of her.

QUI-GON:
And how close you were.

DOOKU:
We still are. Now place the band around my chest. Yes, like that.

Qui-Gon pulls a metal band around Dooku's chest, clicking the ends of the ring together.

DOOKU:
It needs to be tight.

QUI-GON:
It couldn't get much tighter. What is it?

DOOKU:
A medical implement, at least originally, although I believe the Heltraxi use it as a torture device. When pressed, the button on this remote will send an electronic pulse through my chest, not enough to kill me, but uncomfortable nonetheless.

QUI-GON:
I do not wish to hurt you, Master.

DOOKU:
And you won't. Through the Force, a Jedi can endure even the most debilitating pain. Remember the Battle of Nar Shaddaa. Master Crucitorn fought on even after being immolated by the Flame-Wielders.

QUI-GON:
Injuries that would have crippled any warrior. But we live in an age of peace.

DOOKU:
And long may it continue. However, his technique can ease discomfort on any level. The principles I teach you today can be used to soothe any pain, be it physical or mental. Now activate the band.

Qui-Gon clicks the button. There is a slight hum.

DOOKU:
(A LITTLE UNCOMFORTABLE) Good. Turn the dial.

QUI-GON:
Are you sure?

DOOKU:

I wouldn't have asked you if I were not.

Qui-Gon turns a dial.

DOOKU:

(GRUNTING SLIGHTLY) Good. Now ... Reach out with the Force. What do you feel?

QUI-GON:

Your discomfort.

DOOKU:

Hardly surprising. But if I ... focus my thoughts ... and calm my emotions.

QUI-GON:

Master, we should stop.

DOOKU:

No. Pain is only an illusion. It can be controlled.

He steadies his breathing despite the pain.

DOOKU:

I am Jedi. (NOW CALMER) I am Jedi. (CALMER AGAIN) I am Jedi.

QUI-GON:

Your pain. I cannot sense it anymore.

DOOKU:

Nor can I. The pain is still there. I merely deny its power over me.

QUI-GON:

I would like to try.

DOOKU:

You are eager. I like that.

QUI-GON:

I want to learn.

DOOKU:
And learn you shall, my Padawan.

SCENE 81. EXT. ROOFTOP. RAIN.

VENTRESS: (NARRATION)
I shift, not wanting my legs to cramp in the cold. The sky is darkening. Between Ky and the journal, I've lost track of time. I glance down on the street, but it is still deserted. The Crolute hasn't shown. If he doesn't come back soon, I'm going to have to rethink the entire operation. I don't want to think what Dooku will say if I return without his sister. That's if she's even still on Serenno.

Trust in the Force. The words Dooku wrote so long ago bolster my resolve. My first instinct was that Glute would return here. I must stand by my convictions just a little bit longer.

KY NARAC: (GHOST)
Is that the only reason?

VENTRESS:
What?

KY NARAC: (GHOST)
Why you are waiting?

VENTRESS:
You need to stay out of my thoughts.

KY NARAC: (GHOST)
How can I? What did you say I was? A figment of your imagination? No. You thought that, didn't you? How annoying it must be.

She swipes through the datapad, frustrated.

KY NARAC: (GHOST)
But the point stands. You want to know how Dooku was with his Padawan. What kind of teacher he was back then.

VENTRESS:
I know what kind of teacher he is. I bear the scars.

KY NAREC: (GHOST)

But he wasn't always that way. It's there, on the page in front of you. Their travels through the galaxy. Soul's Lament. The waterfalls of Dalna. Station Zeta. Qui-Gon would have become used to waystations like Zeta, and the clientele they attracted. I should have taken you offplanet. There's a freedom about being out in the stars. People take risks that they never would at home, perhaps showing their true nature because they think no one's looking . . .

Fade to:

SCENE 82. INT. SPACE STATION.

Atmosphere: A busy space station, lots of bustle and noise.

Footsteps running through a crowd.

RAEL: (COMM)

Arath? Where are you?

ARATH:

I'm on my way, Averross. I had to see someone.

RAEL: (COMM)

And you chose now? The Plinovian ambassador is . . .

ARATH:

I said, I'll be there—

He barges into someone, knocking them down.

ARATH:

Stang. I'm sorry.

QUI-GON:

No harm is done.

ARATH:

You're a Padawan.

QUI-GON:

And you're a Jedi.

ARATH:

For my sins. The name's Arath.

QUI-GON:

Qui-Gon.

ARATH:

You're here for the peace talks?

QUI-GON:

No. We're passing through.

ARATH:

You and your Master?

QUI-GON:

Yes. Here he comes now.

ARATH:

(GROANS) Today just gets better.

Dooku approaches.

DOOKU:

Well, there's a face I haven't seen in a long time.

ARATH:

Dooku. What a wonderful surprise.

DOOKU:

Careful. You almost sound like you mean it. What brings you out here?

QUI-GON:

Station Zeta is hosting a summit.

DOOKU:

Oh?

ARATH:
Between the Plinovians and the Solodoe. I've taken a diplomatic post with—

There's an explosion nearby. People scream.

QUI-GON:
That doesn't sound good.

DOOKU:
Quickly. (RUNS OFF) We may be able to help.

ARATH:
Ever the hero. (CALLING) Wait up!

SCENE 83. INT. SPACE STATION. CORRIDOR.

Atmosphere: The aftermath of the explosion. People are sobbing. Fires are being extinguished. Rael Averross is attempting crowd control.

RAEL:
Please. Everyone needs to keep back. Yeah. That includes you, lady.

Dooku and Qui-Gon run up.

DOOKU:
Rael?

RAEL:
(SMILING) Master Dooku. I thought I felt your presence.

DOOKU:
You remember my Padawan?

RAEL:
'Course I do. Good to see ya again, Qui-Gon.

QUI-GON:
What happened here?

RAEL:
The peace talks have hit a road bump. The Plinovian ambassador has exploded.

QUI-GON:
He was blown up?

RAEL:
No. He did it himself.

QUI-GON:
I'm sorry?

DOOKU:
Plinovians are a gaseous life-form, similar to Master Oorallon.

RAEL:
The difference being that Oorallon doesn't self-combust when riled. Just look at this mess.

Arath runs up.

ARATH:
I'm sorry. I came as quickly as I could.

DOOKU:
I thought you were just behind us.

ARATH:
I got waylaid. What happened?

SOLODOE AMBASSADOR:
What happened is that damn Plinovian tried to kill me!

MED DROID:
Please, Ambassador Ketas. I must tend to your injuries.

KETAS:
Get your damn pincers away from me.

RAEL:
Let's just calm down, shall we?

DOOKU:

Indeed. Taking out your frustration on a med droid will hardly help the situation, Ambassador.

KETAS:

Then maybe I should take it out on whoever *you* are!

RAEL:

Ambassador Ketas, may I introduce Master Dooku. He has been sent to help with the negotiations.

DOOKU:

I have?

RAEL:

Yes.

KETAS:

The Jedi finally realized you weren't up to the job, did they? Not that it will make any difference. The talks have been a shambles from beginning to end. I knew it was a mistake holding them here. There are too many distractions. We should've held them on Plin, as I originally suggested.

RAEL:

We require neutral ground, Ambassador. If an agreement is to be found . . .

KETAS:

There will be no agreement. I have been insulted and attacked. Terraforming will continue, and that is final.

RAEL:

Ketas, please.

Ketas opens a comm channel, storming off as he speaks.

KETAS:

Tanu? This is Ketas. (BEAT) I don't care where you are. We're leaving. Ready the ship.

RAEL:

(SIGHS) I should've become a librarian. You know where you are with books.

DOOKU:

I never knew you were much of a reader. What can we do to help?

RAEL:

I'd better bring you up to speed. Arath, I need you to coordinate the cleanup. Can you do that?

ARATH:

(ICILY) Of course.

RAEL:

We'll head back to the conference rooms.

DOOKU:

Lead the way.

They leave.

ARATH:

No, that's fine. I'll carry on. No need to say thank you.

SCENE 84. INT. CONFERENCE ROOM.

QUI-GON:

So both the Plinovian and the Solodoe have a claim on Plin Minor.

RAEL:

That's right. But the Solodoe are determined to terraform the planet . . .

DOOKU:

Which would destroy much of the Plinovians' natural habitat.

RAEL:

Everything was going great until Ketas accused the Plinovian ambassador of stealin' his seal of office, which just so happens to be made of solid mythra . . .

DOOKU:

And therefore worth a small fortune. Where was it kept?

RAEL:

On his cruiser, the *Luster*. A real beauty. Top-of-the-line security systems. Cams. Pressure pads in the floor. The works. No one could get in or out.

DOOKU:

But someone did.

QUI-GON:

The Plinovian ambassador.

RAEL:

According to Ketas.

DOOKU:

Able to slip through doors . . .

QUI-GON:

And float over pressure pads.

DOOKU:

But if there is security footage . . .

A door chime bings.

RAEL:

Hold that thought. Enter.

The door slides open.

CHIEF TANU:

You called for me, Jedi Averross?

RAEL:

Chief Tanu. Thank you for joining us.

CHIEF TANU:

Ambassador Ketas is keen to depart.

RAEL:

I'm sure he'll stick around if it means we can find his seal.

CHIEF TANU:

I'm not sure how I can help.

RAEL:

You can give us access to the *Luster*'s security footage.

CHIEF TANU:

I'm not sure that's possible.

DOOKU:

You have reviewed it?

CHIEF TANU:

(UNSURE) I . . . Yes. Yes, I have.

RAEL:

Then ya won't mind if we take a peek. You can use this terminal.

CHIEF TANU:

Very well.

He starts pressing buttons.

CHIEF TANU:

But I don't see what good it will . . . (TRAILS OFF)

QUI-GON:

Chief Tanu?

CHIEF TANU:

This isn't right. The footage. It's . . . It's been deleted.

DOOKU:

By whom?

More beeps.

CHIEF TANU:

It's not possible.

RAEL:

Chief?

CHIEF TANU:

It was deleted . . . using my clearance codes. But I would never . . .
I'd have no reason to . . .

QUI-GON:

Steal the seal yourself?

CHIEF TANU:

Why would I? Ketas is already gunning for me. He told me if I
bomb out again . . .

DOOKU:

An interesting turn of phrase. What do you remember about the
robbery, Tanu?

CHIEF TANU:

Nothing. Ketas discovered the seal was gone. He was furious.
He . . . blamed the Plinovians. Said he was going to have it out with
them and . . .

DOOKU:

And you checked the security footage . . .

CHIEF TANU:

I . . . I must have. I told the ambassador I had . . . but . . .

DOOKU:

But now you're not so sure.

CHIEF TANU:

I would've checked. I . . . I'm sure I would.

QUI-GON:

His mind is clouded.

RAEL:

But I sense no deceit.

DOOKU:

Not about the seal, anyway.

CHIEF TANU:

I'm not sure I like your tone.

DOOKU:

I mean no disrespect, but tell me—what did you mean by "bombed out."

CHIEF TANU:

He's not the easiest man to get on with.

DOOKU:

That much is obvious. But *bombed out* is a phrase from sabacc, is it not? I assume you play.

CHIEF TANU:

Yes. Yes, I do. There's nothing wrong with that.

RAEL:

It depends how much ya lose.

CHIEF TANU:

I can't see how any of this is your business.

DOOKU:

Have you played since arriving on Station Zeta?

CHIEF TANU:

Yes. There's a casino on level twenty. Chance Encounters.

RAEL:

With anyone we know?

CHIEF TANU:

I . . . (STRUGGLING) I'm not sure.

DOOKU:

I think we should take that as a yes. Padawan, I think you should pay a visit to the lower levels.

SCENE 85. INT. LEVEL 20. ALLEYWAY.

A metal fist buries itself in a stomach.

ENFORCER DROID:
Where's the money, Arath?

ARATH:
(WHEEZING) I told you. Your boss will get it. But he has to be patient.

ENFORCER DROID:
No, he *doesn't.*

The droid kicks Arath on "doesn't."

ARATH:
(CRIES OUT) You don't understand. I just need for things to die down . . .

ENFORCER DROID:
Should have thought of that before you cheated!

ARATH:
I didn't.

The droid hits him again.

ENFORCER DROID:
Liar!

ARATH:
(GRUNTS) Oh, what's the point.

The enforcer droid smashes into the wall.

ARATH:
I could get into real trouble for doing this.

There's a crackle of electricity, the enforcer giving out an electronic moan.

ARATH:
But no one cares about droids, do they?

ENFORCER DROID:
(WITH EFFORT) You're ... dead ...

ARATH:
Not if your boss wants me to pay up. So why don't you scuttle off and tell him it's on its way.

QUI-GON: (OFF-MIC)
Arath?

ARATH:
(UNDER BREATH) Stang!

Qui-Gon runs up.

QUI-GON:
What are you doing?

ARATH:
This droid tried to rob me. I was teaching it a lesson.

ENFORCER DROID:
Li—

His vocabulator sparks and gives out.

QUI-GON:
Sounds like there's something wrong with his vocabulator.

ARATH:
There is now.

QUI-GON:
Let him go. I think you've made your point.

ARATH:
Have I, droid? Have I made my point?

The droid burbles electronically.

ARATH:
Good.

He drops the droid.

ARATH:
And don't try anything like that again. Go on. Get out of here.

The droid limps away, joints clattering.

QUI-GON:
You showed him.

ARATH:
Yes. Yes, I did. But . . . we don't need to mention this to your Master, do we? Or Rael for that matter.

QUI-GON:
I'm not sure . . .

ARATH:
You know what a stickler Dooku is for rules and regulation. Although he wasn't always. The stories I could tell you.

QUI-GON:
Perhaps we could discuss them over a drink? Or maybe a game?

ARATH:
Aren't you full of surprises? Did you have anything specific in mind?

QUI-GON:
I was thinking . . . sabacc?

ARATH:
You play?

QUI-GON:
Not exactly. I've never had the chance. Not on Coruscant. But I've watched all the holos and studied the rules . . .

ARATH:
And now you want to break some.

QUI-GON:
Can you get me into a casino?

ARATH:
Not in those robes, but what if we set up a little game of our own?

QUI-GON:
That would be great.

ARATH:
Meet me in my quarters in one hour. Don't be late.

Qui-Gon hurries off.

QUI-GON: (CALLING BACK)
I won't be. Thank you. This is going to be so great.

ARATH:
"I've watched all the holos." (SNORTS) Like stealing slime from a brain-slug.

SCENE 86. INT. ARATH'S QUARTERS.

The door chime trills.

ARATH:
Come in.

The door swishes open. Qui-Gon enters.

QUI-GON:
Where are the others?

ARATH:
They will be here, don't worry. Although I've had to ask Tanu.

QUI-GON:
The security chief?

ARATH:
Security risk, more like. But don't worry. He's harmless enough.

The door chime trills again.

ARATH:

That'll be them now. You ready for this, kid?

QUI-GON:

I was born ready.

ARATH:

Heh. Glad to hear it.

The door slides open.

DOOKU:

I hope you didn't start without us.

ARATH:

Dooku?

DOOKU:

I heard there was a game.

ARATH:

What? Here? No.

RAEL:

Drop the act, Arath. Where is it?

ARATH:

Where's what?

DOOKU:

The Solodoe seal.

ARATH:

I don't know what you're talking about.

RAEL:

Then you won't mind if we search your room.

ARATH:

You can't.

RAEL:

And why's that?

ARATH:
I've done nothing wrong.

DOOKU:
Then why is your heart racing? Qui-Gon. Are you ready to have a look around?

RAEL:
He was born ready.

Qui-Gon starts walking around.

QUI-GON:
You heard that then?

RAEL:
And you're never gonna live it down, kiddo.

ARATH:
You can't do this.

DOOKU:
Stop there.

QUI-GON:
By the bed?

DOOKU:
That's where it is, isn't it?

ARATH:
No. Why won't you believe me? There's nothing here.

RAEL:
Then what are we sensing?

DOOKU:
A guilty conscience.

Dooku turns the bed over.

ARATH:
No. Stop.

RAEL:
Will you look at that?

Dooku picks up a box and opens it.

DOOKU:
The seal.

QUI-GON:
Aren't you full of surprises?

Rael opens a hololink.

RAEL:
We have our culprit, Master Braylon.

BRAYLON: (OVER COMM)
(SIGHS) Arath. Why am I not surprised? What is it? More gambling debts?

DOOKU:
He's done this before?

BRAYLON: (OVER COMM)
Master Dooku, will you bring Diplomat Arath back to Coruscant?

DOOKU:
Happily.

RAEL:
The Solodoe will demand justice.

BRAYLON: (OVER COMM)
Return the seal and see what you can salvage from the situation. We may have to hand this over to the Republic. I doubt either the Solodoe or the Plinovians will trust us now. Braylon out.

The hologram cuts off.

RAEL:
Well, that's just great. Six months of negotiations down the refuse chute.

ARATH:
How did you know?

QUI-GON:
The mess you made of Tanu's memory.

DOOKU:
I assume you had him delete the records so no one could see you using the Force to circumvent the pressure pads. You're a disgrace.

ARATH:
Here we go. Yoda's little favorite . . .

RAEL:
I'd quit while I was ahead if I were you.

ARATH:
Why? It's not like you're going to do anything. Not really.

RAEL:
Not unless I hand you over to the casino? How much do you owe, exactly?

ARATH:
You wouldn't. Would you?

QUI-GON:
He's joking.

DOOKU:
Probably.

RAEL:
Don't worry, Arath, I'll make sure you get what's comin' to ya.

SCENE 87. EXT. ROOFTOP. RAIN.

KY NAREC: (GHOST)
And did he?

VENTRESS:
Another gap in your memories?

KY NAREC: (GHOST)
I wasn't exactly around at the time.

She swipes back and forth.

VENTRESS:
According to this, Arath was assigned to the Archives. Hardly what I'd call a punishment.

KY NAREC: (GHOST)
You've never been there. Besides, you know the Jedi. Always ready with a second chance.

VENTRESS:
More fool them.

She finds something in the datapad case.

KY NAREC: (GHOST)
What's that?

VENTRESS:
Another data disk.

KY NAREC: (GHOST)
In the pad's case? That doesn't make any sense.

VENTRESS:
Perhaps Dooku found it, when he returned to Serenno. Where's that reader?

She slides the disk into a reader. A hologram appears.

KY NAREC: (GHOST)
That's definitely Dooku.

VENTRESS:
Nearer the age he is now.

KY NAREC: (GHOST)
Go on then.

She presses play.

DOOKU: (HOLO-NARRATION)

Jenza. I realize it's been a while since we communicated, but you have a right to know what really happened over the last few days, and my part in it.

VENTRESS:

Sounds promising.

DOOKU: (HOLO-NARRATION)

If I could change what happened I would, but events were in motion long before I discovered Ramil was on Coruscant . . .

SCENE 88. INT. DOOKU'S CHAMBERS.

Dooku is binding his arm, as Lene once showed him.

DOOKU:

For the Force is strong.

For the Force is strong.

There's a knock on the door.

DOOKU:

Come.

The door slides open and Qui-Gon enters. He, too, is older, almost a Jedi Knight in his own right.

QUI-GON:

Master Dooku. I . . . Oh, I'm sorry.

DOOKU:

Don't be. I was just meditating.

QUI-GON:

Are you injured?

DOOKU:

Hmm?

QUI-GON:
Your arm. The bandages.

DOOKU:
(A SHARP LAUGH) Ah, no. It's an old habit. Nothing more.

Calleen trills nearby as Dooku pulls on his tunic.

DOOKU:
Would you mind feeding Calleen?

QUI-GON:
Of course. How long has it been since Master Kostana last saw her?

DOOKU:
I dread to think.

He ties his belt.

DOOKU: (CONT.)
Forgive me, Qui-Gon, but I thought you were assisting Master Oorallon with the Katarr adumbrature this morning.

QUI-GON:
I thought you would be happy that I'm not.

DOOKU:
You know my feelings on seers.

QUI-GON:
And yet you allow me to continue to work with Oorallon, for which I am grateful.

DOOKU:
As with the holocron of prophecy, I would rather you studied such texts with my blessing than behind my back. Is Oorallon sick?

QUI-GON:
No. We've been summoned by the Council. Master Oorallon said he would manage alone.

DOOKU:

From within his tank? Now, that's something I'd like to see.

QUI-GON:

Another time maybe. The Council was quite insistent.

DOOKU:

Do you know why?

QUI-GON:

No. I'm afraid not.

DOOKU:

Then we shouldn't keep them waiting.

SCENE 89. INT. JEDI COUNCIL CHAMBER.

Dooku and Qui-Gon enter the chamber.

BRAYLON:

Ah, Dooku, there you are.

DOOKU:

Master Braylon. Master Aerith. And Jedi Droom, too.

QUI-GON:

Congratulations on your elevation, Gretz.

GRETZ:

Thank you, Qui-Gon.

DOOKU:

You must be very proud, Jor.

JOR:

I don't think so. Pride is a dangerous emotion. We would do well to remember that.

She goes to take her seat.

QUI-GON:

Aerith never changes, does she?

GRETZ:

I honestly thought I'd be able to stop apologizing for her once I was Knighted.

DOOKU:

There is no need. Jor speaks her mind. I, for one, find that refreshing in a Council member.

Nearby, Yoda raps his stick on the floor.

YODA: (OFF-MIC)
Come. Come.

DOOKU:

Shall we?

The Council members take their seats, Dooku, Droom, and Qui-Gon standing before them.

BRAYLON:

Thank you for joining us, Master Dooku. You must be wondering why we called you here.

DOOKU:

I am naturally curious.

JOR:

Well, I'll get to the point. You are to join me in representing the Jedi at the Coruscant air rally, Dooku.

DOOKU:

I am?

JOR:

Unless you have someplace better to be. Gretz and Qui-Gon will accompany us.

GRETZ:

We would be honored, but can I ask—

DOOKU:

Why?

JOR:

You know how popular these races are. The eyes of the galaxy will be on Coruscant. It will not hurt the Jedi to be seen at such an event.

YODA:

Invited by the Candovant ambassador, Jor was.

DOOKU:

Then why am I required?

JOR:

It's quite simple. The place will be teeming with politicians and celebrities. You have a natural affinity for such . . . people.

DOOKU:

I do?

JOR:

You know you do. You're charming, Dooku. Charismatic.

BRAYLON:

Everything Jor is not.

DOOKU:

I hardly think that's fair, Master Braylon.

JOR:

Please. I am quite aware of my shortcomings. As, it appears, is my former Padawan.

QUI-GON:

(SOTTO) Shortcomings that don't include her hearing, it seems.

GRETZ:

(SOTTO) You have no idea.

BRAYLON:

There is another option. We could choose not to go.

YODA:

Master Braylon?

BRAYLON:

Why should the Jedi flaunt themselves in front of the glittering masses? It debases the Order, making us no better than . . . politicians and holostars.

JOR:

I have already accepted the invitation.

GRETZ:

With due respect, Master Braylon, the Candovants are a powerful force in galactic politics.

BRAYLON:

Politics. It's all about politics these days. Your minds are obviously made up. Very well. I'm sure you'll enjoy your day at the races. Just remember that you are Jedi.

YODA:

Trust Master Dooku to remember his place, I think we can.

DOOKU:

Naturally. We will be the souls of discretion.

SCENE 90. EXT. SPEEDER.

A speeder soars through Coruscant's air traffic.

DOOKU: (HOLO-NARRATION)
As always, I played the dutiful Jedi, but the altercation with Braylon had affected me deeper than I realized. I brooded all the way to the air track, forcing a smile as we arrived at our destination.

The soundscape changes to a large hover platform at the starting point of the race. There is the buzz of a party, loud music playing, the clinks of glasses. The partygoers have to shout slightly to be heard.

DOOKU: (HOLO-NARRATION)
I have lost count of the diplomatic functions I have attended since we last saw each other, but for all its glitz and glamour, the hospi-

tality platform was no different from the rest. The Coruscanti jazz band, the obligatory small talk with visiting dignitaries, not to mention the unenviable task of deflecting those who had made good use of the complimentary bar . . .

DIVAD MASSPUR:
(DRUNK) Hey. Divad Masspur, Coco-Town Sports. You're a Jedi, right? Can I see your sword?

DOOKU:
(SMILING THROUGH GRITTED TEETH) I'm afraid not.

DIVAD MASSPUR:
Always wanted to have a go with one of those things. In fact, I've an amazing idea for a show. Wanna hear it?

DOOKU:
Not really.

DIVAD MASSPUR:
"Celebrity LaserSabers"!

DOOKU:
*Light*sabers.

DIVAD MASSPUR:
Whatever. You could be one of the judges. We'll drop contestants into a tank of live animals, I don't know, a pack of valkoths or something, and see who makes it out alive—

DOOKU:
It sounds fascinating, but tell me, isn't that Lekar Hablis over there?

DIVAD MASSPUR:
Lekar? You're right! (RUSHING OFF) I've got to speak to him. But we'll discuss this later, yes? Yes?

DOOKU:
I look forward to it.

DIVAD MASSPUR: (OFF-MIC)

Lekar! Divad Masspur. It's an honor to meet you, buddy. Hey, did you bring your swoop bike?

QUI-GON:

And who is Lekar Hablis?

DOOKU:

The nine-time Devaronian swoopdueling champion.

QUI-GON:

I never knew you were a fan.

DOOKU:

I'm not. I overheard an overexcited Ugnaught working up the courage to ask for an autograph. But what about you? Are you enjoying yourself, Qui-Gon?

QUI-GON:

I'm not sure *enjoying* is the right word. It's very loud.

DOOKU:

A condition that will only worsen once the race is under way. From what Gretz told me, the course is marked out by those large repulsor rings. The airspeeders must pass through them all to avoid being disqualified. Some of the turns will be quite taxing.

QUI-GON:

Master, please. I know you're not happy.

DOOKU:

Not happy? About what?

QUI-GON:

About being here. In this place, with these people.

DOOKU:

Nonsense. It will be an . . . interesting diversion.

QUI-GON:

You can fool the others, but you can't fool me.

DOOKU:

There's a part of me that agrees with Master Braylon. Why *are* we here?

QUI-GON:

It's good . . . what's the term? Public relations.

DOOKU:

And why should we care what the public thinks of us? We have a job to do, and we should do it. Not be wheeled out like exhibits in a freak show.

QUI-GON:

That's a little harsh.

DOOKU:

But it's true. And what good are we doing here, sipping avedamé and making chitchat? Our predecessors pushed boundaries, explored the galaxy. They made a difference, Qui-Gon. Today . . . today we're anachronisms who only act when politicians give their assent. Half the people here think we're nothing more than a glorified police force, enforcers for the Senate.

QUI-GON:

And the other half?

DOOKU:

They don't think of us at all. We're an irrelevance.

QUI-GON:

Master, you cannot mean this. In a few short months, I will face my trials.

DOOKU:

Which you will pass with flying colors.

QUI-GON:

And what then?

DOOKU:

(AS IF THE ANSWER IS OBVIOUS) You'll become a Jedi Knight.

QUI-GON:

To what end? If what you say is true, I might as well give up now. I *want* to make a difference. I want to serve the galaxy.

DOOKU:

And you will. (SIGHS) Pay no heed to me, Qui-Gon, or to Master Braylon. We are old. Past our prime.

QUI-GON:

I hardly think that's true.

DOOKU:

Well, you should. You're the future, Qui-Gon. You and Gretz and, yes, even Ky. Master Aerith is wrong. There's no harm in feeling pride. I'm proud of you, after all. If I never do anything of note ever again, I will watch you rise through the Order, changing it forever.

QUI-GON:

For the better?

DOOKU:

(LAUGHS)

QUI-GON:

What?

DOOKU:

I asked the very same question once. A long time ago. You are wise beyond your years, Qui-Gon Jinn, with a connection to the living Force that may even one day rival Yoda's.

QUI-GON:

I doubt that.

DOOKU:

I have faith in you. And faith in the Force. As for now, maybe we should enjoy the party. I saw a droid serving opala fruit. Have you ever sampled one?

QUI-GON:
I have not.

DOOKU:
Then now is your . . . (TRAILS OFF)

QUI-GON:
Master. You look as if you've seen a ghost.

DOOKU:
Maybe I have . . .

DOOKU: (HOLO-NARRATION)
An air racer was approaching, his drive suit plastered with holographic sponsors and a wine flute in his hand. The hospitality platform was full of pilots, surrounded by equally sycophantic entourages, but this one bore a face I'd thought I would never see again . . .

RAMIL:
Well, well, well. Look who it is.

DOOKU:
Ramil.

RAMIL:
My friends, may I introduce Jedi Knight Dooku.

DOOKU:
Jedi *Master.*

RAMIL:
Master! Going up in the world, eh, Dooku? You and me both.

DOOKU:
Qui-Gon, this is Ramil of Serenno.

RAMIL:
His brother.

QUI-GON:
Brother?

RAMIL:

I know. It's shocking isn't it? I got the looks, he got the . . . well, I would say dress sense, but . . . those robes.

DOOKU:

It was good to see you again, Ramil.

RAMIL:

Don't be like that. Just a bit of fun. Can't we let bygones be bygones, and all that? Unless you're here to fix the race with your magic?

His entourage laugh vacuously.

DOOKU:

Perish the thought. And what of you, Ramil? Are you here representing our father?

RAMIL:

That old gill-goat? Not likely. Why do you think I'm wearing all this?

QUI-GON:

You're racing?

RAMIL:

Indeed I am. (NOTICES ASTROMECH) Ah. You. Droid. My glass is empty.

The droid burbles and whirs over. Ramil takes a glass from the tray.

RAMIL:

Help yourself, boys.

DOOKU:

Do you think that's wise?

RAMIL:

What?

DOOKU:

Drinking before a race.

RAMIL:

Don't you worry about me, baby brother. I have luck on my side.

DOOKU:

And what of Serenno?

RAMIL:

(DRINKING) What of it?

DOOKU:

The trouble with the workers and the droids. Was Father able to reach a resolution?

RAMIL:

(SNORTS) He can barely reach the bathroom, incontinent old grotnix.

DOOKU:

He's unwell? Shouldn't you be by his side?

RAMIL:

Dooku, excuse me for asking, but why do you even care?

DOOKU:

You're the heir of Serenno. Surely you have . . . responsibilities?

ANNOUNCEMENT:

All racers to their speeders. Repeat. All racers to their speeders.

RAMIL:

And that's the end of the conversation. What a pity. Enjoy the show, Dooku.

QUI-GON:

May the Force be with you.

Ramil and his crew swagger off.

RAMIL:

And to you, Qwee-Gin. And to you.

QUI-GON:
(WATCHING HIM GO) It's Qui-Gon, actually.

DOOKU:
Unbelievable.

QUI-GON:
Master?

DOOKU:
It's true what they say. Power is wasted on the powerful.

Gretz and Jor approach.

JOR:
There you are, Dooku.

GRETZ:
The Candovant ambassador requests our presence in his hover-pod. Apparently, it offers the best view of the race.

QUI-GON:
You sound as if you're looking forward to it, Gretz.

GRETZ:
You know . . . I am. Imagine what a Jedi could do at the controls of one of those things.

JOR:
Are you coming, Dooku?

DOOKU:
(DARKLY) Yes. After you.

SCENE 91. EXT. HOVERPOD.

COMMENTATOR: (AMPLIFIED)
Welcome one and all to the forty-eighth annual Dragonfire Air Rally, sponsored by Daystar Entertainment. It's a glorious day and our brave pilots are already at the starting line, waiting for the off.

CANDOVANT AMBASSADOR:
Rika Carno Jedana? [Would you like a drink, Jedi?]

QUI-GON:
Ah. No, thank you.

DOOKU:
What my apprentice meant to say was, yes, he'd be delighted.

QUI-GON:
Absolutely. Thank you.

He takes a glass.

DOOKU:
Refusing a drink from a Candovant is a great insult. Wars have started for less.

QUI-GON:
Thanks for the tip.

DOOKU:
I just wouldn't actually drink any if I were you. Cando brandy tastes like bantha slurry.

COMMENTATOR:
Defending his title is nine-time champion Izal Pre of Cona, who is in pole position just ahead of archrival Thrar of Coachelle Prime.

Thrar, of course, made her name in the Coachelle Burrow Runs before swapping a ground-churner for her trademark M-29 air-speeder.

Next is Drusan of Rodia, flying a Recardian C-18, and Toong Lor Kelasakuroona, former champion and the oldest competitor in the race.

At the rear we find Tanan Vetall of Nithorni and a late entry, Ramil of Serenno, who has been making waves on the Celanon Circuit. Many are suggesting that it is Ramil and not Thrar who could be the real challenger to Pre's crown.

JOR: (TALKING OVER THE END OF THE COMMENTATOR)
Serenno? Isn't that where you come from, Dooku?

DOOKU:
Hm-mm. Yes.

CANDOVANT AMBASSADOR:
Kira caravel von manarecan, Jedana-Mastera . . . [Then we know who you will be rooting for, Master Jedi . . .]

DOOKU:
Don't worry. I will be rooting for all the pilots, Ambassador.

COMMENTATOR:
And the track coordinator has confirmed that the course is clear. Coruscant, are you ready to see the greatest rally in the Galactic Core?

A cheer goes up from the crowd.

COMMENTATOR:
I said: Coruscant, are you ready?

An even bigger cheer.

COMMENTATOR:
Then, pilots, start your engines . . .

Airspeeder engines whine, ready to race.

There are three beeps and then a longer, shriller tone as the air-speeders scream from the starting line.

COMMENTATOR:
And they're off!

We stay with the airspeeders, engines shrieking as they zip around the course, passing through the rings.

COMMENTATOR:
And Pre holds the lead as they speed through the first ring, heading into the Razda straight.

Thrar is on Pre's fin, already pushing to take the Arcona on the bend. And at the back we have Vetall positioning herself right in front of Ramil's T-22. The Serennian can't get past.

JOR:
I've never seen speeders move so fast. The holocams can barely keep up.

QUI-GON:
Can you see, Master?

DOOKU:
Yes. The view is . . . quite satisfactory, thank you.

Back to the speeders who roar on, banking in the air.

COMMENTATOR:
Would you look at that—Ramil of Serenno has passed Tanan Vetall. I thought he was going to plow straight into the marker, but he's leveled up and is accelerating wildly. He passes Drusan above the Karflo Tower and takes the corner to bear down on Kelasaku-roona.

This is thrilling flying from Ramil. Kelasakuroona is swerving in front of the T-22. Ramil can't get past and . . . yes. Ramil of Se-renno has thrown himself into a barrel roll, passing over the head of the former champion. Kelasakuroona can't see Ramil and the Serennian's away, rocketing along the Hesperidium straight to chase down Thrar and Pre.

As we near the end of the first lap, our sponsors would like me to remind you that bets can still be placed until the beginning of the final lap. I for one would recommend a flutter on Ramil. I haven't seen flying like this since the days of Vearacki Dak.

QUI-GON:
Your brother is quite a pilot, Master.

DOOKU:
He is. I hate to say it, but I'm actually impressed.

QUI-GON:

Careful now. You almost sound as though you're enjoying yourself.

DOOKU:

Perish the thought.

The airspeeders thunder past the hoverpod.

COMMENTATOR:

And Ramil hangs on Thrar's tail, but the Lepi won't let him pass. Halfway around the second lap and Kelasakuroona has dropped back into last place, Tanan Vetall picking up the pace. But neither of them stands a chance of catching up with the leaders.

Pre thunders through the Lefex turn, coming up on the Tyerell Ring. He's pulling in hard and—

Pre's airspeeder hits the ring, exploding on impact.

COMMENTATOR:

By the stars! Terrible scenes here on the Dragonfire Circuit as Izal Pre crashes out of the forty-eighth Coruscant rally. His speeder is in flames as it plummets into the Bindai district, fire-skimmers rushing to offer assistance.

There's another explosion as it crashes far below.

COMMENTATOR:

Back on the track, the race continues. Thrar and Ramil are neck and neck, Ramil pulling ahead. What incredible flying. Thrar can't stop him. Just a few more seconds to place your bets and . . . that's it, we're into the final lap and Ramil takes the lead. No. Wait. He's losing ground. Thrar is coming up on his flank and . . . yes, incredible. Thrar has taken the lead.

GRETZ:

What's Ramil doing? He should've kept his throttle open on that last pass.

DOOKU:

I had no idea you were such an expert.

GRETZ:

I've flown enough interceptors.

QUI-GON:

It *is* curious, though. Ramil was looking so strong.

JOR:

Perhaps he's experiencing repulsor problems.

DOOKU: (HOLO-NARRATION)

I had no idea what was going through Ramil's head on that final lap. Maybe it was the roar of the crowd, or the thought of the prize. Or maybe he caught sight of me as he rocketed past the ambassador's hoverpod. I would have been a blur, there one second, gone the next, but perhaps it was just enough to spur him on . . .

COMMENTATOR:

This is phenomenal! Ramil is gaining once more. There's nothing Thrar can do as they zoom down the straight. It's into the Calocour bend and yes, Ramil takes the lead. There can be no doubt. Ramil of Serenno is minutes away from lifting the Dragonfire Trophy. It's on to the Tyerell Ring, Ramil with a twenty-seven-second lead.

There's an explosion on Ramil's speeder.

COMMENTATOR:

And disaster strikes for the second time over Bindai. Smoke is billowing from Ramil's T-22.

Ramil's speeder drops from the sky.

COMMENTATOR:

The leader has gone into a dive and . . .

There is another explosion from the speeder.

COMMENTATOR:
Yes, he's out of the race. Thrar has taken the lead, Drusan pushing for second place. The emergency team has activated a tractor web, but there is no guarantee that they can save Ramil.

On the hoverpod, Dooku races for a speeder.

GRETZ:
Master Dooku. Where are you going?

DOOKU:
Stay here, Qui-Gon.

QUI-GON:
That's not going to happen. Ambassador, may we borrow a speeder?

CANDOVANT AMBASSADOR:
Fara-caneeva mareen? [Where are you going?]

QUI-GON:
We'll take that as a yes?

DOOKU: (HOLO-NARRATION)
We dropped away from the pod, the race thundering on above our heads.

QUI-GON:
(SHOUTING OVER THE DIN OF THE SWOOP BIKES) Do you think he survived, Master?

DOOKU:
(SHOUTING) There is no way to tell.

COMMENTATOR: (ABOVE)
And Thrar of Coachelle Prime has won the forty-eighth Dragon-fire Rally. The crowd is going wild.

QUI-GON:
(SHOUTING) I see them. There. Looks like they brought him down safely.

Dooku and Qui-Gon zoom in, their speeder screeching to a halt.

There are sirens, and the sound of a burning speeder in the background.

POLICE DROID:
Please stay back. There is nothing to see.

DOOKU:
Not for you maybe.

DOOKU: (HOLO-NARRATION)
With a flick of my wrist, I sent the security droid flying into its patrol ship.

POLICE DROID:
Hey!

QUI-GON:
Master!

The police droid gets up.

POLICE DROID:
Assaulting a security droid is a serious offense.

QUI-GON:
He didn't lay a finger on you.

POLICE DROID:
So, what? I tripped?

QUI-GON:
(CALLING BACK AS HE RUNS PAST) Accidents will happen.

DOOKU: (HOLO-NARRATION)
I ran up to the medics, who had already transferred Ramil onto a med-splint.

DOOKU:
Ramil.

MED DROID #1:
Careful.

RAMIL:
(WEAK) Dooku.

DOOKU:
How bad is it?

MED DROID #1:
Who wants to know?

DOOKU:
I'm his brother.

An alarm goes off on the med-splint.

MED DROID #2:
He's going into cardiac arrest.

MED DROID #1:
We need to get him into a shock-cot. Stand back please.

The med-splint whines as it trundles onto the ambulance.

QUI-GON:
Master. We should let them do their jobs.

DOOKU:
Where are you taking him?

The ambulance's ramp rises.

DOOKU:
Which medcenter?

The ambulance takes off.

DOOKU:
Why wouldn't they answer?

QUI-GON:
We can find out.

DOOKU:
Something isn't right here. You sense it, don't you?

QUI-GON:
I'm not sure.

DOOKU:
We must examine his speeder.

The police droid hurries up, putting himself between the speeder and Dooku.

POLICE DROID:
Oh no, no, no. That's evidence, that is.

DOOKU:
But you're already moving it.

POLICE DROID:
If you wish to speak to an investigator, I suggest you submit a request to Jaffkee House.

DOOKU:
I'll do more than that.

SCENE 92. INT. CSF PRECINCT HOUSE. RECEPTION.

DOOKU: (HOLO-NARRATION)
I had never stepped foot in a Coruscant precinct house, and pray I never will again.

Doors slide open and Dooku and Qui-Gon enter.

DESK SERGEANT:
Can I help you, sir?

DOOKU:
A crashed airspeeder was brought in. A T-22.

DESK SERGEANT:
From the Dragonfire, yeah.

QUI-GON:
Where is it, Sergeant?

DESK SERGEANT:
In the evidence bay, but—

DOOKU:
You will buzz us through.

DESK SERGEANT:
I will buzz you through.

He presses a button, and a door slides open.

DOOKU:
You will forget we were here.

They hurry through the door.

DESK SERGEANT:
I will forget . . . Wait? Who the hell am I talking to?

The door shuts.

SCENE 93. INT. CSF PRECINCT HOUSE. CORRIDOR.

We hear them rushing through the corridors.

QUI-GON:
Are you sure this is a good idea, Master?

DOOKU:
No.

QUI-GON:
Interfering with a CSF investigation . . .

DOOKU:
We're not interfering. Yet.

DOOKU: (HOLO-NARRATION)
The doors to the evidence bay slid open to reveal three Trandoshans manhandling Ramil's speeder onto a junk-skiff.

QUI-GON:
That doesn't look like a CSF transport.

DOOKU:
And those don't look like CSF agents. You, stand away from the speeder.

They ignite their lightsabers.

DOOKU: (HOLO-NARRATION)
The Trandoshans took one look at our lightsabers and fired their repulsors . . .

TRANDOSHAN:
Lucumba! [Move out!]

The transporter takes off. Its repulsors are noisy, the chassis rattling.

DOOKU:
They're getting away.

QUI-GON:
Not if we "requisition" a security swoop.

DOOKU:
Now you're thinking like a Jedi. I'll drive.

They jump on the back of the swoop bike and zoom out of the building.

DOOKU: (HOLO-NARRATION)
Within seconds, we were running the gauntlet of Coruscant's rush hour.

Traffic sweeps the other way, horns blaring.

QUI-GON:
Watch out. You nearly clipped that one.

DOOKU:
I'm finding it quite exhilarating.

Qui-Gon's comm sounds. He answers it.

QUI-GON:
Qui-Gon here.

GRETZ: (OVER COMM)
Jinn. Where are you?

QUI-GON:
Chasing a gang of Trandoshans toward The Works.

GRETZ: (OVER COMM)
You're *what*?

QUI-GON:
They've taken the crashed speeder.

One of the Trandoshans fires at them. Dooku avoids the blast.

GRETZ: (OVER COMM)
Was that blasterfire?

DOOKU:
I don't think they like being followed.

QUI-GON:
They're dropping into the lower levels.

DOOKU:
Then so shall we.

The swoop drops down after the criminals.

GRETZ: (OVER COMM)
The Council won't be happy about this.

QUI-GON:
Sorry, Gretz. I can barely hear you. Must be interference from the foundries.

GRETZ: (OVER COMM)
You need to return to the Temp—

Qui-Gon kills the transmission.

DOOKU:
Technical problems?

QUI-GON:
What are the chances?

More blaster bolts whistle by.

QUI-GON:
They really don't want to be caught, do they?

DOOKU:
We'll lose them if they reach the pits.

QUI-GON:
Do you have a plan?

DOOKU:
You take the controls.

QUI-GON:
That's it?

DOOKU:
Not quite.

DOOKU: (HOLO-NARRATION)
I threw myself from the swoop bike, using the Force to propel myself down toward the fleeing skiff.

The largest Trandoshan opened fire as I landed on the back of Ramil's flier.

Dooku ignites his lightsaber.

DOOKU: (HOLO-NARRATION)
The blast ricocheted from my blade to strike the pilot between his scaled shoulder blades.

The skiff spun out of control, smashing into a factory ledge. I threw myself to safety as Ramil's speeder tumbled into the bowels of the planet, taking the first Trandoshan with it. With his compatriots dead, the gang's sole survivor ran into the derelict foundry.

DOOKU:
Stop!

DOOKU: (HOLO-NARRATION)
I threw up a hand, knocking the Trandoshan from his feet. The brute scrabbled for his blast rifle as I pulled him toward me.

TRANDOSHAN:
Jolumba! [No!]

Trandoshan claws screech on the concrete floor.

DOOKU:
For your sake, I hope you speak Basic.

He lifts the Trandoshan from the floor.

DOOKU: (HOLO-NARRATION)
His eyes bulged as I lifted him in front of me.

TRANDOSHAN:
How are you doing this?

DOOKU:
Have you never heard of the Jedi? Do you not know what we can do?

TRANDOSHAN:
Put me down.

DOOKU:
Only when you tell me what you were doing with that speeder.

TRANDOSHAN:
I can't.

DOOKU:
You don't want me to force you to talk.

Force lightning crackles over his hands.

TRANDOSHAN:
What is that!

DOOKU:
Something I've been fighting for years. Something I can control. Most of the time.

TRANDOSHAN:
Rek ka luradan. [The Storm of Nightfire.]

DOOKU:
Tell me who sent you.

QUI-GON: (OFF-MIC, SEARCHING)
Master?

DOOKU:
Quickly!

The Force lightning crackles.

TRANDOSHAN:
The race was fixed. The Serennian was supposed to lose.

DOOKU:
Why?

TRANDOSHAN:
Are you kidding? The bets were flooding in. The boss was going to make a killing.

DOOKU:
So what happened?

TRANDOSHAN:
The boss took out insurance, just in case the Serennian forgot his part of the deal. A detonator in the fuel tank.

DOOKU:
Who is your master?

TRANDOSHAN:
I can't tell you. She'd kill me.

The crackling intensifies.

DOOKU:
And you think I won't?

DOOKU: (HOLO-NARRATION)
A siren echoed around the foundry, lights flashing through the broken glass.

Sirens blare across the factory. Police droids run in the distance and, with them, Qui-Gon.

QUI-GON: (OFF-MIC, CALLING)
Master!

DOOKU:
Qui-Gon! (SOTTO) For the Force is strong. For the Force is strong.

The crackling stops.

POLICE DROID: (AMPLIFIED)
Drop the Trandoshan. I repeat, drop the Trandoshan.

DOOKU:
You can have him.

Dooku throws the Trandoshan to the ground.

TRANDOSHAN:
(GRUNTS)

DOOKU:
He has just confessed to race-rigging and sabotage.

TRANDOSHAN:
Get me away from him. He's *fesssellis* [crazy].

Qui-Gon runs up.

QUI-GON:
Master, the Council has been trying to contact us. They don't sound happy.

Dooku's comm chirps.

DOOKU:
They never are.

He activates his comm.

DOOKU:
Dooku here.

JOR: (OVER COMM)
This is Aerith. Where the hell are you, Dooku?

DOOKU:
In the underground. We have apprehended the saboteurs and are about to investigate the syndicate behind the attack.

BRAYLON: (OVER COMM)
No, Dooku. You are to return to the Temple.

DOOKU:
Braylon?

BRAYLON:
This is a matter for the Coruscant Security Force, not the Jedi.

DOOKU:
But—

JOR: (OVER COMM)
Dooku, why didn't you tell me that the crashed pilot was your brother?

DOOKU:
I didn't think it was important.

JOR: (OVER COMM)
Important? You're emotionally compromised, Dooku. Return to the Temple immediately.

The comm cuts out.

DOOKU:
And it appears I am overruled.

Behind them the Trandoshan runs.

QUI-GON:
Master, the Trandoshan!

POLICE DROID:
He's getting away. Open fire.

DOOKU:
No, wait.

A blast rings out.

TRANDOSHAN:
(DIES)

His body slumps to the floor.

DOOKU:
You could have stunned him!

POLICE DROID:
I thought we were.

DOOKU:
This cannot stand.

QUI-GON:
The Council said we weren't to interfere.

DOOKU:
Then the Council is wrong.

SCENE 94. INT. CSF PRECINCT HOUSE. MORGUE.

Inspector Sartori walks into the morgue, his boots clicking against the tiles. A mortuary droid—QC-ME—turns to him.

QC-ME:
Inspector Sartori. We don't see you in the morgue very often.

SARTORI:

I wanted to examine the suspect, Q-See. What a mess.

QC-ME:

Death would have been instantaneous. I assume there is going to be an inquest.

SARTORI:

I've already filed the report. A malfunction in the police droids. I've had them sent for reprogramming.

The doors swish open behind them. Dooku and Qui-Gon enter.

DOOKU:

Tell me, Inspector, is that normal procedure when a prisoner is killed?

SARTORI:

What the— How did you get in here?

QUI-GON:

You have a very obliging desk sergeant.

DOOKU:

You will surrender the Trandoshan's body to the Jedi.

QC-ME:

This is most irregular.

DOOKU:

So is this.

Dooku activates his lightsaber and slices QC-ME in two, keeping the weapon activated.

SARTORI:

That droid was Coruscant Security property.

DOOKU:

Then why don't you send it to reprogramming.

Sartori pulls a blaster.

SARTORI:

I could arrest you, Master Dooku. You and your Padawan.

DOOKU:

A blaster. Really? You think that will work against this?

He brings up his lightsaber.

DOOKU:

Oh, and another thing.

He pushes out with the Force. Sartori is thrown across the morgue to crash into a wall.

DOOKU:

How do you know my name?

SARTORI:

You can't do this to me. I'm an inspector.

Sartori starts to gag, caught in a Force choke.

DOOKU:

I'll tell you what you are. Nothing. I could snuff you out in an instant.

QUI-GON:

(WARNING) Master . . .

DOOKU:

Tell me who was behind the sabotage. Who's paying you?

SARTORI:

(BARELY ABLE TO BREATHE) No one.

QUI-GON:

Master, this isn't right.

DOOKU:

You gave the Trandoshans access to my brother's T-22. You covered up their crime, ordering your droids to shoot to kill. I want to know why. This is your last chance.

SARTORI:
(CHOKING)

QUI-GON:
Master. Stop!

Dooku holds the gagging man for a moment longer and then . . .

DOOKU:
Oh, very well.

He releases him. Sartori drops to the floor.

SARTORI:
(HOARSE) You're . . . insane.

DOOKU:
I will get the truth, one way or another, Inspector.

SARTORI:
Is that a promise or a threat?

DOOKU:
It's both.

Dooku sweeps from the morgue.

QUI-GON:
Master. Wait.

Qui-Gon runs after him.

SCENE 95. EXT. OUTSIDE THE PRECINCT HOUSE.

Atmosphere: A busy street. Dooku sweeps out the doors, marching down the steps. Qui-Gon bursts out after him.

QUI-GON:
Dooku. Stop.

He grabs Dooku's arm.

QUI-GON:
I said, stop!

DOOKU:
(LAUGHS)

QUI-GON:
I can't see anything to laugh about. You could have killed him.

DOOKU:
Qui-Gon, Qui-Gon, Qui-Gon. I must congratulate you.

QUI-GON:
What?

DOOKU:
You played your part beautifully. The loyal Padawan concerned that his grieving Master is going too far.

QUI-GON:
Because you were.

DOOKU:
Was I?

A swoop bike zooms from a nearby alley up into the air.

DOOKU:
Did you see who was on that bike?

QUI-GON:
Inspector Sartori.

DOOKU:
Yes, I threatened the inspector. Yes, I may have even hurt him a little, and for that, I am sorry. But I was never out of control.

QUI-GON:
You were applying pressure—

DOOKU:
So he would scurry off to whoever has him in their pocket.

QUI-GON:
Then we should follow him!

DOOKU:
(SMILING) We already are.

SCENE 96. EXT. THE SKIES OF CORUSCANT.

Sartori's swoop bike roars as he activates a comm bud in his ear.

SARTORI:
(PITCHING UP OVER THE REPULSOR NOISE) Bagara! I need to see Cenevax now. (BEAT) I don't care if she's busy. The Jedi are on to me. I need protection.

A convor flaps in front of the bike, cawing loudly.

SARTORI:
(CRIES OUT)

He slews the swoop bike across traffic. There's the blare of a horn.

SARTORI:
Stang!

He brings the bike under control.

SARTORI:
What was that? No, I'm fine. It was just a stupid convor. Flew right in front of me. Just make sure Cenevax knows I'm coming. Sartori out.

The comm beeps.

SARTORI:
Stupid bird.

He roars off, and for a moment we stay with the convor—Calleen—flying along.

DOOKU: (HOLO-NARRATION)

The inspector never questioned why an Altiri convor was flying along Coruscant's busiest airlane, or why a nondescript flier was rising up to join the flow of traffic, a Jedi Master at the controls.

Dooku's flier rises up, and we hear the bleep of a tracker.

QUI-GON:

(LAUGHING) A tracker in Calleen's collar.

DOOKU:

A Jedi is prepared for every eventuality, Qui-Gon.

QUI-GON:

And you're okay flying while practicing beast control?

DOOKU:

Animal kinship, my dear Padawan, and of course I am.

QUI-GON:

You never fail to amaze me.

DOOKU:

I'm glad to hear it. Jedi are conspicuous, Qui-Gon, even in this much traffic—

QUI-GON:

But no one would suspect a lone owl.

DOOKU: (HOLO-NARRATION)

The bird led us to the Hythan Quarter, where towering chimneys belched smoke into the darkened sky. Calleen swept over production plants and factories, coming to rest on a window ledge high above Sartori's cooling speeder. We were close behind, our skimmer slowing near a buzzing laser fence.

QUI-GON:

(WHISPER) It looks like it runs all the way around the building.

DOOKU:

(WHISPER) We should be able to leap it easily enough.

QUI-GON:

(WHISPER) Without being spotted by the guards?

DOOKU:

(WHISPER) They'll never even know we're here, thanks to that grog can.

QUI-GON:

What grog can?

A drink can clatters across the street.

GUARD:

What was that?

QUI-GON:

(SMILING) Litterbug.

DOOKU: (HOLO-NARRATION)

We vaulted the fence and within minutes were inside, the heavy doors offering little in the way of resistance to a burning lightsaber. We followed our senses, finally reaching a storeroom that had been converted to a vast treasure trove.

Inspector Sartori paced up and down as a Jenet scampered over a mountain of stolen treasure.

Hiding behind thick velvet drapes, we listened to Sartori's panicked whining . . .

SCENE 97. INT. CENEVAX'S HOARD.

Atmosphere: There is the constant chinking of coins and golden treasures as Cenevax scrambles through her hoard, picking up trinkets and discarding them, her movements quick and scurrying, like the giant rodent she is.

SARTORI:

Are you even listening to me?

CENEVAX:

Like Cenevax has a choice.

SARTORI:

The Jedi came to the precinct. They threatened me.

CENEVAX:

Threatened you, did they? Poor little Inspector-man. Scared was you? Yer blood pumping, yer little boom-box racing? Boom-boom-boom-boom.

SARTORI:

I thought they were going to kill me! You said the Jedi wouldn't be a problem. You promised me.

Cenevax continues to rifle through her hoard.

CENEVAX:

Cenevax promised you, eh? Promises, promises. So easy to break. You promised her, Sartori. Cenevax pays you, you keep her enemies away. Remember that promise, do ya?

SARTORI:

And I have. It isn't easy, you know. Especially when you blow up a speeder with the entire planet watching.

CENEVAX:

He made promises, too, the Serennian, in his furs and his cape. What do you want from Cenevax, Inspector-man? What-what-what?

SARTORI:

I want you to clean up your mess.

CENEVAX:

Clean up the mess. Yes, that would be nice.

She finds something in the hoard.

CENEVAX:

Come here, Inspector-man. Cenevax has found something. Something shiny.

SARTORI:

I don't care about your baubles. I care about my welfare.

CENEVAX:

Welfare, yes. Important it is. Vital. Come and see. Come and see what Cenevax has found. You'll like it. It'll help.

SARTORI:

I don't see how.

He reluctantly walks over, coins crunching like shingles beneath his feet.

CENEVAX:

Nice and shiny. Heavy, too. What do you think?

SARTORI:

It's just an old—

Cenevax whirls around, clubbing him with the lump of precious metal.

CENEVAX:

(BESTIAL ROAR AS SHE HITS HIM).

Sartori goes down, crashing into the treasure.

CENEVAX:

An old trinket box. Told you it was heavy.

SARTORI:

(GROANS)

DOOKU: (HOLO-NARRATION)

Qui-Gon moved to intervene, but I placed a hand on his shoulder, holding him back.

CENEVAX:

Cenevax can't remember where she got it. And now you've gotten blood all over it.

She hits him again with the box.

CENEVAX:

Ruined it is, like you've ruined Cenevax. Leading Jedi to her nest.

She punctuates each of her words with another strike.

CENEVAX:

How. Could. You. Be. So. Stupid?

DOOKU: (HOLO-NARRATION)

It turns out I had been wrong to wait. Trandoshans came out of nowhere, surrounding us before we could reach for our lightsabers.

CENEVAX:

(CALLING OUT) There's no point hiding. Cenevax can smell you. Yeah. She smelled you the moment you sneaked into her den.

Dooku and Qui-Gon are led out.

QUI-GON:

You won't get away with this, Cenevax.

CENEVAX:

Get away with what exactly?

QUI-GON:

We just watched you murder a CSF inspector.

CENEVAX:

Watched it, did you? Yeah. But you didn't stop Cenevax, did you? Strange that. Besides . . .

She kicks Sartori, who groans.

CENEVAX:

He's not dead. Not yet. Take their pretty swords.

QUI-GON:

You can try.

DOOKU:

Let them take them.

QUI-GON:
But Master . . .

DOOKU:
Do it.

CENEVAX:
See. The old one, he has brains.

The Trandoshans grab the lightsabers.

CENEVAX:
That's it. Bring 'em to Cenevax.

She snatches the hilts from the Trandoshans, examining them.

CENEVAX:
Oooh. Very nice. Very nice indeed. Cenevax has heard there's crystals inside, yeah? (GIGGLES) Maybe she add 'em to her collection. Quite the prize.

DOOKU:
You're not going to win, you know.

CENEVAX:
(LAUGHS) Typical Jedi. But you're not in yer Temple now, oh-no-no-no. You'll disappear. How sad. And you won't be missed. Oh no. Not you. Too much like yer brother . . . Yeah, Cenevax knows who you are, Dooku. You and Ramil. Like clones in a vat the pair of you. He couldn't obey orders, neither. Paid the price for it, too.

DOOKU:
My brother lives.

CENEVAX:
Not for long. They told you not to interfere, your Council. They told you leave well alone. But no. You just had to stick your nose in Cenevax's business, didn't you?

QUI-GON:
How do you know what the Council said?

DOOKU:

Because her influence goes far beyond corrupt inspectors.

CENEVAX:

Oh, Cenevax has spies everywhere.

DOOKU:

As do I. (CALLING) Now, Calleen!

DOOKU: (HOLO-NARRATION)

With a screech, the convor swept down from on high, talons bared.

CENEVAX:

Sith spawn! What is that?

The bird flaps around the startled Jenet.

CENEVAX:

Get it away. Get it away.

DOOKU: (HOLO-NARRATION)

The Trandoshans' scatterguns came up, but before they could take a shot, we summoned our lightsabers, igniting the blades in midair.

The two lightsabers blaze, cutting down the guards, who thud to the floor.

There's a pained squawk from the convor, who falls silent.

QUI-GON:

Master. The convor.

CENEVAX:

Tasty. Yes, very tasty indeed.

Cenevax throws the bird's limp body aside.

DOOKU:

You'll pay for that.

CENEVAX:

How? You'll never get out alive.

Cenevax scampers on the treasure hoard to get away.

QUI-GON:
She's running.

DOOKU:
She won't get far.

DOOKU: (HOLO-NARRATION)
I threw out a hand, stopping the Jenet in her tracks. She clawed at her treasure as I hauled her back.

Cenevax scrambles as she's pulled back, trying to hold on to her hoard.

CENEVAX:
No. Stop it. Stop it.

DOOKU:
Not until you've told me the truth.

CENEVAX:
What are you doing?

DOOKU:
It's an impressive hoard you've collected. You're obviously very fond of it. Enough gold to drown in.

DOOKU: (HOLO-NARRATION)
I could feel Qui-Gon's eyes on me. I had played this game before to get what we wanted from Sartori, but was I going too far? Would I really smother Cenevax with her own riches? He didn't know, and the question was, did I?

QUI-GON:
(WARNING) Master.

DOOKU:
She has a contact on the Jedi Council.

CENEVAX:
You have no proof.

DOOKU:
Tell me who it is!

CENEVAX:
You won't kill Cenevax. You're Jedi. It's not in your nature. You're weak.

There's a slight crunch of metal as Dooku presses her into the gold.

DOOKU:
Are you sure about that?

SCENE 98. INT. JEDI COUNCIL CHAMBER.

DOOKU: (HOLO-NARRATION)
Unaware of what had happened not three districts from their Chamber, the Jedi Council was in session, although their deliberations were about to be interrupted . . .

Dooku and Qui-Gon enter the chamber.

YODA:
Master Dooku.

JOR:
About time. We summoned you, Dooku. Did you not receive the message?

DOOKU:
The message was received, Master Aerith. Loud and clear.

Dooku drops Calleen's body on the floor in front of them.

SINUBE:
Is that . . .

QUI-GON:
Lene Kostana's convor, Master Sinube.

JOR:
What happened to it?

DOOKU:
A good question. Perhaps you would like to examine her body.

BRAYLON:
We haven't time for these games, Dooku.

QUI-GON:
Games, Master Braylon? The bird is dead.

YODA:
See that, we can.

DOOKU:
But can you see the tooth marks, Master Yoda? The tooth marks of a Jenet. One of you had dealings with the creature who did this, the creature who tried to kill Ramil of Serenno earlier today.

JOR:
That is a serious accusation.

DOOKU:
For a serious crime. The betrayal of the Jedi Order. Who will admit it? Who will take responsibility?

SINUBE:
Master Dooku. I understand that you are upset.

DOOKU:
Upset?

SINUBE:
Ramil is your brother, after all . . .

DOOKU:
Only by blood.

SINUBE:
But this is not the way. If you suspect there is a traitor on the Council, you should—

DOOKU:

What? Call the Temple Guards? An excellent idea. (CALLING) Bring her in.

Temple Guards march in, dragging Cenevax with them.

CENEVAX:

Get off Cenevax. Let go.

JOR:

What is the meaning of this?

DOOKU:

Cenevax runs an unlicensed gambling ring. She paid my brother to lose the race, and when it looked as if he was about to renege on the deal . . .

JOR:

She scuttled his flier.

CENEVAX:

You can't prove anything.

DOOKU:

Maybe not yet. But we will. We will prove that you have officials in every corner of the Republic. Governors. Inspectors . . . even Jedi.

Who is it, Cenevax? You wouldn't tell me in your lair—

CENEVAX:

Only 'cos you didn't have the guts to hurt Cenevax.

DOOKU:

As you quite rightly pointed out, it is not the Jedi way, but neither is accepting bribes.

CENEVAX:

Cenevax is saying nothing!

QUI-GON:

Fortunately, you don't have to.

DOOKU:

The traitor's own feelings betray her. I can sense her guilt from here.

Dooku activates his lightsaber.

JOR:

Dooku! What are you doing?

DOOKU:

Master Braylon. I've known you all my life. Will you lie to me now? Will you lie to all of us?

SINUBE:

Braylon?

Braylon rises, her lightsaber blazing into life.

BRAYLON:

Do you intend to fight me, Dooku? To strike me down where I stand?

DOOKU:

I intend only to bring you to justice.

Braylon extinguishes her blade.

BRAYLON:

It's true. All of it. I have . . . looked the other way for years, at Madame Cenevax's behest.

JOR:

But why? You have no need for money, dirty or otherwise.

BRAYLON:

She didn't pay me. She didn't have to.

QUI-GON:

Then what was it?

DOOKU:

(REALIZING) Blackmail. What did she have on you, Braylon? What could possibly be so damning that you would abuse your position on the Council?

SCENE 99. INT. JEDI ARCHIVES.

Atmosphere as before.

DOOKU: (HOLO-NARRATION)

Braylon's confession shook the Council to the core. I shared their dismay. We pride ourselves on being one with the Force, and yet none of us had sensed the deception in our midst. Cenevax was dismissed, while Qui-Gon and I had business to attend to in the Archives.

DOOKU:

Arath.

ARATH:

Dooku. I . . . what are you doing here?

DOOKU:

I'm afraid your secret is out.

ARATH:

I . . . I don't know what you mean.

DOOKU:

Cenevax has confessed.

QUI-GON:

We know how you ran up debts with her, Arath. What was it this time? Sabacc? Pazaak?

ARATH:

Batana.

DOOKU:

The trickster's game. Naturally. And then you attempted to talk your way out of it. What was it? You could bring her entire operation crashing down.

QUI-GON:

You have friends in high places.

DOOKU:

The Jedi Council, for instance. But for once, you weren't lying. What did Cenevax do, Arath? Threaten you? Attempt to blackmail you?

QUI-GON:

Until you gave her a bigger target.

DOOKU:

Your own mother.

ARATH:

You don't know what you're talking about.

DOOKU:

Don't I? It's amazing what traits are passed from generation to generation. Mannerisms. Tics. Even emotional states. When confronted Braylon reacted exactly as you did on Station Zeta, before you were sent home, where she could protect you, as she has all your life.

QUI-GON:

How long have you known?

ARATH:

That I was hers? After Zeta, I suppose. I had always seen the disappointment in her eyes, but suddenly . . .

QUI-GON:

It made sense.

DOOKU:

You confronted her.

ARATH:

She was clever, I'll give her that. A Seeker, away for years at a time. Who would question when she returned with yet another baby, strong in the Force? Nobody even batted an eye when she decided to stay, to join the teaching staff . . .

QUI-GON:
All so she could be near you.

DOOKU:
Her son.

ARATH:
What's going to happen to her?

DOOKU:
She will face the Council of Judgment. As will you.

ARATH:
And Cenevax?

Yoda arrives with Temple Guards.

YODA:
None of your concern, Cenevax is.

ARATH:
(LAUGHS) You brought guards. Did you expect me to run?

DOOKU:
I'm sorry, Arath.

ARATH:
Somehow I doubt that.

The guards lead Arath away.

DOOKU:
Go with them, Qui-Gon.

QUI-GON:
Master?

DOOKU:
Make sure they treat him well.

QUI-GON:
As you wish.

Qui-Gon leaves Dooku with Yoda.

YODA:

No harm will come to him.

DOOKU:

Can we be sure? (LAUGHS) Can we be sure of anything anymore?

YODA:

You are troubled, old friend.

DOOKU:

I know what it's like to keep a secret.

YODA:

Hm. I remember.

DOOKU:

She never told anyone, Yoda. All these years, and she kept it to herself.

YODA:

Yes. Worrying, it is.

DOOKU:

Worrying? It's tragic. One of our own makes a mistake, and what happens? Does she come to us? No. Does she confide in us? No. She's afraid. Of what we might do, to her. And to her child.

YODA:

Help. That is what we would have done. What we have always done.

DOOKU:

That's easy to say now.

YODA:

Monsters, we are not. Feelings we have.

DOOKU:

Feelings we suppress.

YODA:

Trusted us, Braylon should have. Different things would be. Learn from this we must.

DOOKU:

And what of Cenevax?

YODA:

To the Citadel, the Jenet will be sent. Dismantled, her operation will be.

DOOKU:

The Citadel? Only Jedi are sent there. (LAUGHS BITTERLY, REAL-IZING WHAT'S HAPPENING) We're not going to the authorities with any of this, are we? What am I saying? We are the authorities.

YODA:

Like this, I do not. But understand, you must . . .

DOOKU:

Oh, I understand, Yoda. I understand all too well.

YODA:

Meditate on all that has passed, I will. And as for you, sorry for your loss I am.

DOOKU:

My loss?

YODA:

Lene's convor. Know how much the bird meant to you, I do.

DOOKU:

Yes. Yes, she did. But what is it you say? We should always let go of the past . . .

SCENE 100. EXT. ROOFTOP. RAIN.

VENTRESS: (NARRATION)

Dooku's gaze didn't waver as he concluded his message . . .

DOOKU: (HOLO-NARRATION)

I understand that Ramil is being transferred back to Serenno. I wish him a speedy recovery. I sense much turmoil in him. Perhaps finally, he will find peace.

As for me, I have decided to accept a position on the Council. Change must come to the Order, and it must come from within.

May the Force be with you, Jenza. Always.

The hologram switches off. Ventress removes the disk.

VENTRESS:
Dooku on the Jedi Council.

KY NAREC: (GHOST)
Is it so difficult to imagine?

VENTRESS:
In all honesty, yes. But what do I know? I'm talking to a dead man.

KY NAREC: (GHOST)
You believe it really is me then?

VENTRESS:
I don't know what to believe.

She notices something shifting on the roof. Servos whine on the street below.

VENTRESS:
But now isn't the time.

KY NAREC: (GHOST)
What is it?

VENTRESS:
Someone's finally decided to come home.

VENTRESS: (NARRATION)
My quarry is trudging toward his door, servos whining so loud that I can hear them from the rooftop. I leap down, drawing my lightsabers as I land behind him.

Her lightsabers ignite. She thuds down behind the Crolute.

VENTRESS:
Glute. I've been waiting for you.

GLUTE:
Wha— Who are you?

VENTRESS: (NARRATION)
The Crolute's voice is little more than a gargle, his breathing labored. He jerks around, corroded cybernetics scraping as he moves.

This won't be a fair fight.

VENTRESS:
Where is she?

GLUTE:
Who?

VENTRESS:
Neither of us has time for you to play dumb, no matter how much it suits you. The woman at the spaceport. Where did you take her?

GLUTE:
I don't know what you're talking about.

VENTRESS:
Really? Let's see if we can jog your memory.

VENTRESS: (NARRATION)
I sweep low, aiming to slice through Glute's mechanical ankles, but the Crolute jumps into the air, my blade passing harmlessly beneath metal feet. He kicks out, catching me in the chest.

Ventress grunts as she is kicked back.

VENTRESS: (NARRATION)
I've been played like a fool. The hissing joints. The wheezing breath. It's all an act to lower my expectations. I won't make the same mistake twice.

I spring back to my feet. Glute is running full pelt toward me, his metal-plated head held low like a battering ram.

I somersault over his back, pivoting to slash at his legs. This time my lightsaber meets armor plating and alloy tendons. Glute bellows in pain, toppling forward to land facedown in an oily puddle.

I use the Force to shove him down into the cracked sidewalk. Dooku may have shown mercy when facing the Jenet, but I have no such qualms. Bones and electrodrivers pop, bubbles breaking out on the surface of the water as he struggles to breathe.

VENTRESS:
Are you ready to talk?

GLUTE:
(MUFFLED) Mff gfff mfff.

VENTRESS:
What was that?

VENTRESS: (NARRATION)
I flip him onto his back, holding the tip of my lightsaber to all four of his chins.

VENTRESS:
Try again.

GLUTE:
I can't tell you. He'll—

A sudden blaster bolt slams into Glute's head, disintegrating it.

VENTRESS: (NARRATION)
One second Glute has a head, and the next it is gone. I look up to see the barrel of a rifle disappearing over the edge of the very same roof I'd used as a lookout.

VENTRESS:
Son of a—

A rocket pack fires.

VENTRESS: (NARRATION)
I bound back up to the warehouse, throwing up a hand to shield my eyes from the glare of the rocket pack. The sniper is already gone, leaving nothing but a trail of acrid fumes and thick smoke. I give chase, leaping from building to building.

KY NAREC: (GHOST)
You'll never catch him, not on foot.

Ventress slows and eventually stops, breathing hard.

VENTRESS:
I don't have to. I know who they are . . .

PART SIX

SCENE 101. INT. FELLIDRONE'S APARTMENT.

A door slides open. Fellidrone enters, the door sliding shut.

FELLIDRONE:
(GROANS AS HE REMOVES HIS JETPACK) My back.

VENTRESS:
Those things weigh a ton, don't they?

Fellidrone pulls a blaster on her.

FELLIDRONE:
Who's there?

Ventress slinks into the room.

VENTRESS:
Don't be coy, Portmaster. You know who I am.

KY NAREC: (GHOST)
Careful, Asajj. We can't trust him.

FELLIDRONE:

How did you get in?

VENTRESS:

You need a new window, but thanks for not asking why I'm here. We're both busy people. It's better we cut to the chase. You hired Glute to abduct Jenza. I just need to know where she is.

FELLIDRONE:

Not why I did it?

VENTRESS:

I don't care either way. Just tell me where she is, and I can kill you and move on.

FELLIDRONE:

How did you know it was me?

VENTRESS:

Your rocket pack. What is that? A Zim-500?

FELLIDRONE:

Five-Oh-One.

VENTRESS:

Impressive. Especially on a portmaster's salary. Runs on what? Refined paralene? Such a distinctive smell.

KY NAREC: (GHOST)

(REALIZING) The village on Rattatak.

VENTRESS:

And to think I mistook it for aftershave. But it all came flooding back when I saw the Zim-Jumper.

FELLIDRONE:

So what happens next? You threaten me? I shoot?

VENTRESS:

No need. You're going to drop the blaster.

The blaster clatters to the floor.

VENTRESS:
Good boy.

KY NAREC: (GHOST)
The mind of the weak. So easy to manipulate.

VENTRESS:
Now you're going to show me where you're hiding Jenza.

FELLIDRONE:
(DREAMLIKE) Behind a fake wall.

VENTRESS:
Through here?

FELLIDRONE:
Yes.

She hurries through to the next room.

VENTRESS:
Tell me how to open it.

FELLIDRONE:
A secret switch, behind the picture.

VENTRESS:
Where is that? Glee Anselm? I must go there one day.

She moves the picture aside to reveal a control panel.

VENTRESS:
And that's more like it. See? That wasn't so difficult, was it? Perhaps I won't kill you after—

She presses a switch and electricity surges through her body.

KY NAREC: (GHOST)
Ventress! Look out!

VENTRESS:
(SCREAMS)

The electricity cuts off and she collapses to the floor.

FELLIDRONE:
I appreciate the sentiment, but it was never in the cards in the first place. (HE CROUCHES DOWN, CHECKS HER NECK) No pulse. I'm almost disappointed.

Fellidrone activates a comlink.

FELLIDRONE:
This is XD-Forty-Five. I need immediate extraction. Dooku sent an enforcer to recover the package.

He enters a code into the control panel.

FELLIDRONE:
No. She's liquidated.

The wall slides back to reveal a secret compartment.

FELLIDRONE:
Copy that. I'll prepare the package for transportation. Forty-Five out.

He cuts off the transmission and walks toward the bound woman he had hidden in the compartment. This is Jenza.

JENZA:
(WEAKLY) Please. No more. I've told you . . . I don't know anything.

FELLIDRONE:
And I believe you, Jenza, but my superiors have gotten it into their heads that you're going to be a valuable bargaining tool or something. It's out of my hands.

A drawer opens and he removes an injector.

JENZA:
What is that?

FELLIDRONE:

The injector? Oh, don't worry. We're going on a journey. This is just a little something to make the time pass quick—

A lightsaber suddenly bursts through his chest.

VENTRESS:

You're going nowhere.

The lightsaber extinguishes.

FELLIDRONE:

(GROANS SLIGHTLY AS HE'S RELEASED)

He slumps to the floor, dead.

JENZA:

You killed him.

VENTRESS:

Looks that way.

JENZA:

Good.

VENTRESS:

Jenza, I presume.

KY NAREC: (GHOST)

You can see the resemblance to her brother.

VENTRESS:

Dooku sent us . . . sent me.

JENZA:

Are you Jedi?

VENTRESS:

Not exactly.

She tries to release the binders around Jenza's wrists.

VENTRESS:
We need to get you out of these restraints. What did that man do to you?

JENZA:
He . . . tortured me. Wanted me to tell him everything I knew.

VENTRESS:
About your brother?

JENZA:
I don't even know who he was.

VENTRESS:
Republic Intelligence, if this equipment is anything to go by. It would explain how he could resist mind control.

JENZA:
Mind control?

KY NAREC: (GHOST)
You knew he was faking . . .

JENZA:
I heard a scream.

VENTRESS:
That would have been me. I spotted Fellidrone's booby trap the moment I broke in. Needed him to think I was out of the picture.

KY NAREC: (GHOST)
So he would open the compartment himself. You could have been killed.

JENZA:
Didn't it hurt?

VENTRESS:
I've survived worse.

She rattles the binders.

VENTRESS:

It's no good. They're stuck fast. I'm going to have to burn them off.

She ignites one of her lightsabers.

JENZA:

He's in trouble, isn't he?

VENTRESS:

Who?

JENZA:

Dooku.

VENTRESS:

He's collecting enemies, that's for sure.

JENZA:

You need to help him.

VENTRESS:

I'm trying to help *you*. Keep still.

JENZA:

I don't care about me. You have to help him . . . like he helped me . . .

We hear the lightsaber burning through metal.

VENTRESS:

I said keep still! One false move and you'll lose a hand.

JENZA:

I couldn't get through to him.

VENTRESS:

Where?

JENZA:

On Coruscant. He'd done what he said he would. Joined the Council, thrown himself into the business of the Temple.

A restraint tumbles to the floor.

VENTRESS:

One down.

JENZA:

I tried everywhere. His holocomm. The Temple. Even the Senate. I'd seen him on the newsnet, addressing the senators. He was magnificent . . .

SCENE 102. INT. THE GALACTIC SENATE ROTUNDA.

ATMOSPHERE AS IN THE PREQUELS.
Dooku—now in his sixties—is standing on one of the Senate platforms, his voice booming around the chamber.

DOOKU:

Senators, on behalf of the Jedi I would urge you to reconsider cuts to the trade route defense program. Not only do the routes guarantee the supply of equipment and resources to the Galactic Core, they also provide an essential lifeline to thousands of worlds on the very edge of the Republic. Time and time again, the Jedi are called upon to protect those using these routes, especially in the Outer Rim. The Hydian Way. The Corellian Run. The list goes on and on. While we gladly serve the Republic, our numbers are few compared with the very real threats that endanger starfarers the galaxy over.

Only a fully funded Republic Guard can provide the security our citizens deserve.

There is applause from around the Senate, but also much jeering.

SENATOR BULGESKI: (SIMILARLY AMPLIFIED)
With all due respect, our honorable friend oversteps the mark. The Jedi Council claims to be a servant of the Republic, and yet here they are attempting to influence senatorial policy. Master Dooku has no business petitioning the Senate on such matters.

DOOKU:

As the senator for Salliche is aware, I speak on behalf of not just the Jedi, but also the billions in need of protection. Indeed, as I'm sure you'll all remember, it wasn't that long ago that Senator Bulgeski called for the Guard to intervene when Salliche was being ravaged by Norkronian raiders. Is he really suggesting that citizens in the Outer Rim shouldn't receive the same security enjoyed by his own planet?

SENATOR BULGESKI:

Salliche is the breadbasket of the Core Worlds. If we fell, how would planets such as Coruscant survive?

DOOKU:

There are plenty of agricultural worlds in the Outer Rim who could supply crops. Perhaps Salliche is afraid of the competition?

SENATOR BULGESKI:

That is a scandalous accusation. Chancellor Kalpana, must I remind you, once again, that Master Dooku stands here not as a member of the Senate, but as an independent adviser.

DOOKU:

And my *advice* is that every planet in the Republic receive the same level of security, no matter how far they are from galactic central.

CHANCELLOR KALPANA:

Master Dooku, the Senate thanks you for your contribution to this debate. Unfortunately, the reality of the situation is that the Republic is growing at an unprecedented rate, fueled largely by the ambitions of the Trade Federation. Unless the viceroy agrees to help fund the Guard . . .

TRADE FEDERATION REPRESENTATIVE:

The Trade Federation already pays more than enough in taxes!

CHANCELLOR KALPANA: (CONT.)

. . . we simply do not have the budget to offer blanket protection to every system.

The Jedi are fond of telling us that the Force is with us, but sadly the Force doesn't repair ships or build new droids. The Force doesn't fund training centers or pay medical bills.

The vote has been taken and I for one intend to honor the will of the people.

Rapturous applause.

SCENE 103. INT. THE GALACTIC SENATE. CORRIDORS.

Atmosphere: Senators milling around. General bustle.

DOOKU:
(TO HIMSELF) For the Force is strong. For the Force is strong. For the Force is—

RAEL:
Hello? It that the future chancellor I see?

Rael approaches.

DOOKU:
Rael?

Rael approaches.

RAEL:
In the flesh.

DOOKU:
What are you doing back here? I thought you were on Pijal.

RAEL:
I'm representing the princess at a meeting of delegates this afternoon.

DOOKU:
Then I hope you fare better than I did.

RAEL:
Don't be hard on yourself. Ya spoke well. You're a natural.

DOOKU:
Not if they won't listen.

RAEL:

At least ya tried. (SPOTS SOMEONE) Actually, there's someone that wants to meet you.

DOOKU:

Now isn't the time. I must return to the Temple.

RAEL:

It'll only take a minute. (CALLING OVER) Senator.

Palpatine walks over.

PALPATINE: (APPROACHING)

Master Averross. How pleasant to see you again. I trust your secondment to Pijal is going well.

RAEL:

It is, thanks to your advice, Senator.

PALPATINE:

I'm glad to hear it.

RAEL:

Master Dooku, may I introduce Senator Palpatine of Naboo.

DOOKU:

It is a pleasure to meet you, Senator.

PALPATINE:

I fear that may not be the case, Master Jedi, especially after the chancellor's remarks. Skor Kalpana is a good man, but he lacks backbone, which is probably why he was voted in.

I hope your experience here today will not discourage you. The Jedi need a voice in the Senate. For all its faults, I've always found that it's better to operate within government, rather than outside. This is where you can make a real difference.

DOOKU:

I'm not sure my fellow Council members would agree, but I thank you for your support.

PALPATINE:

I only wish I'd been able to influence the vote. Well, if you would excuse me. A senator's work is never done. I hope we will speak again, Master Dooku.

DOOKU:

As do I, Senator. As do I.

PALPATINE:

And we must see about getting you back to Naboo, Rael. Queen Ekay has been asking after you.

RAEL:

It would be an honor to see her again. Please give her my fondest regards.

PALPATINE:

(WALKING AWAY) I will. I promise. Until next time, then.

DOOKU:

I didn't realize you were so well-connected.

RAEL:

Oh, Sheev isn't that influential, more's the pity. He's helped me a lot over the last few years.

DOOKU:

So I heard. I would be interested in hearing more about Pijal.

RAEL:

You could come with me.

DOOKU:

A tempting offer.

RAEL:

Then why don't you take it? I'm worried about you, Dooku. I've never seen you so tense. Ever since Qui-Gon flew the coop, you've had a face like a constipated happabore.

DOOKU:

What a captivating image.

RAEL:

I mean it. I'm not sure Temple life is good for you, especially now Qui-Gon's makin' a name for himself.

DOOKU:

And so he should. He's a fine Jedi.

RAEL:

Are you surprised? Just look at his teacher. But something needs to change. At the very least get yourself a new convor, or maybe even another Padawan.

DOOKU:

And leave the Council? What would they do without me?

RAEL:

Find someone else to argue with?

DOOKU:

But what of you? After the *Advent*—

RAEL:

(QUICKLY) I'm fine.

DOOKU:

You should have come to see me.

RAEL:

You were too busy.

DOOKU:

Never for you.

RAEL:

Master, I know what ya did. How you spoke on my behalf.

DOOKU:

The Council vindicated you. For good reason. Your Padawan . . .

RAEL:

Lives forever in the Force.

DOOKU:

We could raise a glass in her memory. I have a bottle of Soulean brandy I've been meaning to open for quite some time.

RAEL:

Now I'm the one being tempted, but I need to head back as soon as today's business is concluded. There is someone who might appreciate the invitation, though.

DOOKU:

Oh?

RAEL:

I saw the *Truthseeker* in the shuttle bay. Lene must be back.

DOOKU:

Hmm.

RAEL:

And Sifo-Dyas, too.

DOOKU:

Yes, I . . . I was aware they'd returned.

RAEL:

And have ya talked to them?

DOOKU:

Not yet.

RAEL:

But ya will . . .

A droid approaches, its servos whirring.

ATTENDANT DROID:

Excuse me. Master Dooku?

DOOKU:
Yes?

ATTENDANT DROID:
Someone is asking for you on the Avenue of the Core Founders.

DOOKU:
Asking for me?

RAEL:
What did I tell ya? Your fame's spreading. Just remember. Talk to Lene. It'll do ya good.

SCENE 104. EXT. THE AVENUE OF THE CORE FOUNDERS.

Atmosphere: A warm pleasant day on the avenue, birds singing as members of the public wander past the statues.

Dooku approaches a familiar droid.

DOOKU: (COMING UP ON MIC)
Dee-Four?

D-4:
Ah. You remember me, Master Dooku. That should make this easier.

DOOKU:
Make what easier?

D-4:
I have been sent to deliver a message.

D-4 activates a hologram.

JENZA: (HOLOGRAM)
Brother. I see Dee-Four has found you.

DOOKU:
Jenza? Are you . . . are you well?

JENZA:

I have been trying to contact you.

DOOKU:

I'm sorry . . . Council business has kept me—

JENZA: (HOLOGRAM)

Please. Don't make excuses. I know you don't wish to speak to me. (THE MESSAGE GLITCHES SLIGHTLY) I just didn't know where else to turn.

DOOKU:

What has happened?

JENZA:

Serenno has been invaded.

DOOKU:

Invaded?

JENZA:

By the Abyssin.

DOOKU:

I find that hard to believe. The Abyssin are . . .

JENZA:

Little more than thugs. Yes, that is what the Senate said. (IT GLITCHES AGAIN) . . . didn't stop them taking Carannia.

DOOKU:

But surely Father—

JENZA:

Father (GLITCH) dead. Ramil has (GLITCH)

DOOKU:

Jenza?

JENZA:

(GLITCH) Need your help. The Republic says (GLITCH) internal affair (GLITCH) beyond (GLITCH) jurisdiction.

DOOKU:

What's happening? Can you boost the signal?

D-4:

I am trying, Master Dooku. The Abyssin are blocking signals to and from the planet. I was smuggled out on a Vandyne freighter.

DOOKU:

And the Senate has refused to help?

D-4:

From what little I know, they insist that as Count Ramil has failed to pay this season's levy, Serenno is on its own.

DOOKU:

Count Ramil. (SHAKES HEAD) Will you come to the Jedi Temple with me? Tell the Council what you know?

D-4:

Will that help, sir?

DOOKU:

I sincerely hope so.

SCENE 105. INT. JEDI COUNCIL CHAMBER.

GRETZ:

I am sorry, Master Dooku, but the Council's hands are tied.

DOOKU:

Droom, listen to me. You heard what Dee-Four said. Serenno has been invaded.

GRETZ:

What we heard is that a few space vagrants have set up camp on your homeworld.

D-4:

A few? There are hundreds. Thousands.

JOR:

We sympathize, Dee-Four, but must concur with the Senate's ruling. From what we have learned, the Count of Serenno has refused to honor his fiscal responsibilities.

DOOKU:

Fiscal responsibilities? Aerith, we are Jedi, not accountants. If Serenno needs us . . .

GRETZ:

Serenno believes they need no one. They have withdrawn their senator, recalled ambassadors. And now, at the first sign of trouble, they call for help. They can't have it both ways.

DOOKU:

But as Jedi, is it not our duty . . .

JOR:

To what, Master Dooku? To rush in, lightsabers blazing? Dooku, remind me. Where were you this afternoon?

DOOKU:

At the Senate.

JOR:

Telling all who would listen that the Jedi couldn't police the Outer Rim.

GRETZ:

A speech, if you recall, the Council strongly advised you not to make.

JOR:

And yet here you are, a few hours later, suggesting we mount an assault on Abyssin raiders. How would you explain that to the senators? To the chancellor?

DOOKU:

The Serennians have asked for our help.

GRETZ:
No. They have asked *you.*

JOR:
Once again, you are allowing your fixation on your birthplace to cloud your judgment.

DOOKU:
My *fixation*?

GRETZ:
The Senate has made their decision and we must abide with it.

D-4:
Well, this is most disappointing.

DOOKU:
Yes. Yes, it is. Master Yoda. I notice you have remained uncharacteristically quiet.

YODA:
Speak only when they have something useful to say, a Jedi should.

DOOKU:
So you agree with the others?

YODA:
Nothing can we do, except intercede on your sister's behalf. Talk to the chancellor, I will.

DOOKU:
Washing our hands of the matter in the process.

GRETZ:
The Council has made its decision.

DOOKU:
Have we?

JOR:
You must respect our wishes, and the wishes of the Senate.

DOOKU:
It appears I have little choice.

He walks to the door.

GRETZ:
Where are you going?

DOOKU:
To accompany Dee-Four to her transport. Unless I need the Council's permission to visit the shuttle bay.

YODA:
Master Dooku . . .

DOOKU:
I didn't think so.

SCENE 106. INT. JEDI SHUTTLE BAY.

D-4 totters after Dooku.

D-4:
But Master Dooku. I have no transport. The Vandyne will be long gone by now.

DOOKU:
I have made alternative arrangements.

BRAYLON:
It's about time.

DOOKU:
Thank you for doing this, Braylon.

BRAYLON:
I take it from your expression that the vote went against you.

DOOKU:
It did.

BRAYLON:
Then I'm afraid I can't take the droid to Serenno.

DOOKU:
But you said . . .

BRAYLON:
Dooku, I can't afford to go against the Council. Not after so many years spent clawing myself back into their favor.

DOOKU:
(NOT HAPPY) I understand.

BRAYLON:
But you don't like it.

DOOKU:
Can you blame me?

D-4:
Excuse me. I'm not sure I understand. What is happening?

DOOKU:
We've reached the end of the road, Dee-Four.

BRAYLON:
Now, I didn't say that, did I?

DOOKU:
I'm sorry?

BRAYLON:
While I cannot get involved, I have a friend who doesn't give a damn what the Council thinks of her.

Footsteps approach.

LENE:
Hello, Dooku.

DOOKU:
Lene. Sifo-Dyas.

When he speaks, we realize that Sifo-Dyas has developed a slight stutter.

SIFO-DYAS:
Your shuttle awaits.

DOOKU:
I . . . I don't know what to say.

LENE:
You could say thank you. Now, or after we arrive in the Outer Rim. It's up to you.

D-4:
You're coming with us?

LENE:
Master Dooku has decided to meditate on the Council's ruling.

SIFO-DYAS:
All the way to Serenno.

BRAYLON:
Now go, before the Council realizes what's happened.

DOOKU:
They're going to be furious.

LENE:
I sincerely hope so.

SCENE 107. EXT. SPACE.

The Truthseeker *flies by.*

SCENE 108. INT. THE *TRUTHSEEKER.*

LENE:
So how bad is it?

DOOKU:
Let me show you.

A hologram shimmers on.

DOOKU:
We can expect resistance the moment we enter the Serenno system.

LENE:
When did the Abyssin obtain an armada?

D-4:
When the Great Houses funded them.

LENE:
I'm sorry?

DOOKU:
From what Dee-Four has told me, Serenno was being raided by pirates. My brother refused to offer protection, holing up in our ancestral seat.

LENE:
And so the houses called in mercenaries.

DOOKU:
For better or worse, Ramil has continued our father's work, dismantling the Serenno military, replacing it with security droids loyal only to him. The other houses didn't have a choice. The Abyssin took their money and decided to stay, claiming the planet as a new base of operations along the Hydian Way.

He deactivates the hologram.

DOOKU: (CONT.)
As communications are being blocked both on- and offplanet, I have adapted our comlinks to operate on a shortwave frequency that should circumvent the jamming signal.

He passes Lene a comlink.

LENE:
When did you become so good with technology?

DOOKU:
(WITH GOOD HUMOR) Didn't you know? I'm good at every-thing. Dee-Four, will you take this communicator to Sifo-Dyas in the cockpit?

D-4:
(SIGHING) If I must.

D-4 totters off.

LENE:
That droid reminds me of someone. I can't think who.

DOOKU:
Lene . . .

LENE:
Dooku, it's okay. We're good. I know exactly why you distanced yourself. Sifo-Dyas didn't exactly make it easy.

DOOKU:
How is he?

LENE:
Honestly? He's barely holding together. The visions have gotten worse. Some days he's lucid, others I find him curled up in a ball in his quarters. Nothing I do seems to help.

A chime of a comm.

SIFO-DYAS: (OVER COMM)
We're coming out of hyperspace, Master.

The ship is suddenly buffeted, rocked by laserfire.

DOOKU & LENE:
(REACT TO THE BARRAGE)

LENE:
Sifo?

SIFO-DYAS: (OVER COMM)
We're under attack. Multiple orb-wings.

DOOKU:
The Abyssin!

SCENE 109. EXT. SERENNO SPACE.

Atmosphere: We cut into the middle of a space battle. The Truth-seeker *is under attack by a squadron of orb fighters. Fire blossoms along its hull.*

SCENE 110. INT. THE *TRUTHSEEKER*. COCKPIT.

Explosions rattle the entire ship as Dooku and Lene run into the cockpit.

DOOKU:
You take navigation. I'll take the guns.

They rush to their stations as the ship takes another hit.

D-4:
(PANICKED) This is hopeless.

LENE:
Calm yourself, droid.

D-4:
That's easy for you to say. I'm getting too old for this.

DOOKU:
You and me both.

Another hit. More sparks.

DOOKU:
(GRUNTS IN FRUSTRATION) Any chance of you holding us steady?

SIFO-DYAS:
Maneuvering thrusters are gone. The power core is at twenty-nine percent.

DOOKU:
I take it that means no.

Dooku lets off a volley of laser bursts. There's an explosion outside.

D-4:
You got one. Oh, well done, sir.

LENE:
Unfortunately, there are still a dozen more.

DOOKU:
Thank you for the encouragement.

There's an explosion from behind. A warning klaxon sounds.

LENE:
What was that?

SIFO-DYAS:
The shields are down.

LENE:
Any good news?

SIFO-DYAS:
We still have propulsion.

There's another strike. The ship is really shuddering now.

SIFO-DYAS:
Propulsion has gone.

D-4:
What does that mean?

LENE:
It means we're dead in the water.

D-4:

Can't you do something?

DOOKU:

We can eject.

D-4:

That's not quite what I had in mind.

DOOKU:

As soon as we enter the atmosphere. Are you ready?

D-4:

No. No, I am not.

SCENE 111. INT. HIDDEN ROOM.

Ventress's lightsaber thrums.

VENTRESS:

Jenza, please. You need to remain still.

KY NAREC: (GHOST)

I don't want to think what Dooku will do to you if you hurt her.

VENTRESS:

The thought has occurred to me. Jenza. I won't tell you again.

JENZA:

You need to listen to me.

VENTRESS:

Do I have a choice?

JENZA:

I knew he wouldn't let me down. Not when we needed him most . . .

VENTRESS:

(SARCASTIC) Yes, he's a real hero.

JENZA:
He is. At least, he was. (LAUGHS TO HERSELF) I should have known his return to Serenno would be suitably explosive . . .

SCENE 112. EXT. SERENNO CAMP. OUTSIDE CARANNIA.

Atmosphere: Wind blowing over open plains.

SERGEANT ESON:
Lady Jenza? There's activity in the upper atmosphere.

JENZA:
Let me see.

The sergeant passes her the macrobinoculars.

SERGEANT ESON:
Looks like a ship coming down.

The whir of macrobinoculars zooming in.

JENZA:
And not just any ship.

SERENNIAN SERGEANT:
Ma'am?

JENZA:
The markings, Eson. They're Jedi. Where will it land?

SERGEANT ESON:
On that trajectory? Somewhere on the Delgaldon Plains.

Jenza is already running.

JENZA:
(CALLING BACK) Then I need a landspeeder.

SERGEANT ESON:
(CALLING AFTER HER) My lady, come back. If you're spotted by the Abyssin—

JENZA:
(CALLING BACK) It's him, Sergeant. I know it is.

SCENE 113. INT. THE *TRUTHSEEKER*.

The shuttle wails as it dives down, everyone's dialogue pitching up to be heard over the noise.

D-4:
I thought you said we should eject.

DOOKU:
The mechanism's jammed!

D-4:
That's bad, isn't it?

LENE:
Unless you enjoy crashing, yes.

D-4:
No, I do not. Not in the slightest.

DOOKU:
There's something else we can do.

SIFO-DYAS:
We're listening.

DOOKU:
Jettison the cockpit.

LENE:
The entire cockpit?

DOOKU:
We could guide it down. Cushion our fall.

LENE:
And by that you mean . . . ?

DOOKU:

We use the Force.

SIFO-DYAS:

That's insane.

DOOKU:

Yes.

SIFO-DYAS:

The worst plan I have ever heard.

DOOKU:

Most probably.

SIFO-DYAS:

I'm in.

LENE:

We'll have to release the clamps manually.

D-4:

Have you done this before?

DOOKU:

No. On three. One.

LENE:

Two.

DOOKU, LENE, & SIFO-DYAS:

Three!

D-4:

Oh, why didn't I stick with Ramil!

There comes a series of resounding clunks, and the cockpit detaches from the shuttle.

SCENE 114. EXT. THE DELGALDON PLAINS.

A landspeeder zips across the terrain.

We move into the back of it.

JENZA:

Can you still see them?

SERGEANT ESON:

It's breaking up. They'll never survive.

There's a crash nearby.

JENZA:

He will. Hang on.

She swings the speeder around.

SCENE 115. EXT. CRASH SITE.

Atmosphere: Burning wreckage. Sparking electrics.

D-4:

(SHORTING OUT) Master Dooku . . . Master Dooku.

Dooku pushes twisted metal off himself.

DOOKU:

(WITH EFFORT) I'm here.

D-4:

My vision . . . is impaired. Are we home?

DOOKU:

Yes. Yes, we are.

D-4:

(AS IF WINDING DOWN) Oh, I am glad. I hated being . . .
away . . .

LENE:

(COUGHING NEARBY)

DOOKU:

Lene.

LENE:
I loved that shuttle. It always got down in one piece.

Sifo-Dyas stumbles up.

SIFO-DYAS:
Until now.

DOOKU:
Sifo-Dyas. You're hurt.

SIFO-DYAS:
It's nothing. How's the droid?

DOOKU:
She didn't make it.

A landspeeder approaches.

LENE:
What's that?

Dooku ignites his lightsaber.

DOOKU:
A landspeeder.

SIFO-DYAS:
More Abyssin?

Lene also ignites her lightsaber.

LENE:
Let's hope not.

The speeder slows to a halt.

JENZA: (OFF-MIC)
Dooku!

DOOKU:
Jenza?

JENZA: (NARRATION)

Before Eson could stop me, I bounded from the speeder, flinging myself into Dooku's arms. He hesitated for a second, unsure what to do, before returning the hug.

JENZA:

You came. You actually came.

DOOKU:

I should never have stayed away.

Jenza pulls away.

JENZA:

Where's the rest?

DOOKU:

The rest of what?

JENZA:

The fleet. The Jedi *are* sending reinforcements, aren't they?

LENE:

You're looking at them.

DOOKU:

Jenza, may I introduce Lene Kostana and Sifo-Dyas.

SERGEANT ESON:

That's all there are? Three of you?

DOOKU:

And you are?

SERGEANT ESON:

Sergeant Eson of Borgin House Guard.

DOOKU:

Then I ask the same of you—where are your troops, Sergeant?

SERGEANT ESON:
I'm all that's left.

JENZA:
That's not entirely true. We have a number of veterans back at camp.

SERGEANT ESON:
Most of whom can barely stand. We were expecting an army.

LENE:
And you've got one. More or less.

JENZA: (NARRATION)
Eson looked as if he was about to argue, when the ground shook beneath us.

The ground shifts beneath them.

SERGEANT ESON:
Lady Jenza!

JENZA:
I'm fine. Really.

DOOKU:
You're still getting groundquakes?

JENZA:
No. Not for years.

The ground shakes again, splitting asunder nearby.

LENE:
It's getting worse.

SIFO-DYAS:
I'm so glad you brought us back.

JENZA:
We should check on the camp.

DOOKU:
Is it nearby?

JENZA:
On the side of the mountain.

SERGEANT ESON:
If the mountain's still standing!

SCENE 116. EXT. SERENNO CAMP.

JENZA: (NARRATION)
Eson's fears were confirmed as we reached camp. A rockslide had demolished half the tents, scattering supplies across the mountain-side. The wounded were everywhere . . .

There is general chaos as the speeder sweeps in, children crying, the wounded groaning.

JENZA:
We must help the survivors.

DOOKU:
I can't believe you're living like this.

JENZA:
It was this or the castle. I chose our people.

JENZA: (NARRATION)
We leapt from the speeder, Dooku and the others fanning out to help the wounded.

HAGI: (CALLING OFF-MIC)
I need a bandage!

DOOKU:
Here, use this.

JENZA: (NARRATION)
Lene moved to stop him as he began to unwind a length of cloth from around his arm.

LENE:
Dooku, do you think that's wise?

DOOKU:
Her need is greater than mine.

He continues.

DOOKU:
Will this help?

HAGI:
Yes, thank you. Can you hold it in place, while I wrap it?

DOOKU:
Here?

HAGI:
Perfect.

They go to work, Hagi winding Dooku's bandage around her patient's head.

PATIENT:
(GROANS)

DOOKU:
Remain calm.

HAGI:
Nice bedside manner. I take it you haven't performed much field medicine.

DOOKU:
And you have, Countess . . . ?

HAGI:
Hagi, of House Malvern. Or what's left of it. You're Jenza's brother. The Jedi.

DOOKU:
I am.

HAGI:

I can see your father in you.

DOOKU:

I trust you won't hold that against me.

HAGI:

Not if you can help us. Press there.

DOOKU:

You've certainly done this before.

HAGI:

My family has mined Serenno for centuries. I've witnessed enough accidents over the years. (TO THE PATIENT) There. Try to rest.

The ground rumbles again.

DOOKU:

Easier said than done.

HAGI:

Must be an aftershock.

The quake passes.

Jenza and Lene run up.

LENE:

Everything okay over here?

HAGI:

Does it look like it?

JENZA:

Hagi. Please. They're only trying to help.

DOOKU:

I had no idea it was this bad.

JENZA:

No one on Coruscant does. Here. Let me show you.

SCENE 117. INT. HIDDEN ROOM.

JENZA:
I took him to the lookout, so he could see Carannia. The city
was . . . (SHE COUGHS)

It was . . .

She descends into a coughing fit.

KY NAREC: (GHOST)
We need to get her out of that restraint. She's not well.

VENTRESS:
Thank you, Doctor.

Ventress burns through the last restraint. It clatters to the floor.

Jenza slumps forward.

KY NAREC: (GHOST)
Catch her.

Ventress's lightsaber snaps off as she catches Jenza.

VENTRESS:
Careful. I've got you.

An alert bleeps.

KY NAREC: (GHOST)
What's that?

VENTRESS:
Jenza. I need to check Fellidrone's security feeds. Can you sit here?

JENZA:
(WEAK) Yes.

VENTRESS:
This won't take long.

She moves to the console, working the controls.

KY NAREC: (GHOST)
Well . . .

VENTRESS:
Fellidrone's handlers. They're on their way.

KY NAREC: (GHOST)
She's in no state to be moved.

Ventress reaches for her holocomm.

VENTRESS:
I'm so glad you're here.

JENZA:
(CONFUSED) I'm sorry.

VENTRESS:
Just talking to myself.

She activates the holocomm, the unit beeping as a hologram shimmers into view.

VENTRESS:
Master.

DOOKU: (HOLOGRAM)
You have news?

VENTRESS:
I've found your sister, but we're about to have company.

DOOKU: (HOLOGRAM)
And?

VENTRESS:
And I can't risk moving her, not on my own.

DOOKU: (HOLOGRAM)
I will send assistance.

The holocomm disconnects.

VENTRESS:
As chatty as ever.

KY NAREC: (GHOST)
You can't trust him.

VENTRESS:
(HISSING) Not now.

She moves to Jenza.

VENTRESS:
Jenza. Jenza, listen to me. Your brother is sending help.

JENZA:
My brother. Yes. I showed him.

VENTRESS:
We just need to sit tight. And be quiet.

JENZA:
I showed him Carannia . . .

SCENE 118. EXT. CARANNIAN HILLS.

Atmosphere: Carannia burns in the distance.

DOOKU:
Look at it. Look at the devastation. And yet the Senate does nothing.

SIFO-DYAS:
That's a lot of Abyssin.

LENE:
Enough to hold the city.

DOOKU:
And that's where they're blocking transmissions?

JENZA:
The comm tower, yes.

DOOKU:
Then that's what we'll hit first.

JENZA:
I'll rally as many fighters as I can.

DOOKU:
We won't need any. Not yet. Sifo-Dyas, how well do you remember your levitation training?

SIFO-DYAS:
What are you thinking?

DOOKU:
Shifting Sands.

SCENE 119. EXT. ABYSSIN OUTPOST.

JENZA: (NARRATION)
(LAUGHS) The Abyssin scouts never saw him coming . . .

ABYSSIN GUARD #1:
What are you looking at?

ABYSSIN GUARD #2:
There's something in the hills.

ABYSSIN GUARD #1:
Pass me the uniscope.

The whir of a uniscope.

ABYSSIN GUARD #1:
You're imagining things. There's nothing there.

A wind starts to whip up.

ABYSSIN GUARD #2:
Like I'm imagining all this wind?

Dirt and sand is blown up all around.

ABYSSIN GUARD #1:
(COUGHING) Must be a dust storm.

ABYSSIN GUARD #2:
Where did it come from?

The storm intensifies.

ABYSSIN GUARD #1:
(CRIES OUT) It's in my eye.

ABYSSIN GUARD #2:
I can't see anything. Oster. Oster, where are you?

A lightsaber strikes in the middle of the storm.

ABYSSIN GUARD #1:
(DIES)

ABYSSIN GUARD #2:
Oster! Oster, what was that? What happened?

DOOKU:
Let me show you.

He spears the Abyssin with a lightsaber.

ABYSSIN GUARD #2:
(DIES)

The Abyssin slumps to the ground.

DOOKU:
(CALLING OUT) That's enough, Sifo-Dyas.

The Force-induced storm subsides.

SIFO-DYAS:
(APPROACHING) Did I pass the test?

DOOKU:
Admirably.

He extinguishes his lightsaber.

Sifo-Dyas raps on the side of a tank.

SIFO-DYAS:
This tank has seen better days.

DOOKU:
It will serve our purpose.

He pulls open a heavy door.

SIFO-DYAS:
(DISGUSTED) Surely there has to be another way. That stench.

DOOKU:
You won't be in it long.

SIFO-DYAS:
I'd rather I wasn't in it at all. Why do I have to pilot this thing?

DOOKU:
We agreed on the plan.

SIFO-DYAS:
You *told* me the plan. There's a difference. Well, if I must . . .

Sifo-Dyas clambers into the tank.

SIFO-DYAS:
I'm warning you, though . . . if I die in here . . .

DOOKU:
You can come back to haunt me . . .

SCENE 120. EXT. ABYSSIN CAMP.

ABYSSIN COMMANDER:
General.

ABYSSIN GENERAL:
What is it, Commander?

COMMANDER:
The sentry tank. It's returning.

GENERAL:
Why?

COMMANDER:
No idea. They're not answering comms.

The general opens a comm frequency.

GENERAL:
Sentry tank. Report. Why have you abandoned your post? Repeat. Why have you abandoned your post?

The tank fires.

COMMANDER:
They're firing on us, sir.

GENERAL:
I noticed! All troops. Return fire. Now.

Multiple blasters fire.

SCENE 121. INT. TANK.

Blaster bolts bounce off the tank's hull.

SIFO-DYAS:
Dooku. I'm still not convinced this is a good idea. When will I know when you've set the charges?

There is an explosion nearby.

SIFO-DYAS:
Actually, scratch that. I've worked it out for myself.

DOOKU: (OVER COMM)
Your distraction worked, Sifo. The jammer is down. Transmissions can get through.

SIFO-DYAS:
So I can pull back?

DOOKU: (OVER COMM)
No. Keep going. Draw their fire.

SCENE 122. EXT. ABYSSIN CAMP.

The sound of the tank taking yet another hit comes over the comm.

SIFO-DYAS: (OVER COMM)
What do you think I'm doing?

LENE:
He won't last much longer in that monstrosity.

DOOKU:
He doesn't have to. We just need to keep them busy.

ABYSSIN MERC: (OFF-MIC)
Hey!

LENE:
You were saying?

ABYSSIN MERC: (OFF-MIC)
What are you doing here?

The Abyssin fires at them.

DOOKU:
Typical Abyssin.

He blocks the shots before slicing the Abyssin in two.

ABYSSIN MERC:
(DIES)

DOOKU:
Didn't even give me a chance to answer.

SIFO-DYAS: (OVER COMM)
Dooku? Are you still there?

A beep of Dooku's comlink.

DOOKU:
I'm here.

SIFO-DYAS: (OVER COMM)
The tank is coming apart.

LENE:
Jam it onto a collision course and bail out.

A groundquake hits.

DOOKU:
Another quake.

SIFO-DYAS: (OVER COMM)
Lene? Dooku?

The ground opens up beneath them.

DOOKU:
(FALLING) Sifo!

SCENE 123. INT. UNDERGROUND CAVERN.

We hear them tumble into a cave, hitting the ground, hard. When they speak, their voices echo in the cavern.

LENE:
(CRIES OUT IN AGONY)

DOOKU:
Lene!

LENE:
Landed on my shoulder.

DOOKU:
It's broken.

LENE:

(CRIES OUT AS SHE MOVES) Of all the stupid . . . Can't even hold a lightsaber.

DOOKU:

You have another arm, don't you?

LENE:

Oh, you're all heart. (WITH EFFORT AS SHE GETS UP) Climbing out is going to be interesting.

Dooku clicks his comlink.

DOOKU:

Sifo? Can you hear us? We've fallen into some kind of cavern.

(NO ANSWER)

DOOKU: (CONT.)
Sifo-Dyas?

LENE:

The rock must be interfering with the signal.

DOOKU:

I could use the Force. Lift you back to the surface.

LENE:

And what about you?

DOOKU:

I can climb.

There's another, smaller groundquake, more rocks falling.

LENE:

If we're not buried first.

The Tirra'Taka growls nearby.

LENE:

What was that?

The monster is in the next cavern. We hear it move, its growl getting louder by the second.

DOOKU:
It's not possible.

LENE:
What isn't?

DOOKU:
Lene, when we first met, you asked me what I'd seen in the Archive . . .

LENE:
Yes. Yes, I did.

DOOKU:
I think you're about to find out.

The Tirra'Taka bursts through the cave wall, roaring fiercely.

LENE:
And I thought rancors were big. That's what you saw?

DOOKU:
(IN AWE) The Tirra'Taka.

LENE:
You know its name?

DOOKU:
An old Serennian legend. The dragon that holds the world together.

LENE:
It hasn't been doing a good job of that recently.

DOOKU:
The statue didn't do you credit.

Another roar.

DOOKU:

No. There's nothing to be afraid of.

LENE:

You're sure about that? Dooku. You can feel it, can't you? The dark side.

DOOKU:

We need to make contact with her.

LENE:

Contact? You want to bond with it?

DOOKU:

As you taught me all those years ago. One mind. Two bodies.

The creature calms, her growl echoing around the chamber.

LENE:

I don't think this is a good idea. We've got an invasion on our hands up there, remember?

DOOKU:

You've always wanted to understand the past, Lene. This is the past. She's been down here so long. Hidden in the rock.

LENE:

How do you know?

DOOKU:

She's showing me. Here. Touch her scales. See for yourself.

LENE:

I . . .

DOOKU:

The Force will protect you.

LENE:

I . . . I hope I don't regret this.

She steps forward, touching the monster's flank.

LENE:
(GASPS)

DOOKU:
There. Do you see?

LENE:
Yes! An army on the march.

As they describe their vision, we hear the sounds of the creature's memories, echoing from the past.

DOOKU:
Armor as black as night. Dripping with blood.

The sounds of a battle, screams, lightsabers slicing through bodies. So many lightsabers.

LENE:
Death on such a scale.

DOOKU:
They used her.

LENE:
Dark siders.

DOOKU:
A beast of war.

The bellow of the Tirra'Taka in the past.

DOOKU:
But it wasn't always that way. They hunted her. Captured her.

Laser blasts. The Tirra'Taka howling in agony.

LENE:
(FEELING THE BEAST'S TORMENT) So much pain.

DOOKU:
Corrupting her . . . into something new.

LENE:
Something malevolent.

She gasps, stepping back, breaking the link.

LENE:
We should stop. The connection is too strong.

DOOKU:
No. Riding into battle. Riding through the stars.

LENE:
Dooku. Break away.

DOOKU:
I can't. The things they made her do. Until . . . until. (CRIES OUT)

LENE:
What is it?

DOOKU:
They fought back. The people. Against her masters. Against her.

More roars. More battle.

FIGHTER: (IN THE SOUNDSCAPE)
For Serenno!

In the past, the Tirra'Taka bays in fear.

DOOKU:
She broke free.

The sound of the Tirra'Taka burrowing down into the planet.

DOOKU:
Buried deep within the planet's crust.

LENE:
Dooku, please.

She goes to grab him.

DOOKU:
Don't touch me.

LENE:
This has gone too far.

DOOKU:
No. You don't understand. This is because of me.

LENE:
You?

In the soundscape, we hear the following exchange from Dooku's childhood.

YOUNG JENZA:
Dooku, what are you doing? Don't—don't touch it, okay? It's supposed to be bad luck.

DOOKU:
She was asleep. All that time. Beneath the surface. She was at peace.

YOUNG DOOKU:
So beautiful.

DOOKU: (OVER HIS YOUNGER LINES)
So beautiful.

YOUNG DOOKU:
(WHISPER) Tirra'Taka . . .

DOOKU:
And then I came home.

YOUNG JENZA:
Dooku—don't!

DOOKU:
It was me. I woke her. She felt the Force within me. (TO THE BEAST) I'm so sorry. You just wanted to be left alone.

The dragon growl is almost like a purr, but then . . .

There's an explosion high above. Rocks tumble down. The Tirra'Taka bays in fear.

LENE:
I don't think it's going to get its wish.

DOOKU:
The Abyssin.

Dooku's comlink crackles.

SIFO-DYAS: (OVER COMM THROUGH STATIC)
Dooku ... Lene ... Anyone!

The Tirra'Taka growls.

DOOKU:
No, no. It's all right. It's just my comlink. Do you see? It's a friend.

There's a beep as he activates it.

DOOKU:
Sifo-Dyas?

SIFO-DYAS: (OVER COMM)
(LOTS OF INTERFERENCE) Whe ... [re are] you? We took the fight to the Abyssin ... They're ... retreating, but re ... [inforcements ...]

Static takes over.

DOOKU:
Sifo? Sifo? Can you hear me?

Nothing but static.

LENE:
We need to get back up there.

The Tirra'Taka roars, not happy about this.

DOOKU:
You can't even lift a lightsaber.

LENE:
We've got to do something.

DOOKU:
And I will. But I need you to stay here . . .

LENE:
I don't need a lightsaber to fight.

DOOKU:
Not to fight. To help her.

LENE:
The Tirra'Taka?

DOOKU:
Keep her calm. Please. She's suffered so much.

Another roar.

LENE:
And what if she won't listen?

DOOKU:
She will, Lene. She'll trust you, as I do.

LENE:
When you put it like that . . .

DOOKU:
I'll be back. I promise.

SCENE 124. EXT. ABYSSIN CAMP.

Atmosphere: A battle is in progress, blasters firing. Sifo-Dyas's light-saber slices left and right, the violence continuing through the sequence.

JENZA: (NARRATION)
On the surface, transmissions started coming in the moment communications lines opened. Remnants of the other houses. Serennians all over the planet. They were fighting back. And so were we.

SERGEANT ESON:
We've got them on the run.

SIFO-DYAS:
(FIGHTING WITH LIGHTSABER) I admire your spirit, but let's not get ahead of ourselves. There's a long way to go.

HAGI:
(SHOOTING BLASTER) Any news from Dooku?

SIFO-DYAS:
No. I can't get through. I don't know what happened to—(CRIES OUT)

JENZA:
Sifo-Dyas!

HAGI:
What's happening to him?

SIFO-DYAS:
I can hear them.

JENZA:
Hear who?

SIFO-DYAS:
Voices. United as one. Doo-ku. Doo-ku. Doo-ku. Chanting his name. The Lost Son. He who will divide.

HAGI:
What's he saying?

JENZA:
I don't know.

A bolt zips through the air and wings her.

JENZA:
(CRIES OUT)

SERGEANT ESON:
My lady!

JENZA:
It's nothing. Just caught my arm. Sifo-Dyas, we need you.

SIFO-DYAS:
I can't. I can't block them out. Doo-ku . . . Doo-ku . . .

HAGI:
(SHOUTING OVER) Jenza! Look out!

A clattering walker, the size of an AT-RT, lurches toward them.

JENZA: (NARRATION)
I looked up to see an Abyssin in a jerry-rigged walker clattering toward us, cannons glowing hot. Sifo-Dyas tried to stand, but his legs buckled beneath him. I tried to pull him clear, but it was obvious that neither of us was going to escape. Not this time . . .

A lightsaber carves through the walker's legs.

DOOKU:
Stay away from them.

JENZA:
Brother!

The walker falls.

JENZA: (NARRATION)
The walker crashed to the ground, its legs sliced away. Dooku loomed over the pilot and . . .

Dooku runs the Abyssin through.

ABYSSIN:
(SCREAMS AND DIES)

JENZA:
Dooku! Help us! Something's happened to your friend!

Dooku runs over.

DOOKU:
Sifo?

SIFO-DYAS:
Dooku. I heard them. I heard the voices. What have you done?

DOOKU:
Nothing . . . But you'll never believe what we've discovered . . .

There's an explosion in the distance.

JENZA:
What was that?

HAGI:
We've taken the Abyssin control tower. They're retreating.

JENZA:
It's over.

SIFO-DYAS:
No. It's just beginning.

DOOKU:
What's that?

JENZA: (NARRATION)
Assault craft had appeared on the horizon, powering toward us. And above them . . .

SERGEANT ESON:
That's the *Windrunner.*

HAGI:
Count Ramil?

JENZA:
He must be joining the fight.

DOOKU:
Then why are their guns trained on us?

SIFO-DYAS:
Dooku . . .

DOOKU:
I know, old friend. I can sense it, too.

JENZA:
Sense what?

DOOKU:
Betrayal.

JENZA: (NARRATION)
The assault tanks ground to a halt, ramps swinging down to deploy dozens of security droids, marching in unison.

DOOKU:
That's an attack formation.

JENZA:
It can't be.

DROID COMMANDER:
All units. Take aim.

BATTLE DROIDS IN UNISON:
Confirmed.

They raise their guns.

HAGI:
What are they doing?

JENZA: (NARRATION)
In answer, an all-too-familiar voice boomed out from the *Windrunner* . . .

RAMIL: (AMPLIFIED)
People of Serenno. This is your count speaking. Lay down your weapons. The insurrection is at an end.

JENZA:
(DESPAIRING) Ramil. No.

SERGEANT ESON:
Insurrection? What's he talking about?

DOOKU:
You.

HAGI:
Us? But we were fighting for freedom.

SIFO-DYAS:
That's not how it will be written.

DOOKU:
Sifo?

SIFO-DYAS:
Help me up. We can't let him take control.

Dooku helps Sifo to his feet.

DOOKU:
We won't.

JENZA:
Then what shall we do?

JENZA: (NARRATION)
Dooku looked at me sadly and then threw his lightsaber onto the floor in front of the droids.

DOOKU:
We surrender.

SIFO-DYAS:
We *what*?

DOOKU:
We surrender!

JENZA: (NARRATION)
We watched, mouths agape, as Dooku walked calmly toward the droids, his head held high.

DOOKU:
Signal my brother. Tell him I am here. He will want to see me.

SIFO-DYAS:
You're giving up?

JENZA: (NARRATION)
He turned and smiled at his friend.

DOOKU:
I was at the Senate when the possibility of a droid army was debated. Units such as these are controlled by a central processor.

SIFO-DYAS:
Which you think is on that ship!

DOOKU:
There's only one way to find out.

DROID COMMANDER:
The count has signaled. A hoverpod is being sent to fetch the Jedi.

DOOKU:
How gracious of him.

SCENE 125. EXT. THE *WINDRUNNER*.

JENZA: (NARRATION)
We were forced to kneel in the dirt as Dooku was led into the pod. It rose into the air, Dooku standing motionless, hands clasped behind his back. I watched him ascend, fearing the worst as he stepped onto the *Windrunner* . . .

Dooku walks onto the wooden deck, accompanied by the droids. We can hear Ramil's labored breathing and, when he moves, the clank of his exosuit.

DOOKU:
Ramil.

RAMIL:
Dooku.

DOOKU:
Cenevax really made a mess of you, didn't she? Please tell me you haven't stamped that face on any coins.

RAMIL:
Guards.

Energy lances through Dooku's body.

DOOKU:
(SCREAMS OUT)

RAMIL:
That's enough.

SECURITY DROIDS:
Confirmed.

The shocks stop, Dooku gasping for breath.

RAMIL:
That's better. On your knees. Where you belong.

DOOKU:
(PAINED) Spoken like a true monster.

RAMIL:
I'm a survivor.

DOOKU:
I'd like to see you survive out of that exosuit.

RAMIL:
Don't you get it, *brother*? This is the way it was supposed to be.

DOOKU:
With you in a walking med-splint?

RAMIL:

With me in charge. Not Father. And definitely not you.

DOOKU:

I have no interest in ruling anyone.

RAMIL:

Tell that to Jenza. The years I've had to listen to her bleating on about you, the brave Jedi. "Why can't you be more like him, Ramil? Why can't he be the heir?" Even after you desecrated Mother's casket. If only she could see you now. I would show her, if it wasn't already too late.

DOOKU:

What do you mean?

The exosuit clanks as Ramil stomps to the edge of the deck.

RAMIL:

Look at them all down there. Ha. Is that Hagi? Her father was the worst. So quick to call in mercenaries to protect him, just like the rest. But do you know the trouble with mercenaries, Dooku?

DOOKU:

They can be bought by whoever has the deepest pockets.

RAMIL:

And Father said I didn't know what I was doing when I let the pirates in.

DOOKU:

It was you. You orchestrated the entire thing.

RAMIL:

You were the one who told me to sort out Serenno. You said it was my responsibility.

DOOKU:

I didn't mean like this.

RAMIL:
But it's so much better this way. Serenno will be stronger than ever before. No more houses. No more infighting. No more Republic. The people will welcome me with open arms, especially when I reveal the sad news that their beloved Jenza has been killed. By a Jedi no less.

DOOKU:
What?

RAMIL:
Activate the holoscreen.

SECURITY DROID:
Confirmed.

A screen appears. We can hear the thrum of a lightsaber over the transmission.

DOOKU:
No!

RAMIL:
Your own lightsaber at her throat. It has a certain poetic charm, doesn't it? Ramil to surface commander. Are you ready to execute her?

DROID COMMANDER: (OVER COMM)
At your command, Your Grace.

DOOKU:
You can't!

RAMIL:
Haven't you worked it out yet? I can do anything I want. Hit him again.

SECURITY DROID:
Acknowledged.

More electricity surges into Dooku.

DOOKU:
(CRYING OUT) She is our sister!

The torment continues, Ramil pitching up his voice to be heard over the arcing electricity.

RAMIL:
And you're about to kill her.

DOOKU:
(PAINED) Don't do this.

RAMIL:
What did you expect? To summon your fancy little sword all the way up here and strike me down? You still don't get it, do you? For all your airs and graces, for all your magic tricks, you're the one who is writhing around the floor at the end of a shock-staff, not me.

You're pathetic.

DOOKU:
(PAINED, QUIET) No.

RAMIL:
What was that?

DOOKU:
I said no. (GETTING STRONGER AS HE PERFORMS THE RITUAL HE TAUGHT QUI-GON) I am Jedi.

RAMIL:
Increase the voltage!

The shocks intensify, as does Dooku's resolve.

DOOKU:
I am Jedi! And I am not alone!

The action moves back down to the ground . . .

JENZA: (NARRATION)
Below, on the ground, Dooku's blade buzzed in my ear, while Sifo-Dyas writhed on the ground beside me, his mind aflame . . .

SIFO-DYAS:
It is now. Coming into focus. The future.

And then, belowground, the Tirra'Taka howling.

JENZA: (NARRATION)
And beneath our feet, Lene struggled to hold Dooku's beast in place.

LENE:
No. You must remain calm.

JENZA: (NARRATION)
For that was exactly what it had become. One mind.

LENE:
(HORRIFIED) No.

JENZA: (NARRATION)
Two bodies.

LENE:
Dooku! Don't!

The Tirra'Taka roars, louder than ever.

JENZA: (NARRATION)
On the *Windrunner,* Ramil staggered over to the side of the ship, his exoframe hissing with the effort. His mouth dropped open as the creature's howl echoed from the depths of the planet.

RAMIL:
What is that?

DOOKU:
Our past. And your future.

Deep below, the Tirra'Taka erupts into the air, bellowing.

JENZA: (NARRATION)
The creature burst from the shattered ground, scaled wings blocking out the sun. Sifo-Dyas laughed as he saw it, his sanity fracturing forever, as the droids looked up in confusion.

But I knew what it was, a legend made terrifying flesh.

Our savior.

I sprang up, barging into the droid that held Dooku's lightsaber, knocking it back.

JENZA:
(SHOUTING) Attack them! Now!

JENZA: (NARRATION)
The refugees snatched up the weapons we had stolen from the fleeing Abyssin, blasting the droids before they could regroup.

We hear the sounds of battle, and the roar of the monster.

SECURITY DROID:
Attack the creature! Attack the—

Force lightning swamps the droid before it can finish its sentence.

JENZA:
Energy burst from the Tirra'Taka's maw, washing over the security droids. The monster swept down, snatching the melting droids from the ground, crushing their bodies between its hooked talons like magella nuts.

A figure clung to its serpentine tail, fingers curled around obsidian scales. She jumped when she saw Sifo-Dyas curled in a ball in the dirt.

Lene lands on her feet, grunting from the pain.

JENZA:
Master Kostana. You are hurt.

LENE:
It's not me I'm worried about. Sifo-Dyas.

She rolls him over.

LENE:
Sifo-Dyas. I need you. It's Dooku. He's taken over the beast. He's controlling it.

JENZA:
He is?

SIFO-DYAS:
Doo-ku. Doo-ku. Doo-ku.

LENE:
Sifo-Dyas, please. We need to break his hold, before it's too late. He's not protected. The dark side will consume him.

SCENE 126. EXT. THE *WINDRUNNER.* DECK.

JENZA: (NARRATION)
I didn't understand her then, but I do now. After the battle was won, I accessed the *Windrunner*'s security feeds and saw what had happened with my own eyes. Dooku twisting, grabbing the shock-staff that had been thrust in his back.

DOOKU:
(ROARS IN FURY)

JENZA: (NARRATION)
His scream echoing the beast he controlled, he unleashed the dark fire he had buried for so long, the same energy that streamed from the Tirra'Taka's mouth. Lightning flowed up the weapon, frying Ramil's security droid to leap from metal body to body. The deck of the airship was ablaze with energy, surging through Ramil's exosuit, the droid's central processor erupting like a supernova.

The processor explodes.

JENZA: (NARRATION)
Ramil convulsed, gripping onto the rail to stop himself from tumbling over the edge, as below his droid army collapsed as one. His mechanical joints frozen, the Count of Serenno stared in disbelief

as a curved hilt flew straight toward the *Windrunner,* turning end-to-end as it returned to its master.

Dooku's lightsaber slaps into Dooku's open palm.

RAMIL:
I cannot move.

The lightsaber ignites.

RAMIL:
Brother. Please . . .

JENZA: (NARRATION)
The lightning was gone, but Dooku's fury remained.

DOOKU:
I have no brother.

RAMIL:
Have mercy.

DOOKU:
For Serenno!

Dooku slices Ramil in two.

RAMIL:
(SCREAMS)

SCENE 127. EXT. THE BATTLEFIELD.

JENZA: (NARRATION)
I couldn't hear Ramil's scream over the cry of the Tirra'Taka. Lene was standing between us and the beast, staring into its coal-black eyes, a shaking arm raised as if in greeting.

The monster roars.

JENZA:
(PANICKED) What are we going to do?

LENE:
There is little we can do now.

HAGI:
We could run!

LENE:
It would cut us down in an instant.

JENZA:
But you said my brother is controlling that thing.

LENE:
He was.

JENZA:
Then it won't hurt us. He won't hurt us.

LENE:
He may not have a choice.

JENZA:
What's that supposed to mean?

The monster growls.

HAGI:
It's going to pounce!

LENE:
Dooku. Hear me. Hear me, for all our sakes.

SCENE 128. EXT. THE *WINDRUNNER.* DECK.

DOOKU:
Lene.

JENZA: (NARRATION)
Dooku told me it was like coming out of a trance. He looked over the side of the *Windrunner* to see the creature stalk toward us, broken droids crunching beneath its feet.

DOOKU:
No. Do not do this. Hear me!

JENZA: (NARRATION)
But the monster wouldn't listen. Not anymore.

DOOKU:
Our minds as one. Let me back in.

The creature bellows far below.

DOOKU:
(REALIZING WHAT HE'S DONE) No. It is too late. I . . . I never meant to hurt you. Not like the others. Never meant to bend you to my will. I'm . . . I'm sorry. So, so sorry.

JENZA: (NARRATOR)
And with that, Dooku threw himself from the ship . . .

SCENE 129. EXT. THE BATTLEFIELD.

The Tirra'Taka continues to growl, ready to pounce.

LENE:
Everyone get ready to run.

HAGI:
I thought you said we wouldn't get away in time!

LENE:
Do you want to die?

JENZA:
What about you?

LENE:
I will hold it back as much as I can.

HAGI:
You'll be immolated.

LENE:

Jedi have lived through worse.

HAGI:

Than being burned alive?

LENE:

Someone take Sifo-Dyas. Look after him.

HAGI:

This is madness!

LENE:

Please.

JENZA:

We will.

LENE:

Get ready. On my mark.

JENZA: (NARRATION)

Something, I don't know what, a sixth sense, maybe even that mystical Force you all talk about, made me look up. I tried to speak, to cry out, but the words died in my throat. A figure was plummeting from the *Windrunner*, somehow guided down in an arc. His lightsaber was held above his head, the hilt gripped by both hands, the glowing blade pointed down like a needle.

JENZA:

(QUIETLY) Dooku.

JENZA: (NARRATION)

His teeth were bared, body taut, ready to strike.

The Tirra'Taka bellows.

JENZA: (NARRATION)

The creature's maw opened, dark fire swirling like a whirlpool in its throat.

LENE:
Go! Now!

JENZA: (NARRATION)
Hagi and the others ran as Kostana braced herself, but I couldn't move. I was rooted to the spot, my eyes locked on my brother.

The Tirra'Taka prepares to unleash its lightning breath as Dooku dives toward it, letting out a bestial roar of his own. The monster begins to scream lightning when, at the culmination of his own cry, Dooku lands on the creature's head, driving his lightsaber down into the monster's brain.

JENZA: (NARRATION)
His lightsaber found its mark, plasma burying deep into the beast's skull. The Tirra'Taka let out one last agonized howl before the fire died on its breath and the once mighty head shook the ground as it fell.

We hear the creature's final roar as its head smacks down.

JENZA: (NARRATION)
Dooku didn't move. No one did. My brother waited, crouched like a statue on the creature's crown, his lightsaber lodged in its ancient brain, waiting until its breathing slowed, and stopped, its eyes closing for the final time.

The Tiri'Takka dies. Dooku extinguishes his lightsaber.

DOOKU:
(QUIETLY) I'm sorry.

LENE:
Dooku?

JENZA: (NARRATION)
Dooku looked up, into the eyes of his friend. His face was a mask, although his eyes betrayed the remorse that raged inside. He jumped down from the dead monster's head, walking not to her, but to me.

DOOKU:
Jenza. Are you—

JENZA:
We're fine. Thanks to you.

JENZA: (NARRATION)
That at least elicited a flicker of emotion, but I couldn't tell what—pride or shame. He turned, his hand on my shoulder, and faced the crowd.

DOOKU:
Ramil is dead. The crisis is at an end.

SERGEANT ESON:
At an end? You can't be serious. Look around you, Dooku. Look at Carannia.

A datapad beeps in Jenza's pocket. She pulls it out.

JENZA:
The Abyssin have retreated. Ramil's droids . . .

DOOKU:
Ramil's droids are no longer operational.

JENZA:
We can start to rebuild.

SERGEANT ESON:
If we can afford it.

HAGI: (OFF SLIGHTLY)
We can.

JENZA:
Hagi?

JENZA: (NARRATION)
She was kneeling where she had run as Kostana held off the dragon, a lump of black rock in one hand and an industrial scanner in the other.

HAGI:

Do you know what this is?

JENZA: (NARRATION)

She rose, walking toward us, holding out the rock for me to take.

JENZA:

No.

HAGI:

It's sacanium.

LENE:

Are you sure?

HAGI:

I don't understand much about what's happened today, but I know my geology.

DOOKU:

As do I. A rare ore. Stronger than zersium when refined, and rarer than phrik. I've seen it before. A long time ago.

HAGI:

It's scattered all across the plain. That . . . creature must have brought it up with it when it broke the surface.

LENE:

But that's incredible. If there's a seam of sacanium running beneath us, the Senate is bound to send a contingent from the Mining Guild. Dooku—Serenno will receive as much help as it needs.

DOOKU:

No.

LENE:

What?

DOOKU:

No help is required.

HAGI:
I don't think that's your choice to make, Master Dooku.

DOOKU:
Not Master. (BEAT) Count.

LENE:
What are you saying?

JENZA: (NARRATION)
Dooku reached into his robes drawing out a holocomm. I recognized it at once. It was the holocomm I'd sent him as a child, still in pristine condition. He'd taken care of it all these years.

Beeps as Dooku enters a code.

LENE:
Dooku. Answer me. What did you mean?

SCENE 130. INT. YODA'S CHAMBERS. JEDI TEMPLE. CORUSCANT.

Far away, in Yoda's quarters, a holocomm beeps.

YODA:
Hm.

He activates the comm, a hologram of Dooku appearing in the room.

YODA:
Dooku. Late, it is. Meditating, I was.

DOOKU: (OVER COMM)
Master Yoda.

YODA:
Concerned the Council is, about your whereabouts.

DOOKU: (OVER COMM)
I am on Serenno.

YODA:

Surprised, I am not.

DOOKU: (OVER COMM)

The Abyssin have been repelled.

YODA:

Gratifying, that is to hear.

DOOKU: (OVER COMM)

The planet is in disarray. Count Ramil is dead.

YODA:

Hm. Talk to the chancellor, I will. Persuade him to send aid.

DOOKU: (OVER COMM)

There is no need. A new resource has been discovered, one that has the potential to restore Serenno to its rightful state. The Serennians will process it themselves, under the supervision of their new leader.

YODA:

Your sister. Jenza.

DOOKU: (OVER COMM)

No.

YODA:

Much conflict I detect in you, my former Padawan.

DOOKU: (OVER COMM)

You are wrong, Master Yoda.

YODA:

What do you wish to say to me?

DOOKU: (OVER COMM)

The Jedi have been my family since I was a child, the Temple my home. But my future lies here, on Serenno.

YODA:

Leaving the Order, you are.

DOOKU: (OVER COMM)
I have no choice. The House of Serenno brought this planet to its knees. It is my responsibility, my duty, to rebuild it, by whatever means possible.

YODA:
And what of your duty to the Republic?

DOOKU: (OVER COMM)
The Republic is changing, Yoda. Has changed. We all know it, even if we won't admit it. A moment ago, Master Kostana told me that the Senate would happily send what is needed to process our new resources. I have no doubt that is true. And yet the very same Senate refused to help when my sister begged them to stand against the Abyssin. The Jedi refused to help. It is Protobranch, all over again.

YODA:
Restored, Protobranch was.

DOOKU: (OVER COMM)
Because of its people, or its commodity? The Senate decreed that Serenno's plight was an internal affair. Its restitution will be likewise. I am the heir of Serenno. I will rebuild this planet, make it stronger. Not for the Republic. And not for the Jedi. But for the people. *My* people. I ask for you, and the Council, to respect my decision in this matter.

YODA:
Hm. Saddened by your decision we are, but honor it we will.

DOOKU: (OVER COMM)
Thank you. I will surrender my lightsaber to Master Kostana.

YODA:
No. Necessary that will not be.

DOOKU: (OVER COMM)
It is the weapon of a Jedi.

YODA:

Which is why keep it you must. More than a name, a Jedi is. More than a title. Strong in the Force, you are. Guide you, it will. Guide us all, it must.

DOOKU: (OVER COMM)

Until we meet again.

The hologram cuts off. We stay in Yoda's chamber a moment longer, and hear the Jedi Master sigh.

SCENE 131. EXT. THE BATTLEFIELD.

JENZA: (NARRATION)

Back on Serenno, my brother's announcement had caused much consternation . . .

LENE:

Dooku, I . . .

HAGI:

I'm sorry. But what just happened?

SERGEANT ESON:

You can't do this.

HAGI:

If you think we're just going to stand back while you waltz in . . .

JENZA:

Hagi. Please.

HAGI:

No, Jenza. He has no right.

DOOKU:

I have every right.

HAGI:

The houses will not stand for this.

SERGEANT ESON:
And neither will the people.

JENZA:
(FIRMLY) No. The people will listen. The houses will listen.

SERGEANT ESON:
My lady . . .

JENZA:
Don't you see? This is our chance. Our chance to stand on our own two feet for the first time in our history. No one telling us what to do. No one telling us what our destiny will be. My brother will make Serenno strong again. He will save us. (RALLYING THE CROWD) Doo-ku. Doo-ku. Doo-ku.

JENZA: (NARRATION)
Around me, the refugees picked up the chant, the battleground ringing to my brother's name.

CROWD:
Doo-ku. Doo-ku. Doo-ku. (AND REPEAT)

SIFO-DYAS: (OFF-MIC)
Chanting his name . . . They're chanting his name.

DOOKU:
Sifo.

Dooku rushes to Sifo's side.

SIFO-DYAS:
I can see you, Dooku. I can see everything.

DOOKU:
Lene. You must take him back to the Temple. Look after him.

LENE:
What do you think I've been doing all these years?

DOOKU:
I'll find you a ship, whatever you need.

LENE:

I will signal the Council. You have enough to do.

SIFO-DYAS:

The futures have become one, Dooku. One path.

DOOKU:

Here. Take this, old friend.

He passes Sifo his holocomm.

SIFO-DYAS:

Take this . . . take this . . .

LENE:

Your holocomm?

DOOKU:

I have no need for it anymore. But one day. (TO SIFO, AS IF TALKING TO A CHILD) If you need to talk . . .

LENE:

Dooku.

DOOKU:

Thank you, Lene for everything. Please, tell Rael and Qui-Gon . . .

LENE:

Yes?

DOOKU:

Tell them the Force will be with them. Always.

LENE:

You can tell them yourself, when we all meet again. This is not the end, Dooku. Only the beginning.

SIFO-DYAS:

The beginning . . .

Jenza and Hagi approach.

JENZA:
Brother?

LENE:
You must go. All will be well.

Dooku walks toward them.

DOOKU:
Sister.

JENZA:
We've received word.

HAGI:
The houses request a summit.

DOOKU:
Then we shall have one.

HAGI:
Where? Carannia is a disaster.

DOOKU:
We shall meet at the castle. Come, Jenza. We have much to do.

They walk off.

HAGI:
Wait. You mean your castle? Castle Serenno?

DOOKU: (CALLING BACK)
Why not? It is my home, after all.

SCENE 132. INT. HIDDEN ROOM.

JENZA:
(SOBBING) Home, Ventress. He said it was his home.

VENTRESS:
Yes, yes. I heard you the first time.

KY NAREC: (GHOST)
She's getting worse. Such confusion.

VENTRESS:
Actually, I think she knows exactly what she's saying.

An alarm sounds. Ventress presses buttons.

VENTRESS:
Damn.

KY NAREC: (GHOST)
What is it?

VENTRESS:
Republic agents in the building. Outside the apartment.

KY NAREC: (GHOST)
Seal the compartment.

VENTRESS:
Don't tell me what to do.

She presses a button anyway. The fake wall slides back.

We hear movement in the outer room. Agents moving about.

KY NAREC: (GHOST)
There're two of them. They're armed.

VENTRESS:
So am I.

She draws her lightsabers.

KY NAREC: (GHOST)
No. The sound will give you away.

VENTRESS:
(HISSING) I know.

We hear footsteps in the next room, the following lines muffled by the wall.

Through it all we hear Ventress's breathing, close to the micro-phone.

AGENT #1:
(MUFFLED) It has to be here somewhere.

AGENT #2:
(MUFFLED) Over here. Behind the picture.

AGENT #1:
(MUFFLED) Glee Anselm? Always dreaming, that one.

The picture is pushed aside and the access code entered.

VENTRESS:
(HISSED) Get ready.

KY NAREC: (GHOST)
For what? I can't do anything to help.

VENTRESS:
Then why are you here?

AGENT #2:
(MUFFLED) Well?

AGENT #1:
(MUFFLED) He must have changed the code.

AGENT #2:
(MUFFLED) Try the over— (GAGS) Can't . . . breathe.

VENTRESS:
(MUTTERED) It's about time.

BOTH AGENTS:
(CHOKING)

Muffled boots are heard walking into the room.

KY NAREC: (GHOST)
That presence . . .

VENTRESS:
You might not be able to help, but he can.

BOTH AGENTS:
(DIE)

Two bodies thump to the floor.

KY NAREC: (GHOST)
It's him.

The door slides open.

VENTRESS:
Master.

DOOKU:
Jenza. Look what they did to you.

VENTRESS: (NARRATION)
He barely looks at me, making straight for his sister.

JENZA:
They wanted me to betray you. But I wouldn't. I want to help, Dooku. You've lost your way.

KY NAREC: (GHOST)
That's an understatement.

VENTRESS: (NARRATION)
Dooku freezes. Can he sense Ky? He turns to me, his eyes cold.

DOOKU:
Did they transfer any data?

VENTRESS:
I . . . I didn't check.

DOOKU:
Don't you think you should?

VENTRESS:
Yes, Master.

She presses buttons.

VENTRESS:
The only transmissions were to Fellidrone's handler, here on Se-renno. No data parcels, only short-range comms.

DOOKU:
Good.

VENTRESS: (NARRATION)
He glances around the room, seeing the rocket pack. He raises an open palm, the Zim-Jumper lifting steadily from the floor. Then his hand becomes a fist, and the fuel tank ruptures.

The metal buckles, fuel pouring from the machine. Fuel splashes as the pack clatters back to the ground.

KY NAREC: (GHOST)
Ventress. Listen to me. This is your last chance. I know what he's about to ask you to do. If you do, that'll be it. You'll be his forever.

VENTRESS: (NARRATION)
Shut up, I think as Dooku walks back toward his sister. *Shut up. Shut up. Shut up.* The count raises her head toward him.

DOOKU:
My darling sister.

JENZA:
Please. If you would just come with me to Coruscant. The Jedi will know what to do. They'll be able to help.

DOOKU:
I have all the help I need.

JENZA:
The hooded man? He isn't helping you. He's corrupting you.

VENTRESS: (NARRATION)
Hooded man? What is she talking about?

KY NAREC: (GHOST)
He's not who you think he is, Ventress. Why can't I make you see?
You need to see.

SCENE 133. INT. VISION. CASTLE SERENNO. DOOKU'S GREAT HALL.

Atmosphere: We cut into a vision. Everything bar Ventress's narration is dreamlike, the voices and sound effects reverberating, the music discordant and eerie.

VENTRESS: (NARRATION)
Everything changes. I'm back in the castle, in Dooku's great hall, but the light is wrong, the room stretched beyond its usual dimensions. The count is hunched over his table, papers and data slates scattered in front of him. This is not the ordered desk of the *Windrunner*, Dooku not the man I know.

KY NAREC: (GHOST)
The affairs of state weigh heavy.

VENTRESS:
This isn't real.

KY NAREC:
(SUDDENLY NEXT TO HER)

VENTRESS:
(JUMPS)

VENTRESS: (NARRATION)
Ky Narec is standing beside me. He is exactly how I remember him. The strip of graying beard, the tattoo creasing on his chin, those warm blue eyes fixed, not on me, but on my new master.

KY NAREC:
You can speak, little one. He can't hear you.

VENTRESS:
Is this you? Are you doing this?

KY NAREC:
You need to see who he is. Who you are.

VENTRESS: (NARRATION)
He nods at the count. Dooku's arms shake as he supports himself. He is tired, his usually immaculate hair hanging lank in front of bloodshot eyes. His cracked lips move. He is muttering beneath his breath.

VENTRESS:
I can't hear.

KY NAREC:
Then move closer.

VENTRESS: (NARRATION)
I'm beside the desk, wrinkling my nose at the odor. Dooku hasn't washed for days.

KY NAREC:
Listen to him.

DOOKU:
(MUTTERING) So much to do. So much to do. Why don't they listen? Why don't they cooperate? Don't they realize I'm doing all this for them?

VENTRESS: (NARRATION)
He sweeps out an arm, knocking the papers and readers from the desk. Glass shatters, casings break, and Dooku yells into the darkness of the empty room.

DOOKU:
(SHOUTING) Why won't anyone listen? Why won't anyone help?

KY NAREC:
Is this the man who so commands you? Is this your future?

VENTRESS:
(UNSURE) I . . .

We hear an ironic slow clap from across the room as someone approaches.

KY NAREC:
What?

VENTRESS:
Ky looks as shocked as I am as another figure crosses the hall toward us.

DOOKU:
I'm impressed. Ky Narec. Back from the grave.

KY NAREC:
I—I don't understand.

VENTRESS: (NARRATION)
It is another Dooku. My Dooku. As he was in Fellidrone's quarters. As he was when we first met.

DOOKU:
You were always a disappointment. Even as a youngling. If I had my way, you would never have even made Jedi Knight.

VENTRESS:
Stop it.

DOOKU:
And when you did, what exactly did you do? You made mistake after mistake.

VENTRESS:
Leave him alone.

DOOKU:
People died because of you, Ky.

KY NAREC:
That's not true.

DOOKU:

And when the Council called for your return, you fled rather than face the consequences. Exiled yourself on a dustball, convincing yourself it was a crusade. And this is the man you have chosen as your conscience, my assassin? This is your hope? Are you like him, Ventress? Will you run?

VENTRESS:

I don't know what you mean!

DOOKU:

(BELLOWING) *Will you run?*

SCENE 134. EXT. VISION. THE GROUNDS OF CASTLE SERENNO.

We hear Ventress running through the night, pushing past branches, slipping on mud.

She's breathing heavily beneath the narration, the soundscape becoming increasingly more nightmarish.

VENTRESS: (NARRATION)

And that's what I'm doing, racing through the forest, my feet slipping on the mud. Castle Serenno looms above me, silhouetted against Mantero's gleaming disk.

KY NAREC: (GHOST)

That's it, little one. You can still make a choice. Run as far as you can.

VENTRESS: (NARRATION)

Ky's voice is everywhere. In the wind. In the trees. But it isn't alone.

DOOKU: (GHOST)

There is no choice. Not for you.

KY NAREC: (GHOST)

Don't listen to him, Ventress.

DOOKU: (GHOST)
Listen to yourself.

KY NAREC: (GHOST)
You need to be strong. Like me.

DOOKU: (GHOST)
You are mine. He is nothing.

VENTRESS:
He rescued me!

DOOKU: (GHOST)
(LAUGHS) Rescued you? From slavery? From the Siniteens? You have no idea what he did to you!

VENTRESS: (NARRATION)
A root snags my foot and I fall . . .

VENTRESS:
(CRIES OUT)

SCENE 135. EXT. VISION. HAL'STED'S BASE.

Ventress lands in sand. There is blasterfire nearby, vultures calling from high above, their cries distorted, maddening.

VENTRESS: (NARRATION)
. . . and land in coarse sand. The castle is gone. The forest, gone. A swollen sun burns high above, strike-vultures wheeling through a shimmering sky.

Ventress scrabbles up.

VENTRESS:
It's Rattatak. I'm back on Rattatak.

KY NAREC: (GHOST)
No.

DOOKU: (GHOST)
Yes. The day Hal'Sted died.

YOUNG VENTRESS:
(CALLING OUT) Master.

DOOKU: (GHOST)
The day he was *killed.*

HAL'STED:
(CALLING) Ventress!

VENTRESS: (NARRATION)
That's him. That's Hal'Sted. The pirate who took me from Dathomir. The Siniteen who brought me up as his own.

KY NAREC: (GHOST)
A daughter in chains.

Hal'Sted runs over.

HAL'STED:
Spince. Have you seen Ventress?

VENTRESS:
I'm right here.

DOOKU: (GHOST)
He can't hear you, remember? There's no way to warn him.

VENTRESS:
Warn him?

HAL'STED:
We need to get her away from here. Go.

The lackey runs off.

HAL'STED:
Ventress! Ventress. Where are you?

A figure jumps down behind the pirate. Hal'Sted whirls around.

KY NAREC:
She'll be safe soon enough, slaver.

HAL'STED:
Jedi scum!

Hal'Sted fires. Ky ignites his lightsaber, deflecting the shots.

KY NAREC:
You'll never use her again.

Ky runs Hal'Sted through.

KY NAREC:
Never again.

HAL'STED:
(SCREAMS)

The slaver collapses to the ground, dead.

VENTRESS:
No!

DOOKU: (GHOST)
You never checked the wound. Sloppy. Not that you would have known the difference between a blaster shot . . . and a lightsaber.

VENTRESS:
It's not true.

DOOKU: (GHOST)
How do you know?

VENTRESS:
He said it was pirates.

DOOKU: (GHOST)
And you believed him?

VENTRESS:
Ky?

DOOKU: (GHOST)

He's not real, Ventress. You know that. He died on Rattatak. You cremated his corpse yourself. No one comes back from the dead. No one.

Thunder rolls above.

VENTRESS: (NARRATION)

The sky turns black, lightning lancing across dark clouds, the same lightning I have felt across my back. His lightning.

A crack of lightning.

DOOKU: (GHOST)

He used you, Ventress. A salve for his loneliness. His failure. They all used you. The Nightsister. The slaver. The Jedi. They define you, because you let them. Because you refuse to be free.

VENTRESS:

No!

The storm intensifies, rain lashing down, the sound distorted.

DOOKU: (GHOST)

Have you learned nothing, child? From the holos. From the journal.

VENTRESS:

The journal?

DOOKU: (GHOST)

You think you found it by chance?

VENTRESS:

The Force guided me.

DOOKU: (GHOST)

I guided you. Everything you have seen. Everything you have heard. Was it for nothing? The past does not define you, Ventress. The future does not define you. *I* define you.

KY NAREC: (GHOST)
Asajj.

DOOKU: (GHOST)
He is not real, Ventress. I am. Who do you choose? Who do you choose?

Thunder bursts overhead, the sound warping as we are thrown out of the vision.

SCENE 136. INT. HIDDEN ROOM.

VENTRESS: (NARRATION)
It's all gone. The storm. Rattatak. Hal'Sted. I'm back with Dooku and Jenza. (WITH HATRED) And *him*, still sniveling in my head.

KY NAREC: (GHOST)
Asajj. Don't listen to him. It's lies. All of it.

DOOKU:
Ventress?

VENTRESS: (NARRATION)
Dooku peers at me, the rat in his maze. I think he's going to speak, but everything has been said. He turns to his sister, her eyes brimming with hope. She has no idea.

DOOKU:
You say you wanted to help me, Jenza.

JENZA:
Yes. More than anything.

DOOKU:
By attempting to betray me to the Jedi. By revealing my plans.

JENZA:
I don't know anything about any plans. And I don't want to know. They're wrong, Dooku. Can't you see that? You said you were going to save Serenno.

DOOKU:

And I have. Serenno will be the beating heart of a new Empire.

JENZA:

An Empire I want no part of. I don't recognize you anymore. You're not my brother.

DOOKU:

I am. Which is why I must release you. Ventress . . .

VENTRESS:

You said you wanted her found.

DOOKU:

A task you performed admirably, but you are an assassin. *My* assassin.

JENZA:

No.

Ventress walks toward her.

JENZA:

Please. You don't have to do this. It isn't you. I know it isn't. I can see it in your eyes.

KY NAREC: (GHOST)
She's right, Asajj.

VENTRESS:

You're not real.

JENZA:

Of course I am.

KY NAREC: (GHOST)
(IN UNISON) Of course I'm not. But I could be. I'm a part of you, Ventress. I always will be. The best part of you.

VENTRESS:
I'm sorry.

The lightsaber ignites, the blade buried in Jenza's chest.

JENZA:
(GASPS IN PAIN) Brother.

We hold on the sound of the lightsaber burning for a moment longer before it cuts off.

JENZA
(DIES)

Jenza's body slumps to the floor.

DOOKU:
You have done well.

VENTRESS:
(QUIETLY) Your will is mine.

DOOKU:
There must be no evidence.

VENTRESS: (NARRATION)
He turns and sweeps from the room, his sister cooling at my feet. I am alone.

VENTRESS:
Ky?

(BEAT)

VENTRESS:
(BREATHES OUT)

VENTRESS:
I have a job to do. I look around, spotting a blaster clipped to a dead agent's belt. I recover the weapon, cranking the power pack. I'll have to be quick. It won't take long to overload.

A piercing whine starts to build as she places the weapon carefully into the seeping fuel.

VENTRESS:

I try not to breathe in the fumes as I place the whining blaster in the pool of paralene. The fuel stings my eyes, tears pricking. It's fuel. Nothing more.

I won't have time to make it to the door. I head back to the window, the catch still smashed from when I broke in.

The window slides open. We can hear the sounds of the street outside.

VENTRESS: (NARRATION)

There's no sign of Dooku, and then I look up and see a shadow in the clouds above. The *Windrunner,* slipping silently home. I wonder how many of Dooku's faithful subjects will see it and smile. The champion of Serenno, protecting his people. I reach into my pocket, drawing out his journal, feeling the cracked leather beneath my fingers.

I throw it back into the paralene.

It lands in the fuel.

VENTRESS:

Time to go.

Ventress jumps down to the street, her feet splashing on the wet sidewalk.

It's stopped raining now. We hear her walking away from the building, the distant whine of the blaster building to a crescendo behind her.

VENTRESS: (NARRATION)

I hate it here.

I hate the lies and the deceit and the fear and the hatred. I hate him and what he's made me do. What he's made *me*.

But where else can I go?

This is where I belong. This is who I am.

I am free.

A massive explosion tears the building apart.

ACKNOWLEDGMENTS

Who do I thank first? Well, I have a great debt to Elizabeth Schaefer for asking me to cast a light on Dooku's past, and to Michael Siglain for both championing my *Star Wars* career and sending me Universal Horror action figures just when I need them. Thanks also to Jennifer Heddle, Pablo Hidalgo, Matt Martin, Kelsey Sharpe, and Emily Shkoukani for their challenging but oh-so-essential notes, Jason Fry for his encyclopedic knowledge of *Star Wars* lore, Alex Davis for guiding the script book into production, and my assistant, Sarah Simpson-Weiss, for keeping my life in order.

Then there is Nick Martorelli, our wonderful producer, and Penguin Random House Audio's amazing publicity manager Nicole Morano, who shared the Dooku love far and wide. Thanks also to our incredible cast for breathing life into these words. Having a script performed for the first time is equal parts nerve-racking and thrilling, but now, as I reread the script, I hear each and every one of their voices.

Mention needs to be made of Claudia Gray and George Mann, who both kept me sane through a rather frenzied writing period, as did my Project Luminous co-conspirators Daniel José Older,

Justina Ireland, and Charles Soule. Claudia, in particular, was a great help as we wrestled with Jedi traditions and new Padawans together.

As always, the largest support came from my darling Clare, who was the first person to read the script and who also kept the Scott house ticking when I burned the midnight oil to hit the deadline. Thank you so much, sweetheart. I couldn't do any of this without you.

But the final thanks should go to Sir Christopher Lee, for first bringing Dooku of Serenno to life (and for terrifying me repeatedly when I was a kid), and Corey Burton, who expanded the count so brilliantly in *The Clone Wars*.

Gentlemen, I raise a glass of Mantero funeral wine to you both.